The
LOVES
and
SORROWS
of
EFFIE FARRADAY

L.A. Williams

ALSO IN THE EFFIE FARRADAY TRILOGY...

The Life and Dreams of Effie Farraday

The Continuing Saga of Effie Farraday

Available on Amazon

*****

Book cover design by Lynn Williams

I dedicate this book to my husband

ISBN 978-1-9995832-2-4

Chapter 1

These days my mind often lingers around old memories, memories that should have faded, but will not be extinguished. Blessed are our lives, and precious are our families, we must value them always, and think often of our dearly departed loved ones. They must never be forgotten.

When I was a young child, I used to believe that if I no longer dreamt anymore that that would mean my life would be over, for surely only the living dream. But now I believe we carry on dreaming, even after we are deceased. For in the darkness of death I had such a dream...

I found myself making my way down to a tiny stream, with the warmth of the sun on my face. Like a child I began running my hands through the silver ripples. Then I watched in awe, as the corn gently swayed in the breeze, causing shimmers of yellow strands to roll like waves on a golden ocean. Humming to myself I passed over fields splashed with crimson poppies and sun kissed wheat. Feeling exuberant I bounded up to the yew trees that clustered together on the hilltops, surrounded with bunches of flowers as white as summer clouds, then through the woods carpeted with a blue sea of bluebells. It was strange but as the wind delicately caressed my face it seemed to be murmuring my name.

I began to laugh. 'What is it wind, what do you want with me?'

Turning north I followed a tiny brook flowing through the woods until I came to the edge, then emerged out into field. I began to run across it as if being pulled along by an invisible hand. On I went down a picturesque pathway that twisted its way through the dense undergrowth until finally I came upon a pretty stone cottage, tucked away from the world. Standing outside was a woman in a green gown, and she appeared to be waving at me.

'Hello there.' I cried out.

With a smile the figure turned away and floated right through the brickwork and into the property. I ran to the cottage and stepped through the open door, padding slowly through the derelict hallway and entering the room nearest to me on the right. The room was devoid of furnishings and was scattered with dry leaves that rustled gently in the breeze blowing in through the open window. Quite unexpectedly I heard the sound of children's laughter coming from the hallway, and feeling intrigued I went to investigate.

'Who's there? I asked in a dreamlike state.

I stood there in the silence, waiting. My eyes darted to the staircase as an object suddenly rolled down and landed at my feet. It appeared to be a stone marble. As I picked it up, I noticed it was cold to the touch, casually I twirled it around in my hand, half expecting it to transform into something else, but nothing happened, it was just a child's marble.

My eyes shot up to the top of the landing as a peculiar creaking noise began to sound in one of the rooms above.

'Hello, is...is anyone up there?'

Yet again the faint laughter of children came into earshot. Gripping the banister, I ascended the stairs, still clutching the marble within my hand. It was only when I'd reached the landing that I realised the noise had ceased. Taking a deep breath, I gently pushed the half open door of the first bedroom and crept in. It was a pleasant, light looking room with a deep fireplace on the far wall and windows on the other. A beam of sun streaked through the windowpane and across onto the floor, highlighting the many dust particles. But there was no one there. I left the room and approached another, hesitating at the door. I could hear the creaking again, louder this time. With shaking hands, I turned the handle and entered. All of a sudden, I became aware that it had gone completely silent. The woman in the green gown was sitting there in a rocking chair, with a faint smile upon her face. Gazing at her I realised she was the woman in the portrait at the church, Florentine Heatherington. I shivered violently as she glided directly towards me and passed right through my body, leaving me standing there all on my own. Suddenly everything went black.

I opened my eyes.

'No, no.' I cried, frantically moving my head against the pillow. 'Why can't I see?' Laying there in the darkness a sudden dread came over me as I began to wonder if it wasn't death that had taken me at all, but instead I was back in my room at the monastery, that sinister, depressive place where unnatural tree roots spread across the ceiling in eager watchfulness, waiting to pounce on its unfortunate victim's whilst they slept. A cool draught drifted over me, as if a ghostly spirit had drifted without restrictions straight through the wooden door and was hovering above me. However, odd at it seemed, it didn't frighten me, for something had changed, something in the air, the breeze that blew over me was fresh, with a distinct scent of sweet honeysuckle, as if it were wafting through an open window. And as I strained my ears, I could hear muffled voices and soft footsteps from somewhere nearby.

'Effie?'

Who was that, did I know the voice, I wasn't sure.

Oh how I wished to open my eyes, but for some reason my eyelids were heavy with sleep, and as I lay there drifting in and out of consciousness I began to wonder if my close encounter with the trees had merely been a nightmare; after all it was common for me to have such dreams, they were part of me, and I was part of them, but although I was accustomed to my night terrors it scared me that the line between dreams and reality was becoming somewhat blurred, and I feared that one day I would awake not being able to distinguish between the two. But even in my sleepy state I was suddenly certain that the trees had been real, for my entire body ached so badly that the pain was excruciating, especially around my middle; I remember how the branches had encircled my waist, tightly squeezing it until I could hardly breathe.

3

'Wake up Effie.'

A moan escaped my lips as I struggled to rise up from the bed and I found myself wincing as a searing pain shot through my stomach. For some mysterious reason I was exhausted, as if something or someone had come along and completely drained all my energy. I suddenly had a vision of a sweet, kindly lady nursing me back to health; she was dabbing a warm flannel over my forehead and stroking my hair. I was suddenly overcome with emotion as I remembered it was my Aunt, but I couldn't recall her actual name. Tears began running down my face and neck as I weakly beckoned for her.

'Aunt, Aunt are you there?'

Once more I heard whispers, only now it was much closer, so near it almost seemed a crowd had gathered in my room. Someone was breathing near my face and I felt a hand lightly touch my forehead. Instinctively I began tossing my head from side to side in terror, wondering if they were spirits from the monastery. I began mumbling incoherently to myself then told them to go away.

'It's only us E.'

With a struggle I finally opened my heavy eyelids, but everything was blurry and indistinct. My eyes began to hurt as an unexpected flash of light passed across my line of vision.

'That's it Effie, you can do it.'

A firm hand covered mine.

'No.' I said, unable to see anything through the blinding light. I snatched my hand away.

'Return to us Effie, don't leave again.'

Leave? I thought to myself, where had I been? And who were all these shadow people surrounding me. Feeling confused I closed my eyes against the light and pressed my face into the pillow. 'What's happened, where am I? I stammered weakly in a croaky voice. 'Is... is this heaven?'

A raucous laughter exploded near my ear making me jump.

'Yes E, it is. Anywhere would seem that way after a spell at the infamous monastery.'

I heard another voice. 'I asked you not to remind Effie of that place.' It was stern and cold sounding. 'It may hamper her recovery.'

'Or, funnily enough, it may actually help.'

'Well, we can at least wait until Effie's up and about before burdening her with such matters.'

A hand caressed my forehead, brushing away the hair from my face.

'If you say so wise one.'

A strange silence followed

'Why don't you go downstairs and fetch some water, Effie must be thirsty.'

Someone sighed heavily then said 'Yes sir' in a growling voice.

I heard footsteps thudding across the floorboards, and then a door slamming.

'Be quiet.' Someone hissed.

Once again, I opened my eyes and was able to focus on the figure sitting by my bedside. It was Noble.

He smiled at me apprehensively. 'You're going to be alright Effie.'

I tried to lift my head. 'What...what's wrong with me?'

His eyes momentarily flickered to the bedspread before meeting my gaze. Nothing.' He uttered softly, bending over me and tenderly stroking my hair. 'You've been very poorly, that's all.'

Determined to sit up I attempted to lift myself out of bed. 'Really?' I uttered in a surprised voice. I gasped as pain shot through my left side.

'Careful does it Effie.' He reached forward and placed one arm round my waist and one about my shoulders, and carefully lifted me up, pulling the pillow up with his hand and resting me back against it. 'One step at a time.' His face came near to mine, and briefly our eyes locked, before I averted my gaze, focusing on the bedspread. 'Is that comfortable for you?'

'Yes, yes thank you.' It was a lie, for my back ached, as did my arms and my whole body, but the worst pain was around my middle; it felt like something had clenched my waist so tight that it had practically cut me in two. 'Where am I...what happened to me?'

His eyes widened, and he took my hands. 'I shall answer your questions later, but first how about some tea, and perhaps soup?'

'Very well.' My voice was raspy and sore, and my lips felt dry. I stared into his face, realising how much I'd missed him, those unusually beautiful eyes returned my gaze, completely unwavering, and suddenly I felt rather giddy.

'Good.' Squeezing my hands momentarily, he released them and stood up. 'I shall inform father and...and.' He suddenly looked uncomfortable. 'Everyone shall be overjoyed that you've awoken.

I watched as Noble hesitantly started towards the door, he paused for a little and stared back at me, and I sensed a hint of pain in his eyes. For a second, I thought he was going to say something but then thought better of it. Slowly he turned and gradually stepped towards the doorway, colliding with Mace on the way out.

'Why must you always run Mace? You act like a young child frantically darting about the place. No wonder you have so many accidents.' Noble was wiping something from his jumper. 'Half the water has gone down me.'

Mace threw him a sheepish grin. 'My apologies.' He held the cup of water away from Noble, as if worried he'd spill it again. 'I was eager to get back to Effie, now that she's finally awake.' Striding confidently into the room he placed the cup on the bedside table and sat down on the edge of the bed, grinning at me from ear to ear.

'Welcome back sleepyhead.' He briefly glanced at Noble. 'If it's not too much to ask, could I please have a few moments alone with my best friend?' He said, laying emphasis on his words.

I could see by Noble's expression that the animosity between the two of them hadn't improved; his eyes showed a mixture of alarm and suspicion as he glared at Mace. 'Very well.' His face softened as he turned to me. 'I shall go and prepare the soup, Effie.'

I smiled weakly as he turned and marched out the room. Staring after him, I heard his footsteps stomping down the stairs, followed by the slamming of a door, and then the distant sound of muffled voices.

'Well, that's got rid of him.' Mace said with a smile on his lips. 'He clings to you like one of the tree roots at the monastery.' Widening his eyes, he swiftly placed his hand over his mouth. 'Whoops. Sorry about that E. You probably want to forget about that place.' He reached for the cup and placed it near my lips. 'Have some water E, you must be parched.' Slowly I took a sip. 'There' he said plonking the cup back on the table, 'better?' Smiling, he took my hand, his large eyes peering at me anxiously. 'You do know where you are don't you?'

I looked pensive for a moment. 'Yes, I'm at the cottage in Briarwood.' Coughing slightly, I held my hand to my throat in an attempt to take the pain away. 'We travelled here, didn't we, from Harland. When did we arrive, last night?'

Mace sighed, his face looking grim. 'Effie, you've been gravely ill. For days now you've been slipping in and out of consciousness, and running a high fever.'

A cold feeling came over me, shivering I bent forward, trying not to wince with pain.

'Oh.'

'If it wasn't for Caleb concocting a medicine...well you'd be a goner.'

'Well Mace, thanks for being so honest and blunt with me.' I tried to laugh but ended up coughing violently.'

With a chuckle he moved his arm around me. 'Yeah, well I didn't see the point of beating around the bush.' He began gently massaged the top of my back. 'Noble probably would have held back.'

I smiled and gazed down at the covers.

'Well, I feel much better now, I should get up and go downstairs.'

'Oh E.'

'No really, I should.' My breath came unsteadily as I tried to lift my legs, but they were like weights. 'I must thank Caleb for...for helping me get better.'

Mace looked alarmed. 'No, no E.' he exclaimed in a firm voice. 'You need to rest in bed and get your strength back.'

I grimaced. 'Do I really have to?'

'Doctor's orders.'

A laugh escaped my lips. 'I didn't know there was a doctor in Briarwood.'

Mace's voice sounded odd. 'There isn't. If we were home in Abercrombie you would have made a swifter recovery.' His eyes glazed over. 'You would have been in hospital and seen a proper doctor and had the necessary antibiotics immediately. Instead you had to make do with some ancient remedy that people had to rely on in the dark ages.'

'I see you've been reading your notebook.'

He looked at me rather solemnly. 'Yes well, just lately it's the only thing that's kept me sane.' Reaching out he clasped his hands in mine. 'Once you're up and about I suggest we start searching for a way back home.'

My eyes widened in surprise. 'Are you so eager to return?'

'Well yes, aren't you?'

'All in good time.' I swallowed in pain. 'Once everything is sorted out here.'

I watched as he rose from the bed and paced across the room, gazing out of the window. 'You mean once you've decided whether or not to give up on Gideon.'

'I...I haven't really thought about it.'

He swung round to face me. 'Or is Noble your main concern now?'

A mixture of apprehensive and excitement suddenly coursed through me.

'Please Mace, stop it.'

He grinned. 'Sorry E.'

I leant back a little against the pillows, ignoring the searing pain around my waist.

'For now, I'd just like to talk about the events that lead me here.'

He sighed heavily. 'Well, after I fled from the monastery, I decided to come back for you Effie, along with...with Croft and his other feathered friends.' I watched as his face glazed over. 'We got there just in time before...before you were eaten alive by one of those hellish tree creatures.'

I shivered and lay there thinking for a moment.

'How is that possible? Croft couldn't have stood a chance against such enormous strength.' My eyes stayed focused on his face. 'And how was I pulled free, and why? It just doesn't make any sense.'

He shrugged his shoulders. 'A lot of things in this world don't make sense Effie.'

My hand reached over my mouth as I had another coughing fit.

Mace swiftly leapt forward and passed me the cup of water. I gulped some back before sinking down onto the pillows, gazing up at the beams across the ceiling.

'You're right about Croft.' Mace said glumly, sitting back on the bed. 'He didn't stand a chance. The trees killed him.' He began tracing the pattern on the bedspread with his finger. 'Luckily for us we managed to clamber on one of the other birds and escape.'

My voice was quiet as I spoke. 'Poor Gideon, he must be heartbroken.' A wave of heartache swept over me. 'He loved that bird.'

'Ah yes, poor old Gideon. So, what do you actually remember about the last time you saw your beloved?'

My heart began thudding in my chest. 'As I recall Gideon was nearby just before The Elder trees took me. I remember him shouting.' I paused for a moment as I noticed how my hands were covered in little scratches.

'Then what?'

'Well...perhaps I imagined it but I think Gideon ran after me, and...and pulled me from the trees.' I laughed. 'Of course, knowing me I could have dreamt up that part.'

Mace narrowed his eyes and scratched his head.

I threw him a quizzical look. 'Mace?'

'Well actually E...'

The door swung open and Noble stood in the doorframe carrying a tray.

'Time to eat Effie.' Placing the tray down on the dressing table he briefly glanced at Mace. 'My father requires your assistance in the kitchen. He's just about to serve dinner.'

'Now?'

'Yes, this very minute.'

Mace stretched out on the bed and I felt the weight of him pressing down painfully on my legs. 'I'm not really that hungry.' He lay there looking bemused for a moment before pulling himself up off the bed. 'Well alright, maybe I could manage a small dinner.'

'Well, run along then Mace.' Noble said, as if speaking to a child.

Mace bent forward and kissed my forehead. 'I shall be up later to tuck you in E.' he grinned at me and winked before striding towards the door.

Noble glowered at him but remained composed. 'Well.' He said, turning his attention to me. 'Would you like some chicken soup?' He reached for the tray. 'I've already eaten, so I shall sit with you Effie until you are asleep.' He smiled charmingly at me. 'Would you like me to read to you after dinner?'

Reddening a little I gave him a smile, and nodded my head.

Sleep came easy that night and I dreamt Gideon was wandering through the countryside of Briarwood, endlessly strolling through meadows and woodlands before arriving in the heart of the village, where he took an axe to the tree in the village square, hacking it down like a madman, until it was a mere stump.

I heard a loud thump.

'Morning E.' said Mace bounding through the door.

'What...what time is it?'

'Just gone nine.' He said casually. 'Time keeping has been much improved around here since I wound up the grandfather clock downstairs. Caleb hates it of course; says he doesn't need to know what time it is.'

Very carefully I lifted myself up and began to cough violently.

He leapt over and placed his hand on my back. 'Steady on old girl, you'll do yourself an injury.'

'I already have.' I replied croakily.

With a grin he energetically strode towards the window and flung back the curtains.

'Let's get some air into this room, shall we.'

I watched sleepily as he unlatched the window, and flung it open.

'Whatever you say Mace.'

'It's a mighty fine day out there my friend.' For a minute he leant on the windowsill, staring outside, deep in thought.

With a yawn I moved up a little in the bed.

'Well, perhaps I should go and sit outside.' I uttered in anticipation. 'Some fresh air will do me the world of good.'

Mace turned away from the window and faced me. 'Yeah, well maybe you should ask Caleb, he's adamant you should spend at least one more day in bed.'

Trying to ignore the pain I began pulling myself up.

'Okay, well perhaps I should have a word with him.'

'Oh Effie you are stubborn. One more day in bed will hardly kill you.'

'I shall be very sensible and rest in one of the garden chairs. Then later I could have a soak in the bath, dress and join you all for supper.'

He groaned.

Reaching for the bed covers I drew them back and slowly moved my legs down to the floor, determined not to wince from the pain around my waist and back. As I adjusted my nightshirt, I noticed the hideous claw- like marks on my lower legs. I stared at them in horror.

'They're just scratches E.' Mace said softly. 'They will fade in no time at all.'

'I know.'

He stared at my solemn face. 'Come on E.' Looking sympathetic he helped me back into bed and arranged the bed covers neatly around my waist. 'Let's not go and infuriate Caleb, shall we. He's been in such a jolly mood since…. since.'

I raised my eyes at him. 'Since what?'

'Since…since we returned from Hartland.' He said rather vaguely, avoiding my eye.

'Oh, I see.'

There was something Mace wasn't telling me; I could tell from his demeanour.

And it struck me odd why Caleb should be in such a jolly mood when we failed to return with Gideon.

He looked at me with a sheepish grin. 'Have you noticed how Noble takes after his father for his mood swings, he really can be quite sullen at times.'

'No, I've not.' I mumbled impassively. 'Talking of fathers, you haven't told Caleb that you're his long-lost son yet then?'

'I don't think that would be wise E, especially as I'm leaving soon.'

'You're serious about going home then?'

He didn't answer me immediately but just stood there looking at me.

'Just lately I can't stop thinking about home. Every time I look in my notebook, I'm reminded of it, and sometimes I want to throw my notes on the fire and burn them to oblivion.' A haunted expression crossed over his face. 'The truth is Effie I really miss Abercrombie, and my foster parents. They must be sick with worry.'

I bit my lip but said nothing.

'Just like your Aunt must be sick with worry about you.'

My face clouded over. 'Oh yes, my Aunt.'

I stared forlornly at him, wondering if this was the right moment to tell him that his foster parents were dead, it would be such a crushing blow that perhaps it would be kinder to wait, but perhaps I'd waited too long.

'Also E, going home is the only way to rid me of this terrible guilt I feel at leaving Clarice to rot in that hideous monastery, and will make me forget that I didn't have the guts to go back

12

and rescue her.' He sighed heavily. 'Which, by the way, makes me a spineless coward.'

'Mace, how can you say such a thing? You did your very best in trying to save Clarice, just as I did in trying to save Gideon, but sometimes in life one must accept defeat. Besides, you've shown great courage in rescuing me, which I'm very grateful for, thank you, and for leading Lucinda to safety.' My eyes widened in concern. 'You did bring Lucinda back to Briarwood, didn't you?'

He looked perplexed. 'Lucinda?'

Staring into his blank face, I became worried. 'Yes, Lucinda, the young girl who fled with you through the tunnels, don't you remember?'

'No, I don't.' He began to talk slowly as if speaking to a child. 'I ran ahead Effie, on my own, through the tree infested tunnels, and you decided, like a fool, to stay with Gideon. There wasn't any girl called Lucinda with me.'

With a worried look on his face he pulled up a chair and sat beside the bed.

'How strange.' I muttered in a distant voice. Suddenly, feeling chilly, I clambered back into bed and pulled the bedcovers over me. 'Did you not see her in my room the night we were going to escape, did you not hear me mentioning her name?'

Placing his fingers on his lips he gazed up at the ceiling, deep in thought. 'Mm. Now you come to think of it I vaguely recall you mentioning a Lucinda.' He lowered his eyes, focusing on his hands. 'But I never actually saw the girl.'

A look of despair crossed over my face. 'Well, didn't it cross your mind to ask me who she was?' I could feel my face turning scarlet with anger and frustration. 'Were you not curious?'

Shrugging his shoulders, he began to fidget on his chair. 'No. Not really. Perhaps the tonic did have an effect on me after all.' He laughed rather falsely. 'I did you a favour really E.'

'How?'

'Well, we were all on edge, weren't we, living in that environment. If I'd made you aware of...of the girl who wasn't really there, then it could have tipped you over the edge of sanity and plunged you into the depths of madness.'

I leant forward in the bed, so I could make closer eye contact with him. 'Don't speak gibberish Mace. I can't believe you're using that foul tonic as an excuse. And as for not mentioning to me that you couldn't see Lucinda that was hardly for my benefit, you just couldn't be bothered to say anything.'

'Calm down Effie.'

My eyes drifted off towards the window. 'It all makes sense now. She was always appearing from nowhere and was very good at hiding, as if she.... she was invisible.' I let out a cry and hid my face in my hands. 'She was a ghost. Lucinda was a ghost.'

I felt an arm about my shoulders. 'There, there E, don't fret about it. That diabolical monastery plays tricks on the mind. Some ghostly entity used to creep up behind me every night, and each time I turned round to confront it, the thing would retreat back into the shadows' He shuddered. 'But that wasn't the worst of it. There was a far more repugnant creature stomping those corridors, with beady eyes and a ghoulish face, its name was Proctor.'

I tried to smile. 'But Lucinda wasn't scary, she was a sweet, melancholy girl, who needed a friend. She helped me Mace, Lucinda showed me the secret passage down to the tunnels. How desperate she was to leave with me.' My eyes became tearful. 'But it seems she can never leave the monastery, not now, not ever.'

The door opened and Noble came into the room, immediately noticing my tear stained face. He threw Mace a nasty glare. 'What is it Effie, has Mace upset you?' He came over towards the bed and sat on the edge, and tenderly touching my face he wiped away a tear with his thumb. 'Why have you been crying?'

For a minute or so I was speechless.

'Effie?'

'No, Mace hasn't upset me.' I said. 'It's nothing, really.' Much to my embarrassment, I began to snivel. 'We were just discussing a friend of mine.'

Mace gave me a knowing smile. 'Yes, a friend from Hartland, a quiet girl who apparently helped us to escape.' He winked at me and kissed the top of my head before striding towards the door.

I looked puzzled. 'Where are you going?'

'Oh, I have chores to do E. I shall leave you in the capable hands of Gideon.' He gasped and put his hand up to his mouth. 'Sorry...I mean Noble.' He banged his hand against his forehead as he stood in the doorframe. 'The two of you are so alike I keep getting you mixed up. I should remember, Gideon is better looking, isn't he.' Before Noble had a chance to retaliate, Mace was bounding down the stairs.

To my surprise Noble seemed unruffled.

'Would you like some breakfast Effie?'

I nodded. 'Yes please.' My eyes fixed on his. 'Mace doesn't mean any harm, you know. Don't pay any attention to his taunting.'

'And does he do the same to you Effie?'

'Oh yes, almost all the time. I just tend to ignore him.'

He grinned.

A breeze came in through the open window and I shivered.

'Would you like me to close the window?'

'No, I like the air. Please would you pass me the shawl over on the dresser?'

He hesitated then went to fetch it. 'You must keep warm.' He ordered stoically.

'The last thing you need is another chill.'

'That's true.'

As he handed me the shawl, I shifted a little in the bed, causing the arm of my nightshirt to fall down, exposing my bare shoulder. I felt his eyes linger on it as I adjusted the material and arranged the shawl. Without a word he pulled the latch on the window so it was only slightly ajar then went downstairs to prepare my breakfast.

Chapter 2

As I crept outside the night was still and clear. The cool air seemed new and strange as if it had been a matter of years since I'd last been outside rather than a few days, and although it was a little chilly, I embraced the freshness with vigour and eagerness. All day I'd languished in bed, becoming increasingly restless, until finally it had become unbearable, and I had sneaked out the cottage when everyone was asleep.

Familiarising myself with the garden I meandered down to the stream and sat on the edge of the bank, listening to the soothing trickle of water.

My thoughts drifted to Gideon and how I must resign myself to never seeing him again, he was more lost to me now than he'd ever been; the man I had grown up with in my dreams had taken a different path now, one separate from mine. Septimus had been victorious in taking his grandson and moulding him into what he wanted, he had stripped him of his heart and soul and replaced it with a cold stone of emptiness, and now Gideon would spend his life at the monastery, wasting his days, without love or friendship, ignorant and oblivious that there was a brighter, rosier future elsewhere. And then there was Clarice, how utterly wretched I felt at not being unable to save her, and how she'd never be able to return to normal, to go home or see her mother. Discovering the haunting truth about Lucinda chilled me right to the bone, that sweet, quiet girl who spent most of her time in the library, so clever at hiding away and not being seen, now I understood why. The only positive outcome was Isaiah and his incarceration in that ghostly cell, I pondered if he was still alive, or whether he had already been strung up from the rafters in the great hall as Septimus had proclaimed. It's strange but I felt no loss or regret about his passing, my heart was empty.

There was a sudden rustling of bushes nearby, and as I stared in the direction of the noise, a dark mass seemed to appear from behind them, and as it moved nearer it materialised into a shadow-like figure.

I froze.

'Mace, Noble, is that you?'

It seemed that an endless silence hung in the air.

Not waiting to see what it was, I sprang up from the ground and scurried back up the garden, aware that something or someone was following me. Strong arms grabbed my waist from behind and with a scream I dug my nails deep into its flesh. It let out a groan and momentarily released its grip before clutching my arm. For a few seconds we wrestled with one another until the thing stumbled back and fell onto the grass, pulling me down on top of it. My eyes grew wide with horror as I stared into a pair of dark eyes glaring back at me, those oh so familiar eyes that I knew so well, and had admired since a small child when we used to play games in the forest.

'Gideon?'

Time seemed to cease as we continued looking at one another, without moving. I felt the warmth of his breath on my cheek and the beating of his heart against mine.

'Please move Effie, you're hurting my shoulder.'

His words returned me to reality and I moved away from him and sat down on the grass, not knowing what to say, trying to work out in my mind why he was here.

'What are you doing here Gideon?' I murmured in a questioning voice.

I watched him steadily as he raised himself up and sat beside me on the grass, his eyes boring into me. 'I heard a noise and came to investigate.'

A mixture of trepidation and bewilderment coursed through my veins as I tried to come to terms with him being here.

'Have you just arrived in Briarwood?' My eyes suddenly darted around the garden in panic. 'Did you come alone?' I gulped in fear, half expecting Septimus and Proctor to creep across the grass, ready to drag me back to the monastery, but I could see no one. 'I'm sorry Gideon but if you've come to take me back to Hartland you've had a wasted journey.'

There was a long silence.

'No Effie, I haven't just arrived. I've been here for a while now.' He paused. 'And I have no intention of taking you back to my home. I do not believe that my grandfather would be overjoyed to see you.'

I lowered my eyes to the ground. 'No, no he would not.' Looking up I gulped. 'So, are you back to stay?'

When he spoke, his voice was solemn and serious.

'No, I don't think so.'

'But I don't understand, what made you come back?'

'When I saw you being taken by The Elder trees at The Giver ceremony something inside of me snapped and I took it upon myself to save you.'

My eyes widened in shock. 'You... you did run after me that day.'

'Yes. Did you not realise.'

'Sort of, but it's all a little hazy. I remember the great birds swooping down, and then everything went black.' A shiver ran through my body. 'One of The Elder trees had me firmly in their clutches, but apparently Mace and the birds freed me.'

He was silent for a moment. 'I was the one that freed you Effie.'

'How?' I shook my head in complete disbelief. 'The trees are far too powerful.'

'Yes, yes they are. I'm not sure why but the trees didn't seem to put up much of a fight, they just shuddered for a moment then it was relatively easy to pull you away from them.'

I stared at him in disbelief. 'How strange.'

'What also struck me odd was how abnormally still they were, all the same I did wonder if they would snatch me, but for some reason they left me alone. Then by some miracle we all managed to clamber onto the birds and flee.' His face clouded over. 'Unfortunately, the trees had already caught Croft within their clutches.'

Instinctively I reached out and rested my hand on his arm, but he immediately flinched away from my touch.

'I'm so sorry about Croft, I know how much he meant to you.'

'Croft was foolish to enter the domain of Hartland as it is treacherous to any flying creature. I feel no sadness of his passing.'

His lack of compassion was a cold reminder that just because he was free of Hartland didn't mean he was free of the tonic. But I didn't want to think of that now, I was just grateful he was here, he had returned home.

'Well, I'm glad you decided to travel with us.'

'It was a rash decision, but before I had the chance to change my mind, I was being carried over the landscape away from Hartland.'

A smile spread across my face. 'And back to your home of Briarwood.'

I stood up and began pacing up and down, feeling angry that the others hadn't warned me that Gideon had returned to his rightful home. I wasn't surprised of course that he hadn't visited me whilst I'd been convalescing, just because he was back didn't mean he suddenly cared for me.

'I'm glad you've returned Gideon.'

He rose from the grass and stepped over towards me. 'Effie, just because I am here now doesn't mean I am staying. My actions on the day of The Giver ceremony have cast a dark shadow over my future at the monastery, but I have faith that grandfather will forgive me if I return.'

Leaping forward I grasped his hands in mine. 'Gideon I'm...I'm sure your grandfather will manage without you, for a while. Now that you're back in Briarwood you should take time to re-acquaint yourself with your father and brother, both of them have missed you greatly.' I hesitated for a moment. 'Perhaps you came back here for a reason, because you were homesick.'

I felt his hands gradually slip from mine. 'I sincerely doubt that. Since my arrival here I've been trudging the fields, trying to take my mind off Hartland. For I crave the routine of the monastery, and...and.' His voice became unsteady. 'I greatly miss my daily tonic.'

'Then why are you still here?'

He shrugged his shoulders. 'A small part of me was concerned for your health. But now you've recovered I feel easier in my mind, and will be returning to Hartland shortly.' He began to stroll towards the cottage, then paused and half turned to me. 'Maybe you'd like to join me tomorrow, we could take a stroll in the countryside.'

My throat suddenly felt dry and when I spoke my voice sounded gruff. 'Yes, yes of course.' I began to walk towards him. 'But I should warn you, my legs are a little out of practice.' I chuckled.

His face remained straight. 'We won't go far. Come, it's cold out here. You must go back to bed before you catch a chill.' He stood there waiting for me to pass and go into the cottage.

After rising just before dawn I went and had a wash then padded back up to my room to get ready. It was a little early for me, especially as I wasn't quite myself yet, but just as we'd gone back inside the cottage last night Gideon had mentioned meeting up just after dawn, and I had agreed without question, fearful that it wouldn't take much for him to change his mind.

I groaned with pain as I accidentally collided with the corner of the dresser, catching my waist exactly where the branches had gripped me. Holding my middle, I slowly made my way to the wardrobe and peeked inside. The few clothes I'd brought with me from home were in my rucksack at Hartland, and had probably been discarded by now, along with Isaiah. I wasn't surprised when I saw the same old pale lilac dress, belonging to Florentine, and the crimson one I'd worn that sultry night of the festival. As I touched the silky material it reminded me how deliriously happy I'd been the last time I'd worn it, but then the mad woman had made an appearance and taken all my joy away by reminding me that I didn't belong in Briarwood. Trying to ignore the feeling of acute melancholy flooding over me, I swiftly reached for the crimson dress, and reluctantly put it on.

Gideon was already waiting for me in the back garden. A strained smile appeared on his face when he saw me and I noticed how his eyes briefly scanned my dress.

'Ready for a walk?'

My legs suddenly felt heavy, like weights. I felt exhausted, as if my energy was all used up for the day.

'Yes, I think so, a short one. Would you mind taking my arm Gideon?'

His eyes widened in alarm, as he stood there staring at me, uncertain of what to do.

'If you prefer, we could delay our walk.'

'No.' I uttered quickly. 'I'd love to go for a stroll.'

So serious and tense was his expression that it seemed I'd asked him to do something terrible. Taking matters into my own hands I moved forward and linked my arm with his.

'Shall we go?'

Without saying a word, he walked slowly forward, seemingly angry that he had to make physical contact with me, as if it repulsed him. And for some time, we walked along quite quietly, arm in arm as if we were a loving couple taking an early morning stroll in the countryside. I noticed how he seemed pre-occupied, and strode forward with the unconscious motion of a sleepwalker.

Quite abruptly he withdrew his arm from mine and turned to face me.

'Effie?' he said, looking directly into my eyes. 'There is something I must ask you.'

I studied his face carefully. 'Very well.'

He half-opened his lips as if to speak but changed his mind.

'Yes?' I uttered, unable to bear the suspense.

He paused for a moment, looking nervous and confused, and when he spoke his voice was hoarse and unsteady. 'You shall have to forgive my hesitation, it's just that I'm not finding this very easy.' Placing his hand over his mouth he cleared his throat. 'As I told you last night I shall be leaving very soon for Hartland and have no intention of taking you back with me. But... but I've thought the matter over and have decided that you should accompany me.'

'Pardon?'

'I'd like you to come and live with me at the monastery.'

Standing there I felt unable to respond, and when I finally spoke my voice sounded garbled. 'You want me to...to go back with you. To that horrid place.' My voice became louder. 'But why Gideon?' Do you not recall what happened last time I was there, how your grandfather had me sacrificed to The Elder trees?' I shook my head, feeling exasperated. 'I could never be happy there Gideon, never. And even if I did become acclimatised to the strange way of life in the monastery, your dear grandfather would see to it that I conveniently disappeared.'

He suddenly moved forward and grasped my arm. 'Not if we were to marry.'

I was stunned. 'Marry?' looking up I saw his eyes, wide and intent upon my face.

'But I thought you couldn't stand the sight of me.'

'No Effie, that's never been true. During The Giver ceremony when you mentioned the forest, I finally realised what you really meant to me.' An agonised looked crossed over his face. 'That's why I ran after you, to try and save you. I...I just need to try and adapt to life with you Effie. And then I think that we can be happy together. Grandfather will accept you; I know he will.' He paused. 'So, will you marry me?'

'Oh Gideon.'

I stood there pondering for a moment. After all this time he had finally asked me to marry him, how ironic it should have to come at a terrible price. I would not survive the deadly monastery, not a second time. I recall how he'd almost asked me before on the day of the festival, but circumstances beyond our control had prevented him. I would have accepted his proposal then, but now it wasn't events that had got in the way it was the tonic. Nevertheless, his proposal did give me a tiny glimmer of hope, for despite the tonic he must still love me, and where there's love there's a way.

'But we can be together here in Briarwood, Gideon. This is your true home.'

He suddenly looked desperate. 'Not Effie, it is not.' He shook his head viciously. 'I feel weak and unhappy here.'

'It's the tonic Gideon; you need to rid yourself of it. Stay here with me, with your family. We will all help you get better.'

He glared at me. 'I don't think you've listened to a word I've been saying.' He snarled. 'Now I've asked you a question, so please be good enough to give me an answer.'

I pictured myself back at the monastery, living a sorrowful existence, addicted to the tonic. Gideon would be by my side, we would love one another but it would be without passion, without tenderness, without feeling; I would be dead inside, just like all the other inhabitants. And Septimus would watch me like a hawk, biding his time, before doing away with me, and then the darkness of the trees would ensnare me, and I would be no more.

With a gasp I stumbled away from him. 'I cannot marry you Gideon, not if you expect me to return to Hartland.' I gulped. 'It will destroy me, just as it's destroying you.'

His face darkened. 'So be it.' With a twisted grin he approached me, his face close to mine. 'I should have known that you never truly loved me. Grandfather was right, love is for fools.' I watched as his eyes travelled down to the ring on my finger and rather swiftly, he snatched my hand, moving his thumb roughly over it. 'Noble gave you this did he not?'

Transfixed, I stared down at the ring, trying to recall the story behind it.

'Yes, but it doesn't mean anything.'

'You're not a very good liar, Effie.' He said in a stony voice. 'Noble told me that the two of you are engaged to be married and that is what prompted me to ask you, before it was too late. But I can see now how foolish I've been.' Releasing my hand, he slowly moved a few paces away. 'I hope the two of you shall be very happy together.'

'I'm not engaged to Noble.'

'Is that really the truth, Effie?'

'Yes.' I glared at him. 'Did you only ask me because you thought Noble had?'

'No, of course not.' He snapped. 'But I do realise it was inappropriate of me to ask you, knowing you could be engaged to another, and for that I apologise.' He casually shrugged his shoulders. 'Let's put the whole matter behind us now. I shall be leaving within the next few days and we shall never see one another again.' He bent his head towards me. 'I bid you good day Effie.'

I watched as he marched back down the hill and through the corn, knowing there was nothing I could do. Feeling despondent and weary I lay down for a while, my arm shielding my face from the sun. It would have made me most content to stay like this for a while and take a nap, however during these past few days I had slept enough. Perhaps I should have returned to the cottage but I was too agitated and needed to distant myself from them all. With a sudden burst of energy, I lifted myself up and began striding out towards the village, there was nothing like a good walk to clear the mind, and with each step my legs seemed to be improving.

After passing through a shady avenue I came upon a lane of cottages, which I'd not seen before. With their picturesque exteriors and soothing charm, they blended in snugly to their surroundings. I strolled up the cobbled lane and saw an old man smoking a pipe, sitting outside one of the cottages.

'Good morning Miss Heatherington.'

I paused and stared at him.

His face relaxed into a slow smile. 'I'm glad to see you're back with the living.'

'I'm not Miss Heatherington.'

As he chuckled his pipe almost fell from his mouth. 'Are you sure?'

Reaching forward I placed my hand on his shoulder.

'My name is Effie.'

'Nay.'

I whispered in his ear. 'Please be good enough to inform the other villagers that I am Effie, and I'm very much alive. Oh, and if you could also mention that it's rather rude to keep staring at me all the time. I'm afraid if it continues, I may be forced to put a curse on the village.'

The pipe dropped into his lap.

I smiled smugly at him. 'Do have a good day sir.'

I'm not really sure what possessed me to say about a curse, and on reflection I could see that such a thing would make matters worse. Instead of a ghost I would now be known as a witch. As I walked away, I suddenly felt remorseful and turned to go back and apologise to the man, and explain I was just joking about the curse, but a sudden noise made me stop in my tracks.

A bent figure was peering at me, smiling peculiarly.

'Sister, I've been waiting for ye.'

I looked startled. 'Gilbert.'

He beckoned me forward. 'Come sis, won't you take some tea with us?

With an anxious smile I found myself stumbling back. 'Perhaps another day.'

I didn't mind so much but the thought of having to see the mad woman, let alone speak to her filled me with a horrible dread.'

From out the corner of my eye I could see the old man with the pipe peering at us.

'Oh, come on sis. I be in need of the company.'

I stared into his bony face. 'But your... I mean our sister. Will she not mind?'

'She's not ere.'

'Oh.' My face relaxed a little. 'Very well then Gilbert.'

We sat in the parlour having tea and cake. For some reason the curtains were drawn closed and apart from the glowing fire the room was shrouded in darkness.

'So, where is Verity?'

He carried on eating the cake, spilling crumbs all over his trousers. 'Went on one of her trips, she did. Left me all alone again.' He wiped the side of his mouth with his sleeve. 'My sister thinks it's her right to go travelling when she feels like it.' He took a gulp of tea. 'Folks round here don't take kindly to it. Warned her they have, told her that she should stay in the village or else.'

'Or else she'll be banished?'

'Yep. Just like father.'

I finished my cake and took a sip of the tea, lowering my eyes. 'What a shame.'

We sat in silence for a moment, watching one another.

I began to laugh. 'So, who else is here?'

'What?'

'You asked me to take some tea with…us. So, I assumed you had company.'

He drained his cup. 'Oh, I meant father.' Once more he wiped his mouth, then noisily clanked the cup back down onto the saucer. 'Want another slice sis?'

'No, no thank you.' I replied rather perplexed. 'Gilbert…your father, he isn't…'

Not waiting for me to end my sentence, he sat there staring longingly at the cake as he spoke. 'I should save some for father. He won't be best pleased if I scoff it all.' He exploded into hysterical laughter.

I almost dropped my cup. 'Please Gilbert, stop this foolish talk- your father isn't in Briarwood.'

His face grew strange. 'Yes, he is sis. I'm not supposed to say anything to the villagers, but you being my sister and all, I know you won't tell.'

With a great sigh I closed my eyes and began taking deep breaths.

'He wants to see you sis.'

I opened my eyes and stared into his narrow face. 'I see.'

'Shall I go and fetch him sis?'

My hand was trembling as I placed my cup on its saucer. 'No Gilbert, I really should be on my way.' I rose unsteadily and made my way towards the door. 'Thank you for your hospitality.'

'But sis, you can't go without seeing father.'

I suddenly felt a little nauseous. I'm not sure if the cake was to blame, or the annoying way Gilbert kept calling me sis, or his disturbing behaviour, thinking Isaiah was in the cottage, but whatever it was I was desperate to leave and get some fresh air.

Rather swiftly I made my way to the door. 'Good day Gilbert.'

'Wait sis, please wait.'

I swung round to face him. 'Gilbert your father's gone away. I understand you must be lonely but…. but pretending your father's here in the cottage, well it really isn't healthy.' My eyes filled with compassion. 'You're welcome to visit Caleb's cottage whenever you like, and I shall make a point of calling in on you in the next few days.'

He made a strange groaning noise.

'Until next time Gilbert.'

Just as I reached the door my attention was drawn to the pile of shoes and boots in the corner, haphazardly thrown there in a heap, and beside it was a rucksack, my rucksack. In a daze, I stared at it intently with strange fascination, trying to figure out how and why it was there. Tentatively, I shakily reached out to touch it with my hand, half expecting it to vanish at my touch.

'Effelia?'

With a gasp I stood bolt upright and slowly turned to see a still figure, standing there like a ghostly statue.

When it spoke, I felt a chill go down my spine.

'We've been waiting for you Effelia.'

I couldn't take my eyes away from his face- it was Isaiah.

'No.' I cried between sobs. 'No, it's not you.'

Suddenly it was all too much for me and I opened the door and fled. Without looking back, I staggered over the uneven cobbled stones and through the village green, passing hurriedly by the market stalls, pushing my way through the villagers as if they didn't exist, not noticing or caring how they stared at me.

'Effie…Effie wait.'

I ignored whomever it was calling my name and carried on running, too scared and upset to speak to anyone.

On reaching the avenue leading from the village I stopped to catch my breath, then at a steady pace I proceeded in the direction of the cornfields and followed the footpath leading to the church and went inside. I'm not really sure what possessed me to automatically head for the place of worship; perhaps I felt safe on sacred ground, no monster or supernatural being could enter this holy place, or so I was led to believe. But it was cold in the church and as I hunched forward on one of the pews, shivering from head to toe, I allowed my paranoia to overwhelm me- what if one of the unnatural beings from the monastery had followed me to Briarwood; I could almost feel its presence creeping towards me, reaching out with its icy hand so it could drag me back to its home, and finish its task of turning me insane. And then I would lurk in the darkness of those foreboding corridors, screaming and muttering to myself like a woman possessed, until the trees of Hartland silenced me forever.

A piercing scream erupted from my mouth as I felt something clasp my shoulder, and in complete and utter fright I scrambled along the pew and fell to the floor, burying my face in my arms.

'Effie? Please don't be scared it is only me, the parson.' He cleared his throat. 'Is everything alright?'

I remained on the floor for a moment trying to regain my senses. The pressure was on my shoulder once more, but this time I didn't become hysterical. With a deep sigh I pulled myself up and shakily sat back on the pew and sheepishly peered into the face of the parson.

'Please excuse my strange behaviour parson.' Embarrassment came flooding over me as I saw how he stared at me in bewilderment. 'I...I forgot where I was for a moment.'

He sat beside me on the pew and gently patted my hand. 'It wasn't my intention to startle you Effie. I should have been more considerate of your delicate state.'

Looking into his eyes I saw they were full of pity. What a poor thing he must think me, weak from my illness and broken from my experience at Hartland, a shadow of my former self. Of course, the parson most likely sided with the villager's, and seeing how I flitted from one world to another with careless abandonment had come to the conclusion that I didn't belong here.

I did my best to smile at him. 'Really parson there's really nothing wrong with me. I'm just a little on edge.' Feeling awkward, I bent my head and began twisting the engagement ring on my finger, trying to think what to say.

'Forgive me for asking Effie, but are you betrothed to someone?

My head rose and I stared at him quizzically. 'Whatever gave you that idea parson?'

He glanced at me expectantly. 'The ring you're wearing.' His eyes fell to my hands. 'It is a love token, is it not?'

I stared at him blankly without saying a word. A picture of Noble materialised in my head, gazing endearingly at me; we were in a garden, surrounded by people, on a gloriously warm summer's day.

'It's...its nothing really, just a friendship ring.'

The parson cleared his throat and looked away. I'm sorry Effie, it's really none of my business.' He rose and moved over to a narrow table to the right of the pulpit. 'It's just that I always imagined you and Gideon would marry...well before the both of you left the village and went to Hartland.' Unable to answer I watched as he began gathering hymnbooks from the table. 'However, the situation must be rather different now that he is changed so.' Carrying an armful of the books he turned to stare at me. 'He comes here, you know. Not to pray or speak to me.' One by one the parson began to unload the hymnbook along the pews. 'All he does is sit here, gazing ahead at the altar, like a lost soul trying to find his way.' He shook his head violently. 'I've tried talking to him, but he seems completely reluctant to confide in me. It's a sorry sight, sorry indeed.' His face looked grim as he approached me, and when he spoke his voice was but a whisper. 'The question is can you and Gideon find the happiness that the two of you once shared?'

'To be quite honest parson I have absolutely no idea. I always imagined we would end up together but now...'

'But he did return home, so there is hope. If it was meant to be the lord will find a way to reunite the two of you. You must have faith Effie.'

I smiled rather weakly, giving him a half- hearted nod.

'Do you believe in ghosts, parson?'

'I most certainly do.' He said with a gentle smile. 'Why do you ask?'

Clasping my hands tightly together, I hunched forward on the pew, trying to ignore the pain around my middle. 'I saw one this very day.'

'Did you recognise the ghost Effie?'

'Yes, it was....'

The parson was looking at me attentively. 'Yes?'

I suddenly cast my mind back to the trial, here in the church, when Isaiah had been banished from the village. Perhaps I shouldn't reveal whom it was I saw today, even if it was merely my father's ghost. What if word got back to the village folk, and just for good measure they decided to investigate? Gilbert was clearly already distressed at the loss of his father, and the last thing he'd want is a barrage of people descending on his home.

'It...it was my descendant Florentine Heatherington.'

He gave me a knowing smile. 'Ah yes dear old Florentine. She manifests herself to many in the village, especially here in the church. Sometimes her shimmering figure is seen floating up the aisle and through the old door that is now blocked up.'

I gave him a timid smile but did not comment.

'Where did you see her?'

'In the village.' I said feeling desperately uncomfortable. 'Never mind. I...I more than likely imagined it anyway.'

He peered into my face. 'They say the rare few that manage to escape the clutches of Hartland suffer terribly, and the trauma of it all is more than likely causing you to hallucinate.'

I stared back at him, pondering over what he had just said. 'Yes, yes you're absolutely right parson.'

'I trust you feel better Effie.'

For a minute I was tempted to blurt out the truth, the parson had such honest eyes, and appeared to be someone you could confide in, but in the end, I decided to leave the matter be.

'Yes, thank you parson, your wise words have helped tremendously.'

Clasping his hands together he beamed at me. 'Oh, I'm so glad.'

I rose from the pew and shook his hand enthusiastically. I'd convinced myself that he was right- my mind was playing cruel tricks that is all. Isaiah had gone and wasn't coming back.

Mace was right it was time to go home. Gideon was leaving and not coming back. Caleb had apparently saved my life, and for that I was grateful, but he didn't want me here, he tolerated me. The majority of the villagers still threw me strange unnerving looks, and apparently, I was seeing visions of my dead father. But Noble infuriated me the most -how dare he tell Gideon we were engaged, it was a lie, and I almost hated him for it.

Feeling suddenly weary I traipsed back home, hoping to sneak back upstairs but Caleb called out to me.

'Effie? Effie thank god, we were all becoming concerned about you. Noble saw you in the village and said you seemed distressed.'

I stood and glared at him. 'I went for a walk that is all.'

He wrinkled his brow as he wiped his hands with a cloth. 'Well I hope you didn't venture too far. The sun's healing qualities will not work if you over exert yourself.'

'Right.' I muttered. 'Well thanks for the warning.'

'Is something amiss Effie? You seem rather vexed.'

My hand rested on the banister. 'No, not really, apart from discovering that Gideon is here and nobody bothered to tell me.' I sighed. 'My other troubles are my own.'

'I only didn't tell you about Gideon because I feared it would delay your recovery. I'm...I'm sorry it wasn't my intention to upset you Effie.'

'I know Caleb.' As I ascended the stairs, I half turned to him. 'By the way-I've not had a chance to speak to you before now, and I'd like to say thank you, thank you for making me well again.'

He smiled, nodding his head in acknowledgment. 'Effie?'

'Yes Caleb.'

'I'm worried about Gideon. He won't talk to me about anything. Would...would you try and speak with him?

I suddenly noticed faint shadows underneath his eyes. I wondered if he knew that Gideon intended to leave. If he didn't should I be the one to give him the news? The chances of persuading his son to change his mind were almost none existent, and yet I felt I owed it to Caleb to try.

'Very well then Caleb, but I cannot make you any promises.'

I went to my room and unlaced my boots, and fell asleep instantaneously.

The conversation at supper was kept light, with very little laughter. Occasionally I would meet Gideon's eye and then we would both look away awkwardly. I purposely avoided Noble's gaze, as I was still annoyed with him about the engagement. All through the meal I made a point of hiding my ring, which I intended to prise from my finger later.

Caleb cleared his throat. 'There is to be a celebration in the village green tomorrow eve, Rose Green and Frederick Chambers are finally to be wed.'

My eyes flickered to Gideon and then to Noble.

'Have they been engaged for long Caleb?'

'Oh yes, for a time now. At one point I thought they were calling the whole thing off.' He clasped his hands together. 'Anyway, the entire village has been invited to their wedding feast, so it would be very pleasant if we all attended, do you not agree?'

Mace responded with a mouthful of food. 'I'm up for it Caleb. And so is E, aren't you?'

I smiled at him. 'Why not.'

Noble responded hastily. 'I shall attend father.'

Gideon looked steadily at his father then dropped his gaze to his plate. 'Very well then.'

Caleb clapped his hands together in glee. 'Wonderful.'

'Then it will be time for me to leave Briarwood for good.'

'What? No Gideon no.' Caleb gulped nervously. 'You're not going back to that place, are you?'

'That place father is my home.'

I watched as Gideon abruptly rose from his seat, sending it crashing to the floor, and as he strode to the back door, he froze for a moment. 'I heard you earlier father, discussing me with Effie. There is no point her speaking with me, she will not change my mind, no one can.'

I watched as a frantic Caleb went running after him.

'Well, another jolly night in Briarwood, eh.' Exclaimed Mace. 'And you wonder why I can't wait to leave.'

The last thing I thought of as I drifted off that night was my rucksack, and how it had mysteriously turned up in Briarwood. I imagined it had grown wings and flown all the way from Hartland. This rather outlandish theory was most favourable to the other explanations I had floating around inside my head and for a short while it eased my troubled soul, allowing me glide effortlessly along the path of sleep. However, in the dead of the night something awoke me, a noise perhaps I'm not sure, but as I half opened my eyes, I saw the form of a man standing by the window staring at me.

I cried out and clamped my hand over my mouth.

As my eyes acclimatised to the dark, I stared wide-eyed into the ghostly face of Isaiah. With a whimper I dived underneath the bedcovers and told him to go away, mumbling it over and over again. It seemed like a lifetime before I felt brave enough to emerge from the covers, and check the room. The figure had gone, along with the darkness, and the early morning light was flooding through the crack in the curtains, that were gently swaying in the breeze from the open window. Thinking it must have been a nightmare I slumped down into the bed and fell back to sleep.

Chapter 3

It is said, by some, that when a person looks death in the face that their life from that point onwards is completely changed. Their little world that once existed is shattered into tiny fragments and scattered to the wind, and everything that once seemed important doesn't matter anymore, and all those niggling worries and insecurities that make us who we once were will disappear. They will have a fresh new outlook on life, a deep appreciation for their second chance at living. For life is like a precious and delicate flower that can wither and die so easily, but with careful nurturing it can flourish until old age descends upon it. However, as I mulled this theory over that morning, I came to the conclusion that for me this wasn't so. I may have survived Hartland, and narrowly escaped with my life, but that didn't take away my demons; they were still skulking close by, watching and waiting to pounce, and until I completely dispelled them from my life, I hadn't a hope in hell of starting a fresh one.

I licked the blood from my finger as a thorn tore through my thumb. It was late morning and I was in the lane leading up to the cottage, picking blackberries for a pie, and had already filled an entire basketful.

Noble was coming out the gate and heading directly towards me.

I frowned.

'Mace is looking for you.'

'Oh. That's nice.'

Gathering the basket, I began walking towards the cottage.

'You're angry with me, aren't you Effie'

I spoke without looking at him, knowing that his gaze always distracted me.

'Just a little. You know Noble, it wasn't right for you to tell Gideon that we were engaged.' I glanced at my ring. 'I'm not sure if you did it to aggravate him, but it really was unnecessary was it? Especially when it's a big fat lie.'

There was a silence.

'Well?'

I stole a quick glimpse at him. He was staring glumly down at my basket. 'Effie, I'm truly sorry. Perhaps it was my intention to annoy Gideon, he always has a way of bringing out the worst in me, and sometimes...well sometimes my mouth has a way of running away with me. Especially when it's to do with you.'

Our eyes met and I saw he was smiling.

'Please say you forgive me Effie.'

With the sweetness of his smile it was impossible to be cross with him.

'I forgive you.'

He grinned. 'Wait there, I shall be right back.'

'But I'm going back to the cottage.' I shouted after him.

'No, stay where you are.'

I frowned then laughed to myself as he leapt over the gate to the cottage and disappeared inside. He emerged almost immediately carrying a package.

'Here, I have a present for you. I didn't want to give it to you in the cottage. Father wouldn't approve it he saw me giving you a gift.'

I took it from him and unwrapped the cloth, gazing down at the silk gown.

'Well...do you like it? A lady in the village is a dressmaker and I asked if she'd make you a new dress. I...I wasn't sure about the size. I chose the material as I thought it matched your eyes.

I removed the green gown from the cloth and ran my fingers over the fine silk.

'Thank you Noble, it's lovely.'

'I thought you might like to wear it to the wedding.' He laughed. 'The one being held tonight in the village, not our wedding.'

My face broke into a smile.

'Unless of course you'd like to wed me today?'

Startled I gazed into his serious face then playfully hit him. 'Very funny.'

'It wasn't meant to be a joke.'

For a brief moment we stared at one another.

Mace came bounding towards us with a big chunk of bread in his hand.

'Sorry to interrupt your cosy little chat but I really need to speak with you E.' He took a bite out the bread. 'Why don't we take a walk in the spectacular countryside Effie?' With his mouthful he took the basket from my hand and handed it to Noble. 'Be a chum and take this back to the cottage will you.' His eyes rested on the gown. 'What's this a new dress...very fancy.' He tried to snatch it from me.

'Leave it Mace.'

Noble went to take the dress, his hand brushing over mine.

'Give it to me Effie. I shall go and hang it up for you, ready for tonight.' Throwing me an intense stare he turned and paced towards the cottage.

Mace and I strolled down the lane and out into the field. He commented how Noble was irritatingly attentive towards me and was attempting to entice me with lavish gifts and lingering looks, and now that Gideon was almost out the picture he was reeling me in, ready to devour me. I scoffed, telling him he was being an idiot.

'So, what did you want to discuss Mace?'

'What? Oh yeah...two things actually. Firstly, I wanted to talk about our going home.'

He went on to ask me if I had any idea how we're going to get back to our world, and looking slightly embarrassed he told me how he kept getting an overwhelming urge to burst out crying, because he was so bereft at not being able to return. Every single night he'd flick through his notebook so he could remember his foster parents and Abercrombie. Just hearing the name made me feel melancholy, it was like a blow to the chest. The notebook was more of a curse than a blessing, it reminded us that we didn't belong in this world and urged us to go back, and yet without a safe gateway it was hopeless. Last time we had crossed over into Briarwood between the trees, but would we be risking our lives returning that way, would we yet again find ourselves in an interface between worlds, where lost souls roamed about in utter torment, searching for a way out that they could never find. The mere idea made me shudder with fear.

We reached the spot that looked down into the valley, an area of outstanding beauty that never failed to take my breath away.

In unison we both sat down on the bank.

'Mace?'

'Huh?' he uttered looking distracted.

'What...what if we have to stay here, would you be awfully unhappy?'

'Is that a trick question E?'

I threw him a half smile.

'It's just that if we can't find a portal...gateway or whatever you'd like to call it, then we would have to make our lives here. If you destroyed the notebook it would make it easier.'

Looking indignant he swung round to face me. 'It's because of him, isn't it...Noble.' He laughed mockingly. 'I knew it.'

'No...no it's not him. This has something to do with you.'

'What?'

I began biting my nails.

'Spit it out Effie, it can't be that bad.'

'Can't it?'

He studied my face carefully. 'Effie.' He snapped. 'You can't keep me dangling like this, now what is it?'

I reached for his hand and held it in mine. 'It's...it's your foster parents Mace. There was an accident, a gas explosion in their house. They...they didn't make it.'

He sat there for a while without saying a word, and gazed blindly into the forest beyond.

'Mace?'

A strange laugh erupted from his mouth. 'Effie, are you sure your minds not becoming unhinged through lack of use, or if this is some kind of joke then it's not a particular amusing one.' His hand left mine and rubbed his face. 'And how would you know all this, you've not been home for ages. So, if this has just happened then....' His voice trailed off. Effie...Effie look at me.'

Looking shamefaced I stared into his eyes. 'The accident occurred when I was last home. I'm so dreadfully sorry Mace, for not mentioning it sooner, it was wrong of me. It's just that I knew how it would upset you so.'

As his face became overcome with grief the tears started to fall down his cheeks.

He buried his head in his hands, and as he sobbed, I leant over and placed my head on his back, wrapping my arms around him. For quite some time we remained there, it was a good place to mull over your worries and contemplate life...or mourn.

He raised his head and stared at me with his red eyes.

'I...I can't take it in Effie. Are you sure it was an accident?'

Rather swiftly I lowered my gaze to the grass. It wouldn't help telling him the truth. The perpetrator was dead.'

'Well...yes I presume so Mace.'

I would have remained there all night with him if he'd wished it, but eventually he rose from the bank, pulling me up with him, and without a word we returned to the cottage. He went to his room and I asked the others not to disturb him, I didn't tell them why, only that he wasn't feeling well and wouldn't be attending the wedding feast.

I stared at my reflection in the mirror. The gown that Noble had given me fitted me well, rather too well for my liking, it clung snugly around the bodice and waist, accentuating my figure. Suddenly I wanted to grab a shawl so I could hide beneath it, but Noble would be hurt, and it wouldn't be right to conceal such a beautiful gown.

I let my hair fall loose over my shoulders and ran the brush through it, noticing how it gleamed in the fading glow of the sun that streaked through the open window.

The gown rustled as I stepped out onto the landing, and rather slowly I made my way down the staircase, mindful of falling flat on my face. Gideon and Noble were waiting for me downstairs and stood there staring at my gown as if I were some kind of phantom. It took me back to when I'd first worn Florentine's dress, and I had rendered father and son speechless.

My eyes lowered to the ground and I laughed nervously.

'I...I was wondering whether to take a shawl. It may become chilly later.'

'Nonsense.' Replied Caleb as he entered. His eyes ran over my gown. 'Is that a new dress Effie?'

My eyes travelled to Noble then back to him. 'No...I found it stuffed right at the back of my wardrobe. It seemed a shame not to wear it.'

Noble strolled forward and kissed my hand. 'You look truly radiant Effie.' He winked at me and mouthed a thank you. 'Would you do me the honour of being my partner at the wedding feast?'

I nodded slowly.

The door suddenly swung open and crashed into Gideon. It was Mace.

'Oh, sorry Gideon, I didn't realise you were standing there.' As he looked at me, I saw his eyes were still rather bloodshot. 'Well, don't you scrub up well E?'

'Mace, I thought you were ill'

He looked suddenly lost. 'No Effie, I feel a little better now.' His face brightened. 'And you know me, I'm not the one to miss a good old knees up.'

'You just want to try Mr Quantock's cider, don't you Mace?' chuckled Caleb. 'I warn you though, it's a particular potent brew.'

'Well Caleb, that sounds just the thing to make me feel better.' He came up close beside me and lowered his voice. 'Nothing like a drink to drown one's sorrows.'

There was the murmur of hushed voices as we approached the village green, with the usual stares of astonishment. Strangely enough it didn't bother me anymore, it was something I'd become accustomed to. There seemed to be much frivolity at the feast, with drinking and dancing and plenty of food. A couple of the villagers were playing a violin and an accordion, and people was dancing arm in arm to the music, including the bride and groom who were directly in the centre, their eyes intently fixed on one another. Evidently, they had married in the church earlier that very afternoon and were now enjoying their wedding feast.

Noble and I had remained together since leaving the cottage and it was only when Caleb pulled him away to speak to a couple of the villagers that I found myself standing alone. Gideon was sitting on one of the benches staring broodingly across at me. I pondered whether or not to go and join him but after our conversation yesterday I wasn't sure if he'd be very welcoming. He reiterated his plans to leave at breakfast this morning, despite Caleb's heartfelt attempts to make him stay. Deciding I should at least give it one last go I began to stroll towards him.

Someone grasped my arm.

'Here.' Said Mace, passing me a tankard. 'You should really try this cider E.'

He stumbled forward, spilling some of the contents over my boots and narrowly missing my gown.

With a frown I took a sip. 'You really should slow it down Mace.'

He hiccupped. 'Why? Everyone else seems to be drunk.' Laughing he snatched the tankard from me and swigged back the contents. 'So E, why are you standing here all on your lonesome. Where has your faithful puppy gone?'

'If you mean Noble, then he's talking with some villagers.'

A jovial looking man with a white moustache joined us and passed Mace another tankard of cider, and as he mumbled something under his breath he patted his arm. Mace passed me the tankard and thanked the man, before shaking his hand. As the man wandered off we both stared after him.

'That's Mr Quantock, who brews the cider.'

'I see.'

'He's a nice old gent. Shame I can't understand a word he says.' He glanced at me. 'Look E. You brought me sad news today the least you can do is join your friend for a drink.' He moved the tankard up to my lips. 'Now drink my girl and be merry.'

With a reluctant smile I knocked back the liquid.

I'm not sure at what point we got up and joined the others for a dance, but I can't recall a time when I'd laughed so much. Mace twirled me round so fast that everyone's face became a blur, and as I found myself falling someone else linked arms with me and then another. Everyone had laughing faces; they were all so jolly, as was I. A thickset man with a beard lifted me up into the air, swinging me round in a circle and as he set me down he grasped my hands and kissed them. I beamed at him.

'I don't care what folks say. You're no witch.'

My face dropped for a moment but then I grinned at him. 'Are you sure about that?'

He stared at me before bursting into laughter.

A woman took his hand and led him away. She threw me a look.

'Witches get burnt at the stake my dear, so be on your guard.'

I stared after her as she disappeared into the crowd with the bearded man. Suddenly my head began to spin and I began to panic.

'Mace, Mace where are you?' I shouted; my voice barely audible above the music.

Someone took a firm hold of my hand and led me away from the throng of dancers.

I began to laugh as I realised it was Noble.

Were you dancing too?

'No. I've never danced in my life.'

'Oh.' I exclaimed. 'That really doesn't surprise me.' I laughed again, and then started to giggle.

He came to a halt and grasped my arms. 'Effie, have you been drinking the cider?'

'Only a drop, unlike Mace.' I peered back towards the green. 'Talking of my friend, have you seen him?'

'Unfortunately, yes. He's slumped over one of the tables having a snooze.'

It only then occurred to me that I'd intended to speak with Gideon that was until Mace had intervened.

'I should go and see him.'

'Effie, he is fine. I thought you might like to take a walk and clear your head.'

'So that's why we're so far from the green.' I smiled.

He released my arms and took my hand, leading me up a bank.

'I also thought you may like to get away from the village folk. It never ceases to amaze me how they never tire of talking over old times.'

'Oh, I think it's rather endearing. Everyone should talk about their past, if they can remember it.' I giggled for a moment and then became serious. 'Noble, does Briarwood really burn witches at the stake?'

'Whoever told you that Effie is making it up.

'Did it ever happen in the past?'

'The old life will always remain here, and our ways never change. The subject of witches has never been mentioned, to my knowledge. Our toughest penalty is naturally for murder.

Feeling a little woozy I stopped and leant against him for a brief second, and as I pulled myself up straight, he steadied me with his hands.

'And what pray is the punishment for that?'

'The accused will be hanged in the village square then placed in a gibbet as a warning to others.'

'I can't imagine you have many murders in the village.'

We carried on walking.

He smiled. 'No, the last one was many years ago, and he was a visitor. Your father of course narrowly escaped through lack of evidence. But everyone knows he killed his wife, and many others.'

We had arrived at the top of the bank and had a good view of the village green. I could hear the music drifting towards us.

'You know Noble. I keep seeing visions of Isaiah.' I swallowed. 'Do you think I'm going mad?'

He lifted my chin so I was looking into his face. 'Effie, no of course not, you've been through a terrible ordeal at Hartland; it's bound to affect you. But it will pass, I'm sure of it.'

As I allowed my head to rest on his shoulder his arms came about my waist. For some while we remained like that, gently swaying to the music in the background. I lifted my head and looked up into his face, mesmerised by his eyes. Without warning he put his hand to the back of my head and moved my face nearer to his. His mouth began caressing my lips and for one surreal moment all sense left me and I responded by kissing him back, it was a long lingering kiss that became more urgent as we carried on. As he murmured my name, he pulled me closer but just as he did so I felt his body being wrenched from mine.

'Get off her Noble.'

It was Gideon, and he looked furious.

'Why? You'll be going back to Hartland tomorrow, what do you care?'

Without replying Gideon suddenly shoved him back. In a daze I stood there looking in bewildered as they began fighting on the grass, reigning punches down upon one another. As they rolled from side to side Gideon viciously pounded his fist into Noble's stomach and he cried out in agony.

'Stop.' I yelled, taking hold of Gideon's arm and tugging him away from Noble.

He pulled free of my grasp, throwing me a fierce look. 'Move out the way Effie. You'll only get hurt.'

I frantically looked around hoping that someone was nearby, and to my relief I suddenly saw two figures rushing towards us at a tremendous speed. It was Mace and Caleb.

'Quick. Please stop them.'

I watched the two of them prise the brothers apart but as Gideon mumbled something under his breath Noble lurched forward and struck him on the side of his jaw.

Caleb looked startled. 'Noble, stop that this instant.' He stared at the both of them. 'Whatever possessed you two to start fighting?

Mace widened his eyes. 'They're fighting over Effie. Noble is in love with her as well as Gideon.'

'Please be quiet Mace.' I whimpered, sinking to the grass. This is not helping.'

'Oh, come on E. I actually think it will help a great deal.'

Caleb put his hand up to silence Mace.

'Is this true Effie?'

'Well...I think so yes.' I stammered, suddenly feeling embarrassed and a little agitated that he was asking me rather than Noble.

'Don't flatter yourself Effie, this isn't all about you.' Shouted Gideon unsteadily. 'This goes way back doesn't it Noble, to when we were children.'

'Does it?'

'Before I go home to the monastery why don't we have this out once and for all.'

Noble wiped his blood-smeared face. 'Okay Gideon, let's talk about our mother, shall we, and how you were always her favourite son. You made her take the two of you on that trip to Hartland. She didn't even say goodbye to father and me. It's because of you that I never saw her again.'

'No, it wasn't like that Noble. Mother practically dragged me there against my will, and when father came to rescue me I begged her to return with us to Briarwood, but she wouldn't listen. She didn't care about me Noble; she didn't care about anyone but herself.'

Mace's face darkened. 'That's not true.'

'Keep out of this, it has nothing to do with you.'

'Oh, is that so Noble? Well for your information mother cared for us more than her life. Just like Gideon, there was an uncontrollable force dragging her back to Hartland, and she could do nothing about it. But she escaped in the end, only it wasn't Briarwood she ended up in, it was another world...Effie's world.' His eyes glistened with tears. 'Our time together may have been short but mother truly loved me, just as she truly loved the both of you.... and Caleb.'

Caleb staggered back in a daze.

'You're...you're Sabina's child?'

Mace gulped. 'Yes.'

'But...but I don't understand.'

'Sabina was carrying me when she left Briarwood for the last time and after fleeing Hartland with Effie's mother she gave birth to me.'

'Is...is Sabina dead?'

'I'm afraid so. What with the journey across worlds and giving birth, she became very weak...and passed away when I was a baby.'

Caleb stood there staring in bewilderment at Mace.

'Son...you're my long-lost son.' He began to sob uncontrollably.

My eyes welled up as I watched Caleb reach out to Mace and take him in his arms, and together they stood there weeping together. Gideon and Noble looked completely dumbfounded. Then something extraordinary happened, Noble placed his hand lightly on Mace's shoulder and as his tear stained face turned to his brother they embraced.

'I've always wanted a younger brother.' Exclaimed Noble.

Mace laughed at him between his tears. 'That's good.'

'Well Gideon, aren't you going to greet your new found brother?' asked Caleb.

'Of course.' He shook hands with Mace. 'Welcome to the family Mace.'

'I can't believe I finally told them.' Said Mace, shaking his head in disbelief.

It was late and all the others had gone to bed. The both of us were sitting in the garden, wrapped in blankets with mugs of tea. After the nights events Mace had been unable to sleep and asked me to come outside with him for a chat.

'Well, it was about time.' I said laughing. 'You know, I do believe Caleb half expected you were his son.' My eyes darted to his. 'But only when you weren't breaking his precious china or tripping over something.'

He grinned. 'Yeah, you're right about that E.' with a slurp of his tea he turned and looked at me. 'What a day for revelations, eh. Little old you finally decided to tell me about the death of my foster-parents and I accidentally let it slip to Caleb and my brothers that Sabina is my mother.' He began tapping annoyingly on the side of his mug. 'The thing is E, this changes things.'

In the darkness I could scarcely see his face but I knew he was mulling something over in his mind.

'What things.'

'You know how I've been rambling on about wanting to go home. Well...I've decided to stay in Briarwood with Caleb.' Placing his mug down he plucked a blade of grass and began chewing on it. 'Without my foster parents there's nothing really for me back at the old homestead.' He paused for a few seconds. 'Only rubble I imagine from where my house used to stand.

'I understand Mace.'

'If you want my notebook E, you can have it. It's no use to me anymore.'

'Thanks, but no.'

Apart from the hoot of a nearby owl it was silent.

'So, Effie what are you going to do now Gideon's leaving. Continue searching for a gateway out of here or...or perhaps marry Noble? He suddenly leapt to his feet in excitement. 'You realise we'll be related. I can start calling you sister in law.'

Although I couldn't see his face, I sensed he was grinning.

I giggled. Oh, I don't know Mace.' I said rising to my feet. 'I suppose if I did find a way out, I would go and see my Aunt, but if not...who knows.'

'Well, if you happen to stumble on a gateway and want to return, I'm coming back with you E, just for a short visit mind. I'll not have my best friend traipsing across worlds without her loyal companion.' He placed a kiss on top of my head then looked closely into my eyes. 'I'm still trying to make up for that time I pushed you through the portal; it was unforgivable of me Effie.'

'Oh Mace. That was a long time ago. And you know I'm not one to hold a grudge.'

'You realise that cursed father of yours put paid to you going home via Browning's Wood when he obliterated the portal. Don't tell me you forgive him too.'

'Perhaps not, but I won't speak ill of the dead.' I said, trying not to think of Isaiah's apparition.

'Huh.'

Wrapping his arm around me, Mace and I headed back inside the cottage. We didn't notice the two shadowy figures lurking by the riverbank, closely watching us.

Chapter 4

That night, such was my tiredness that I fell onto the bed without undressing. The cider, it seemed played a large part in what occurred tonight. If it hadn't been for the drink I wouldn't have danced with the villagers, Gideon wouldn't have lashed out at Noble, and Mace wouldn't have revealed his true identity.

In my dreams I saw Isaiah's lifeless body swinging upon a gibbet in the village square. His bloodshot eyes were peering at me through an iron mask. Suddenly his entire body began to twitch as if returning from the shadows of death, and as he extended his arm, I saw something drop from his blackened hand onto the ground – it was the ledger.

My first conscious thought as I opened my eyes was there must be a storm, as I could hear the rain pelting against the windowpane but as I swung back the bed covers and padded over to the window, I saw that the night was still and dry. I shot backwards as a spatter of pebbles made contact with the pane of glass, and it was only then I realised someone was trying to gain my attention. Moving forward I peered out into the darkness and could just make out the shadowy figure of a man. Initially I thought it was Gideon but as he stood there staring up at me, I managed to get a clearer look at his face, and saw that it was my brother Gilbert. I shook my head in bemusement and flung open the window.

'What is it Gilbert? I whispered, not wishing to wake anyone.

He didn't say anything but gestured for me to come down and join him. Why on earth it couldn't wait until morning I didn't know, but not wishing to be unkind I nodded at him and gave him a quick smile. Then wrapping the shawl around my shoulders, I crept out the cottage.

'Whatever is it?' I asked. 'Has something happened?'

'Nay sis.'

I held my hands out in confusion and laughed. 'Then what is it Gilbert?'

He looked unsettled, rather shifty. 'Can we go to the church sis? There's something I need to show you. It won't take long.'

Although I really didn't want to visit the church in the dead of night he had sparked my curiosity, and giving him another nod, we slowly made our way down the garden and through the cornfield. It was a cloudless night and the moon was full, bathing the church in a midnight blue.

'Mason didn't give you my message then?'

'Huh?' I said looking nonplussed.

'Your friend...Mason.'

'Oh.' I exclaimed smiling. 'You must mean Mace.'

He bent forward, rocking with laughter. 'What kind of name is that? Mace is a spice the last I heard.'

'Yes, I grant you it is rather strange. But I happen to think it rather suits him.'

As we reached the church doors he told me how he'd bumped into Mace in the market that morning and asked him to pass a message on to me, a message of great importance – I was to meet Gilbert in his cottage before noon. I suspected that was the other thing Mace was going to tell me when we were on our walk, but after I broke the news about his foster parents he must have forgotten, and who could blame him.

The door creaked eerily as he opened it.

'After you sis, go and take a pew.'

As I walked along the shadowy aisle my footsteps sounded hollow on the stone floor and sent out a strange echo around the building. A single candle was lit on the altar, emanating a soft gleam. I was suddenly taken back to that night of the thunderstorm, when the mad woman was waiting for me, to bring my world crashing down around me. How she revelled in showing me the portrait of Florentine, and reminding me of where I truly belonged. I fell to pieces after that, and scurried back home. But if my mad sister happened to be here this night, I would hold my ground and be strong, she wouldn't win this time.

'Gilbert?' I asked turning back. 'Why are you standing by the door?'

He let out a nervous laugh. 'Just so you don't run sis. It be father's idea, not mine.'

A cold chill crossed over my heart.

'This isn't funny Gilbert, it really isn't.' Shivering I turned round and made my way back to the entrance. 'Now let me out this instant.'

'Hello again Effelia.'

I stopped in my tracks. 'No...no it's not true.' With a cry I swung round and stared into the face of my father.

His face looked strangely old in the half-light, almost ghost like, but I now knew that it wasn't a ghost, and it wasn't the after effects of Hartland making me see things that weren't there, if I reached out and touched his cheek it would be warm, for he really was standing before me, he was flesh and blood.

'I can tell that you're stunned to see me Effelia. And why not.' He laughed. 'You must be wondering how I could possibly have escaped that dreary cell at the monastery and found my way back to Briarwood.'

'Yes, as a matter of fact I am.'

'That's a story for another day.' He ran his hand across the stubble on his chin looking suddenly deep in thought. 'What matters now is going home. If I have to stay hidden away in that cramped cottage for another day I swear I shall go mad. He lowered his voice to barely a whisper. 'One can only take so much of living with an imbecile.'

I dragged my eyes away from his face and glanced back at Gilbert, who was waiting dutifully in front of the doors.

Isaiah went on to tell me how he'd already been banished from Briarwood twice, and if he was discovered to be back in the village they would surely hang him this time. He would certainly not be welcome back at Hartland, and that leaved him only one option –travelling home to Rawlings. Just hearing the name of my house again made me feel homesick, I could suddenly picture the great house in my mind and it filled me with a strange sense of longing. After telling me to snap out of my daydream, Isaiah began moaning about being extremely hurt that I'd not come to visit him today and that I was selfish. But in the circumstances he'd forgive me, as now was not the time to have some petty squabble because he needed to focus on returning home.

'And how do you propose going home Isaiah?'

He grinned. 'Oh, it's not just me that's going home, you're coming with me Effelia.' With a devious smile he reached into his back pocket and produced a small notebook, waving it in front of my face. 'I should thank you for leaving me this. I can't tell you how informative it's been.'

My eyes lingered on the notebook for a moment then looked into his smug face.

'You didn't answer my question. How can we reach home?'

'Ah...so you do want to go back.' He smacked the notebook against his thigh. 'I knew it. But pray tell me dear daughter, do you plan on dragging along a certain young man by the name of Gideon, or will Noble be the man of your choice.' He threw his head back and laughed. 'Decisions, decisions eh? Yesterday I would have put my money on the older of the two brothers but after tonight shenanigans I'm not so sure.'

'You were at the wedding feast?'

'Oh yes. I saw everything. Gilbert and I were watching from afar.' He stepped forward looking stern. 'How dare Noble put his hands upon you, he took advantage because you'd been drinking. And I must say that your behaviour was rather deplorable. God knows I detest all three of Caleb's sons, especially the youngest one, but even I felt sorry for Gideon tonight. You cannot go flitting from one man to another Effelia; it's extremely common and unladylike.'

I lowered my gaze to the floor suddenly feeling a little humiliated. What Isaiah said was right to a certain extent; my conduct at the wedding feast had been inappropriate. However, love was such a complicated emotion and I was hardly an expert on affairs of the heart. Ultimately, I was very attracted to Noble but wasn't sure if it was love, for how did one know when their heart had always belonged to another.

'Effelia? Please stop daydreaming and speak to me.'

My eyes glared at him. 'If it's all the same with you Isaiah, I'd rather not discuss what happened at the wedding feast. And you can hardly stand here and preach to me about my behaviour after the way you've treated the woman in your life.' Glancing across at Gilbert I dramatically lowered my voice so he couldn't hear. 'Violet wasn't it, your first wife who was bludgeoned to death here in Briarwood, then there was Sabina, were you not mixed up with her in some way shape or form, and last but not least there was my poor mother, whose life you ruined. Tell me Isaiah, is that everyone, or have you another wife stored away somewhere.'

A strange expression crept over his face and for a minute he stood there motionless.

'Have you quite finished your ranting Effelia?'

'Yes.'

'Now about going home.'

'How exactly do you propose we reach home without a gateway to travel through?'

'Oh, that's easy Effelia. We will journey through the mirrors.'

I laughed. 'What mirrors?'

He frowned. 'Take a seat whilst I quickly explain.'

I went and rested on one of the pews and tried to listen attentively as Isaiah told me all about it. Apparently when they were boys, Caleb had shown Isaiah a mirror in his home and said how it had special powers. Isaiah had forgotten all about it until the both of us had been discussing the subject of mirrors whilst locked in the cells at Hartland. After I had gone to the Giver ceremony, he begun flicking through my notebook and suddenly came to the conclusion that my ancestor, Florentine Heatherington had travelled through the exact same mirror when she had stayed in the cottage at Briarwood, the same home that now belonged to Caleb. Whether she knew what she was doing, or it was merely an accident, we will never know, but somehow Isaiah deduced that she must have exited through another mirror, the one now housed in the attic at Rawlings. Apparently, he'd sneaked into Caleb's cottage last night to see if it was still there and found the mirror in my bedroom. He apologised for scaring me.

'This is all just supposition Isaiah. Are you really willing to risk our lives on such flimsy evidence?'

'Oh ye of little faith, Effelia. I fully intend to give it a trial run beforehand. If it works then I will return without delay and take you back with me.' He smiled rather ingratiatingly. 'And you need not have any doubts about me returning to collect you. You know I wish you in your proper home, at Rawlings, with me your father and dear Aunt Constance.' He looked at me. 'And perhaps Gideon.'

'Gideon is returning to Hartland tomorrow. I tried to make him stay, but he's adamant on going back to that hellish place. It will be practically impossible to make him change his mind, especially at such short notice.' Looking despondent I shrugged my shoulders. 'Anyway, what would be the point when the tonic has already taken him.'

He pursed his lips. 'It's an addiction alright, an addiction that cannot be cured.' Coming closer he peered into my face. 'Not in this world anyway.'

I stared back at him. 'What do you mean?'

'Travelling across worlds is a dangerous business Effelia, and if you're not careful it can destroy your mind and send you insane. We will be taking a risk when we return; a big risk, but frankly I don't have a choice, and if you return with your precious Gideon, we can save him.'

'You mean the tonic will be wiped from his mind, just like all his memories of Briarwood?'

'Precisely.'

I stood there contemplating for a while.

'But won't the tonic still affect him physically?'

'Only a little, I imagine.' His eyes strayed from mine and rested on the pew. 'Gideon is a strong, healthy young man, and is certain to recover in no time. And don't believe that ridiculous notion about journey's making you dramatically

54

age. Take a look at me. I was about Gideon's age when I left this land and all I got was a few grey hairs.'

'And the limp.'

'Yes, but that injury was from Briarwood.'

I looked at him unwaveringly. 'Your other daughter shot an arrow in Gideon's shoulder. If I take him home the wound will be re-opened.'

'He shrugged looking suddenly disgruntled. 'Oh Effelia, you are over complicating the matter. They do have hospitals back home, so I'm sure they can mend your precious Gideon.'

'How can you be so sure, by taking him with us we could be placing his life in serious danger.'

'If he returns to the monastery he might as well be dead anyway, and once he's guzzled down more tonic he will forget you even existed. If you persuade him to come home to Rawlings we can make him better, plus both of you can finally be together, and live happily ever after. Or would you prefer to give up on your one true love and take his arrogant brother Noble back instead, if indeed he's willing. He has many admirers in the village, you know. Only yesterday I saw him with....'

'Isaiah please.' I snapped, interrupting his sentence. 'Noble will not be returning with me, nor will Mace, just in case you're wondering.'

'Huh. Well thank the Lord for that.' He studied my face carefully. 'So, are you coming alone or will you be in the company of Gideon?'

I stood there without saying a word. All of a sudden I had a million different thoughts invading my mind, and I couldn't think straight.

'Why are you so keen for Gideon to come back with us, what's in it for you?'

His face remained reticent. 'Nothing, nothing at all, apart from wishing my daughter to be happy; I understand that it would be selfish of me to expect you to leave Briarwood without the man you love.' He paused. But whatever you decide you know I shall be there to support you.'

I raised my eyebrows.

'You may be surprised to hear Isaiah, but I would've been prepared to do this trip without Gideon or Noble. Just seeing Aunt would make me happy.'

'Good.' He nodded his head frantically. 'That poor woman, it fills me with sorrow to think of her sitting there in that big old house with only ghosts for company.' He let out a harrowing sigh. 'And you, her only living relative....'

A dull ached flickered over my heart.

'Yes, thank you Isaiah.'

'I just thought you might need a reminder.' He glanced at the notebook. 'So then Effelia have you made a decision about Gideon?'

I realised then that although I had serious doubts about the whole thing working, it could be my very last chance to make Gideon normal again, so I had to take it. If it all came to nothing then at least I had tried, and he could go on his merry way back to Hartland.

'Yes.' I said decisively. 'If I can persuade him to journey with us, then yes. He will of course have to be kept in the dark about us trying to cure him, if he knew that was our plan he'll never agree to it.'

'Certainly Effelia, I totally agree.' He clapped his hands together in glee.

I glanced back at Gilbert as he started to yawn loudly. He was slumped on the ground half asleep, leaning against something, and as I peered closer, I saw it was my rucksack.

Isaiah yelled across to him. 'Do try and stay awake Gilbert, we'll be going home in just a tick.' With a groan he looked at me. 'Be sure not to mention our plan to Caleb, that wiseacre will only cause problems. It's the weekly grocery market the day after tomorrow, so that should keep him out the way. I also suggest you ensure Noble and the boy Mace stay clear of the cottage; those two will only cause complications. When the coast it clear I will sneak over to Caleb's and we can leave immediately.'

I began to laugh. 'So, you intend on making the journey the day after tomorrow?'

'Yes Effelia.' He said rather sharply. 'I've just told you that. Please pay attention.'

'But...but that's extremely short notice.'

'Yes, sorry about that, but it's best we leave as soon as possible. Oh, and good luck in changing Gideon's mind about Hartland.'

I grimaced as he sauntered over to the door and wrenched the rucksack from underneath Gilbert's arm, causing him to lose his balance and topple sideways. 'Here,' he said tossing the bag towards me. 'You'll need this.'

I caught the rucksack in my arms. 'Thanks.'

With a nod he and Gilbert went to leave the church. At the door he turned and peered at me. 'Shall we escort you back to the cottage?'

'No, I'm perfectly capable of finding my way back, thank you.'

'Suit yourself daughter.' Without looking back, he bid me goodnight.

Gilbert started waving frantically. 'Bye sis.'

I smiled and gave a little wave.

'Oh, do come on.' Cried Isaiah, clouting his poor son over the head and hurrying him out the doors.

I stood there for a few moments to make sure they'd left then ran up the church to where the portrait of Florentine was displayed. In the half-light my ancestor and the dummy seemed hauntingly real, and I half expected them to suddenly come to life and exit the painting. With shaking hands, I reached behind the canvas and felt for the ledger. I don't know why but it had only just occurred to me to retrieve it, and when it was safely back in my possession I would throw it on the fire and watch as the flames lapped across the pages until it was merely a pile of ashes. 'Where is it?' I whispered urgently to myself, as I fumbled further along the wooden ledge at the back. In my panic I somehow managed to dislodge the canvas, and my free hand immediately shot out to steady it. Suddenly feeling impatient I lifted the painting right off the wall and carefully examined the wooden part at the back, then I fell to my knees and began frantically searching around on the ground directly beneath it. There was nothing there- the ledger was gone.

Chapter 5

After returning to the cottage I flung my rucksack down and slumped onto the bed, staring at the mirror in confusion. I'd often thought that there was something mysterious about it, but would never have guessed it was a portal. I wondered how it was activated, and assumed that Isaiah must know the key to working it.

How on earth my crafty father managed to escape Hartland was unfathomable, not unless he managed to convince Septimus he knew where the ledger was located, after all he was bound to have read my notebook, the notebook I had foolishly left behind in my rucksack when we'd been incarcerated in the cells. He could have been set free to return to Briarwood and collect the ledger from the church. However, Isaiah wouldn't be foolish enough to return the ledger to Hartland, and Septimus wasn't gullible enough to believe he would. But if this theory was wrong then how did Isaiah escape, and who had taken the ledger? I began to convince myself the parson here in the village had put it away for safekeeping after discovering it by accident. Tomorrow I would visit him and reclaim it.

My stomach was aching with worry and apprehension; there was so much to do before I left, and I still wasn't entirely convinced that I should leave. It's true to say I had a yearning to see Aunt, but as for Gideon, how on earth could I stop him from going at such short notice; time may move slower here in Briarwood but not slow enough. I imagine we were well into the early hours of the morning by now which would mean I probably only had until about dawn. And I was tired, so tired I felt dizzy. With a yawn I decided to rest for a while, and snuggled down onto the bed. Everything would be clearer with a little sleep.

'Come on old girl. Get yourself up.'

I gradually opened my eyes and peered at Mace. My first thought was to tell him not to call me old girl. Every so often he'd come up with some new name to call me, and it seemed this was his favourite one at the moment. I preferred E, or my proper name of course. Numerous times over the years I'd told Isaiah not to address me as Effelia but he never did listen, he said it sounded more refined and that he was sure my mother had meant to call me this.

'What a grand day it is out there... mistress Farraday.'

Not answering I drew myself up from the bed and stared wide eyed at him as he stood with his back to me at the window. He was very still, unusually still for him.

'Mace. Why did you call me that?'

He didn't answer.

'Mace?'

I wasn't sure whether to laugh or cry when his head slowly began turning, all the way around until it was looking at me, only the rest of him was still facing the window. It was still Mace's body but his face was no longer human, it was Gilbert my childhood dummy. His arms and legs moved awkwardly as he wobbled towards me, and as I stared into his unnaturally wide eyes, I realised that his remaining hair had now turned grey. As he moved his mouth the wood around it began to crack.

'Do I look like Mace?' He growled in a raspy voice.

Unable to answer I merely shook my head.

'Now listen mistress Farraday to what I have to say....'

'You left me at home all alone to moan when I wanted to roam. Can't you see you neglected me; just how selfish can you be? I'm not a toy that you should forget, it's not as if we haven't met. You're the dummy who can't even find her mummy. She's far away, or so they say, perhaps you'll find her one fine day. The tonic for Gideon is such a craving but ask yourself is he really worth saving? Going through the mirror could be a killer. You'll get old, or so I'm told, and what you see will leave you cold. That father of yours is a devious critter and will leave you

feeling rather bitter. So, think what you're doing before it's too late, hurry now we can't afford to wait.'

His face began to crack further until it split directly down the middle, causing the left side to fall away and smash to the ground with a thundering crash.

'Good morning sunshine.'

I began to scream.

As I opened my eyes I saw Mace coming into the room.

'Sorry old girl did I make you jump? I didn't mean to open the door so violently and crash it against the wardrobe.'

Trembling I sat up in the bed, rubbing my eyes. 'What...what's going on?'

'Bad dream?' He said, flinging the window open in his usual manner. Glancing at me he began to rock with laughter. 'Really E, you could at least have changed out of your gown from last night old girl.'

I groaned, looking exasperated. 'Please Mace, stop calling me old girl.'

He pulled a face.

Taking a deep breath, I tried to compose myself. 'It seemed I did have a bad dream. You were in it Mace.'

'Really, was it particularly gruesome?'

I smiled. 'Yes.' Smoothing down my hair. 'It was rather.'

'Tell me all the gory details.'

'No.' I replied bluntly. 'I'm too weary.'

'Well you shouldn't be E, you had a good sleep in.'

With a sudden gasp I dragged myself out of bed. 'Oh, my goodness, what time is it Mace?'

'According to the grandfather clock downstairs, it's just gone eleven. Although Caleb always forgets to wind it up so I wouldn't take that as gospel. You know how he detests timekeeping devices.'

Mumbling to myself I hurried over to the door and then stepped further back into the room, not knowing what to do. I'd only meant to sleep for a few hours. What if Gideon had already left?

3

Mace stood there watching me with amusement. 'You're in a strange mood this morning.'

Without replying I ran outside onto the landing and made my way to Gideon's bedroom, and began hammering on the door. When there was no reply I barged in and glanced around the empty room. I began biting my nails.

Mace poked his head around the door.

'Effie? What's got into you? Did the cider from last night have an adverse effect on you? Or are you just eager to see Gideon?'

'Has he gone?'

'What?'

'Gideon.' I snapped. 'Has he already left for Hartland?'

He looked at me blankly. 'Not I'm aware of. But he was in a foul mood last night after...after that kissing thing with you and Noble. Perhaps he crept away without saying goodbye to anyone. Pretty rude if you ask me, I mean we are family, and you're his...his good friend.'

Frowning, I barged passed him and ran downstairs. Caleb was sitting in the kitchen, glumly staring down at the table, his face white and strained.

'Good morning Caleb.' I mumbled. 'I wonder if you've seen Gideon.'

He briefly glanced at me before lowering his gaze again.

'So, you've finally plucked up the courage to venture out your room, have you Effie. I wouldn't have blamed Gideon for leaving without saying goodbye to you, as you certainly don't deserve it. But as it happens, he is still in Briarwood.' He sighed. 'You'll find him down by the stream at the back of the garden.'

So intense was my relief that I felt the tension inside of me flooding away. Forgetting Caleb was there I rushed urgently towards the door.

'Oh, and Effie?'

Turning very slightly I half glanced at him. 'Yes.'

'I appreciate you've never been able to turn to your parents for guidance, so as a father allow me to give you this piece of advice. Those of us who play games with people's hearts will seldom find lasting love. In other words, I suggest you make up your mind whom you truly wish to be with and stand firm with that decision otherwise you will end up alone.'

I stood there wobbling slightly.

'I understand what you're saying.' I met his gaze. 'Thank you for your advice Caleb.' 'Giving him a brief smile, I turned away and rushed outside.

Gideon was crouching down on the bank, gazing into the stream as if his thoughts were lost within its depths. I was scared to go near him, mindful of his reaction at seeing me. So, for some time I stood close by, watching him, thinking what I was going to say.

'I can see you lurking there Effie. I'm not blind.'

Laughing nervously, I approached him. 'Gideon?'

He tossed a stone into the water.

'I decided to take a walk early this morning before I left, and I just so happened to bump into your father.' He rose from the bank and came near to where I was standing. 'Don't look so worried I've not breathed a word to anyone that Isaiah's here. He said how mortified you'd be if the villagers discovered he was in Briarwood. Although I must say I'm rather surprised the two of you are now on such good terms.'

'We are?'

'He nodded. 'Isaiah told me all about how you broke down in the church last night and poured your heart out to him. How sorrowful you were when you believed your father to be dead, and when he turned up in Briarwood you finally realised what he meant to you.' His face clouded over. 'I also learnt the truth about you and Noble.'

My eyes grew wide. 'You...you did?'

'You only embraced Noble to enrage me, and was overcome with remorse immediately afterwards.' He looked up into my face. 'I accept your apology Effie and I'm pleased to say I agree to your stipulation.'

'My...my stipulation?'

'Yes. Although I must make it crystal clear to you Effie that our visit to your home must be an extremely short one. Our wedding of course will be held at the monastery, and when you become my wife you will be expected to partake in the tonic, just like everyone else.' Looking suddenly agitated his eyes drifted away from me.

All I could do was stand there. I didn't know what to say, what *could* I say in the circumstances. I pictured Isaiah, wallowing in self- satisfaction at having found a solution to our problem with Gideon. It seemed he had it all worked out in his head. Only what if his sneaky plan didn't work and we couldn't reach home.

'You're awfully quiet Effie. Is something wrong?'

'No.... no, it's just I'm surprised you agreed to the stipulation.' I laughed nervously.

'Your father can be a very persuasive man when he wishes to be Effie, and he was most emphatic that this is what you truly wished for.'

I stared into his eyes, searching for a hint of warmness, but they remained cold.

'It is Gideon. It truly is.'

After lightly touching my arm Gideon had casually strolled off into the countryside for one last walk before we left tomorrow. Isaiah had informed him of when we were to travel through the mirror, and he was apparently very eager to depart. Caleb was already angry and hurt that his son was going back to Hartland and there was no need to complicate matters by telling him about going through the mirror to visit my home. Gideon had simply told him he had delayed his journey to the monastery by a day.

I had a bath and changed into one of the dresses hanging in the wardrobe. Taking particular care, I took the green gown Noble had given me and hung it in the wardrobe, luckily it wasn't too crumpled. For a moment I allowed my thoughts to dwell on our kiss last night. How awful I would feel at just leaving without a word, without an explanation, I pondered whether it would be kinder to tell him what I was doing, but that could make the matter worse. My thoughts kept returning to the advice Caleb had given me in the kitchen earlier. Isaiah might not think him very wise but there was no denying his words of wisdom made perfect sense.

I went and gazed out the window. Mace was with Caleb beside the vegetable allotment on the land to the right of the cottage; they were picking runner beans for dinner. Since being in Briarwood Mace had taken over the maintenance of the vegetables and according to Caleb was very green fingered. There were rows upon rows of cabbages and cauliflowers and in the cold box there were lettuces and marrows. He had even created a scarecrow out of old clothes and straw, crows would come along and peck away at it and rest on its lumpy shoulders. It warmed my heart to see them together, laughing and chatting. Suddenly Noble strolled over and joined them, and as I gazed down upon him, he caught me looking, he smiled and gave me a little wave. I staggered away from the window and crouched on the floor, where I remained for some time, just staring into space.

'What am I doing?' I mumbled underneath my breath.

Hoping some fresh air would clear my head I laced up my walking boots and ventured downstairs and out the front door, hoping not to be seen by anyone. I strolled down a shady lane and smiled as the small birds darted swiftly back and forth amongst the wild rosebushes. I crossed into a field where cattle were grazing in the distance then made my way towards some large oak trees that were so full of summer foliage that they made an unbroken arch as I passed through and caused the earth beneath my feet to be dark and green. I ventured into the violet wood up ahead, a place so captivatingly charming in its vivid splendour of bluish-purple that I truly wondered if I had stepped into an oil painting. There were harebells on the field banks and copses brimming with bluebells, and as I peered closer I could see all sorts of wild flowers tucked away amongst the damp grass. I'd become so accustomed to the ways of Briarwood that it wasn't a surprise when I found myself wishing to linger in the delicious calmness of the wood. Only my conscience was calling for me to return to the cottage. As I made my way back I picked a bunch of poppies from the cornfield then sat and watched the sun glittering on the water in the stream. Feeling somewhat melancholy I trudged through the back garden and into the cottage.

Mace was sitting at the kitchen table eating cake.

'Oh, you shouldn't have E.'

'Pardon?'

His eyes rested on the poppies clutched in my hand.

'The flowers?'

Trying to smile I went to find a vase from the cupboard. 'I thought they might brighten up the kitchen a little.'

'Noble's been looking for you, and Gideon. Tell me E, don't you find it strange suddenly being so sought after?'

I filled the vase with water from the jug. 'It's more aggravating than strange.' I placed the vase on the table and arranged the flowers in it.

'Oh dear E, man trouble again?' he took the remains of the cake and stuffed it into his mouth. 'Times against you E, I mean you're not getting any younger old…sorry, I mean Effie, not old girl.' He smiled at me cheekily.

The back door opened and Gideon strolled in. When he saw me a very faint smile hovered over his lips.

'There you are Effie. I trust everything is still satisfactory.'

'Of course, I've just been for a walk.'

His large eyes held my gaze. 'Good, that's good.' Looking a little uncertain he nodded at Mace before striding to the door. 'I'm going upstairs to prepare for my trip.'

We both stared after him.

'He's still determined to go back to hellish Hartland then.' Commented Mace as he rose from the table. 'Still, there's something different about him, don't you think? Placing his empty dish on the side with a clatter he wiped his mouth on the cloth.

'He seems rather more…. happier, considering he's still possessed by the tonic.' Bending down he put his muddy boots on. 'And I thought he'd still be mighty angry with you and Noble after witnessing your little display of affection.' He hovered by the back door. 'It's odd though that he even reacted in that way. I mean the tonic is supposed to turn you into an unemotional zombie.'

My thoughts drifted back to the time Gideon had destroyed the portrait I'd been painting of him. He'd been confused and furious both at the same time. I don't believe anyone truly knew how the tonic really worked, and if it affected individuals differently. Mace and Isaiah had apparently been immune to it, I can only ascertain they didn't take enough.

'Ah well, I'll leave you to it E. I can see you're in one of your uncommunicative moods.'

'Where are you going?' I piped up.

'To the garden shed my friend. Care to join me?'

I followed Mace out into the shed and leant against the workbench with my chin in my hands, watching as he began planting seedlings in tiny clay pots. He stooped forward over them, his unruly hair practically covering his face.

I took a deep breath.

'You were right about Gideon. There is something different about him.'

'Huh?' he murmured only half listening.

'Mace, please stop what you're doing for a moment there's something I need to say.'

He flung his hair from his eyes and straightened up, asking me to fire away. I told him everything that had occurred since the night of the wedding feast; it all came gushing out. After I'd finished we were both silent for a while. I felt better for telling him, relieved. However, that soon changed when he began shouting at me about how he had finally settled in Briarwood with his father and brothers and how it was his duty as my best friend to go back to the very place he didn't want to return to anymore. In frustration he threw one of the clay pots across the floor and stomped to the shed door. I grabbed his arm and pulled him back, and in a quiet voice I informed him that as my best friend he must promise to stay here with his father and brother Noble, otherwise I wouldn't speak to him ever again. For a moment he seemed to calm down.

9

'What about Noble, you are going to tell him, aren't you Effie?'

'I...I don't know if I can Mace. Initially I was going to write him a letter but then I thought not. So...so I was wondering if you would have a word with him after we've left, if indeed we do, for I still have doubts about it....'

Mace's eyes were blazing.

'No, no I won't tell him E. You can do the decent thing and tell him yourself.'

'I...I don't know if I can do that.'

With a drawn-out sigh he glared at me. 'The way I see it Effie, there are two kinds of people in life - The doers and the ditherers. Now you fall into the category of the ditherer.'

I opened my mouth to speak but his finger rested on my lips.

'Silence. I haven't finished yet. Ever since I've known you E, you've been aggravatingly indecisive. But that's okay, over the years I've grown used to it. Only, I have to say E, I'm sick of this business with my brothers. One minute you're all over Noble and then next you're going to marry Gideon.' He threw his hands up in despair. 'I just can't keep up. For heaven's sake E, if it is going to be Gideon then at least have the decency to tell Noble yourself, and put the poor boy out his misery.' He widened his eyes at me, waiting for a response.

'Yes, yes of course. I suppose you're right.'

'There's no suppose about it E. It is the right thing to do.' Looking incensed he flung the shed door open and went outside. 'Now make sure you tell Noble.' He slid a little on the wet grass before striding towards the cottage. 'See you later.' He stopped for a second and turned to scream at me. 'Old girl.' With a huff he marched indoors.

'Tell me what?'

I turned to see Noble standing behind me.

I jumped.

'Noble. You...you shouldn't creep up on people like that.'

'Sorry, it's just I heard raised voices.' He looked over towards that cottage. 'You've had an argument with Mace.'

I stared into his face, taking in his features. It never ceased to amaze me what a remarkable face he had, so like Gideon, only different in a way I couldn't really put my finger on.

'Effie? What is it you need to tell me?'

I opened my mouth to speak then decided against it. Mace was right I was a ditherer. The way I always hesitated about everything that I wasn't sure about, important matters that could be put off until the following day, or much longer in the case of his foster parents. However, my dithering was usually done with the best intentions, and would give me time to do or explain something easier. But now I didn't have the luxury of time, and it wasn't going to magically slow down just because of being in Briarwood.

I had to tell Noble now. I just didn't know how, not without hurting him. I couldn't bear to see that lost, wounded look in his eyes, knowing I had been responsible for putting it there.

'Noble I...There's something you must know.'

'Yes?'

'Please promise me not to lose your temper. Just...just listen carefully to what I'm going to tell you.'

He laughed. 'You're scaring me Effie.'

'Gideon and I will be leaving tomorrow...with Isaiah. We've found a way to return to my home. Isaiah believes that the journey across worlds will cure your brother of the tonic addiction. Obviously, we haven't told him that this is the reason for taking him with us.'

Yet again he laughed but a slight quizzical looked crossed over his face. 'Effie if this is some kind of joke, it's...it's not very funny.'

I didn't reply.

It came then, that wounded look, the look that would haunt me for a long while.

'It's not a joke, is it Effie. You really are leaving.'

'Yes Noble.'

'So, you weren't seeing apparitions of your father, he really is in the village.'

'Yes, Gilbert has been hiding him.'

He turned away. When he spoke not only did his voice have a hint of bitterness about it but it also sounded unsteady, as if it were breaking up.

'And what's going to happen if it all goes wrong, and you can't return to your home.'

I thought for a moment, then realised I couldn't back out of this if we didn't make it through. I had chosen Gideon and therefore I should stand firm with my decision, whatever the outcome.

'Then I shall face the consequences and return to Hartland with Gideon, and…. and make the monastery my home.'

'You would risk ruining your life just because that father of yours thinks he can cure Gideon?'

'Yes, I suppose so. On the other hand, if it works, Gideon's life will be saved, he will be normal again and no longer reliant on the tonic. You may not see eye to eye with your brother but surely you wish him better?'

He paused. 'Yes, yes of course. I just wish it didn't mean you going away again.'

'Sorry Noble, but I really haven't got a choice.'

I half expected him to swing round and confront me and tell me I did have a choice, and that I could stay here in Briarwood and make a life together with him, but instead he remained silent, with his back to me. I wanted to move nearer and rest my hand on his shoulder, but I held back knowing it wouldn't help the situation.

'So… so I'd like you and Mace to accompany your father to the market tomorrow. I really think it's for the best. I beg you not to mention anything of this to Caleb until we have gone.'

Initially he didn't show any emotion, but merely stood there motionless. But then to my astonishment he suddenly began laughing silently as if he didn't wish me to hear.

Although I still couldn't see his face, I suspect he had tears in his eyes.

If that's what you wish Effie, whatever makes it easier, after all Gideon comes first, he always has and always will.' Still avoiding my eye, he strode over to the cottage, and in a low fierce voice he bid me farewell.

Chapter 6

There wasn't really anything to pack. My rucksack still contained all my old clothes and had been washed and neatly folded up in the bag. I wondered if this had been Isaiah's doing or my brother Gilbert's. Just saying that name in my head made me shiver. My nightmare of this morning had been terrifying to say the least. Unsurprisingly my notebook wasn't anywhere to be seen, it made sense that Isaiah would hold onto it.

Since speaking to Mace and Noble I felt wretched, and there was an ache within my stomach that wouldn't leave me. Because of what was said tonight there was now a dark stormy cloud hanging over our relationship, and I couldn't see how it would clear by tomorrow morning when we left. But there was no going back now, I would do what I had to do, I would stick by my beloved Gideon, and together we would weather the storm.

That night Noble came to me in my dreams, we were standing on a cliff edge and below the thunderous sea was crashing against the jagged rocks. In the moonlight his eyes looked dark and brooding, and as a blood red tear trickled down his cheek he transformed into a great raven. With his talons he caught hold of my shoulders and we took flight over the cliff, gracefully swooping over the crashing waves. Without warning he released me and I fell like a stone into the dark depths of the ocean, and as I gradually began to sink, he fluttered over me for a moment before taking off towards the sunset.

All of us breakfasted together that morning. For the very last time Caleb attempted to make Gideon stay, but it was to no avail; at one point he hinted on travelling to Hartland with his son, to try and bargain with Septimus, but Gideon was quick to dismiss this idea, saying it would make no difference, and his trip would be wasted. As Mace upset the milk all over the table he cursed underneath his breath and began frantically dabbing up the liquid with a cloth. No one laughed like they usually would. Not this day.

'Perhaps I shouldn't go to the market today.' Announced Caleb.

Gideon quickly caught my eye then turned to his father. 'Nonsense father, you must continue your daily routine.' He got up from the table. 'I will be leaving very soon regardless.'

Caleb sighed then rubbed his eyes. 'Yes, yes of course you will.'

Mace patted his father's shoulder. 'Noble and I will be coming to the market today, to keep you company. Maisie Fellows will be there to brighten it up.' He winked at Noble. 'Eh brother?'

Looking disgruntled Noble rose from his seat and began clearing away the plates. 'Come on, we should get going.'

'Effie, will you also join us?' asked Caleb quietly.

Mace spoke before I had the chance. 'My delightful friend Effie here has already made plans, crucial plans of the utmost importance.' He glanced down at my jumper.
'And only scruffy old clothes will do for such an undertaking.'

I gulped as they all stared at me.

'Well' said Mace. 'Aren't you going to explain what you are up to Effie?'

I pretended to laugh as I glared at Mace. 'As usual my friend here is completely over dramatizing things.' I lowered my eyes. 'I....I'm going for a long walk in the woods.' I stared down at the clothes I'd taken from my rucksack this morning. 'That's why I've put these on, I didn't want to ruin one of my gowns.'

'Oh.' Mumbled Caleb 'I wondered why you were dressed differently. I thought you'd lost all of your old clothes when you were at Hartland.'

'Yes, yes I did. But I...I must have stuffed these into the dressing table ages ago and completely forgotten about them, until now.' I gave Mace a stern look, hoping he would be silent. 'And besides, I thought wearing them would make a change.'

'A change for the worst.' Said Noble as he left the room, slamming the door behind him.

As we all stood in the front garden Caleb pulled Gideon towards him and gave him a hug, trying not to sob as he looked into the emotionless face of his son. Mace and Noble shook their brother's hand then all three of them went and stood by the gate, leaving Gideon and myself standing by the honeysuckle.

Caleb turned at the gate and gave Gideon an agonised stare.

Mace took his arm. 'Come on father, let's go to the market. Don't make this hard on yourself.'

As I stood there in a daze Noble gave me a lingering look before marching ahead of the other two, and as they disappeared from our view I had to hold back the tears.

Suddenly Mace came bounding back towards us. Gideon stepped back as he flung his arms about me.

'Love you friend. Always have always will.' With a gulp he looked into my face. 'You'd better come back and see me E, or they'll be trouble.' He kissed the top of my head before nodding at Gideon. 'Take good care of her brother.'

Seldom had I felt so alone, for although Gideon was with me, he wasn't really there, his mind was far off in the monastery and was merely waiting for his physical being to join it. I had an overwhelming urge to run after the others, to scream at them to wait. But of course I didn't.

'Here they are.' Said Gideon nonchalantly.

Isaiah emerged from the side of the cottage, along with Gilbert, trailing behind him in his three-quarter length trousers that hung baggily around his bony legs. They were both rushing, as if time was at the essence.

'What a heart-breaking farewell that was.' Isaiah said with a sly laugh. 'I almost came over to watch Caleb wallow in his misery.'

Gideon threw him a stern look. 'Come, let us go'

Isaiah grinned. 'Eager, are we? He turned to Gilbert and patted him on the head. 'You're the master at home in my absence, so be sure to act in a grown-up fashion.'

Gilbert looked forlorn. 'You won't be long father, will you?'

Isaiah ruffled his hair. 'Of course, not son.' He took a deep breath and began to speak slow and steady. 'As soon as I've got everything sorted in Abercrombie, I'll be straight back to Briarwood to make everything right.'

'You'll speak to the parson?'

'Yes, yes. That's what I said, and your father doesn't lie Gilbert.'

'Nay father, nay.' He began jumping up and down. 'He don't.' with a giggle he gave him a tight hug. 'Then you can live with me without having to hide away like a bad man.'

Isaiah firmly pushed him back. 'Yes, now calm down, time to run along home.' He gave him one last look then barged into the cottage. 'Come along Effelia...and Gideon. I shall meet you upstairs by the mirror.'

Gilbert screwed his face up and began to sob. 'Don't leave me sis.'

I put my arms about him. 'There, there, don't fret. We'll be back before you know it. Your father is very grateful to you Gilbert, for taking care of him, you've saved his life.'

He looked up into my face. 'Really sis?'

I nodded. 'Really brother.'

His face brightened and he grinned. 'You come back soon sis. Then never, ever leave again.' Laughing, he glanced at Gideon then skipped along to the gate and down the lane, whistling to himself.

I felt Gideon grasp my hand. 'Let's go Effie. 'Without another word he led me inside and up the stairs, guiding me by the shoulders to my room as if I didn't know the way. He stopped within the doorway. 'Where is your father?'

In bewilderment I looked around the empty bedroom, my eyes focusing on the mirror. It looked very much like it always did, accept it was misted up, and when I lightly touched it with my finger the glass was cold.

'Isaiah must have already gone through, to see if it works.'

Gideon frowned at me before turning to stare out the window.

'Then we will have to wait.'

16

I nodded at him and sat on the edge of the bed, my heart pounding in my chest. What if Isaiah had never intended to come back for us, what if this whole thing had just been a ploy to gain access to the mirror? Only why bother arranging this, when he could have sneaked through any old time, like the other night when he'd been in my room. The bed creaked as I leaned forward, and staring down at my hands I clasped them together and began to pray, pray that Isaiah would come back. But with every passing moment I became more uncertain and scared, scared that instead of going home I would have to endure a life of misery at the monastery.

Gideon strode forward and held out his hand. 'Come Effie. Your father has gone, and is not coming back. Let us leave for Hartland.'

'No.' I gritted my teeth. 'Wait for goodness sake. Give him time.'

Taking my wrist rather tightly he pulled me up. 'We haven't got time Effie. This was a foolish undertaking anyway; I can see that now.'

I wrenched my wrist free and glared at him. 'Don't be so impatient.'

He closed his eyes for a moment then gave me a menacing look.

'You lied, didn't you Effie? You have no wish to return with me to the monastery, and only agreed to all of this because your father seems to think going back to your home will cure me, did you really think I didn't realise?'

'Then why go through with it Gideon.'

He began banging his fist against the wall. 'Maybe part of me wanted to be cured so...so that you'd truly want me. I'm not really sure. You confuse me Effie and cloud my judgement.' Looking agitated he paced forward and grabbed my hands. 'Everything will fall into place when we're back in the monastery. Trust me Effie, the tonic will be your salvation.'

As he began to pull me towards the door, I heard a strange sound, rather like a gentle rumble of thunder. Then I realised it was emanating from the mirror. I began to shout at Gideon, to try and tell him Isaiah was on his way back, but it seemed an unknown force had suddenly taken him over, and he screamed back at me that we were going to Hartland this instant. As I broke free he grabbed my hair and I cried out then slapped him across the face, hoping it would bring him to his senses.

I was suddenly aware of a shadow beside the mirror.

'Now children, don't fight. Rawlings awaits.'

We both stopped and stared at Isaiah.

'You...you made it home.'

'Of course, Effelia, where do you think I've been, fairyland?' He gave Gideon a sly look before grabbing my hand. 'Well come on then, what are you waiting for.'

I smiled tentatively at Gideon. 'Come with us.'

'No.' he replied stubbornly.

Isaiah stepped forward. 'Leave him Effelia.'

'I...I can't.'

'Oh, for heaven's sake.' Look Gideon if you come with us I can whip you up a concoction that is very similar to the tonic. I have all the necessary ingredients stashed away at Rawlings.' He glanced at me. 'Effie can vouch for my expertise in such medicines.'

I nodded eagerly. 'Please Gideon you have nothing to lose. If you really hate it there I give you my word we will return immediately, together.'

'Very well, let's get going.'

With a sigh of relief I reached for my rucksack and approached the mirror. I took Gideon's hand and held it tight just in case he changed his mind.

'How do you activate it Isaiah?'

'My dear Effelia, the mirror is already activated; I did it whilst you were wasting time downstairs with Gilbert, and that's how I managed to go through. However, it only lasts for a short while and then reverts back to normal, so I suggest we get a move on'

I looked slightly agitated. 'But I'm just intrigued to know.'

'Well don't be Effelia.' He snapped. 'I shall save the story of how it all works for a rainy day. But I can tell you it was your sister Verity who told me all about it; she's rather an expert on these sort of matters. It's just a shame she's so sadly lacking in other areas.'

Reluctantly I allowed Isaiah to clench my hand. We all had to remain holding hands the entire journey as that way we wouldn't become parted. He was to go first then I would follow and then Gideon. I listened attentively as Isaiah told us that to arrive in our desired destination, we as passengers must focus completely on the place we wish to go, whether it be Aunt, the house or even the gardens, it didn't matter. The only thing I could think of was the old tumble down shed that Noble had been hiding out in. I allowed my mind to momentarily drift, wondering what would have happened if we'd never left my home, would we be together?

'But what will Gideon focus upon when he's never been to my home?' I asked feeling perplexed.

'If he concentrates on you Effie that should be sufficient. Just make sure you don't let go of each other's hands. Otherwise Gideon could drift off anywhere and never be found. And during the journey we must look straight ahead, under no circumstances be tempted to look around, for there are many creatures out there, skulking in the shadow worlds, just waiting for the right moment to pounce.' He went closer to the mirror. 'Ready?'

My eyes widened as I looked back at Gideon. I'd never be ready, for this was terrifying. Only oddly enough I had faith in Isaiah to get us through safely, and as he stepped inside the mirror I followed without hesitation, pulling Gideon along behind me. Journeying through was rather like being immersed in an impenetrable fog that wouldn't lift, I could feel its coldness creeping over my body, slowly suffocating me. Isaiah was right, there were creatures, and I could hear their strangled cries calling my name. The shed I thought, trying to concentrate, the tumbledown shed was full of cobwebs and was where all my painting material was stored, along with discarded garden furniture and an old mower. Stacked along the sides of the walls were canvases, mainly landscapes. One day I had carved my name in one of the walls, and had swiftly covered it with a painting, fearful that my Aunt would scold me if she saw what I'd done. It's where I had painted my mother, and I remember believing that when it was completed she would somehow find her way back to me. I was just a young girl then and my wild imagination held no bonds, and anything seemed possible. It's sad that when we grow up it all just disappears.

I began to fall. A blinding pain suddenly shot through my head that was so excruciating that I collapsed onto the ground, and curled up into a ball. I cried out as pain enveloped my middle, as if something was gradually wrapping itself tightly around my waist, and then my ankle began to ache. I could hear someone groaning nearby, but as I peered up everything seemed to be a blur.

'Gideon?' I croaked. 'Is that you?'

There was no reply.

As my eyes became accustomed to my new surroundings, I saw Isaiah sitting beside me, grasping his left leg in his arms.

He inclined his head to the corner of the room. 'Over there.'

Although I felt like my entire life force had been drained away, I somehow managed to crawl passed him and make my way to the huddled form, lying beside a bureau. Suddenly my hand slipped on something wet and slippery, then I realised it was blood, Gideon's blood. I could see it now, trailing along the wooden floor to where his body lay. He must have crawled along the floor when we'd toppled out of the mirror.

'Oh, please god no. Gideon? Gideon speak to me.'

Still unable to rise I made my way along the floor on all fours, slipping and sliding in the blood, and when I reached his still form my heart gave a lurch as I saw the blood pouring from the wound in his shoulder, the wound the mad woman had put there. A wave of nausea swept over me as I remembered she was my sibling, a fact I hoped would soon fade from my memory. Nearby there was a scarf draped over one of the chairs, I scrambled to my feet and grabbed it, then pressed it up against Gideon's shoulder.

'Is he still breathing?'

My eyes darted to Isaiah for a second then back to Gideon.

'Just. I can see his chest moving.' The blood was seeping through the scarf. 'I...I can't stop the bleeding.'

Isaiah hobbled over towards me. 'Here, allow me.' he crouched down and put his hand beside mine. 'I shall hold it firmly in place, you go and call for an ambulance.'

'Can't you help him?'

His eyes met mine. 'It's too late for that Effelia. He hasn't got long to live.'

A whimper erupted from my throat. I pulled myself up and staggered across the room, with Isaiah's words ringing in my ears. I hadn't even had time to see where we were, but it certainly wasn't the attic at Rawlings. But as I stumbled into the spacious hallway, I thought I recognised the large cabinet, only it was now white instead of mahogany, there was a new coat stand, and a small desk, with a telephone. With my hands shaking uncontrollably I rang for an ambulance.

The ambulance had arrived almost immediately and after we'd arrive at Oakland hospital, the crew had whisked Gideon off on the stretcher, leaving Isaiah and I sitting in the waiting area.

Isaiah patted my hand. 'It shouldn't be long now.'

I glared at him. 'What do you mean, until Gideon's dead, you mean? I'm sure it wouldn't break your heart if he were.'

'Oh Effelia. I meant it shouldn't be long until we hear word from the doctor.'

As I bent forward the pain around my waist began to increase.

'It may surprise you Effelia but I actually want your beloved Gideon to survive. As I told you, the main reason I made him come back home with us was to make you happy.'

'Is that true Isaiah, really?'

'Yes, most certainly. Without him you would have moped around Rawlings for a while with your Aunt and I, then gone trotting back to Briar...Briarwood to seek him out.' He paused. 'Or you'd go running after one of your other little pals. You see Effelia, gone is the day when I try to make you marry someone from Abercrombie. We tried that once and look where it got us.'

Despite my pain and heartache, I laughed.

'Poor Duncan, he must have cursed the day he ever set eyes on me. He's probably married someone else by now, someone with poise and glamour, someone who doesn't live in a dream world.'

He scoffed. 'He was rolling in money, you know. It makes me sick to the stomach to think how I almost managed to make him my son in law.' A far-off look appeared in his eyes. 'Rawlings would have resembled a palace if you'd married him.'

I was about to respond when I saw the doctor approaching us with rather a grim expression etched across his face. He briefly glanced at his clipboard before meeting my eye.

'Are you Miss Farraday, Gideon's friend?'

I nodded silently. 'Please, call me Effie.'

'I'm Dr Mason. May I have a quiet word with you?'

Isaiah rose from his seat and placed his hand on my shoulder. 'I shall go and fetch some tea.'

As he stumbled off awkwardly, I suddenly realised his limp had returned. A small price to pay for being safe and back in the place you loved, I thought.

My gaze turned to the doctor as he coughed.

'Sorry...sorry Dr Mason, you were saying.'

Looking hesitant he cleared his throat and took a seat beside me.

'Gideon is extremely weak and requires an urgent blood transfusion.' He paused for breath. 'The problem we're having is finding a match for his particular blood type.'

I stared blankly at him. 'But, but surely there must be someone, somewhere suitable.' I could feel my voice becoming desperate. 'Have you not got a supply of different types kept within the hospital?'

Dr Mason gave a short laugh. 'Well yes we do keep some here, but only the types we know about.' He narrowed his eyes and shook his head. 'Effie, your friend doesn't even have a rare blood group.' He took a deep intake of breath. 'To be frank, I've never seen this kind in my entire time as a doctor.' I watched as he leant forward in the chair, his head bending closer. 'It may be a strange question, but where does your friend come from?'

In a daze I glanced Dr Mason. 'Gideon originates from...from overseas.' I stammered nervously. 'And he doesn't have any living relatives in this part of the world.'

'Huh. I see. How very odd.'

As Dr Mason scribbled something down on his clipboard, a brief thought flickered through my mind of darting through the mirror and dragging someone back who could give Gideon blood. But even if I did follow through on this absurd idea it didn't guarantee that their blood would be a match.

Looking apprehensive Dr Mason met my eye.

'I'm extremely sorry Effie but under the circumstances there's nothing we can do.' His voice became low. 'We can keep Gideon comfortable until...until the end.'

A profound sense of anguish swept over me.

'Nothing can be done?'

Looking sympathetically into my eyes he shook his head. 'No, not without a suitable donor, Gideon has lost far too much blood.'

My heart began to ache. 'How...how long has he got?'

'I very much doubt he will last the night.'

Saying nothing I stared down at my hands in a daze.

'Perhaps you would like to go and sit with him, Effie. I can call for a nurse if you need some support.' His eyes flicked up the passageway. 'The gentleman who was just sitting here, is he a friend?'

'Yes, my father.' I muttered croakily. 'I shan't need support.' I rose up from my seat and staggered forward. 'I'd like to see Gideon on my own please Dr Mason.'

'Of course, Effie, allow me to show you the way.'

As we walked down the corridor, I only half listened to what Dr Mason was saying. He seemed extremely intrigued to know how Gideon had received his shoulder wound, and looked disappointed when I pretended to be baffled by the whole incident; the perpetrator could never be brought to justice anyhow, so there was little point in telling him what had truly happened, if indeed I could remember it all.

We entered a ward down the far right and I tried not to stare as we passed a series of patients who all looked rather poorly. Many were connected to machines and were covered in tubes, and some appeared to be in comas. An elderly woman with some type of breathing apparatus over her face was coughing violently; her eyes followed me as I wandered by. We stopped at the very end of the ward and went into a small room.

Dr Mason lowered his voice considerably. 'Just to warn you Gideon keeps coming in and out of consciousness, so he may not be aware you're here.' He said plaintively. 'If you require a nurse there's one by the entrance to the ward.'

In a daze I barely nodded.

He hovered there for a moment as if wishing to ask me something, but then he turned on his heel and marched off.

My eyes fixed upon the still figure lying there in the bed. Gideon appeared to be sleeping peacefully, his complexion a deathly white. His injured shoulder was neatly swathed in bandages and only a little blood had seeped through. Shakily I crossed over and sat beside him, resting my hand over his, it was cold to the touch, as if his life had already started to ebb away.

'Gideon? Gideon can you hear me?'

There was no response. I sat there for a while, wondering whether or not to speak again or just remain there, holding his hand. Suddenly his lids began to flicker and as his eyes opened I saw a strange, distant look within them. With a struggle he began to move his lips.

'Effie.'

'Yes Gideon, I'm right here.'

'Where...' He gulped. 'Where are we?'

'At the hospital.'

'Is that what it's called?' He let out a weak cough. 'Is it a place people are sent to before travelling to heaven?'

I smiled serenely at him, trying not to cry. 'Sometimes, yes. But it is also a place that can make you better.' I lowered my eyes, focusing on his hands in an attempt to control my emotions. 'The standard of care here is extremely high... I'm sure they can make you well again.'

'Effie?' His hand moved in mine. Effie, look at me.'

Gradually I raised my eyes and looked into his face, unable to speak.

'I know I'm seriously ill, and that soon I shall be in heaven.' He ran his tongue over his dry lips, his breathing laboured. 'But...but I want you to know that it's all right. I remember everything now, our long years in the forest, and our love for one another. I feel fortunate to have had you in my life, and...and I want you to promise me.' He swallowed and caught his breath. 'Promise me you'll not be sad, that you'll meet someone new and be happy.'

I stared into his bloodshot eyes. 'No, no I will not.' With a cry I threw my head forward onto his chest. 'You're not going anywhere.' I began weeping silently as his hand gently caressed my hair.

Realising I must have dropped off I abruptly raised my head and peered at Gideon. He was seemingly fast asleep, but I couldn't see him breathing. A surge of panic swept over me as I realised he could be gone. With trembling hands, I reached forward, trying to find a pulse on his neck, praying that he was still alive. I almost jumped out my seat when he let out a rasping breath and moved his head slightly on the pillow, struggling to open his eyes.

'I'm still here.' He said hoarsely. 'Just.'

With a smile I leant over and kissed his forehead. 'Don't try and speak if you don't want to, just rest.' I said quietly. 'I shall be here all the time.'

As he drifted back to sleep, I sat there staring at him, hoping and praying for a small miracle.

Someone tapped on the door and entered.

'I must speak with you urgently Effelia.'

Reluctantly I glanced over at Isaiah.

'Whatever you need to tell me it can wait.' I uttered in a low voice, turning my attentions back to the Gideon. Every second with him was sacred and I didn't want Isaiah tainting the memory of my final moments with the man I loved. 'Please leave.'

'Oh, I don't think so Effelia.'

Feeling the pressure of his hand on my shoulder I shot up and spun round to confront him. 'What is it?' I hissed at him. 'What do you want?'

He didn't reply at first but just watched me. Suddenly a slow sly smile appeared across his face. 'I can save him, you know. Your precious Gideon.'

My eyes widened with surprise. 'What do you mean?' I said in a whisper, so as not to disturb Gideon. 'Have you some mysterious concoction hidden away that can miraculously restore him back to health?'

'No, not exactly.'

'This is all some game to you isn't it Isaiah. All the time you knew he wouldn't make it, and now you're deliberately making me suffer.' Trying to hold back the sobs I turned away from him and focused on the sleeping figure of Gideon.

'Now's not the time to throw a tantrum Effelia.' He sighed deeply. 'Gideon's life is in your hands.'

Feeling mystified I turned to glare at him. 'What do you mean?'

'Gideon doesn't have any relatives hereabouts, so it seems you're his closest acquaintance and therefore the burden of responsibility falls upon your shoulders.'

'What are you getting at Isaiah?'

'Oh Effie, have you not caught on yet.' He said in a mocking tone. 'In order to carry out the procedure the doctor has to have our consent.'

'Consent?' I retorted with a mocking laugh. 'Consent for what?'

'For me to give your precious Gideon my blood.'

I stared at him open mouthed. 'You've the same blood type?'

'Yes, yes of course.' Isaiah replied rather hurriedly.' He took my arm and began dragging me away from Gideon and out of the room. 'I've already supplied the doctor with a sample of my blood and it's a perfect match.'

26

'But I...how can that be?'

In silence we swiftly passed the other patients, and it wasn't until we were standing in the corridor that he answered me.

'Did you forget that Gideon and I are both from that delightful village called...called. Oh, never mind' he said gruffly. 'You know which one I mean.' An ingratiating smile spread across his face as he turned to see Dr Mason approaching us. 'Ah doctor. I've explained the situation to my daughter and quite naturally she will sign the forms.'

Dr Mason smiled at me and gave a little nod.

I stared vacantly back at him, not yet able to digest what was happening.

'Now Effie, although the procedure should be straightforward, I must inform you that on occasions there can be complications.'

Isaiah looked alarmed. 'Complications. What sort of complications?'

'With the patient Isaiah, not with the blood donor.'

'Oh.'

'They're listed on these consent forms, which I'll require you both to sign.'

He swiftly handed me some papers from his clipboard and produced a pen from his pocket. 'Have a quick read through Effie then sign and date the bottom of both pages.

My eyes briefly flicked over the small print before scribbling my signature on the forms. I paused before writing the date and stared up at the doctor in alarm. 'Sorry to dither but...but what's the date today?'

'Oh, it's the ninth.' Noticing my blank expression, he laughed nervously. 'The ninth of October.'

I could feel the colour rising in my cheeks. Although I could remember what year we were supposed to be in I had a nasty feeling it had passed me by whilst I'd been away.

'And...and the year?'

Dr Mason narrowed his eyes in puzzlement, and letting out a short laugh he told me the year.

I exchanged a look with Isaiah then stared straight ahead for a second or two. Then with a shaking hand I completed the date on the forms and handed it back to the doctor, who examined it for a moment before handing the paperwork to Isaiah, but he brushed it away dismissively.

'Before I sign doctor, I need to have a brief discussion with my daughter.'

'Very well then, but please be quick, time is of the essence. I shall ask nurse King to come and find you in a few moments.' His eyes travelled across to me. 'After you've spoken with you father, Effie please sit in the waiting area by the restaurant, and I will come and find you immediately after the procedure.' Then with a nod he turned and began marching down the corridor.

I called after him, still trying to process what was happening.

'Is it possible to see Gideon once again before he has the transfusion?'

He replied without turning. 'Yes, yes of course Effie. Pop in quickly now.'

Still in a daze I rose and started making my way to Gideon's room.

'Well, that's gratitude for you.'

I stood still for a moment then turned to face Isaiah, rubbing my hands across my tired eyes. 'I'm sorry Isaiah.' I took a deep breath. 'You must know that I am extremely grateful for what you are about to do. So...so thank you.'

He stared at me without saying a word, and when he spoke his tone was surly.

'Thank you, who?'

'Thank you...father.'

He raised his eyebrows. 'That's better.'

Unable to look at his smug grin I turned to go.

'Wait a moment Effelia. Aren't you forgetting that I need to speak with you?'

'Please be quick.' I said anxiously. 'We haven't much time. I swung round to face him. 'What is it you need to discuss?'

He leaned in close and whispered in my ear. 'Saving Gideon's life will come at a price, dear daughter.'

My heart began thumping loudly in my chest as a sense of foreboding crept over me. 'What price?'

'As your father I shall be content to live at Rawlings as a welcomed guest until your Aunt passes away, but after that I want you to sign the entire estate of Rawlings over to me. You will of course be welcome to stay whenever you wish, but ultimately it will be mine, all mine.'

I looked stunned. 'This is ridiculous.' With a huff I began walking away from him. 'We can discuss such matters after Gideon has recovered.'

He came after me and clasped my arm firmly. 'No, we shall discuss it right now. You will go and sit down and complete a written testament, stating you are handing the house over to me, and I shall have it signed and witnessed by some of the staff at the hospital.' His grip tightened on my arm. 'Without it I will not part with one single drop of blood.'

I glared at him. 'Yes, yes alright.' I said in a hurried voice. 'I shall agree to anything. Please just give Gideon your blood.'

A broad smile swept over his face. 'Give me your word and we have a deal.' Releasing my arm, he extended his hand out to mine. 'Let us shake on it.'

Reluctantly I shook his hand. 'I give you my word.'

Without warning he embraced me then drew back and gazed into my face, his eyes bright with exultation. 'Oh Effelia. What a wonderful day it is.' He tapped my nose with the tip of his finger. 'No run along and get writing, and I shall go and save your beloved Gideon.'

In his excitement he must have forgotten about his limp, for as he bounded along the corridor he suddenly stopped and groaned in agony, he bent down and clutched his knee, and then rather awkwardly he carried on walking.

After a brief few emotional words with Gideon I wearily ambled along to the waiting area and took a seat in the corner. How strange, I thought wistfully, that in order to save the life of my greatest love I had to sacrifice another- my beloved Rawlings. However, as I sat down in the waiting area

I wondered if Isaiah could actually get away with stealing my home from me, and did he need to? My Aunt was very fond of him and it was quite feasible she had already drawn up a will, leaving him a large chunk of the estate. I shook my head and sighed. Or perhaps she had written me out of her will altogether after I had run off and deserted her for a second time, I wouldn't blame her. With a groan I covered my face with my hands.

'Are you alright young lady?'

I looked up into the face of an elderly lady sitting opposite and tried to muster a weak smile. 'Yes, thank you. 'I'm just rather anxious at the moment.'

'Waiting is the worst part isn't it?' She dabbed her eyes with a tissue. 'Time seems to grind to a halt.' Her eyes glazed over. 'Being in hospital is like being in another world, and everything outside this building ceases to exist.'

I stared at her intently for a moment, then my eyes glazed over as I looked forlornly down at the ground. 'Yes, I suppose it is.' I widened my eyes and released a drawn-out sigh. 'A world like no other.'

She told me how her sister was having severe breathing difficulties and how she was fearful of her not pulling through, and as I sat there and listened I realised her sister was the lady I'd seen in the special care unit, with the breathing apparatus. We discussed all manner of things, including the best method to remove bloodstains from my clothes. 'They'll be as good as new.' she said smiling at me with her kindly eyes. I nodded slowly at her, and a lump came to my throat as I stared down at my jumper, realising Gideon's blood was on my hands too, both literally and metaphorically.

The lady reached forward and took my hand, holding it softly in hers. 'Will you pray with me?'

I looked up at her with a sad smile. 'Yes, yes I will.'

As we both sat there, I prayed for the recovery of Gideon, and asked god to forgive me for placing his life in jeopardy. After we had finished praying I sat crouched forward in the chair willing myself to have faith, faith that Gideon would be back to normal and we would all go back to Rawlings. My Aunt would accept me back into her life, wouldn't she? My thoughts turned to the silly testament Isaiah wanted me to complete, and I reassured myself that it was inconsequential, as Aunt had a strong constitution and would be around for years to come, and when she did eventually pass away Isaiah could have Rawlings, because it wouldn't be home without my dear old Aunt. I would, however, put a proviso in the statement, stipulating that if she should die under suspicious circumstances then the house would revert back to me.

I'm not sure how long I waited there. The elderly lady had already left to visit her sister, as apparently she was much better now. I'd given her a hug and asked her to send her sister my best wishes. With the testament completed, I leant back on the seat and tried to relax, but every time I heard the sound of approaching footsteps my heart would lurch uncontrollably, fearing it was Dr Mason with bad news. As another hour ticked by my mind began to wander hopelessly into a swarm of dark thoughts: What if Isaiah blood wasn't compatible after all, or he had changed his mind about being a donor, maybe there had been complications, as Dr Mason had mentioned, or maybe it had simply been too late to do the transfusion and Gideon's heart had stopped beating. And then there was my Aunt. She didn't appear to be at the house when we came through the mirror. What if she no longer resided at Rawlings but had found a new home in Abercrombie churchyard.

I found myself drifting off into a most peculiar dream. Somehow I'd become trapped inside an oil painting at Rawlings. I was standing amongst the trees in a mystical looking autumn forest, full of vibrant yellows and burnt oranges. Every single day my Aunt would walk passed the picture, and I would scream out to her. 'I'm here, why can't you see me Aunt. I haven't gone away, not this time.' But she never heard or noticed me. As the years drifted past, we both grew older, until one day I no longer saw her, and realised she must have gone. As the tears streamed down my face I began to melt into the oils, until I became completely combined with the colours of the trees, and henceforth lost for evermore.

'Effie, Effie, please wake up.'

With a jolt I opened my eyes and stared up into the face of Dr Mason.

'What...oh sorry doctor.'

'The transfusion was a success and Gideon is recovering well.'

My face broke into a broad smile. 'That's fantastic Dr Mason, I can't thank you enough.'

'Thank your father Effie, he's the one that saved his life.'

'Yes, yes of course.' For a moment I stared down at the crumpled piece of paper in my hand, the testament that gave my father Rawlings. 'How long before they can be discharged?'

'Your father is a little weak so we'll keep him in for tonight. I imagine it will be a few days before Gideon can be discharged. We need to run a few routine tests.' He seemed suddenly hesitant, peering back and forth from me to his clipboard. 'That was a nasty wound on his shoulder. Do you really have no idea how he received it?'

I shook my head slowly. 'No none whatsoever. I...I found him unconscious on the floor of my home.'

'And there was no sign of an arrow?'

'No.'

I watched as he hurriedly scribbled something on his clipboard.

'Well obviously, taking into account the nature of Gideon's injury, we will have to get the police involved. I'm sure they'll need to interview him and take a statement to ascertain what actually happened.' He began tapping his pen on the paper then glanced at his watch. 'It's rather late for visitors but I'm sure the nurse won't mind if you pop in and see them both for a moment. Then I suggest you go home.' He said with a smile.

'Well yes I am... but can't I wait at the hospital overnight, just in case...'

'You look exhausted Effie.' Exclaimed the doctor with a chuckle. 'A goodnight's rest at home will do you the world of good, and then you can return tomorrow nice and refreshed.'

'Yes Dr Mason. You're right.' I murmured, rising from my chair. 'I shall go home.'

Gideon and Isaiah were in beds next to one another and appeared to be asleep. Wary of waking them I crept quietly over to Gideon and wiped the hair from his brow, and bending down I kissed his forehead.

'Your beloved is sleeping like a baby.' Isaiah said drowsily. 'He drained enough blood from me, I can tell you. It's left me so weak I can hardly move.'

I struggled to smile.

'Well, rest is the best medicine after what you've had to go through. Dr Mason thinks that after a good night's sleep you'll be able to go home.' I said, doing my utmost to act friendly and appreciative towards him. 'I shall return in the morning Isaiah.' Once more I glanced at Gideon, then edged my way towards the door.

'Effelia?'

My heart sank.

'I trust you've written your testament?'

'Can it not wait until tomorrow?' I muttered wearily.

'No, I insist we go through it now.'

With a deep sigh I retrieved the paper from my pocket and handed it to him.

Chapter 7

As luck would have it, one of the nurses knew Rawlings and offered to give me a lift home, and kindly drove me all the way up to the house. During the journey the lull of the car made my eyelids want to close, and as I tried not to drift off to sleep, I thought of Isaiah and how he'd meticulously gone through my written testimony, picking out a few minor spelling errors and making me correct them. He howled with laughter when he read the condition I'd added regarding the manner in which my Aunt must pass away, in order for the testament to be valid. He had called for two of the nurses to sit with us whilst I wrote down and swore on oath that my testament would still apply in the event of my Aunt making a fresh will, and under no circumstances could my statement become non-and void. I watched as the nurses both signed and dated the piece of paper, wondering if they thought this whole business a little strange. And after they'd left, he grinned from ear to ear, saying how perfect everything had turned out. Apparently, his next step was to put my testimony in the hands of his solicitor for safe- keeping. For one surreal moment I wanted to snatch that ludicrous testimony from his hand and tear it into little pieces, just so it would wipe that smug smile from his face.

'I really appreciate that, thanks.' I said wearily to the nurse as I clambered out the car. Kindly she had offered to give me a lift after overhearing me discussing with the doctor about going home. I thought for a moment that she was going to ask if she could come in, and was relieved when she bid me goodnight.

I hovered by the grand front door, suddenly afraid of entering my own home. What if there really were new owners, I thought, they'd hardly be happy to let me stay in a house that no longer belonged to me, especially after discovering all the blood in the study, at least I think it was the study. In all the commotion I'd hardly been in a position to inspect the room. But I was too exhausted to go anywhere else, and it was dark now and a bitterly cold wind was blowing across from the east, making the trees sway and rustle, like the gentle soothing sound of rain. Taking a deep breath, I reached for the brass handle and began to knock. I'm not sure what I expected. Perhaps my worries of earlier had been justified and my Aunt was in her grave, perhaps she was under the impression I'd never return and my claim on the house had long since passed, or perhaps she was still alive and kicking and simply wouldn't allow me in the house.

As the door began to edge open, I prepared myself to look upon an unknown face, and was rather taken aback when I gazed at the elderly grey-haired lady standing in the doorframe. Her face, I thought seemed rather gaunt, but her skin displayed a healthy glow and her green eyes were bright and alert. There seemed to be an air of serene calmness about her, as if she'd cast aside her troubles in favour of a new life, a life without me; but in doing so I feared our time apart had wiped away our entire relationship, and we were now merely strangers.

'Hello Aunt.' I said in a soft low voice.

Instinctively I went to throw my arms about her, however as I did so she recoiled, her eyes running over me in disgust. 'What on earth has happened to you Effie, why are your clothes covered in blood?

I hesitated, staring down at my bloodstained attire and then in a rather garbled way explained to her about Gideon's injury and how he was rushed to hospital and given a blood transfusion from Isaiah. I omitted the part where we'd travelled through mirrors and didn't mention how Gideon had obtained his injury, as it was rather complicated to explain and too outlandish to be believable.

'I see.' She said in a composed voice. 'Well I suppose that would explain the blood splattered floor in the study.' She scowled. 'It took me forever to clean it up.'

'I'm so sorry Aunt.'

Well, do come through to the living room.' After looking me up and down again she pointed towards the far left of the hallway, as if I'd forgotten my way about. 'I shall go and fetch something for you to sit on.' Her slight figure headed towards the kitchen. 'And I suspect you're in need of some tea.' She yelled, not bothering to turn round.

I croakily called after her. 'Yes, yes please Aunt.'

Relaxing a little I entered the living room, expecting it to be familiar. I gasped. Apart from the fireplace everything had changed. Each armchair and sofa had been upholstered in a deep luxurious green, with curtains to match, and expensive looking cabinets and dressers were cleverly positioned around the large room, which was bathed in a soft glow from the elegant table lamps.

I jolted a little as my Aunt came into the room carrying a sheet and watched as she spread it across the seat of the armchair closest to the fire.

'Sit on this please Effie.' A strained smile appeared on her face. 'I will just go and fetch the refreshments.'

As I sat down on the chair, I carefully folded my arms, mindful of touching anything not protected by a sheet. I moved nearer towards the warmth of the fire, closing my eyes, and as the heat penetrated my body it soothed my aching limbs. My eyelids became heavy and for a moment my head jolted forward. A loud crash came out of nowhere and as I opened my eyes, I saw my Aunt had placed a tray of tea and cakes on the coffee table beside me.

'You can't go to sleep yet Effie.' She said. 'It's far too early for bed.' A slight frown appeared across her face. 'I would like to know where you've been hiding these past four years.' With a slightly shaking hand she poured the tea and handed me a cup. 'Do try not to drop it dear, it's bone china.'

Without saying a word, I continued to stare as she took a sip of her tea. I placed the cup and saucer back on the table. I remember the sinking feeling that had washed over me when Dr Mason told me what year it was, but it was only now I could properly digest the fact.

'Well?' She scowled at me. 'What have you got to say for yourself?'

My eyes glazed over. 'I really can't believe it's been four whole years.'

'Why? Was the place you've been to so enthralling that you lost track of the time?'

I stared into her face. 'No...I'

'Oh, do stop dithering Effie and get to the point.'

Laughing a little, I suddenly thought of Mace, and how he'd accused me of being a ditherer. It seemed he wasn't the only one.

'I fail to see what's so amusing Effie.'

'Sorry Aunt, it's nothing.' With a sigh I stared up at the large chandelier hanging ominously above my head. 'The truth is I didn't intentionally lose track of time. To me it only seemed I'd been absent a matter of months.' I focused on her face. 'The reason for this is that time passes by at a much slower rate in...in'

'In?' she narrowed her eyes. 'In where?'

I suddenly felt agitated and began shifting about in my seat. 'The...the name of the place has slipped my mind.' My eyes travelled above the fireplace and I noticed the portrait of my mother. 'I see you've bought my painting back from Mr Lombard.' I gazed at her. 'Oh, Aunt I'm so glad.'

'Mr Lombard died Effie. He left the portrait to you in his will'

My face dropped. 'Oh. Poor Mr Lombard.' Suddenly feeling subdued my gaze drifted to the fire. 'I've been gone far too long haven't I Aunt. I'm sorry for leaving you all this time, and I'm sorry the explanation for my absence is such a poor one.' Leaning back slightly I clenched my hands together, digging my fingernails into my palms. Despite the heat from the fire I could feel myself shivering. 'But I'm back home now where I belong.'

She stared at me intently, her face only showing a hint of shock. 'How convenient for you Effie.' With a sigh she rose and moved across to the far window, her arms folded across her chest. 'Well, I know you've returned with Isaiah and this Gideon chap, but what about Noble, what happened to him?'

I opened my lips several times to speak but nothing came out.

'Effie?'

Noble, why did his name seem vaguely familiar? My notebook, I had to get it back from Isaiah. It was the only way I could fill in the missing pieces. But as I gazed into Aunt's face, I felt myself lying.

'Noble's gone home Aunt.' I muttered unconvincingly.

'Oh, that's a shame I liked him. I thought the two of you were extremely well suited.'

'We were? I gulped. 'I mean...perhaps we might have been but now I'm with Gideon.'

'Oh Effie. I really wish you'd settle down and stop jumping from one man to another. First there was Mace, then Duncan, then Noble and now Gideon.' She laughed. 'For such a shy little thing you surprise me.'

My face reddened. 'Aunt, Mace has always been merely a friend, that's all. And as for the others' I shrugged. 'I wouldn't have made Duncan happy; we're too different. Noble was...was.' I let out a short laugh when I suddenly recalled seeing him at the garden party here at Rawlings. 'He's a dear friend that is all.' I said in a faraway voice. 'I most likely won't see him again.' A lump came to my throat.

'We shall see.' Aunt asked in an odd sounding tone, as if she doubted me. 'After all you are still wearing his engagement ring?'

My eyes darted down to my hand. 'Oh. It...it was only ever a friendship ring. And besides the emerald stone is so beautiful I really couldn't part with it.' I began twisting it, trying to remove it from my finger. 'You should have it back Aunt, it really belongs to you.'

'Keep it Effie. What's mine is yours.'

'I'm so glad you said that Aunt, I said laughing, 'because I'm having trouble removing it.'

'Perhaps that's a sign, telling you it should remain on your finger for a reason.'

I smiled poignantly at her. 'Perhaps.'

'So, where did you meet this Gideon chap?

I wasn't sure if telling her the truth was the best option or lying. In the end I decided to keep to the facts but omit the parts she wouldn't believe.

'Oh, I've known him for years.' I said rather candidly.' We lost touch for a while, but have now been reunited.'

'Really.' She retorted bluntly. 'It's funny how you've never mentioned him before, and didn't consider allowing me to meet him.'

'Oh he's...he's rather a loner and not comfortable meeting new people.' I replied, unable to prevent myself from yawning. 'So, I've never brought him to Rawlings before.'

The grandfather clock in the corner chimed.

'You look weary Effie. Why don't you go upstairs to your room and rest? Your bedroom's just as you left it.' She smiled serenely. 'In fact, it's the only room in the house that's not been altered.'

'I'm glad Aunt.' Heaving myself up from the armchair I stepped closer to where she was standing by the window. 'Thank you.' I wanted to run up and hug her, to hear her say that everything was all right. But she wasn't ready yet; I could sense it in the way she looked at me, the tone of her voice. I hadn't been forgiven yet. 'Thank you for being so understanding.'

Avoiding my eyes, she turned and gazed out the window. 'You're my niece Effie, that's the only reason.'

I nodded dejectedly. 'I do hope you'll find it agreeable for Gideon to stay here for a while. He should be discharged in a few days. I of course will make his bed up in one of the spare rooms. And you will be pleased to know that Isaiah is coming home tomorrow.' I laughed half-heartedly.

Aunt waved her hand casually in the air. 'Gideon can stay for a while.' Turning from the window she peered into my face. 'But Isaiah is no longer welcome at Rawlings.' A strange smile appeared on her lips, almost like a grimace.

'What?' I asked, looking straight at my Aunt in bewilderment. 'But...but you adore Isaiah.'

'Any foolish adoration I had for your father has disappeared completely.' She smoothed her hand over her hair. 'I don't know what was wrong with me in the past, and to be quite frank, I don't really care.' She pursed her lips. 'What's important is that I've regained my senses and in doing so have come to realise what a beast that man really is.'

I stared at her open-mouthed. 'What, what have your learnt about him that's so bad?'

She widened her eyes at me and then shook her head. 'Oh Effie, do not treat me like a daft old fool. You may have been able to pull the wool over my eyes before but not now.' After a momentarily pause she came closer, her face a mixture of pain and anger. 'What hurts the most is your betrayal Effie. All these years my mind was shut against the truth and yet you didn't find it in yourself to reveal what was going on?'

'Oh Aunt.' I said, feeling wretched. 'Please believe me I did try, but Isaiah had such a powerful hold over your mind that any attempt to reach you was in vain.' I stepped forward and reached for her arm but she turned her back and walked over to the window. 'Whatever I said, you...you nearly always sided with him.'

'You should have kept trying Effie. Sooner or later I would have listened to you.' Bending forward she gripped the window seal and stared outside. 'But you're just like your mother, weak willed and foolhardy.' Her voice broke a little as she spoke. 'And just like her you decide to run away rather than facing up to reality.'

'I didn't run away Aunt, I had to go.' I retorted distraughtly. 'And mother did come back, when she was carrying me, and would have stayed had it not been for Isaiah smuggling her out of Rawlings in the dead of night and then making her disappear somewhere.' I gulped nervously. 'That is what happened, isn't it Aunt?'

'Yes, yes that is right Effie.' With a grim smile she turned round and looked into my face. 'But that still makes her weak for falling in love.' She held her hands up in despair. 'And now she's lost in heaven knows where, probably forever.'

I could feel myself becoming angrier.

'Being in love doesn't mean my mother was weak.'

'Perhaps not weak but stupid, stupid for falling for a man such as Isaiah.'

'That's hardly fair Aunt.'

'Life isn't always fair Effie, haven't you realised that yet. And you may have returned but you'll go, just like before, leaving some half-hearted, pathetic note of forgiveness and expecting me to wait here patiently, year after year until you once again grace me with your presence.' Her face grew scarlet as she began shouting. 'Well I've had enough Effie. I have a life too, and intend to enjoy it, with or without you.' With a determined stride she went towards the door and hovered there for a moment, her fingers gripping the handle. 'You can remain here as long as you like. It is your home too. I shall not be annoyed or distressed if you decide to depart once more, just have the decency to tell me to my face that is all I ask.'

I stared back at her, trying to take in what she was telling me.

'Very well then Aunt, I replied rather feebly, 'Can we discuss matters further in the morning?' I asked, curious to know how she'd discovered what had been going on, and if she was aware of the full story.

She glanced at me, running her eyes over my clothes. 'Yes, all right. I can see that you're tired. And Effie, please discard your clothes in the bin, they're completely ruined.' Not waiting for a reply, she turned and left the room, leaving me standing there in a daze.

My first impression of my Aunt tonight had been wrong. That look of contentment was misleading, a façade that she showed to the outside world. Speaking to her tonight there had been a bitter note in her tone, a deep- rooted resentment I'd not seen before. It was evident being away from Isaiah had finally triggered her memory, and now she remembered everything.

As I wearily pulled my aching body up the stairs, I realised that the strain of the day had finally taken its toll on me. Too weak to even change my clothes I flopped down onto the bed and immediately slipped into a dreamless sleep. Come morning I hardly felt any better, and had to drag myself out of bed. After a long soak in the bath I brushed my hair and cleaned my teeth, then changed into some of my old clothes from the wardrobe. They smelt a little stale but at least they were clean. Knowing my Aunt would be mortified if she found out I'd fallen asleep in my blood-stained clothes, I hurriedly retrieved them from the bathroom floor and stuffed them into a paper bag.

My Aunt was in the kitchen making some toast. Murmuring a greeting to her I hastily placed the paper bag in the bin and sat down at the table, before she had a chance to turn round. My eyes travelled across the room, taking in the new wooden cupboards and marble work surfaces, the old rusty fridge had been replaced with a larger model, and beside it stood a solid oak dresser, adorned with an array of matching crockery, hand painted in delicate yellow flowers. The range was still there, the heart of the kitchen, homely and warm.

'Well you certainly had a long lay in Effie.' Said Aunt, glancing at me. 'What time are you going to the hospital to see Gideon?'

'At midday.'

She stepped closer and began scrutinising my face. 'You look better this morning, less drained. But you have a slight red mark on your temple. Have you knocked into something?'

Instinctively I covered my forehead with my hand. 'Oh. I don't know. It appeared yesterday when…. when I arrived at Rawlings. My left ankle aches too.' I rose from the table and walked slowly over to the window. My eyes were immediately drawn to the grand conservatory, attached to the far rear of the property. 'I hope you don't mind me asking Aunt, but all these changes to the house must have come at a price.'

'Well, you have your father to thank for that Effie.' She said with a snigger. 'He needed to pay for all those years he….'

'Deceived you?'

She turned and glared at me, looking rather bemused. 'Yes, that's right Effie. Isaiah leaving Rawlings for four years was the best thing he could have done. His absence finally cleared my head and made me remember the past, as well as what he'd been up to in the present.'

My thoughts turned to the Davenport sisters, wondering if my Aunt was aware Agnes had left her home to Isaiah in her will. 'So, you're saying Isaiah paid for the repairs?'

A haunted look came about her. 'I knew both Lydia and Agnes Davenport had left your father a substantial amount of money in their wills, but of course I didn't have access to any of it, or at least I didn't believe I had.

My face looked stunned. 'How did you find out about their wills?'

'I worked it out myself Effie. I'm not as dizzy as you thought, am I?'

'I never thought you were dizzy Aunt -it was Isaiah's doing. I think he put something in your tea, some type of potion that made you disorientated.' My face grew serious. 'He did the same to me by placing a potent bundle of herbs underneath my pillow that made me forget what had happened.' I choked up. 'I thought I was losing my mind.'

She patted my hand, her face filled with compassion. 'I know. You and me both.'

We stared into one another's eyes, and for a moment we remained silent.

Her face suddenly lit up. 'Anyway, one day, when I decided to clear out your father's room, I found wads of notes all over the place, underneath his mattress, on top of his wardrobe and in a box underneath the floorboards. After counting it out carefully I discovered he had a small fortune, more than enough to cover the repairs needed for Rawlings.' She clapped her hands together in glee. 'So, I decided to spend it.'

'But where do you suppose Isaiah got all the money from. Do you think it was the proceeds from the Davenport's house?'

She poured the hot water from the kettle into the teapot.

'No, the money from the sale of the Davenport's house and all their savings was delivered to the door by some nice solicitor, some weeks after you all left. Evidently Isaiah had asked for the money to be given to him in cash, so when the package came for your father, I decided to open it, and....in his absence I decided to take possession of the money.'

I watched her carefully as she continued to make the tea.

'Did you spend any of it?'

'Oh yes.'

My face took on an expression of astonishment as I stared intently into her eyes.

'But Aunt, how could you think of using it.' I gulped, barely able to get my words out. 'Knowing it was their money, and that Isaiah had murdered them both in cold blood.'

She let out a small ironic laugh. 'It's all right Effie. I know how they died.' Placing the teapot on the table she leant towards me and stared into my eyes. 'You see Isaiah didn't just leave money under the floorboards, I also found a bundle of old diaries, crammed with notes he'd made, dating back to when he first moved to Abercrombie, explaining every single detail of the dishonourable life he led.' Her eyes widened in amusement. 'So, you see I know everything.' She straightened up and turned away. 'And with my mind clear I was able to move forward with confidence and strength, my judgement no longer clouded, and my life no longer governed by your father.' Taking a seat beside me she reached for the teapot. 'Now how about a lovely cup of tea.' She chuckled. 'Don't worry I've not added anything extra.'

I nodded at her, unable to muster a smile.

'What happened to dear Lydia and Agnes was dreadful and I intend to see that your father pays for his crimes.' She took a sip of her tea, and began to butter some toast. 'However, I cannot pretend to feel guilty about spending the Davenport's money on Rawlings. They had no living relatives and would more than likely had left the money to some animal sanctuary.' She banged her fist on the table. 'More fool them if they were sweet talked by Isaiah into leaving him all their money. I wasn't simply going to stand around and let Rawlings decay and crumble, now was I?' She stared into my face, her eyes willing me to agree with her. 'Effie?'

I sunk forward slightly over the table and shook my head, looking despondent. 'No Aunt, of course not.' Rising from the seat I went towards the window, gazing out onto the immaculate garden. 'I know how precious Rawlings is to you; it's your life.' Suddenly tearful I strode to the doorway. 'And you will even use money tainted with the blood of your murdered friends to save it.' Briefly I caught sight of the look of shock in her eyes before I left the kitchen, slamming the door behind me.

I wandered from room to room, mooching about the place like a sulky child who had just had an argument with their mother and was stubbornly waiting for them to come along and appease them, to say everything was all right. Perhaps my comment about the tainted money had been too rash, perhaps I was being silly and melodramatic, and perhaps my Aunt still did have a conscience, she had just temporary mislaid it. Perching on the velvet window seat I gazed out onto the wide sweeping lawns and watched as she chuckled to the gardener, not a care in the world. Apparently, the garden was becoming too much for her so she'd employed a daily help, named Ambrose. 'Why not' she had told me, 'I can easily afford it now'

A door suddenly slammed and a bellowing voice could be heard outside. It was Isaiah. With haste I rushed to the front entrance and looked upon his beaming face as an ambulance man helped him up the driveway. They mumbled something to each other and then the man handed him a walking stick, then with a nod he drove off.

My Aunt had joined me now, her arms tightly folded in defiance. With a glint in her eye she turned and glanced at me. 'This shall be fun.'

Isaiah looked elated as he looked from me to my Aunt.

'Ah my two favourite girls in all the world.' He said jubilantly. 'What a blessing it is to finally be back home.' Pressing down on the walking stick he hobbled over towards us. 'My dearest Constance.' He held out his arms to embrace her.

She immediately stepped back - a look of revulsion spread across her face. Never before had I witnesses such a display of disgust towards the man she had once idolised.

'Keep away from me.'

Isaiah's ingratiating smile slowly slipped from his face and he stumbled backwards in dismay. 'But Constance, it's me.'

'Yes, I'm well aware of who you are Isaiah. 'I know what you are.' She shrieked. 'And I know what you've done, you despicable man. You're banned from ever again setting foot inside Rawlings and its grounds.'

Ambrose, the gardener had joined us now and was standing there looking puzzled. He was a jovial looking man with a cloth cap and a rather red patchy face, probably from the time he spent outdoors.

Isaiah's face was seething as he turned towards me. 'Whatever Effelia has told you is a pack of lies.'

My Aunt began to laugh rather hysterically. 'But it wasn't Effie, you stupid man.' She glanced up to the window where his bedroom used to be. 'I found your diaries underneath the floorboards. They made for very interesting reading.'

His face took on a look of horror. 'What?' Taking a few steps forward he glared directly into my Aunt's face. 'They're private.' He snapped. 'You had no business looking at them. Where are they?'

'Oh, they're in safe hands, don't you worry.' She stepped back, laughing. 'I've left instructions for the diaries to be taken immediately to the police if you enter Rawlings or if Effie or I come to any harm.'

He stood there with his mouth gaping, and then a simpering smile appeared on his face. 'Oh Constance, please. Those diaries are full of drivel, surely you're not taking them seriously.' Approaching her again he stared endearingly into her eyes. 'It's me Isaiah, your trusted friend. I've come back. Now let's go inside and forget all this nonsense.' He took her hand in his. 'I must say how well you're looking; you're new clothing is very becoming.' Releasing her hand, he brushed passed her and limped towards the door. 'Let me make a nice cup of tea for us all.'

A momentarily look of happiness and admiration swept over my Aunt's face, the look I remember and had seen so many times, the look I always expected. But it disappeared in an instant, and was replaced with fury and hatred. I watched as she snatched his walking stick and began repeatedly bashing it against his legs.

He cried out in apparent agony. 'Please Constance, please stop.'

She held the walking stick still for a moment. 'You're not only despicable Isaiah, you're insane. Perhaps I should have you admitted to The Manor.'

He stared at her not quite able to digest what she was saying, then collapsed to the ground on his hands and knees and began pleading with my Aunt, telling her what he'd done was all for the sake of Rawlings, her beloved home. 'Please Constance, say you'll forgive me.'

With a look of fury, she tossed the walking stick away from the house. 'If you do not leave this very moment, I shall be forced to ring the police.'

Seeing that my Aunt wasn't going to change her mind he rose from the ground and stood there, his face looking pitiful. 'What about my belongings? I'll need to go and fetch them from my room.'

She stepped towards the gardener and mumbled something in his ear. He nodded and disappeared into the house.

'I took the liberty of clearing out your room when I had it refurnished. Everything has gone to either charity or the local skip, apart from one bag of your clothes, which Ambrose has just gone to fetch.'

'But...but my herbs, and... money.'

'If you mean all those tiny bottles full of dried flowers and leaves, then yes I discarded them. And as for the money, well some of it has been spent on Rawlings and the remainder is in my bank account, safe and sound.'

Ambrose appeared from inside the house and handed him the bag of clothes and stood next to my Aunt defiantly, waiting for him to leave.

For a moment Isaiah appeared so distraught I thought he was going to burst into tears. 'So be it.' He mumbled moving away from the house, turning once to look at my Aunt. 'I do hope you'll reconsider Constance, just think about what you're doing.' Realising she wasn't going to reply he sighed deeply. He came and stood beside me; his mouth close to my ear. 'Don't forget the testimony Effelia, it still stands.' He whispered. 'And if you need me, I shall be in Hudson's café every Wednesday at noon.' For a brief moment he placed his hand on my arm. 'Look after yourself dear daughter.'

With the walking stick forgotten Isaiah limped down the gravel driveway, carrying his bag of clothes underneath his arm, his head bent in defeat. My Aunt asked Ambrose to dispose of the walking stick and then she trotted back into the house. I stood there for a while and watched until my father disappeared amongst the shadowy branches of the great oaks, and out of our lives.

I spent most of the afternoon by Gideon's bedside, and although he was still a little tired, he was lucid enough to hold a conversation. We discussed Isaiah and I told him what had happened at Rawlings, and how my Aunt had attacked him with the walking stick. The doctors made their rounds, and lingered for rather a long time, asking him awkward questions that he couldn't answer; they seemed extremely curious about his blood type, and hinted that they'd like to perform tests. I pictured them using Gideon as a type of guinea pig to experiment on, poking and prodding and giving him injections; little by little they would drain all his blood, and then they would dissect him. How convenient for Isaiah that they couldn't locate him. I know he had long since sold his old house, so where he was living now was a mystery.

'Effie?' asked Gideon, caressing my hand with his.

'Yes.'

'We didn't just come back to your home to see your Aunt, did we? I sense there was another reason for our journey, and even though we knew it would be risky we had to do it. But I can't for the life of me remember what it was.'

I beamed at him. 'I don't know either Gideon, and I don't care. The important thing is you're better, and in a couple of days you'll be up and about.'

His eyes glazed over. 'I'll be back to normal.'

I stared at him for a brief moment, trying to work out what was so odd about what he'd just said, but then my face broke into a smile. 'Yes Gideon – you'll be completely normal again.'

As I made my way back through the ward, I spotted the elderly lady who'd had difficulty breathing. She looked better today and was free of the breathing mask. Rather tentatively I approached her and smiled shyly. 'Hello.' I uttered. 'You don't know me but I was chatting with your sister yesterday in the waiting room.'

She looked at me blankly. 'My...my sister?'

I laughed nervously. 'Yes...she was so lovely and kind, I would very much like to say thank you to her. She made me feel so much better.'

'I'm sorry dear but you must be mistaken. I only have one sister and she passed away many years ago, in this very hospital.'

Looking puzzled I stared at her, wondering if I had indeed made a mistake. It was all too strange. Deciding it wouldn't be wise to enquire further I retreated from the bed and told her I was dreadfully sorry to have bothered her.

On arriving back home from the hospital I decided to take a stroll around the gardens. How odd I thought that in the next few days Gideon would be living here, it was like a dream, a dream that had become reality. But I was nervous and apprehensive in having him stay: would he be happy living here, would my Aunt accept him, would we both be able to make a life together at Rawlings, or would circumstances get in the way that were beyond our control, causing my dream to be shattered.

For some unexplained reason I found myself wandering towards the garden shed at the very back of the garden, eager to go inside. But to my horror it wasn't there anymore; it had been replaced with a large summerhouse. My heart sank for a moment. Trying not to think about it I ambled around the rest of the garden amazed and shocked by the changes. The great trees that once enfolded the house had been cut neatly back and the brickwork of the property was free from the creeping ivy that we had never quite managed to destroy. The terrace had new garden furniture and was full of potted plants, cleverly arranged to look neat, and I noticed the porch and everything that went with it was gone. The wide sweeping lawns were perfectly maintained, and in the middle of the back lawn was a sunken fishpond, surrounded by ornamental statues. The outer edges of the entire garden had brilliant borders filled with colourful mixtures of late flowering shrubs, such as roses, hellebores and dahlias. My eyes were then led to the outer walls which were adorned with clematis and rambling roses, creeping decoratively over the brickwork. Even the untamed parts of the garden, furthest away from the house were filled with plants and flowers. No one could deny the improvements greatly enhanced the beauty of Rawlings, it was truly splendid, and yet it made me feel a little uncomfortable, as if I was a guest in my own home; for me it was too perfect, and Rawlings was never meant to be perfect, it was meant to be flawed, just like me.

Chapter 8

There was a distinct chill in the air that October morning. I gazed out at the sunbeams streaming through the silvery mists of the early morning, bringing a radiant burnt orange glow upon the leaves of the trees. Gideon was coming home today and I was full of nervous excitement. I had prepared his bed in one of the spare rooms and lit a fire in the living room and the study in readiness for his return. My Aunt had insisted on rising at dawn to do baking, commenting how Gideon would probably need feeding up after his spell in hospital. She was also preparing a roast with all the trimmings. Although I sensed our shattered relationship was slowly mending, at times she'd make comments about me being away for so long, and how irresponsible and selfish I'd been. Isaiah was rarely mentioned; it was almost as if Aunt had pretended he no longer existed. I however didn't have the ability to completely block him out. Yesterday morning I'd found a package on the table addressed to me, and when I ripped it open I saw it was my notebook, the one with all my notes about this world and the other. Laughing to myself I pulled out the letter that was poking out the first page.

Dearest daughter

I thought it was time I returned this to you. Had the situation been different I would have gladly handed it to you in person, but sadly your Aunt Constance has not yet forgiven me, I live in hope that she shall!

How is the dear old homestead? I hear from various sources that it is now looking splendid. What a decent sort those Davenport sisters were, god rest their souls. Their money has been well spent, and it's all thanks to me!

Talking of being thankful I hear Gideon is making a good recovery. How lucky he will be to convalesce at Rawlings with the both of you. Oh, and by the way you'll be glad to know your testament is in the safe hands of my solicitor.

Please remember I shall be in Hudson's café every Wednesday at noon.

Much love, your father.

In a daydream I stared at the notebook, trying to decide whether to read it or not. However, as I picked it up my mind suddenly became clear, and I knew what to do. With purposeful strides I took the notebook up to my room and stuffed it at the back of the wardrobe, next to Gilbert. Reading it would only confuse me, of that I was certain. And why would I even think of looking in it when everything I ever wanted was right here with me in Rawlings. It was my past, another life, another world, and it was my choice to forget it.

Hearing a car door, I ran down the stairs and out the front door. Gideon was standing there looking anxious and lost. He reminded me of a poor little boy who'd been sent away to boarding school for the very first time, and was already missing his home. When he saw me, his face broke into a grin. I smiled back at him and gently took his arm and led him into the house. He was trembling slightly, through nerves I thought, as well as still being very weak. My Aunt greeted him rather gingerly, shaking his hand with an awkward smile.

'Do come through to the dining room Gideon. Lunch is almost ready.'

He nodded and gave her a weak smile.

During our meal Aunt made a point of staring at him rather ungraciously, especially for someone so keen on good manners. 'It's rude to stare Effie.' She would always tell me as a child and yet now she was doing precisely that.

'You have a very impressive house Constance.'

'Why thank you Gideon.' Her eyes followed him closely as he helped himself to the food. 'Do tell me, where do you actually come from?'

'Well I...I'

'And how did you injure your shoulder?' She asked, 'did someone try and murder you?' Her eyes grew wide. 'Was it Isaiah?'

'Aunt please.' I cried. 'Gideon has just had a live saving operation and here you are bombarding him with questions.' I saw she was still peering at him curiously. 'What is it Aunt, why do you keep staring at him?'

'Oh dear.' Looking rather abashed she lowered her gaze to her plate. 'I didn't mean to; it's just Gideon looks so much like...like Noble.'

Gideon suddenly clattered his knife and fork down onto the plate and gazed curiously at her. 'Noble?'

I sighed and closed my eyes. 'That's because they're brother's Aunt.'

'Oh, I see.' She answered, coldly. Looking solemn she rose from her seat. 'If you excuse me, I have a headache and shall be retiring to my room. I shall leave the clearing up for you to do Effie.' Without another word she left the room.

We both stared after her.

'How could I have forgotten about my own brother or where I come from?' Gideon said quietly. 'And what about my shoulder injury, why can't I remember anything about it.' Grimacing he rubbed his hand over his eyes. 'What's happened to me Effie, where have all my memories gone?'

It struck me odd that he was completely clueless as to the reason why he couldn't remember anything. He'd been so wise and knowledgeable about such matters, and had always been the one to do the explaining, and yet now the tables had been turned. I wondered if the journey through the mirror had cleared his mind more thoroughly than Isaiah's and mine. Whatever the reason, it had left Gideon somewhat frightened and vulnerable.

I rose from my seat and went to kneel beside him, gripping his hands tightly in mine. 'Gideon this is all perfectly normal for someone who travels across worlds. It's happened to me too, and Isaiah.'

'But how, and why?'

I went on to explain the theory behind it all. It all came out rather muddled and when I'd finished he just gazed at me in bewilderment.

'How odd it all sounds Effie, and unbelievable.'

With a laugh I got up and gave him a light hug, mindful of his wounded shoulder.

'Yes, I know. It's important not to dwell on the subject, and just concentrate on the here and now. And besides, with your injury it wouldn't be wise to go leaping back into that mirror.'

He looked up into my eyes. 'I'm not leaping anywhere without you.'

'Good.' I said looking amused. 'Now I suggest you go and have a rest.' I helped him up from his seat. 'I'll show you up to your room.'

'What about your Aunt, why did she suddenly become upset on learning Noble and I were siblings?'

I shrugged my shoulders and looked down at the table. 'I...I don't know.'

He looked confused. 'When was my brother here?'

'Oh um... he turned up one day out of the blue and stayed at Rawlings for a while.'

'Then where did he go?'

'As far as I can remember Noble went back home.' I replied rather rapidly. 'To wherever that is.'

'And you didn't wish to return with Noble, to stay with him?'

'No of course not.' I snapped. 'Otherwise I wouldn't be here with you now, would I?'

He stared at me intently for a moment before lowering his head and laughing.

'Sorry Effie, I didn't mean to pry. And you're right I should get some sleep.' As he leaned heavily on my arm we walked slowly towards the door in silence.

Whilst Gideon was resting, I cleared away the dishes and began to wash them up in the kitchen. My Aunt appeared, looking decidedly cross. I'd already resigned myself to what was coming, and I was right. She scolded me for leaving Noble in the lurch and moving onto his sibling; in her view it was completely inappropriate and unseemly. I was to seriously consider my future if I wished to stay living in this house, and it was time I started acting like an adult. Gritting my teeth, I tried to tell her yet again that Noble had only ever been a friend but she wasn't at all convinced. I urged her not to say anything to Gideon about how Noble had stormed into the chapel that day, and how the two of us had become engaged at the garden party, all be it a fake engagement. There was little point dredging it up and would only confuse matters. She'd stood there frowning at me and said she couldn't make any promises, she wasn't accustomed to lying and if something happened to slip out about my relationship with Noble it wouldn't be fair to hold her accountable.

The rest of the day I showed Gideon around Rawlings, even the attic room, which I'd always associated with fear. Like the rest of the house it had had an overhaul, and the boxes and trunks were now stacked in neat piles up against the walls, and apart from a few old suitcases and hats the space in the centre was empty and uncluttered. The mannequin wasn't there anymore, which I was rather glad about, as it had always scared me, and the mirror of course was now downstairs in the study.

As the days past by Gideon's shoulder carried on healing well and a district nurse would visit every day to change the dressing. We had several visits from the local police, and they took a statement from Gideon in regards to his injury. Also, much to my annoyance, various doctors kept ringing about his unusual blood type, and kept urging Gideon to come in for tests. It hardly surprised me that they couldn't locate Isaiah, and I almost told them he could be reached in Hudson's café at noon on Wednesdays, but something prevented me, my consciousness perhaps, for despite everything, it would seem a little mean of me when he had saved Gideon's life.

For me the nights were the worst, quite frequently I would wake up in a cold sweat, panicking about something, but I didn't know what. One night I awoke to find Gilbert sitting at the edge of my bed, gawping at me with his bulbous looking eyes. My Aunt and Gideon assured me they hadn't placed him there, but I rather wished they had. After that I almost took him along to the jumble sale in the local church, but something held me back, maybe a sense of loyalty, or possibly I believed the dummy would become enraged if I attempted to get rid of him, and seek his revenge.

Gideon and I were married on Christmas Eve in a quaint little church, surrounded by frost-covered fields, on the outskirts of Abercrombie. It didn't seem fitting to have the ceremony in the chapel where my previous wedding had been, for one thing it held too many painful memories and, although extremely unlikely, I feared history repeating itself. The congregation was full of my Aunt's chums from the committee and several of my old friends, including Rosemary who was heavily pregnant and due at any time now. She'd always been popular and outspoken at school, and despite us being so different we seemed to bond over our love of art. Then there was Cassandra, who'd I'd never been particularly close to, but had made a point of inviting herself, saying how she missed out the time before. 'What a catch Duncan would have been.' She said raising her eyebrows. 'I can't believe you let him slip through your fingers Effie.'

The reception was held at Rawlings and the entire house was adorned with wreaths of holly and ivy that trailed down the grand banisters as if nature had taken over. An impressive Christmas tree stood in the grand hallway, decorated in silver and gold, and I'm not sure if it had been planned but wedding gifts from the guests were nestled beneath it. My Aunt had a catering firm in to take care of all the food, and a lavish feast was laid out in the dining room, along with rows of tables, covered in crisp white linen tablecloths and soft candlelight. After we'd all eaten, toasts and speeches were made, and Gideon and I presented Aunt with a large bouquet in thanks for all her hard work. An instrumental band were playing in one of the large rooms leading off from the hall and everyone watched whilst Gideon and I had had the first dance, before being joined by a number of smiling guests. Never before had I seen that amount of people in the house, it was full to the brim. Not so long ago being the centre of attention would have made me nervous, however today of all days I hardly felt awkward and uncomfortable at all. Perhaps it was the wine, or perhaps I felt so giddy with happiness that no other feeling stood a chance. I was finally with my beloved Gideon, the kind, virtuous and impressive looking man I had grown up with.

'Do you not remember anything Gideon?' I asked, suddenly feeling sad that none of his family were here to see us get married.

We were dancing together in the summerhouse, swaying together to the distant music that was drifting over from the house. It was the middle of the evening and the party was in full swing. Gideon and I had sneaked out to escape the unrelenting questions being asked about our courtship, and if indeed my new husband was the mysterious stranger from my previous wedding. I could see by the look on his face he was becoming overwhelmed and needed a break.

'About what Effie?'

'Your past life.'

'Very little.' He lifted his head from my shoulder and moved his face close to mine. 'It doesn't matter anyway. My life is now with you, we are bound to one another for the rest of our lives.'

I giggled. 'That's a very serious declaration.'

He nuzzled his face into the nape of my neck. 'Well, I'm a very serious person, and extremely serious about you.'

But aren't you curious about your family?'

'No Effie, the past is in the past. Let's leave it there where it belongs and concentrate on our future.' He mumbled, raising his head and looking into my eyes. 'When precisely are the guests going to leave?

'I don't think they'll be leaving quite yet.'

'That's a shame, I was very much hoping it was time for bed.' He grinned.

My face began to redden.

His arms tightened around my waist and we began to kiss.

Without warning a gentle tapping came from the glass door. I pulled away from him and looked towards it and saw Mrs Lapworth peering in through the glass, waving frantically at me.

'It's Clarice's mother, I should go and speak with her Gideon.'

He reluctantly stepped back and sat down in one of the chairs. 'Don't be long.' I threw him a quick smile before going outside.

'Hello Mrs Lapworth.' I glanced down at the sherry glass in her hand. 'I...I didn't think you could make it. I'm so glad to see you here.'

She took a gulp of her drink and when she spoke her speech was slurred. 'Well, don't you look the sophisticated bride.' Her eyes travelled over my lace gown. 'All dolled up for your new husband.'

I scoffed, not knowing how to respond.

With a dry laugh she began shaking her head. 'Yes, sorry I'm late it's just that I was looking over some old photos of my daughter.' She swayed a little and my arm shot out to steady her. 'Remember her do you Effie? Clarice used to be your best friend, she went out one day and never returned.' With a laugh she stabbed me with her forefinger. 'What right do you have to be happy when Clarice is out there somewhere, lost.' She gripped the tops of my arms and her glass tumbled to the ground. 'You're to blame Effie Farraday, I don't know how or why, but you took her away from me.'

'Please Mrs Lapworth I...'

'Don't interrupt me.' she snapped. 'Didn't the righteous Constance teach you any manners?'

Gideon popped his head outside. 'Is everything alright?'

'Ah the groom.' She released her grip on me and tottered over towards Gideon, who was now standing beside us on the lawn. 'Oh my, it's true what everyone's been saying, you are indeed handsome. What a lucky girl Effie is.' She turned away from him and glared back at me. 'It's all worked out so well for you, hasn't it Effie.' Suddenly there was pure hatred within her eyes. 'Isaiah was right about you being selfish. The poor man is completely heartbroken he didn't receive an invite to the wedding, he was hoping you'd ask him to give you away, and yet you cruelly snubbed him, your very own father.'

I stood there in silence, staring back at her.

Gideon came forward and put his arm around me protectively. He looked solemnly at Mrs Lapworth. 'I suggest you go home madam. You're upsetting Effie.'

She stumbled back with a loud laugh. 'I don't care.' Suddenly she lost her footing and fell down amongst the bedding plants.

With a desperate sigh I rushed forward to help her.

'Come on Mrs Lapworth. You're not yourself. Allow me to take you into the house and make you a strong coffee. You'll feel better after....'

'No.' she hollered. 'The only thing that can make me better is seeing Clarice again.' With a hiccup she clutched onto my dress, half pulling me down beside her. 'Where is she Effie, just tell me, just tell me she's...she's not.' A whimper escaped her lips. 'I couldn't bear it if she was dead.'

As she began to sob I pulled her into my arms so her head was resting on my shoulder. 'No, no Mrs Lapworth, Clarice is very much alive. I've seen her at....' My whole body suddenly went tense. 'She had to go away for a while, and...and I'm sure she'll come back home soon.'

Sniffing she rose her head and stared into my face.

'Really?

'Yes.' I said with a nervous gulp. 'I am so sorry Mrs Lapworth I should have come and told you the news. It's just that...' My eyes darted to Gideon then down to the lawn. Since my return I'd been so preoccupied with Gideon and the wedding arrangements that my friend had been far from my thoughts, as had Mace. I could hardly blame my memory, as I could remember both of them, I just chose not to. Isaiah was right about me being selfish. 'It was very wrong of me, please accept my apologies.'

'But where exactly is Clarice? Could I go and visit her?'

I exchanged a desperate look with Gideon. How could I tell Mrs Lapworth I couldn't remember where she was? I only knew her daughter was alive, and that was all. With a reassuring smile I stared into her blotchy eyes. 'I think it's best we leave Clarice alone for now. She'll come back when she's ready.'

Her expression remained agonised.

Someone was shouting my name from the terrace, and sounded very much like my Aunt. With another gulp I rose up from the lawn and held my hands out to Mrs Lapworth.

'How would you like to stay the night - we can put you up in one of the guest bedrooms?'

She shook her head vigorously as if I'd suggested something terrible. 'No, I prefer the safety...I...I mean the comfort of my own bed.' Allowing me to pull her up she stood there, wobbling from side to side. 'Forgive me Effie, for the nasty comments I made towards you tonight, I didn't mean them. My emotions are all over the place.'

I gave her a broad smile and told her it's fine. Gideon and I helped her into the house and gave her a strong black coffee. For some time, we sat together at the kitchen table, and I held her hand as she lamented over how overzealous Clarice was as a child, and how she was always getting herself into trouble. After Ambrose had kindly driven her back home, I went to find Gideon. He was perched on the edge of the window seat in the morning room, whilst Cassandra and a few other guests hovered over him. I bit my lower lip then with a deep breath I went to join them.

As the last guests drifted towards the door, Rosemary clutched my arm.

'Who'd thought it Effie. Little old you marrying someone like him.' She smiled charmingly at Gideon then with a chuckle she whispered in my ear. 'I always imagined you'd end up with that gangly boy. Do you remember how we used to call him mouthy Mace at school?' She gave a thoughtful sigh. 'Since that gas explosion at his foster parent's house, I've not seen him, have you?'

'No, he.... he moved away Rosemary.'

'Probably married now with ten children.' She giggled. 'You had a lucky escape there Effie. With his sarcastic nature I would have ended up throttling him' Frowning she reached for her coat. 'Best get home, that husband of mine is outside becoming impatient.'

'Thank you for coming Rosemary, it's lovely to see you after all this time. Good luck with the baby. We...we should keep in touch.'

'Well of course Effie, although I may have my hands full with this little one.' With an endearing smile she rubbed her stomach then gave me a hug.' She opened her mouth to speak but then changed her mind, and began glancing around as if she was about to discuss something secretive. Pursing her lips, she spoke in a low voice. 'Have you seen anyone in the house?'

In puzzlement I laughed. 'Pardon?'

'Any spirits, ghosts whatever you want to call them. There's been talk all over Abercrombie about the sightings at Rawlings. Well just the other day the postman....'

'Rosemary.' Someone shouted nearby. 'Come on, it's getting late. We should go home.'

I glanced behind and saw a rather thin man with a beard standing in the doorway, looking uncomfortable. He gave me a brief smile before widening his eyes at Rosemary.

'Oh Henry, very well then.' She pecked me on the cheek. 'Take care Effie.' Rushing over to Gideon she gave him a hug before having a few words with my Aunt. Then taking her husband's arm she yanked him out the door.

After all the guests had departed and the catering firm had cleared everything up and gone on their way, my Aunt flopped down onto a chair in the hallway, looking exhausted. I thanked her for making our day so memorable then insisted she go straight to bed. I was most emphatic that tomorrow she would spend the day resting whilst Gideon and I tidied up, then later on we would all open the wedding and Christmas gifts over afternoon tea. My husband had insisted on cooking the Christmas dinner, and we would dine early tomorrow evening.

Whilst Gideon was placing the rest of the presents under the tree, I sat by the fire in the living room, reflecting over the day. Apart from a few minor hiccups it had gone wonderfully well, I thought. The subjects of ghosts that Rosemary had mentioned didn't really worry me, Rawlings had always been renowned for being haunted, and I personally had never seen an apparition, or ever wished to. I can't recall my Aunt ever witnessing such things, other than when she saw my mother that time. No, it was all just mere speculation that had been embellished by certain townsfolk to make my ancient home sound creepier than it actually was.

I was however slightly disturbed by something else this evening. After everyone had left, I'd gone upstairs to fetch some presents to place underneath the Christmas tree, and had been stunned to see my notebook lying there on the centre of my bed. I know for certain it had been stuffed at the back of my wardrobe, and completely forgotten, for I intentionally wanted it that way. Whoever the culprit, it was becoming apparent they wished to play silly mind games with me; first Gilbert had been flung on the bed, and now my notebook. Perhaps I should be concerned about ghosts, did Rawlings have its very own poltergeist? After pondering for a moment, I picked the book up and took it downstairs and into the living room, seriously contemplating if I should read it. But what would I glean from its contents, and would it help or hinder me? It may contain the whereabouts of Clarice, however how would that comfort Mrs Lapworth, when she realised her daughter was completely out of reach, for that much I knew. Gideon was right: The here and now was what counted. I no longer needed the memories of my old life in the other world; they would only stir up unwanted feelings and confusion.

With an air of complete resoluteness, I tossed the notebook onto the fire and watched as the pages darkened and curled amongst the flames.

'What are you doing?'

I turned around to see Gideon standing there smiling.

'Oh, nothing really. Just burning an old book I don't need anymore.'

Kneeling down beside me he grasped my hands. 'That's not like you, I thought all your books were sacred.' He bent his head and kissed my hands then tenderly stroked them.

'They are, but this was just a notebook.'

He raised his head and looked deep into my eyes. 'What did it contain?'

My voice was hoarse and trembling as I spoke. 'It contained unimportant notes from the past. Like you mentioned earlier - it's the future that's important, mine and yours.'

His face became serious and staring into my eyes he rose up from the floor, pulling me up by the hands. Without saying another word, we left the warmth of the living room and went upstairs to my bedroom.

Chapter 9

During the following months Gideon and I slipped effortlessly into married life and we were both happy and contented. My Aunt's spirits had lifted and she was back to her old self. Occasionally she'd take to her room complaining of a headache, but reassured me it was nothing serious. By early spring I discovered I was going to have a baby, which made us all joyous. The prospect of being a mother was quite daunting, and occasionally I still felt like a young girl who was barely capable of looking after herself let alone anyone else, but that was the frightened, insecure part of me, where the tiny demon on my shoulder would try and fill my mind with doubts. On the whole however I felt quietly confident that everything was going to go well, and with Gideon and Aunt by my side it made it all the easier.

Gideon crept up behind me and wrapped his arms around my stomach, nestling his face into the nape of my neck. 'Let's have an early night.'

'Another one?' I said amusingly, turning to face him. 'But we've only just had dinner, and I promised my Aunt, I'd do the washing up.'

'I'm sure in your condition Constance won't mind. The doctor recommended more rest.'

I ruffled his hair. 'But Gideon I'm only a few months pregnant.' I smiled. 'And besides, if we retire early will I actually be resting?

His nose touched mine. 'Probably not.' With a grin he rolled up his sleeves and lifted me up gently by the waist, shifting me over to the right. 'I'll wash you wipe.' Kissing me quick he handed me a tea towel. 'It'll get done quicker that way.'

I giggled.

My Aunt poked her head around the door. 'Now remember you two I'm at the village hall all tomorrow morning and then I shall be shopping in town.' She glanced down at my stomach. 'I must remember to purchase some wool for those booties I'm going to knit for the baby. What a shame you don't know what you're having Effie, then I could get the appropriate colour.'

'Sorry Aunt, but we'd rather it was a surprise.'

'Get blue Constance, I'm sure it's going to be a boy.' Said Gideon with a laugh.

She raised her eyebrows. 'Surely that's not wishful thinking because you want to carry on your family name? Otherwise why use Farraday?' She began to cackle. 'The ladies at the village hall still can't believe it you know.'

Gideon and I exchanged glances.

'No, it has nothing to do with my family name Constance, I can just feel it in my bones.' He grinned.

Having no clue about Gideon's surname, we had decided to pretend on having mine for now. It seemed a practical solution in the circumstances, and besides I was rather glad to still have it. My Aunt, on the other hand, had been astonished when we told her. 'What a controversial decision.' She had declared. 'It won't do you know - it really won't do at all.' After much complaining she finally gave up trying to dissuade us and even commented how wise it was to keep the name Farraday in our family home of Rawlings.

She let out a little squeal and studied his face intently.

'Oh, Gideon you are a hoot. You know at times you really remind me of...' she paused. 'Well, someone I used to know.'

'It's alright Constance, I really don't mind you discussing Noble.' Looking amused he glanced at me. 'I'd already learnt he put a stop to your previous wedding Effie, and how the two of you staged a fake engagement.'

I looked stunned. 'But...but how did you find out.'

'Several of Constance's friends told me all about it at our wedding reception.' He suddenly looked sheepish. 'Sorry Effie, but when we discussed Noble on the day I returned from the hospital I sensed you found the whole subject more distressing than me. So, I thought it wise not to rake it all up again.'

My eyes flickered to my Aunt then back to him. I laughed nervously, suddenly feeling rather queasy. 'Oh, it doesn't matter now anyway.' Moving away a little I glanced at her. 'Be sure to be home by teatime tomorrow, won't you Aunt.'

She smiled serenely. 'Certainly dear.'

Tomorrow was her birthday and we'd arranged a surprise get together with a few of her friends.

Suddenly an acute wave of nausea came over me and I rushed to the bathroom.

The following morning I wandered into the garden to find Ambrose and ask if he'd like to attend my Aunt's birthday party. Gideon was busy baking in the kitchen for her birthday surprise and insisted I allow him to do it all. It was rather a welcome relief to get some fresh air, as I still felt rather nauseous from yesterday evening.

'Why don't you invite your wife over Ambrose, she's very welcome.'

He removed his cloth cap and scratched his head. 'Thank you miss, for your kind offer but the missus won't be able to make it up to the house.'

'Oh, I could arrange for transport.' I said, knowing he cycled each day. 'I could go and collect her in my car.'

He lowered his eyes to the ground and cleared his throat as if he was nervous. 'It's not the travelling miss.' With a drawn-out sigh he met my gaze. 'It's...it's them ghosts. She's petrified of seeing one.'

My eyes grew large with surprise and I laughed.

'What ghosts?'

'Them that lurk in and around the house.' His eyes suddenly darted about as if he was scared they would hear him. 'There's always been talk about Rawlings being haunted but I never took notice before, but now I've actually seen one with me own eyes.'

I tilted my head a little to the right, trying to act composed.

'Can you describe it?'

He stared blankly at me. 'No miss, I don't hang about to see what it looks like. But it's usually a tall, willowy figure that appears. Watches me it does, watches me from afar.' With a long deep sigh, he replaced his cap and picked up the rake. 'Best get on miss, there's lots to do.'

Nodding at him I smiled faintly and swallowed. 'Well I do hope it doesn't put you off gardening here Ambrose. My Aunt is more than happy with your work.'

'Oh no miss. They're just apparitions aren't they. They might be a bit scary looking but they can't hurt the living.' He chuckled to himself as he began raking the soil.

My eyes drifted across the lawn and towards the house. 'No Ambrose, no they cannot.'

My Aunt's birthday party was a great success, and she was quite delighted to see all her friends waiting for her in the living room. We all had afternoon tea together then watched as she opened her presents. The forthcoming baby was discussed at length and also the latest goings on in Abercrombie, including the shocking sudden departure of Mrs Monaghan's son, who had just upped and left without so much of a goodbye to his mother, and had simply said 'there's a better life out there for me,' evidently it was all down to some woman, who'd been seen in his company recently. Gideon frequently joined in the conversation and took a genuine interest in what the ladies were discussing, he was courteous and charismatic as ever, and with his rich sounding voice and captivating eyes he held everyone's absolute attention. Other the past months he had come into his own and had settled well into life at Rawlings. He had his confidence back and was merrier than I'd ever seen him before, more so because of the baby I think but also because that dark cloud of forgotten memories had completely cleared away, and now there were nothing but blue skies and sunshine.

After the party Gideon and I had cleared up whilst my Aunt rested in the living room. I was just removing the tablecloth from the dining room table when I heard a piercing scream.

'Aunt?' I uttered, running out into the hallway.

'We're in the morning room.' Shouted Gideon.

I rushed in to see Gideon holding Aunt's hand as she sat hunched forward in an armchair. Drawing closer I saw she looked decidedly distressed.

'Whatever's happened Aunt?'

With a nervous gulp she looked up into my face. 'There's strangers in the house Effie, wandering about the place as if they live here.' With a gasp she clutched Gideon's arms. 'We should call the police -they could be burglars.'

Glancing at me Gideon widened his eyes then turned back to my Aunt. 'Where did you see these strangers Constance?'

'They were just in the hallway. I...I'd been in the library getting a book and when I came out the room, that's when I saw them.'

'Did they see you Aunt?' I asked.

She looked at me in a daze. 'I'm not sure Effie, I'm really not sure.' With a whimper she buried her face in her hands.'

I went over and placed my arms around her. 'We should call the police Gideon.'

He looked at me blankly. 'What?'

Suddenly I realised he'd never used the telephone.

'I'll go and call them. You must stay with my Aunt, Gideon.'

'No,' Gideon said sternly. 'It could be dangerous Effie. You two wait here, whilst I search the house. If I can't find anyone then perhaps we should think about calling them after.' With a half-smile he looked at my Aunt. 'Perhaps you imagined it Constance. Night's falling and the shadows could be playing tricks on your eyes.'

Rather reluctantly I let Gideon go and look around the house. I pulled up a chair and sat close to my Aunt, trying to pacify her. She was adamant about what she'd seen, but as the minutes ticked by I began to wonder if it had indeed been a figment of her imagination, or ghosts perhaps. Everyone else seemed to think my house was haunted, why should we be exempt from seeing spirits. When Gideon returned a few moments later he shrugged his shoulders and shook his head. Apparently, he'd searched the entire house, including the attic room, and found precisely nothing. My Aunt began to get agitated, stumbling around the room and talking to herself. When I tried to reassure her, she screamed at me angrily. 'Do not try and mollify me Effie. I know what I saw. I'm not going mad, not quite yet anyway.' After she persuaded me to call the police we waited patiently whilst they too checked the house, and yet again there was no one there.

Things took a while to settle down again after that particular incident. My Aunt was on tenterhooks, waiting for another occurrence, almost willing it to happen just so she could prove that she was right. By early summer however the disturbing incident had faded with the inevitable march of time and for a while life at Rawlings became relatively normal again. I did however still receive long letters from Isaiah, pleading with me to meet with him at the usual time and place; sometimes I would read them and others I would simply tear them up unopened. My pregnancy was going well and I no longer felt nauseous, but with the birth date looming I began to feel rather anxious at the thought of becoming a mother, an emotion that I certainly didn't need, for little did I know a shattering blow was fast approaching.

I'd been resting on the window seat in the morning room, breathing in the heady scent of roses and honeysuckle wafting in through the open window. It reminded me of a forgotten memory long since passed and out of reach, yet so familiar. I sat there for a moment, lost in my thoughts.

The shrill ring of the telephone brought me back to reality and placing my hand over my belly I made my way slowly to the hallway.

'Hello.'

'Can I speak to Gideon please?'

It was Dr Mason.

'It's Effie here doctor, Gideon's popped into town. May I take a message?'

There was a long pause at the other end of the line.

'Yes, I was just calling about Gideon's missed appointment with the specialist, I wonder if he would call me back.'

I suddenly realised what it was all about. 'Please doctor, I know Gideon has an unusual blood type but I would really appreciate it if you would not persist in pestering him. Are you really not able to contact my father?'

There was silence at the other end.

'Mr Penhaligon?' the doctor asked in a confused voice.

'Yes.' I retorted a little impatiently. 'My father was the blood donor for Gideon.'

'I'm sorry Effie but I think there's been a misunderstanding. I have suggested both to Gideon and your father that they should come and give blood just in case it is needed in the future, an offer I'm sorry to say they have so far both declined. But that's not the reason I am calling now.' He cleared his throat. 'Gideon was supposed to come in for tests on his heart.'

The receiver nearly dropped from my hand. 'His...his heart?'

'Yes, I'm sorry, didn't he mention the subject?'

Suddenly the room began to spin and I dropped down into the chair by the phone, pressing my hand across my eyes.

'No, no he did not.' My voice became increasingly shaky. 'And what exactly is wrong with his...his heart?'

'I'm not exactly sure. We discovered the abnormality during routine tests when he was being treated for his shoulder wound. Which reminds me, did you hear from the police?'

'What? Yes, the matter was closed due to lack of evidence.' I answered rather vaguely. 'Is it serious, the problem with his heart?'

'I'm not sure at this stage Effie. So please try not to worry.'

Worry, how could I not worry after hearing news? I was silent for a moment, trying to work out why Gideon had kept this information secret from me.

'Well, I shall make sure Gideon contacts you as soon as possible, Dr Mason.'

'That would be wise, thank you Effie.'

I calmly replaced the receiver and sat there, staring into space and trying to digest what the doctor had just told me. A dull ached appeared in the pit of my stomach that wouldn't go away. A range of thoughts darted through my mind, as I tried to make sense of it all. Had Gideon always had this condition, or was the harm done recently, when he travelled over to this world, had the loss of blood been a strain on his heart and permanently damaged it. Was he going to die? I carried on sitting there, the ache in my stomach becoming worse.

'Why didn't you tell me about your heart Gideon?' I asked immediately as he came through the front door.

He seemed shocked. 'What?'

I pulled him into the study and shut the door so as Aunt wouldn't hear. 'I've just had a phone call from Dr Mason about the appointment you missed. He says there's something wrong with your heart.'

He reached for my hand but I moved away.

'You should have told me Gideon.'

'I wanted to Effie, but it would have only worried you, and when you announced you were having a child I knew my decision not to tell you had been right.'

'No, your decision was wrong.' I shouted at him angrily. 'Marriage is about sharing everything, the good and the bad.'

He slunk down in one of the armchairs and gazed pensively down at the floor. 'I'm truly sorry Effie.'

With a sigh I went and placed my hand on his shoulders, then moved my face against his hair. 'It's okay Gideon, really it is. What...what do you think is wrong with your heart?'

'I'm not sure. Obviously, I can't remember much, but I sense it's a condition I've had for a long while.'

'But if you think you already knew about it why did you risk travelling here.' I said in a raised voice.

As he looked up at me, I saw the tears in his eyes. 'I would have risked anything to have a life with you Effie that much I know. We must have come to your home because we had to, because it was necessary, and if I had to do it all over again I would.'

I stared into his face, then with a sob I knelt down and flung my arms around him. As we both hugged one another I felt the baby move inside me.

We both went to see Dr Mason the following day. After several tests we had to wait a week before he gave us his verdict. Gideon had a slight heart disorder that was probably hereditary, but without confirmation from his parents the doctor couldn't be sure. Apparently, the condition could be controlled with pills, which he gave us a prescription for. He did however stress that Gideon shouldn't put undue strain on his heart, just in case it aggravated the situation; he gave random examples such as climbing a mountain or running a marathon. This immediately sent alarm bells ringing and I almost asked the doctor if Gideon should refrain from travelling through portals.

As the days past by I tried desperately to put the matter out my mind, but it lingered there all the same. Gideon seemed happy enough but I wondered if he was just very good at hiding his concerns. We sat down with my Aunt one night and told her what had happened. She was very sympathetic and understanding and said how ultimately we had to carry on, we had done what needed to be done, and dwelling on the causes of his heart trouble would only cause unnecessary suffering for both of us.

To take my mind away from my troubles I decided to do some light gardening, and ambled into the conservatory to retrieve the trowels been left there by my Aunt. She was in Abercrombie with Gideon collecting the crib for the baby, and Ambrose was going to give them a lift back in his truck. The room had a wide range of windows and housed white wicker chairs carefully positioned amongst the vast amount of well-established plants that caused the room to be dark and shady. Large containers of ferns and exotic looking fruit trees, many of them citrus and fig, were laid out ready to be placed outside, along with the masses of bedding plants on the shelves. My gaze was drawn to the vines with their brilliant foliage of yellow leaves spread across the glass ceiling, drawing warmth from the sun. For some inexplicable reason I half expected the vine to come alive and imagined it reaching down and strangling me.   Feeling suddenly giddy from the warmth and humidity I reached across and opened one of the little windows, breathing in the warm spring air. A breeze caused a gentle rustle within the conservatory and the distinct sound of laughter drifted over to where I was standing. That's peculiar, I thought, both my Aunt and Gideon were in Abercrombie and Ambrose wouldn't come into the house.

There was nothing but a hushed stillness.

'Hello?' I uttered quietly. 'Who's there?'

Feeling unexpectedly chilly I closed the window and ambled towards the entrance of the conservatory, realising my mind was playing tricks on me. Perhaps this was a side effect of pregnancy, hearing voices that weren't there.

'Effelia.'

My whole body froze. It wasn't hearing my name that petrified me it was the way it was said. It was a woman's voice and she had sung my name; it was so eerie that it chilled me to the bone. I turned and frantically scanned the conservatory, feeling an overwhelming surge of heat creeping over my body, making me giddy. At first, I thought the ferns had come alive but then I saw a figure emerge from amongst them, a tall willowy apparition was gliding towards me. Everything was blurry now, a mass of green and grey mist. I was falling, and all around me there was darkness.

My Aunt discovered me, unconscious on the terracotta floor with an arrow lying across my stomach. I was shaken up but unharmed. After begging her she promised not to breathe a word of my ghostly encounter to Gideon. It seemed wrong to worry him unduly, for despite his continual reassurance that he was well I had this tiny niggling doubt at the back of my mind that wouldn't leave me.

One day when no one was looking I went into the garden and buried the arrow, hoping this would banish the memory from my mind, and remove the vision I had of her face, the woman with the callous eyes.

Chapter 10

By the end of summer, I decided it was time to pay someone a visit, someone who could perhaps provide me with answers, someone who was at Hudson's café every Wednesday at noon.

'Hello Effelia.' Isaiah said as I came up to his table. He stood up to greet me and eyed my stomach. 'Congratulations.'

Struggling to smile I took a seat beside him.

'Thank you, Isaiah.'

As he settled back down into his seat I was surprised at his dishevelled appearance. He was decidedly thinner than the last time I'd seen him and had grown a beard. Suddenly I wondered if he was sleeping rough and pictured him curled up on a park bench covered in newspaper for warmth.

'I do hope you're eating healthily Effelia.'

My forced smile faded. 'Yes, yes of course.' I replied sternly, observing the food stain on his bow tie. 'How are you keeping?'

He rolled his eyes. 'I'm surviving.' With an ironic laugh he handed me the menu.

A young waitress came over and stood beside us, staring down at a notepad.

'May I take your order?'

Isaiah snatched the menu from my hand and glanced at her. 'We'll have the cream tea for two, with extra cake please.'

'Anything else?' she asked, not bothering to look up.

'Yes, where's Mrs Worthington today?'

She threw him a vacant stare. 'Who?'

'Oh, never mind, I can see that you're new.' He growled at her. 'Just go and get our food please.'

Nonchalantly the waitress moved away and ambled over to another table. She must have known the people sitting there as they all started chatting and laughing. Isaiah suddenly shot up and shouted across at her to hurry up with their order, causing her to scurry off towards the kitchen area.

'Why are you so irritable Isaiah?' I said, looking at him in disbelief. 'You did manage to find alternative accommodation, didn't you?

He grunted, loosening his bow tie. 'Yes, yes. But it's a far cry from the peace and calmness of Rawlings.'

'Where are you staying?'

'That's really none of your business is it, dear daughter.' He replied sarcastically, glaring across at me, but then his face softened. 'Apologies, lack of sleep is making me grumpy.' With a heartfelt sigh he leant forward and spread his hands out onto the table. 'I'd like to think you've come to see me because you've missed me, however I suspect that's not the reason.'

Looking bashfully at him I averted my gaze to the window. It reminded me of the time I was sitting here with Mace, and Gideon had been waiting outside for me in the pouring rain, with a chilling warning that she was after me. All that seemed such a long time ago now, and yet somehow it had all come back to haunt me.

'I've seen Verity.' I said without emotion. 'She visited me a few weeks ago.'

He stared at me for a moment then roared with laughter, clapping his hands. 'Do you know, I'd almost forgotten about your older sister.' With a look of animation, he moved forward in his chair. 'How is that evil daughter of mine?'

'I don't know, we didn't have a conversation' I said with a sigh. 'Heaven only knows what she wants with me.'

'Mmm.' He said, tapping his finger against his lips. 'Perhaps she's just being nosey and wants to see you and Gideon enjoying your life together, or maybe she just wants to spook you. But I shouldn't be too concerned, even Verity wouldn't be capable of projecting herself for longer than a minute before disappearing, it takes deep concentration and a very strong will.' His tone changed as the waitress plonked a large three-tier cake stand, full of sandwiches and cakes on our table, and the tea and cups on the tray beside it. 'At last.' He uttered coldly, looking her up and down as she sullenly marched off. 'The service here has gone downhill dramatically.' He began to pour the tea, glancing at me. 'Well come on, eat up Effelia.'

'You were telling me about Verity.'

'What?' he muttered with a mouthful of sandwich. 'Ah yes Verity. If anyone can project themselves to another place and time, it's her. She has exactly the right mentality to manage such a thing.' He watched me as I buttered my scone. 'It's a shame she's so sadly lacking in other areas.'

'The strange thing is I have a feeling she's found a way to maintain her physical being in this world for much longer than a minute.' I took a quick sip of tea. 'I sensed she was in the conservatory at Rawlings for a while before leaving me the gift of an arrow.' My mind drifted back to the occasion she had tried to kill me in the kitchen, and had left an arrow dent in the fridge. 'I don't understand it.'

Isaiah was silent as he munched on his sandwich, helping himself to more. 'I don't either, he answered, wiping a crumb from his chin. 'But if I had my diaries I could more than likely provide you with an explanation.' He wiped his mouth with a serviette.

'From your diaries?'

A look of irritation crossed over his face and he leant forward and stared straight into my eyes. 'Yes, the one's dear old Constance took. They were more than day-to-day accounts of what was happening in my life. They also included my findings on a number of experiments I'd made over the years including various ways in which a person can transport themselves to another time and place.' Relaxing a little he leant back and grabbed a cake. 'If you can persuade your Aunt to give me back the diaries maybe I can help you.'

Gazing out of the window I drifted off into my own thoughts. 'No, I don't think that would be wise.'

'You've discovered Gideon's got a heart problem, haven't you?' He narrowed his eyes and smiled slyly at me. 'I've always suspected he's had it.'

76

I shot an angry look at him. 'You have?'

Someone greeted him from the other side of the café and he waved at them, cursing something underneath his breath. He then turned his attention back to me. 'It's a weakness he inherited from his mother.'

'You should have warned me before we returned to Rawlings.'

He held his hands out and shrugged his shoulders. 'Why? If you'd not brought him to this world he would have been permanently changed by the tonic and you certainly wouldn't be carrying his child. And you seem to forget your beloved Gideon must surely have been well aware of his condition before we travelled through the mirror and yet he failed to disclose it to you.'

I narrowed my eyes. 'What is this tonic you're talking about?'

'It's a vile substance that your beloved was addicted to. You see unlike you dear daughter I took the liberty of scribbling it all down whilst I was in hospital, so I wouldn't forget.' Looking smug he reached for a cake and crammed it into his mouth, his eyes directly on mine. 'Look at it this way, at least you will have a few blissful years together before Gideon dies of heart failure.'

I looked at him in alarm. 'Don't say that, don't you dare say that.' Dread swept over me and my face grew red with anger. 'You had this planned all along, didn't you Isaiah. That's the reason you were so keen for Gideon to travel with us.' I dug my nails into the palms of my hand, trying to control my temper.

'Oh, please Effelia. I really do want you to be happy. But Gideon has served his purpose now can't you see that? It was because of him that you returned to your true home, and I thank him for that.' With a smile he glanced at my stomach. 'And for providing me with my very first grandchild.' He took a gulp of tea. 'Enjoy the time you two have together then move on. There are several affluent men in Abercrombie, Effelia, I'm sure I could arrange...'

'Be quiet.' I snapped at him. 'I've forgotten how truly evil you can be.'

I watched as he took the last cake and placed it on my plate. 'Practical not evil.'

Suddenly I was tempted to pick up my fork and prod it into his eye. Only I didn't just want to hurt him I wanted to kill him.

'You look tense Effelia. Being stressed is bad for the baby.' He poured out my tea. 'Or so I've been told.' He cleared his throat. 'So, what is it to be, a boy or a girl?'

Ignoring his question, I peered into his face. 'How bad was Gideon's mother's heart?'

He paused for a moment and brushed the crumbs from his trousers, as if purposely making me wait. 'Are you sure you want to know Effelia?'

I nodded.

'Well I imagine the strain of travelling across worlds didn't help, but that wasn't what ended her life.' He lifted the cake stand onto the empty table next to us. 'It was the boy that finally done her in.'

My cup clanked loudly into the saucer as I lost my grip of the handle.

'Boy? What boy?'

He raised his eyebrows. 'Come on Effelia, surely you've not forgotten that impetuous friend of yours.'

'You mean Mace.'

'Yes, I most certainly do mean Mace.' He screwed his face up in disgust. 'A pathetic name for a pathetic boy.'

The waitress returned and Isaiah ordered her to clear the table and to bring the bill. As she sullenly started to walk away with the tray full of crockery, he clicked his fingers, telling her to remove the crumbs from the tablecloth. She glowered at him, but reluctantly obliged. I found myself adverting my gaze in embarrassment, and peered out the window until she had gone.

'You were saying about Mace.'

'Ah yes.' He yawned then stretched out in the chair. 'When your mother left Rawlings, just after you were born, I sought

Sabina out.' His face became grave. 'It didn't take long to find her.' With a sigh he glanced at his watch and frowned. 'She was in a pathetic state, tired and breathless, her complexion an unhealthy paler. And after she gave birth to that moron, she became so weak that she wasn't capable of taking care of him. I pleaded with her to put him up for adoption but she wouldn't agree to it. Every day I visited her, I fed and dressed her, I did everything I could for her.' He looked suddenly repulsed. 'I even helped her with the baby.' His eyes misted over. 'Until one day I found her.... stone cold dead.'

We both turned towards the waitress as she accidentally dropped a plate, which shattered to the floor in small pieces.

Isaiah frowned at her. 'That waitress appears to be clumsy as well as insolent.' He mumbled under his breath.

'So, what happened after you found Sabina's body?'

Stifling a yawn his eyes rested on mine. 'The boy was on the bed beside her, bawling his head off. I should have ended it there and then, when I had the chance, it would have been so easy, but instead I left him with a nurse at the local hospital, and told her he was an orphan.' He laughed hysterically. 'Imagine my horror when five years later he winds up in the same school as my daughter. For years now I had to endure his presence, watching him grow into a rude and obnoxious little brat.' A dark cloud fell over his face as he stared grimly down at the table. 'And knowing all the time he was responsible for killing my Sabina. Many times, I've tried to dispose of him, to make it look like a car or train accident, but he just wouldn't die.'

The waitress came over with the bill and laid it on the table, and without saying a word she marched off to serve another customer.

'You cannot blame Mace for her death, he didn't ask to be born.'

'But all the same I do blame him.' With an abrupt movement he rose from his seat, his chair screeching along the floor. 'As much as I'd like to continue this conversation, I'm afraid I have to go.' Looking irritable he glanced at the bill and sighed.

'Have you a meeting or something? I asked curiously.

'Not exactly, no.' He suddenly looked shifty. 'Let's just say I have to be somewhere to collect…. something.'

I searched his face. 'It all sounds very cryptic and mysterious.'

He raised his left eyebrow. 'Believe me it is not. I would much rather stay here with you.' Embracing me lightly he whispered in my ear. 'Would you mind paying the bill, I forgot to bring my wallet.' Avoiding my eye, he buttoned up his raincoat and casually waved to the ladies sitting over on the far side of the café before turning back to me. 'Take care of yourself Effelia. I shall be here the same time next week, do try and make it.' And with a raised voice, so that everyone could hear, he told me to look after that grandson of his.

My son Gabriel was born when the trees were at their most radiant, with the splendid colours of autumn. Everything had gone well with the birth and after a few days in hospital we brought him home to Rawlings. How strange it was having a baby in the house, strange in a delightful way. Suddenly this tiny being became the centre of our world, and everything else went by the wayside, turning our lives upside down. Gideon seemed deliriously happy and would spend every waking moment with his son. It was uncanny how alike they both were with their dark curly hair and deep brown eyes.

With a baby taking up all my time it was easier to push unwanted worries out my mind, and it was only when I couldn't sleep that they forced their way to the forefront. I would often dwell on what Isaiah had told me in Hudson's café, for since our meeting my concerns for Gideon's health had magnified; it took a while for me to realise, or rather convince myself that my father couldn't be certain about what would happen to Gideon, he was guessing; just because Sabina had died of heart failure didn't necessary mean her son would suffer the same fate. After all Dr Mason had already reassured us that Gideon would be perfectly fine as long as he didn't over exert himself and carried on taking the medication. Gabriel had been tested for any abnormality and thankfully his heart was extremely healthy.

As the months slipped by, I embraced my new life wholeheartedly. Young mothers, such as my old school friend Rosemary was suddenly keen for me to be part of her social circle. And so we began meeting up about twice a week in café's or parks and chatting for an hour or two about our babies sleeping patterns and eating habits, and how often they cried. Finally, I had found some common ground that I could comfortably discuss with ease, and I didn't care that our conversations were primarily centred on our children, for it gave me a warm fuzzy feeling to feel normal and accepted.

However, I soon came to realise a single incident can totally destroy it all. At the time of the occurrence, Rosemary, Eve and myself had been picnicking with the children under a large weeping willow in Montgomery Park.

'I think Gabriel wants to crawl over and join those boys playing football.' Remarked Rosemary. Laughing she turned her attentions back to her young daughter, who was sitting on the blanket beside her, pretending to feed her dolls a sandwich.

With a smile I glanced across the park. 'Yes, I think you're right.' I said with a casual laugh. I kissed the top of Gabriel's head as he tried to escape my arms. 'You'll a little young yet darling.'

He was very good at crawling now and at Rawlings I would allow him to move about freely, but there were too many people about in the park today, for even though it was late summer, the day was particularly hot and everyone seemed to flock to the park or beach to make the most of the weather, as if their life depended on it. I felt stifled with so many people about and wanted to go home to the calm, peacefulness of my garden. My Aunt and Gideon were probably having tea now, under the great oak.

'You wait until Gabriel starts to walk.' Exclaimed Eve. 'I had to put my oldest in reigns when he started, otherwise I'm sure I would have lost him somewhere.'

I smiled at her and watched as more people came and sat down in the park. I had never seen it more crowded, or noisy. A family of six had spaced themselves out directly in front of us and were unpacking a large hamper, chatting and laughing loudly to one another. For a minute I drifted off into a world of my own and as I gazed ahead everyone became blurry and indistinct.

Rosemary let out a loud laugh. 'That woman's a little strangely dressed.'

With a contented sigh I began bouncing Gabriel on my lap. 'What's that? I asked, only half listening.

Looking amused Rosemary pointed ahead to where a mass of people were sitting and laying about. 'I was just saying to Eve how odd that woman over there is dressed.' Her face dropped suddenly and she widened her eyes. 'Ah, I think the woman saw me pointing, she's staring straight as us, and she doesn't look too happy.'

'Don't stare at her Rosemary.' Said Eve in an urgent voice. 'There maybe something wrong with the woman.'

I began surveying the groups of people nearby, scrutinising each one carefully, and as my gaze turned left my eyes rested on a particular woman. A dread swept over me. For a moment our eyes locked and I saw a cruel smile creep slowly across her face. It was the mad woman.

'Rosemary, will you take care of Gabriel for just a minute. I have to go somewhere.'

Before she had a chance to answer I handed her Gabriel and darted across the park towards the mad woman as fast as I could. I knew my behaviour would seem odd to my friends, but I didn't care. They didn't have a mad half-sister following them about. Put in my position they too would act on their instinct and chase after her. For I had to know what the mad woman wanted, did she mean to harm me, or worst still did she intend to hurt my child. My eyes remained fixed upon her as I made my way through the throng of people, doing my best to dodge them. I heard someone moan at me as I spilt their pitcher of drink and another shouted angrily as I accidentally barged into them as I sped by. 'Sorry' I muttered, not even bothering to look at them. I was nearly there now, to where she was standing. Unable to stop myself I began to shriek. 'What do you want, what do you want with me?' I'm not sure how, but I stumbled, falling forward onto the grass, my arms splayed out in front of me. I heard peals of laughter from several people nearby and for a minute I wanted the ground to swallow me up. Suddenly I noticed someone hovering over me, and glancing up I saw it was a middle- aged man wearing a straw hat.

'Are you alright?' He said, smiling down at me. 'Please, allow me to help you up.'

With a weak smile I gave him my hand and he pulled me up.

'Thank you, sir.' I uttered, feeling embarrassed. I swiftly glanced over his shoulder, frantically looking for the mad woman in the crowd.

'Are you chasing someone?' He asked his expression rather perplexed.

I didn't reply straight away, as I was too busy searching everyone's faces, just in case she was hiding amongst them. People were looking at me strangely, raising their eyes and shaking their heads.

The man cleared his throat. 'Miss?'

When I finally spoke, my voice was subdued. 'Yes, but she's gone.' Impassively I stared straight ahead. 'That awful woman is trying to scare me, to make me go mad.' I sighed heavily and stared gloomily down at the grass.

'Perhaps you should contact the police.'

Looking up into his face my expression turned to amusement. 'They won't be able to help. She has a habit of vanishing you see, right before your very eyes.'

'I see.' Said the man, with a knowing look. He retrieved something from his pocket and handed it to me. 'If you need to talk, just give me a call.' His eyes were suddenly filled with compassion. 'It might do you the world of good to spend some time at our establishment.' Patting me lightly on the arm he turned on his heel and walked away.'

In bewilderment I stared down at the tiny piece of card in my hands. It had a contact number for a Dr Stirling, psychiatrist and in the top right-hand corner was his address.

THE MANOR
Sycamore Street
Abercrombie
Great Elms

I vaguely recall Isaiah mentioning he knew a Dr Stirling. Some years back when he was keeping me at his house after I supposedly had a breakdown, I remember being quite petrified when he told me he'd arranged with the doctor to have me sent to The Manor. As it turned out Isaiah was just trying to frighten me, but all the same it made me a bag of nerves. How strange that I should bump into this doctor, the doctor I didn't really believe existed until now, and how ironic that he should think me in need of a stay in his lovely mental institution. I wondered what the psychiatrist would make of Verity, if he should ever be unfortunate enough to meet her; would he be skilled enough to spot her psychosis, or would she cleverly deceive him into thinking she was sane.

With a shudder I threw the card into a nearby bin and swiftly made my way back to the willow tree, where Gabriel was bawling his eyes out on Rosemary's lap.

'I'm so sorry Rosemary.' I took a nervous gulp when I saw her bewildered face. 'I...I saw someone I knew. But she must have ran off.'

'Who?'

My.... my half-sister, Verity. She's a little deranged.' I watched her eyes grow wide with alarm. 'I don't think she meant us any harm.'

'Is this sister of yours dangerous?'

My eyes travelled over to where her daughter was playing with Eve's twins. They were all giggling as they pulled funny faces at one another. I realised there and then that I had no choice but to be honest. Even if the chances of it were remote, I couldn't take the risk of them becoming a victim of the mad woman.

I stared directly into her eyes. 'Yes, more than you can ever know.'

Rosemary glanced at Eve then gave me a slow nod. 'We have to be leaving now Effie.' Rather swiftly she handed me Gabriel and turned away.

I watched as they swiftly packed up their belongings in silence before grabbing the hands of their children.

'I.... I do hope we can still be friends.'

Rosemary eyed me with a look of cold indifference. 'I don't think so Effie.'

Without another word they all marched off, leaving me standing there with a crying Gabriel.

I watched as Gideon blew raspberries on Gabriel's stomach, and as he lifted him up in air he giggled relentlessly, his eyes gleaming with joy.

'We should put him down in a minute.' I uttered in a subdued tone. 'But first I need to feed him.' Without smiling I took Gabriel from him and went towards the door.

'Effie, is something wrong?'

I paused at the door. Perhaps I should have told Gideon what had happened in the park today but I held back. What good would it do; it would only cause him to worry needlessly. Whether it was necessary or not, since finding out about his condition, I felt he needed protecting.

'No, I'm just tired that's all.' I smiled. 'It's been a long day.'

After Gabriel fell asleep, I joined Gideon and my Aunt in the kitchen for hot chocolate, where we all sat and chatted. They told me about a discovery they'd made whilst in the garden that afternoon, a most peculiar finding according to Aunt. Whilst taking tea they'd noticed a carving in the bark of the great oak, the type of carving made by young sweethearts. It read "Verity and Gideon forever" With great amusement

Gideon told me how he believed someone had put it there as a practical joke, and how he was completely in the dark as to who the lady in question could be. Aghast I stared at the two of them as they laughed together, almost envious of them for being completely unaware of the chilling and disturbing nature of their find. Maybe I should have warned them of the danger we were in, but I wasn't sure how I'd even begin trying to explain it all. Perhaps I believed the burden of responsibility should be mine and mine alone; evil had seeped its way into Rawlings, evil in the name of the mad woman, and it was up to me to banish it.

That night in bed I laid there for some time, staring up at the ceiling and unable to rest. Gideon had been unusually tired and had dropped off almost immediately. It struck me odd that he had no recollection of the mad woman, even after seeing her name carved into the bark of the great oak. Perhaps he needed to see her in person to have his memory jogged; surely no one could forget a face like hers, for it was unique in the worst possible way.

Just as I was beginning to doze, I heard someone calling my name, someone close by. Suddenly my blood ran cold. With a jerk I opened my eyes and looked into the face of the mad woman. She was sitting beside the bed cradling Gabriel in her arms. I stared at her and swallowed hard.

'Let him go.' I whispered urgently. 'Please Verity put him back in his cot. I beg you.'

Paying no attention to my pleas she continued to sit there, gently rocking the sleeping Gabriel from side to side in her arms and watching me with her sadistic eyes.

I frantically shook Gideon, but he wouldn't stir.

'He won't wake Effelia I sneaked some sleeping tonic into the glass of water by his bedside.'

'Why...why are you here?'

She laughed mockingly at me. 'I wanted to see my tiny nephew again before I left.' With a snigger she lowered her head and kissed Gabriel's forehead then lowered him back into his cot. 'I've been visiting him for weeks, you know.'

'You have?'

'Oh yes, he's extremely used to seeing his Auntie Verity.'

I shuddered. 'Please get out of my house and never return.' I demanded in a raised voice.

With a cackle she turned and strolled towards the door, turning her head just a little.

'If that is what you truly wish for Effelia.'

'It is Verity.'

'Then I shall depart dear sister.' She hovered in the doorframe, smoothing down her gown. 'But first I have a surprise for you.' Extending her arm, she beckoned me to follow her.

I sat up rigidly in the bed. 'What surprise?'

'Come with me and I'll show you.'

'I don't trust you.'

'Of course, you don't. I wouldn't expect you to. It will only take a moment of your time.' She took a few steps back into the room and held out her hand. 'Come. Surely you must be intrigued.'

I gulped. 'And afterwards you promise never to return to Rawlings or Abercrombie?'

Her thin lips twisted into an unnatural smile. 'Hand on heart hope to die, if I ever tell a lie.'

With shaking hands, I pulled back the cover and put on my dressing gown, momentarily glancing at Gideon and Gabriel, who were still both sleeping peacefully. I crept barefoot out the room, following the mad woman down the staircase. On reaching the foot of the stairs she turned a sharp right as if she knew the house well, and proceeded into the study. Slowly and rather tentatively I entered the room. From the window I could see the light from the moon peeping through the trees, sending streaks of pale light upon the writing desk and wooden floor. I peered around looking for her.

'Verity?' I whispered. My heart lifted a little as it occurred to me she may have already left. Perhaps there wasn't a surprise, and she was merely toying with me just for fun. But why lead me to the study? Something didn't ring true about the way she seemed able to come and go so easily, and how she had the ability to make physical contact. I was missing something crucial.

A glimmer of light suddenly caught my eye in the corner of the room and I felt myself slowly wandering towards it. In the distance I could hear the muffled sound of Gabriel wailing, and I remembered thinking that I should go and see him. Stepping nearer I realised the strange glow was emanating from the mirror. For an instant I stood rigidly before the glass, realising a little too late that it was a trap. Before I had a chance to turn and run a pair of outstretched arms were clutching me tightly within their grasp, pulling me through the mirror.

Chapter 11

Shivering with fear and shock I huddled on a cold stone floor, gasping in agony from an acute pain that seemed to cover my entire body. I appeared to be in a room on my own and it was pitch black. A terrible dread came over me as I slowly began to comprehend that all this time the mad woman had been using the mirror as a means of travel. I cursed myself for being so slow in realising it, and because of my stupidity I had now been torn away from my family and home.

'Hello?' I called out on the off chance that there was someone nearby. 'Verity, Verity are you there?'

The room remained silent.

Slowly I began to crawl on my hands and knees across the stone floor, feeling my way as I went, until finally my fingers fell upon a door handle. But as I twisted the knob I realised it was locked. 'Please? I called out desperately, banging on the door. 'Can someone help me?'

There was no sound.

'Verity please don't leave me here.' My voice trailed off as I heard something above my head. The noise had a distinctive sound about it that was both familiar and sinister. My heart turned cold as I recognised the abnormal screech of the tree roots creeping across the ceiling.

I began to scream.

Against all odds I somehow drifted off to sleep for a while, and on awaking I began praying that what I'd just experienced had only been a nightmare. However, on opening my eyes I saw my prayers had not been answered. I was in a living nightmare that confirmed my worst fears; I was back at the monastery. But how did I arrive here when the other mirror was at Briarwood? What was going on? There was a slight possibility, I suppose that the mad woman had somehow managed to sneak me out of the village without anyone noticing; perhaps we had ridden on one of those great birds such as Croft. She must have drugged me though, for I didn't recall any of it. Only why had my sister come here when this wasn't her home, she didn't belong here; had she dropped me off then fled? The entire situation was completely unfathomable. One thing was certain; it was evident my memory of this world had returned, frighteningly quickly.

Hearing the key in the lock I struggled to my feet, and standing back I grabbed a tiny wooden stool in the corner, with the intention of bringing it crashing down on whatever evil individual came through the door. Such was my fury at being in this dreadful place that I would do anything to get away. No man or beast or unnatural being would hold me back this time. I was stronger and more resilient than my previous visit, and most importantly I was a mother who'd been unwillingly parted from her child. I realised now what my mother must have endured in the early days of our parting, the intense pain and suffering of not knowing when we would be reunited. I wondered if the pain lessened with each passing year, or was it just as intense and raw as in the beginning. I hoped to God I didn't have to find out.

As the bolt went back, I readied myself for attack. The hinges squeaked and the door flew open and Abel stood before me, grinning from ear to ear.

'Hello again Miss.' His voice trailed off as he saw me raising the stool up in the air, ready to strike out. 'Miss Effie, it's me Abel.'

I was almost disappointed. The thought of using the stool as a weapon was extremely appealing. With a drawn-out sigh I lowered the piece of furniture and placed it on the ground. 'Abel.' Despite my mood I couldn't help but smile. 'How are you?'

Blundering forward he hugged me awkwardly then stepped back with a friendly chuckle. 'I'm doing alright Miss. Especially now you've returned.' As he grinned again, I noticed one of his front teeth was chipped. 'Things will get better now.' He began to nod his head frantically, as if he was trying to convince himself.

'What's going on Abel, why am I here?'

'No one tells me nothing Miss.' His eyes became solemn and he lowered his gaze to the floor. 'I just got ordered to bring you to the hall.' For a moment he disappeared outside the door and on returning he carried a neat bundle of clothing. 'Your robes Miss.' As he passed them to me his eyes travelled over my attire. 'Best get changed quickly Miss. You'll stick out like a sore thumb dressed like that.' He laughed. 'I will wait outside the door. Give me a holler when you're ready.'

With a frown I changed into the robes, those oh so familiar clothes that resembled an old sack and made everyone appear that they were devout monks, dedicated to a life of prayer and solitude. I wondered why they even bothered to keep up the pretence of dressing in such a way when in truth the residents were merely poor misguided sheep following orders from Septimus. They existed only to serve him and to take their daily tonic, waiting for the day when they could be sacrificed to The Elders.

As we left the room, I gently took Abel's hand. 'You and I are friends are we not Abel.'

He nodded eagerly. 'Oh yes Miss. You be my very best friend.'

I smiled, peering down the dark corridor just in case we were being watched.

'Once I've been to the hall and seen what this is all about, I intend to leave as soon as possible.' My thoughts suddenly turned to Clarice, and I wondered if she was still about somewhere. Being back at the monastery was a poignant reminder of my friend. Her poor distraught mother was understandably very keen to have her back home; that much I remembered. 'I need your help finding my friend, and once we have found her all three of us must leave in secret.' I studied his face in eager anticipation. 'Will you help me Abel?'

'You bet Miss.' He replied, his face beaming. 'I won't chicken out like last time. Now that the masters gone, I don't get treated so good.' He let out a shallow laugh. 'Even Proctor weren't so bad.'

I looked confused. 'Where has Septimus gone?'

He looked around warily. 'We should get going Miss.'

I shuddered as we continued along the narrow foreboding corridors.

'So, Abel, when you said that Septimus has gone, did you mean he's left Hartland?'

'No Miss, he'd never do that.' He looked solemn. 'The monastery was his only home.' He stopped momentarily and peered into my face. 'Septimus be dead.'

'Oh.' I exclaimed, rather taken aback. 'Was it natural causes?' I asked, recalling how sick he claimed to be.

He scratched his head. 'I don't rightly know. He died in his sleep just after the wedding.'

'The wedding?'

Two burly looking men in robes were striding towards us and must have alarmed Abel, as he suddenly seemed extremely nervous and agitated.

'I be going now Miss.'

Looking subdued he lowered his head and proceeded cautiously towards the men, then as they grew closer he stepped aside so as not to get in their way. I noticed how much alike they were, almost as if they were twins. They both shared the same large frame and long limbs, and what hair they had left was lank and greasy, and fell forward in dark streaks upon their forehead, as if they had purposely arranged it that way. Totally disregarding Abel, they both stopped before me with a flicker of malice in their cold deep-set eyes.

'You must be Miss Farraday.' One of the men said as he passed his tongue over his lips. 'We've been asked to chivvy you along.' He threw Abel a sideways glance. 'If you want a job done, do it yourself. That's my philosophy.' His eyes bored into mine. 'I'm Wilding by the way and this is my brother Craddock.'

The other man nodded rather abruptly and I noticed a faint scar running from his left eye to the corner of his mouth. He stared at me rather peculiarly before suddenly taking my arm. 'Come on now, we need to get moving.'

I snatched my arm away. 'I'm perfectly capable of making my way to the hall by myself thank you.' Giving Abel a faint smile I began marching down the corridor ahead of them.

With steely determination I flung the doors open and stared in. The lay out was much the same, with rows of tables running the length of the room and a head table for the more important residents situated over on the far wall. Despite my apparent fearless attitude, I still found myself blushing profusely as everyone turned to stare at me. The room appeared to contain more residents than I'd ever remembered seeing before, and to my astonishment some of them began talking quietly amongst themselves and laughing, their eyes alive with animation. However, as I peered closer, I noticed several vacant faces in the crowd, the hauntingly familiar expression of those who had taken too much tonic. Perhaps in different circumstances I might have been intrigued to know what had happened, but my only interest was leaving.

I felt hands on my back, pushing me forward.

'Take a seat at the head table. The mistress will be along shortly.'

With a scowl I turned round and glared at the brothers. 'And who exactly is the mistress?'

One of them came closer, breathing over me with his foul breath. 'You'll see.'

I stepped backwards into the room.

Don't be afraid.' He said looking upon the crowd. 'They won't bite.' As he smiled, I noticed how yellow his teeth were. 'Their tame compared to our leader.'

In some kind of dream, I crossed the hall. My eyes wandered about the room searching for Clarice but I couldn't see her. Mechanically I went and sat at the head table and stared out upon the throng of people eating and drinking. Taking a sip from the goblet in front of me I was surprised to discover it was wine, at least that's what it tasted like. A sudden realisation that it may be the tonic should have stopped me from taking another sip, but in my present state I didn't care. I observed Wilding and Craddock guarding the door, carefully watching the residents; ever so often they turned and stared at me, as if checking I hadn't run off. Taking a large gulp of wine my eyes were drawn to the small group of people who had just entered. At first, I couldn't see them clearly as they appeared to be flanked by guards, but as they came into clear view my heart sank then skipped a beat. I wasn't surprised to see the mad woman, but as I glanced at her companion my goblet dropped from my hand. It was Noble.

The mad woman looked down in disdain at the table. 'Oh Effelia, how clumsy you are.' She gestured to Abel who had just entered the hall, snapping her fingers impatiently. 'Clean this up immediately.' The loudness of her voice echoed around the room, causing some of the residents to look our way. She glared back at them. 'Continue with your supper please everyone.'

I watched as Abel hurriedly scurried off towards the door. I'm sure I had never seen him move so fast. He was afraid of the mad woman that's for sure, and for that I couldn't blame him. With her acid tongue and scornful expression, she seemed to relish picking on people, especially the weak and vulnerable. Some may deem her outward appearance to appear relatively normal, but her eyes always betrayed her, they were so cold and malevolent that even a blind man would feel their viciousness and sense she was the devil in disguise.

I stared into Noble's face. With a look of astonishment, he held my gaze for a moment before sitting beside me.

'What are you doing here Effie?'

Before I had a chance to reply the mad woman's voice could be heard in my ear, loud and shrill. 'Effelia is our honoured guest.' She sat the other side to me, so I was wedged in between them both. 'I invited her to stay for a while.'

'Invited?' I retorted angrily. 'Is that what you call it?'

She reached forward and grasped my hand. 'Very well then I admit it, I deliberately took you away from your beloved

Gideon and child.' Her eyes flitted to Noble before turning back to face me. 'But I missed you so- you are my dearest and only sister.'

I wrenched my hand away from hers. 'You'd no right to bring me here without my permission, and you maybe my half-sister but there's certainly no love lost between us.' Trying to keep my voice steady I rose abruptly from the chair, knocking it over. 'I demand you return me home immediately.'

She erupted into a fit of giggles. 'Demand eh.'

Noble narrowed his eyes at her. 'Verity, what are you playing at?'

Before she could answer I butted in. 'Noble, this awful woman should be locked away in a dungeon somewhere and forgotten about. She's evil, pure evil.'

There was utter silence throughout the hall.

As she glowered at me the mad woman's face grew red with anger. I stood there with my arms folded waiting for her to explode with fury, but to my surprise she held back. Suddenly I understood the reason for her composure, it was Noble. I moved back a little as I saw her reach forward and cup his cheek with her hand, gazing adoringly into his face.

'Noble my love, Effelia may not realise or admit it but she requires a short holiday. For months now I've been watching her from afar, observing her struggling to cope with the demands of a new-born baby.' She glanced up at me. 'Look how pale she is, so worn from the endless sleepless nights.' Her eyes darted back to Noble. 'Forgive me for my selfishness, but I only had my sister's best interests at heart.'

I closed my eyes and rubbed my temple, trying desperately to put the apparent affection they shared to the back of my mind. Without realising I began stumbling back against the wall.

'See Noble, how Effelia is struggling, the poor woman can barely stand.'

I opened my eyes and scoffed. 'I was perfectly fine before you brought me to the monastery.' My breath caught in my throat as Noble reached for my waist and gently guided me forward, gesturing for me to sit back down. 'You believe me, don't you Noble?'

'I can see that you are tired.' His eyes looked deeply into mine. 'At least sit down for a while and eat some supper. Afterwards you can have a good night's rest.' He paused. 'And then return home.'

Temporarily thrown by the richness and warmth of his voice, I stood there gazing at him. I'd forgotten how appealing he was, and how he transfixed you with his eyes. But he was with the mad woman now, which made him the enemy.

I turned away from him and stoically stared ahead.

'Effie, please.' He implored.

Abel had returned and with his head bent began mopping up the spilt wine. I tried to catch his eye but he failed to look at me.

'Don't forget the floor as well.' Snapped the mad woman.

He nodded his head frantically. 'Yes mistress.'

With a drawn-out sigh I sat back down and glanced at Noble, who was carefully watching me. 'Very well, I shall remain here tonight but wish to go at first light.' Reluctantly I turned to the mad woman. 'Do I have your assurance that I can return home tomorrow?'

The mad woman narrowed her eyes. 'Is that what you truly desire?'

I nodded, pouring myself some more wine. 'Yes. Most definitely.'

She bowed her head in acknowledgement, but didn't reply.'

Taking a gulp of the drink I saw two of the residents laying out food on our table. Compared with previously there seemed an abundance of it, with large serving platters of rich succulent looking meat, potatoes, vegetables and bowls of crusty bread on every table. There were puddings too, steamed sponges and custard.

The mad woman watched me closely. 'Well do tuck in Effelia. There's plenty enough food to go around. Septimus was always a little frugal when he was alive.' Her eyes gazed ahead as if her thoughts were elsewhere. 'But we no longer have the need to tighten our belts now that I am in command.'

'How did you come to be in charge of the monastery Verity?'

She paused as she contemplated my question. 'Through my love for a wise man.' With a flick of her hair she gazed adoringly at Noble, and he in turn stared back at her. With a flippant laugh she turned her attentions to me, glimpsing down at my plate. 'Is the food to your liking Effelia?'

'Yes, thank you.' I replied bluntly.

She began caressing Noble's hand 'You especially like the venison don't you my love.'

Without speaking he gave a solemn nod and carried on eating. I noticed how he discreetly moved his hand away from hers.

'You mean to say we're eating the Hartland deer?'

'Yes Effelia, did you not realise?' Many of the Hart deer were roaming too near to the grounds and were becoming a nuisance, so it seemed a logical solution to use them as a food source. Septimus was initially reluctant as he always said that they were sacred to Hartland. But I persuaded him otherwise.' I could feel her eyes boring into me. 'The deer are also easy prey for The Elder trees, but unlike some of the residents they are not so eager to die.'

Pushing the remainder of the meat to the side of the plate with my fork I shakily placed my hands on the table. It was my first reminder of the trees. Their memory had been deep rooted within my mind and yet I'd not allowed them in until now. A vision of The Givers face Cuthbert suddenly came to me-how proud and strong he'd been, how willing to sacrifice his life for the greater good of the trees; how greedily and swiftly the branches had seized him, eager to return his body to their lair where they would devour him. I had often hoped and prayed that death came swift for all of those poor wretches that sacrificed themselves, for to suffer a slow painful death would be an unimaginable horror and no amount of tonic could distinguish their fear in the end.

Hearing a child's laugh I looked across at one of the tables. The boy in question was laughing with another older child, his sibling perhaps. They seemed normal and happy.

I sudden shiver went through me.

'So, the sacrifices are still being held?'

The mad woman seemed taken aback. 'No absolutely not, I abolished that inhumane ritual as soon as Septimus had passed. I could not allow innocent people to be slaughtered in such a barbaric fashion.' She laughed rather nervously. 'As Noble will tell you I treat the residents like one big family. Some do try my patience on occasions but they are reprimanded with the appropriate punishment. The Giver ceremonies and tonics are a thing of the past.'

Staring into her dark eyes I couldn't quite comprehend what I was hearing.

'So, what do The Elder trees feed on, apart from the odd deer?'

'Effelia they are trees, and trees do not require food to survive.' With a mocking stare she held my gaze for a moment before turning her attentions to Noble. Slowly she began running her fingers through his hair, and then laughing she leant over and whispered something into his ear.

My stomach began to churn.

She kissed him on the cheek. 'How well everything has fallen into place for us both, you have Gideon and I have won the heart of Noble.' Her eyes held mine. 'I am pleased for you dear sister and you must be pleased for me.'

With an impulsive movement Noble jumped up from his seat. 'I have some reading to do in the library.' His voice was low, hardly above a whisper. 'I bid you both goodnight.'

Without glancing at either of us he began to stride across the hall, almost colliding with a resident who was heading our way in rather a rush. The man in question approached the head table slightly out of breath. He had a rather portly frame and a round pleasant face that beamed at the mad woman a little ingratiatingly

The mad woman's face clouded over in a sudden fury. 'What is it now Hector?' She hissed at him.

'I beg your pardon your Excellency but someone has yet again been stealing from the kitchens.' He dusted some flour from the apron covering his robes. 'Several cakes have gone missing.'

The mad woman rose from her chair and leant forward over the table, with her hands splayed out in front of her. 'I've told you time and time again Hector to address me as mistress.' She spoke through gritted teeth. 'And as for the cakes, are you sure you've not scoffed them yourself; you look even podgier than ever.'

A high- pitched giggle erupted from his mouth, causing his whole body to shake. It was a sound that I imagine the mad woman would find extremely irritating.'

'No, no your Ex.... I mean mistress Verity. It's one of those pesky children, I'm sure of it. Could you not have a word with them?'

The mad woman lost her temper. 'Go away Hector and stop bothering me with such trivial matters.' She bellowed at him, completely losing her composure of earlier. 'If you continue to be so bothersome I shall....' She glanced around the room and realised that everyone was staring at her. 'I shall be forced to put you on a diet.' A strange, forced laugh came from her mouth. 'Now away with you.'

He giggled again and with a look of recognition he stared at me, his eyes wide.

'Hello Miss Farraday, how are you keeping?'

'I'm sorry –Hector? But do we know one another?'

I heard the mad woman groan softly under her breath. 'Hector comes from Briarwood Effelia, along with some of the other residents.' She ushered him away with her hand, and with a bow he shuffled off.

'You made some of the villagers of Briarwood come here?'

'No, most came at their own free will. Others needed some coaxing.' She smiled at me, placing her hands upon my shoulders. 'You see little sister we needed to make the numbers up, and what better way than to bring willing volunteers from other lands.' A cruel twisted smile spread across her face. 'I even collected some people from Abercrombie.' She was whispering now, her mouth close to my ear. 'You didn't really believe I kept crossing over to your world just for you, did you Effelia? Rawlings is such a large house; it was so easy to smuggle people into the study without being detected and take them with me through the mirror. That old Aunt of yours spotted us one day and we nearly scared her half to death. Still, who's going to believe a dotty old lady eh?'

'How…how did you persuade them to come here?'

'When I told them what was going to happen many jumped at the chance. It has given them the opportunity to make a new life, away from their mundane little lives. All they had to do was step from mirror to mirror.'

'Has the mirror at Briarwood been moved to the monastery?' I asked. 'Is that how I arrived so swiftly?'

She ran her finger down the side of my face. 'No Effelia, I have another mirror you see, hidden away in the monastery. I stumbled across it one day, along with other ancient relics that have laid undiscovered for many years, relics that I'm sure you'd be very interested to see.' Her fingers rested on the side of my chin and she dug her nails into my flesh. 'Without the mirror I wouldn't have been able to reach you and bring you to the monastery. And now that you're here I'd like to say thank you Effelia for making my plan a reality.'

I grasped her hand and pulled it away from my face. 'Surely you didn't drag me to hell Verity merely to say thank you.' My face looked exasperated. 'What on earth have I done to deserve your gratitude?'

She smiled, her eyes widening in amusement. 'Can you not guess dear sister?'

I stared at her open-mouthed, shaking my head in confusion. 'Whatever little plan you've hatched has nothing to do with me, and I certainly wouldn't have helped you make it possible. What was your plan exactly- to repopulate Hartland?' My heart began to ache. 'To capture the heart of Noble?'

'Oh Effelia, Effelia. That was only the start- the main aim of my plan has not yet come to fruition.'

'And what is your main aim?'

Her eyes looked strange, almost compassionate. 'All will be revealed soon enough dear sister. You won't have long to wait.'

I moved away slightly. 'You're not going to allow me home tomorrow are you Verity?'

'No Effelia, but you may leave soon, with my blessing.' She laughed. 'In the meantime, please treat the monastery as your home.' Reaching forward she planted a kiss on my cheek. 'I'm off to seek out Noble in the library. Abel or one of the other guards will escort you to your new quarters. I don't expect you to spend another night in the resident's accommodation.' As she made her way around the side of the table she turned and whispered. 'Oh, and Effelia. Just in case the trees do finally decide to make a meal of you, don't go roaming the grounds or tunnels. It's imperative to me that you stay alive.'

I watched as she turned on her heel and glided away, her dress rustling along the floor. Being who she was I suspected she felt too important to wear robes like the common folk. Even Noble, it seemed, wasn't exempt from having to wear the sack like material. Although his behaviour seemed rather ambiguous that wasn't what concerned me, it was his mere presence here at the monastery that was severely unnerving me, and the growing possibility that he may be wed to my vile sister. Abel had mentioned a wedding, one that had occurred just before Septimus passed away and it seemed logical that it was theirs. Such a thought was totally abhorrent, and yet in some warped way it made total sense.

The hall had emptied out now and a couple of the residents were clearing the tables. For a while I sat there twiddling my thumbs, hoping that Abel would suddenly appear, but to my dismay one of the brothers I'd been introduced to earlier begun marching towards me.

'Mistress Verity has asked me to direct you to your room.' His eyes briefly ran over my face and hair. 'You two don't look much alike for sisters.' He extended his hand and ushered me across the hall. 'Your colouring is totally different.'

'Yes, well we have different mothers.' I said coldly, walking a little ahead of him. 'We also have opposite personalities.'

When we'd emerged from the hall he stopped and folded his arms.

'Really?' He peered around to check no one was eavesdropping. 'Are you saying that Verity is cold and unpleasant and you're warm and friendly?'

Unable to stop myself I smiled at him. 'Something like that yes.' As he held my stare, I felt myself desperately wishing to distance myself from him. 'If you'd please show me to my room.'

To my relief he began plodding his way along the dimly lit passageway.

'Me and my brother Wilding are alike in every way, but then we share the same parents.' He headed in the opposite direction to the library. 'Before my folks perished they were farmers, and we all lived out in the wilds just beyond Hartland.' For a second, he stopped and glanced at me before turning a corner and proceeding down a narrow corridor. 'We were so well hidden that no one knew we ever existed.'

'What made you and your brother travel to Hartland?'

He came to a halt at the end of the corridor, just before a large door. 'In the end we had no choice but to leave. When our parents died the farm had already gone to rack and ruin, we might have lasted a while longer but lands around these parts are always so cold and barren, and the food was running out, so my brother and I thought we'd try our luck at Hartland.' He turned the handle and flung the door open. 'Here we are Miss, your rooms. They've all been cleaned and there's fresh linen on the bed. In the two rooms opposite you'll find a bathroom and a small room that can be used for dining in if you don't want to join the other resident's in the hall.'

I stepped into the vast bedroom, it was so large and airy compared with my previous room, and was fully furnished. My eyes took in the oval window on the far fall, which I could clearly see would be far too small to crawl out. I crossed over and stared out into the night, hoping to see the moon, but all I saw was blackness.

'What's the view like in the daytime?'

'Icy fields and trees beyond.' He said, hovering within the doorway. 'If you've got good eyesight you can see the moving branches. Creepy they are and dangerous.' He glanced over towards the bed. 'I should let you get some rest. Unless you require anything else Miss.'

'No, no thank you Craddock, it is Craddock isn't it?'

'Yes Miss, I'm the one with the scar running down my face.'

'How did you come by it?'

'When I was a young boy, I came across a stranger when I was out hunting with my brother. We attacked and robbed him, and left him for dead. But as I went to swipe his valuables he lashed out with his dagger and sliced my face.' His expression became aggressive. 'I made sure he was a goner after that.' With a short laugh he looked me in the eye. 'No one lays a hand on Craddock and gets away with it.'

Trying not to show any emotion I simply nodded at him slowly. 'Well goodnight Craddock.'

Relief flooded over me as he left and closed the door. Finding out Craddock and Wilding were cold bloodied killers perhaps shouldn't have shocked me, but it did. They had the look of thugs about them, and unfortunately that's exactly what they were. How well suited the brothers were to serve the mad woman. I imagined the other guards were exactly the same. Not Abel though, he was different, he wouldn't hurt a fly. It still puzzled me how he had changed from the horrid little boy who would pinch me and pull my hair when we were children. I suppose circumstances had changed him, as they could with anyone, even me.

Chapter 12

Gazing at the inviting bed in the middle of the room I wanted nothing more than to sink down into it and forget my troubles; weary from the effects of the travelling, my entire body ached, including my heart, and only sleep would ease my pain. But I couldn't. This wasn't a hotel on holiday at some pleasant seaside town with views of the coastline, where you were relaxed and happy. This was a place of death, where monstrous trees took people away, and where vengeful spirits skulked around in the shadows, waiting to pounce. Only they were nothing compared to the mad woman- she was the most petrifying of them all by far. Whatever scheme she was cooking up was undoubtedly an evil one, and I wasn't prepared to hang about to witness it. I was fleeing this dreadful place and I was going tonight.

As I stood there plotting my escape, I thought of how my sister had already warned me of entering the grounds and tunnels. I remembered from first-hand experience how treacherous those underground passages could be. That fateful night when Mundy had been taken, the look of horror on his face as he clung to me, just before being dragged away to his death. It had been my turn then, only with the aid of the knife I'd somehow managed to successfully dislodge the mass of roots firmly coiled around my boots and ankles, allowing Gideon the opportunity to free me. It was a horrifying thought having to go back there again, but to my knowledge it was the only means of escape, unless of course I could locate the mirror.

With a shudder I turned my mind to home, which was rapidly becoming a faded memory. Would Gideon realise where I had disappeared to, and even if he did would he be able to activate the mirror? I visualised little Gabriel sobbing his heart out in his cot, desperate for his mother to cradle him in her arms, and a sense of complete hopelessness came about me, knowing I couldn't be there for him.

For a while I sunk dejectedly onto the bed, my head bent forward in utter misery.

I wondered what Mace and Caleb would make of the villagers that had left their snug little life in Briarwood and set out for Hartland. Surely it would seem odd to the two of them, but was it odd enough for them to take matters into their hands and investigate? Mace I sensed was petrified of the monastery, although he'd never admit it, and wouldn't even risk returning to rescue Clarice, poor Clarice who I hadn't yet seen. Her absence made me extremely concerned and fearful. It seemed there had been many changes in the monastery, including the presence of Noble: seeing him again had stirred up old feelings, however I had to accept he was with her now, for it seemed they were man and wife, and as far as I could tell he was totally under her influence. He was lost to me.

With a weary sigh I poked my head into the other two rooms. The bathroom had a cast iron bath and a small sink with a mirror above it. As I glanced at my reflection, I was rather shocked at my appearance: despite my hair being tied back into a ponytail, it was obvious it hadn't been brushed in a few days, and my complexion was an unhealthy pallor and accentuated my large tired looking eyes, that seemed to stare back at me in a perpetual state of alarm. With a harrowing sigh I looked into the other room and noticed a tiny table that had a length of rope upon it, and two chairs. Staring up at the hook attached to the centre of the ceiling I pondered if it was intentionally put there to enable someone to hang themselves; all they had to do was take the rope and place it through the hook, then once they'd made a noose it was all ready for the unwilling victim, or willing victim. Maybe it was meant for me. Shivering I returned to the main room and began to wander around restlessly, contemplating my next move. I ran my finger over the neat row of prayer and psalm books on the shelf, wondering to whom they belonged to-some one of religious faith it seemed, probably long gone. In the middle was a large brown vase with a set of rosary beads draping over the side. For some reason it made me feel sad. As I turned away one of the books fell to the floor with a dull thud. Curiously I picked it up, flicking through the delicate looking pages of old hymns, not recognising any of the sacred songs. I carefully placed the book back on the shelf and shut my eyes for a moment, trying to convince myself that there wasn't a ghost lurking in my room, and that the book dropped to the floor purely by accident. Then I remembered Lucinda; the poor girl who it seemed was stuck in the monastery for all of eternity, never finding the peace that she so rightly deserved. She would be in the library, I was sure of it, and Lucinda could travel anywhere in the monastery without being seen, even to the room that housed the mirror.

As I tried the door, I didn't really consider what I was doing, I didn't really care, desperate people take desperate measures, and I was more desperate than most. Glad to find it unlocked I gradually opened the door and peeked outside into the blackness. It was impossible to see if there were any guards stationed outside, but I suspected not, otherwise Craddock would've merely locked me in my quarters. There wasn't any need to keep an eye on me; only an insane person would go wandering about a ghostly monastery in the dead of night, either that or a desperate one. An icy blast blew across my face but choosing to ignore it I grabbed one of the lanterns from my room and ventured outside. I crept along the end of the corridor then took the passageway in the direction of the library. Although it was late, I was conscious of bumping into someone, especially Craddock or Wilding. They were bad, without a shadow of a doubt. My thoughts turned to Proctor or rather 'The Gorgon' as Mace had so aptly named her. I recall her malicious looking eyes peering at me with utter contempt, especially after throwing me in the cells with Isaiah. She too had vanished, only unlike Clarice it didn't matter what had become of her.

As I approached the library something suddenly attacked me from behind, clamping a hand tightly across my mouth and dragging me along the passageway and into the library. Somehow, I'd managed to cling onto my lantern and for a moment was tempted to smash it into my assailant's face, but as the doors closed behind us, I felt the hand slacken a little over my mouth, giving me the opportunity to bite down hard on one of the fingers. There was a cry and then I was released.

'What was that for Effie?'

It was Noble. His face looked agonised as he held his injured finger, which was dripping blood on the floor.

'I'm…I'm sorry. I thought you were one of the guards.'

I watched as he retrieved a cloth from the pockets of his robe and wrapped it around his finger, his thick hair falling down over his eyes. For one brief moment I couldn't think what to say.

'If I were a guard you'd be in big trouble.' He mumbled under his breath. 'When I crept up on you in the corridor my main priority was keeping you silent.' With his finger secured in the cloth he looked angrily into my face. 'The slightest noise would have alerted them.'

As we stood staring at one another in the soft glow of the lantern I saw how disgruntled he seemed, his large eyes staring broodingly into mine.

'Why are you here Noble, rather than with your wife?'

His expression lightened and he began to shake his head, laughing softly.

'Effie, what are you talking about? I haven't got a wife.'

I stumbled backwards, leaning up against the large desk in the centre of the room. Clasping the edges with my hands I glared at him. 'Verity, you're married to Verity.'

'No.' He replied in a firm voice. 'I am not married to Verity or anyone else for that matter.' Looking perplexed he moved closer to the desk, hovering over me. 'Whatever gave you that idea?'

A surge of heat enveloped my body. 'Then who…who was Abel talking about.' I lowered my head, as if talking to myself, and then with a nervous gulp I stared back into his face. 'Someone was married, here at the monastery, just before Septimus died.'

Realisation flooded his face. 'Ah yes. You must mean *their* marriage.'

'What.... whose?'

Before he had a chance to answer we heard the distance sound of voices from outside the door. Firmly taking my arm, Noble led me over to the far right so that we were half hidden by a stone column.

'We should be careful not to be seen. Guards prowl the monastery late at night, just in case anyone decides to take a wander.'

I flinched slightly as his arm brushed against mine. 'And what happens if they catch someone, are they scolded and sent back to their rooms?'

Extinguishing the lantern, he looked into my eyes. 'If only that were true, there's many rumours flying about this place Effie, but anyone that's captured by the guards at night are never seen again. Verity makes a point of telling the residents that roaming the monastery at night is strictly forbidden. It's one of her many rules that must be obeyed or there will be consequences.'

'Which are?'

There was noise at the door and Noble pushed me back a little so we were right up against a wall behind the stone column.

'Guards.' He whispered, shielding my body with his. 'Don't say a word Effie.'

The sound of voices became louder and the library door crashed shut.

'Hurry up Wilding, there's no one in here. Let's go down to the kitchens and swipe a cake.'

There were plodding footsteps. 'I'm sure I heard something. 'If I catch the little devil it'll be extra helpings for The Elder Trees tonight.'

'You shouldn't speak about it out loud brother. You know Verity doesn't want anyone finding out the truth.'

'Oh, to hell with her Craddock. If anyone's stupid enough to be roaming about the monastery at night then we'll find them and toss them to the beasts.

I felt the tips of Noble's fingers in my hair, his breath close to mine, and when I met his gaze in the darkness his eyes looked suddenly hollow and weary. He had known all along what happens here. Nothing had changed or improved, in fact with the mad woman running the monastery matters could only get worse.

'What a shame eh? I was looking forward to seeing the look on a resident's face just as they realise they're going be tree food. I'm tempted to go and get the simpleton just for the fun of it. What do you say brother?'

'I've got a better idea Wilding. Let's go and visit that nice Miss Farraday.'

They sniggered. 'Leave off Craddock. Are you soft on her or something?'

'No, she's not really my type, too skinny. Maybe if she put a bit of meat on her bones I could take a fancy to her. I'll go and bring her a cake or two from the kitchens, I'm sure she'd invite me in.'

As we heard laughing I felt Noble clenching his fists, and impulsively I placed my hands around his shoulders and held him firm, frightened he would do something stupid.

'Verity will be on your back if you go anywhere near her. Best stay clear of trouble brother. Our time will come.'

I heard a grunt.

'Come on Wilding let's go.

As the door crashed shut I felt Noble's body relax against mine. And for a while we remained cradling one another for comfort, breathing in one another's scent. Maybe I should have drawn back sooner, but I couldn't. At that moment we were like two desperate souls clinging to a sinking ship, knowing in our hearts that we were about to fall into the deep dark depths of the ocean.

Unexpectedly a book dropped from one of the bookcases, jolting me back to earth and I reluctantly removed my arms from around his shoulders and looked up into his face.

'How did we reach this point Noble? What is to become of us?'

I could see tears slowly forming in his eyes. 'I don't know Effie. You must realise that Verity isn't going to let you go home willingly.'

'Yes, I know. That's why I need to locate the mirror. Do you know where it is?'

He shook his head. 'Verity has told no one. We must find it so you can escape Hartland, before it's too late.'

I shook my head in confusion. 'Too late for what Noble?

His face looked agonised and lost. 'Everything.'

'What's happened Noble, why are you involved with Verity?' I bit down hard upon my lip. 'She seemed very loving towards you at supper this evening.'

'Verity believes I return her love but I do not. Unbeknown to her I'm completely aware of her vile nature and grave intentions.' He moved away a little. 'Oh, I was taken in at first by her charm. She can be very entrancing and persuasive when she wishes to be. And when I first arrived at Hartland she did her utmost to hide the truth from me. But as time progressed her real character emerged, and little by little I began to put the pieces of the puzzle together. When I saw you in the great hall today, I had to pretend to be surprised to see you. I deliberately acted cold towards you so Verity would not be vexed. If she'd seen one hint of affection or warmth between us she will make your life a misery.' As he gazed into my face his eyes grew darker. 'I don't care what happens to me, but you.' He paused. 'You've got a family who need you.' His hand cupped my cheek. 'And unless you leave the monastery soon, you'll never see them again.'

'What...what do you mean Noble?'

His eyes clouded over. 'They'll be nothing left Effie, no lands, no people, even entire worlds will vanish. Verity plans on destroying it all, and if she succeeds the only kingdom left standing will be Hartland.'

I slid down the wall and sunk to the floor. 'Verity has the ledger; she was the one who stole it from Briarwood church. That's the only way she could even consider her plan.' Beginning to laugh I glanced up at Noble. 'You don't truly believe in that absurd theory, do you? My eyes grew wide with bewilderment. 'I remember Septimus speaking about it with such enthusiasm, what a shame he can't be present to witness its spectacular failure.'

'You're entitled to your opinions Effie, and I respect them. But you should try and see it from my perspective. You and I come from different worlds, and in my world folk tend to take such happenings seriously.' I watched as he gazed down upon me. 'I'll help you locate the mirror tomorrow but for now I suggest you return to your room, it's the safest place.' He hesitated and lowered his eyes. 'Just promise me you'll lock the door.'

A wave of sickness suddenly enveloped me as I pictured Craddock barging his way in with a tray full of cakes, grinning at me with his stained teeth. With a renewed sense of determination I rose up from the floor.

'No, I promised myself I would leave tonight. We cannot pin our hopes on finding the mirror tomorrow, or any other day. So, I shall leave through the tunnels.' With a frown I glanced around at the bookcases, searching for where Lucinda had shown me the lever that would reveal the location of the concealed passage.

He reached forward and grabbed my arm. 'Effie, the tunnels are no longer safe. By each passing day the trees become greedier. They have already begun extending their branches up the steps of the secret passageway and before long they'll break through the heavy door and enter this library.'

'That's a chance I'll take Noble.'

He began to laugh. 'I'd forgotten how stubborn you can be.'

My eyes darted instinctively to his. 'Stubborn and desperate.' I retorted without smiling.

I saw the anxiety deepen within his eyes. 'Effie, you're not thinking straight. At least stay a day or two longer. Verity won't be acting on her plan until she's gathered more followers. If we find the mirror your return journey will be swift and safe. Surely that's better than perishing in the tunnels.'

'And what if we can't locate the mirror Noble?'

'Then I'll think of something else. There's always an answer to a problem, if you search hard enough Effie.'

I furrowed my brow, trying to recall who had said something similar to me, but I just couldn't remember.

'Effie, are you alright?'

'Yes, yes as well as can be expected under the circumstances.'

'So, have you seen sense? He grinned at me. 'If you don't return to your room I'll sling you over my shoulder and carry you back.'

I smiled. 'I'd like to see you try.' My face grew solemn. 'Please Noble don't stay here, not with her. Your worth more than that.' My hand nearly reached out for his, but I held back. 'Come back with me.' I began stumbling over my words. 'I...I mean...go back to Briarwood, and be happy.'

For a second, he didn't speak, but stood there studying my face closely. Then his face broke into a smile. 'It's all right Effie. I don't need saving.' His finger lightly flicked my cheek. 'Someone has to stay here and keep an eye on your sister.'

There was a sudden commotion outside the door. Noble grabbed my hand and we darted behind the desk. Hearing a muffled cry I poked my head around the side of the desk and saw the shadowy figures of Craddock and Wilding dragging someone along the floor, a man, I think.

Craddock spoke in an amused tone. 'Don't worry mate. It'll all be over in a matter of minutes. The roots will probably strangle you before digestion takes place, that's a slow old process.'

I saw one of them removing some books and plunging his hand into the gap, and as he did so another section of the bookcase sprung open. I could see by their swiftness that they had done this many times before and I shuddered to think how many residents had perished in this manner. As they carried the poor man into the opening between the books he began kicking and screaming. All three of them disappeared from sight and the library became silent.

Without warning Noble pulled me up, and with no time to lose we fled swiftly through the library doors.

112

A sudden piercing scream made me shudder.

Noble glanced at me and swallowed. 'They must have been lying in wait for their victim on the steps. I told you it was a bad idea escaping through the tunnels.'

Chapter 13

I'd intended to lay awake the remainder of the night and attempt to make sense of what was happening, to try and find some clarity. However, my desire for sleep became unendurable and I found myself drifting off almost instantaneously.

As the natural light flooded into the room I came too and mechanically rose from the bed and padded over the cold stone floor in my bare feet and peered out of the window. Thick grey mists drifted across the fields in a ghostly shroud that floated low over the icy ground, and I could hear the faint sound of wind whistling mournfully across the landscape as if in perpetual torment. I imagined monks of another age slowly emerging from the vapour, wailing sorrowfully over what had befallen their sacred homeland. Although I couldn't see them, I knew The Elder trees were beyond the fields, watching and waiting.

I freshened up in the bathroom as best I could and went and sat on the bed, my hands neatly folded in my lap. Just for a short while I felt the need to compose myself before heading out to the grim misery that awaited me. Glancing over to the far wall I noticed a single pitiful frame containing a scroll with faded handwriting; I crossed over to examine it closer but realised it was unreadable. Looking at it reminded me of the ledger, and my heart sank. Why oh why did I not destroy that cursed book when I had the chance, for now it lay in the deadly hands of the mad woman. There had always been a sinister strangeness about the ledger that had almost caused me to burn it, but for some reason I couldn't. Of course, I wasn't certain it was in my sister's hands but I suspected that's why she'd thanked me yesterday- I'd made her preposterous plan possible. But regardless of the so-called plan, my decision to safeguard the ledger had caused terrible repercussions for me and my family, it had torn us apart without warning, and now I was in this world and they were in theirs, and it was all my fault.

In a surge of wretchedness, I threw myself down onto the bed and buried my face in the pillow, crying tears of frustration. Through my sobbing I barely heard the soft tapping on the door, but as it came louder I slowly crawled off the bed, wiping my tears with the sleeve of my robes. Rather unsteadily I stumbled across the room.

'Yes?' I asked feebly with my face pressed up against the wood.

'It's me Miss. It's Abel.'

With a sniff I turned the key in the lock and opened the door. Abel was standing there looking bashful, his right eye red and swollen, and studying him closer I saw a cut on the side of his lip with a trickle of dried blood underneath.

'Abel, what happened. Has someone attacked you?'

He threw me a weak smile. 'Oh no Miss Effie.' For a moment he avoided my eye and his face began to twitch nervously. 'I accidentally slipped Miss.' He took a large gulp. 'Tumbled down those steep stairs, I did. The one's by the resident's quarters.'

Instinctively I reached out and gently touched the side of his mouth. 'Come inside and let me clean your face.'

'No, no Miss.' His eyes darted anxiously along the corridor. 'Best you come along to the great hall. The mistress if waiting for you.'

I took hold of his arm and began pulling him into the room. 'Verity can wait.'

With a sharp intake of breath, he bounded backwards into the corridor. 'The mistress don't wait for anyone Miss. And if you'll late she'll blame me.' He glumly lowered his eyes. 'Everyone blames me for everything.'

I sighed. 'Someone gave you these injuries didn't they Abel. Was it one of the guards?'

Without uttering a word, he slowly began to nod.

'Was it Craddock or Wilding?'

He gave me a knowing look. 'Don't tell Miss. Please don't tell. It will only cause more grief.' A flicker of brightness appeared in his eyes. 'I be getting out of here soon, remember Miss? Once we get your friend we can all leave together.' He reached out and grasped my hands in his. 'That's what will be keeping me strong Miss.' Gulping, his gaze darted up the corridor before meeting my eye. 'Any idea when and how we are leaving?'

I stared at him blankly. Last night I had been so desperate to leave that I'd completely forgotten about Abel and Clarice. My face began to redden when I realised how selfish and inconsiderate I'd been.

'I shall tell you as soon as I know Abel. I give you my absolute promise we shall all leave together.'

His face beamed as he shook my hands. 'Bless you Miss Effie. Bless you.'

I smiled. 'Before we do anything, we need to find Clarice. She's about my age with light hair and very pretty. Have you seen anyone like that?'

He shrugged his shoulders. 'I'm not sure Miss. But don't fret, we'll find her.'

My heart sank for a moment, thinking the worse.

As the dull chime of the bells sounded Abel's eyes widened in horror.

'Cripes Miss we won't be going anywhere if we don't get our backsides down to the hall. If Proctor was here she'd scolding me something chronic.'

Unable to prevent myself I began to laugh. 'Where is Proctor?'

'Mistress Verity took a big disliking to her. One night she had Proctor bound to a stake that had been specially put into place on top of one of them barrow mounds where we used to hold The Giver ceremonies. By morning there was nothing left but the wooden stake and a bit of tattered rope.'

As we approached the hall, I gave him a sideways glance. 'Oh. Poor Proctor.'

'Yes Miss. She weren't nice to me but I didn't wish her dead.' He slowly opened the doors to the hall. 'I won't be surprised if she's still here in spirit. Haunting the corridors at night and checking her rooms are all in order.'

A chill suddenly crept across my body. 'What rooms did Proctor have Abel?'

'Why the rooms you're staying in Miss.'

I began to shiver.

Sitting at the table I caught Noble's eye and for a fleeting moment we shared a knowing look, and then he lowered his gaze to the table, looking sullen.

The mad woman seemed rather preoccupied as we ate our breakfast and thankfully didn't really speak to me much apart from asking me how I had settled into my new accommodation; with a smirk she told me how much pleasanter I was than the previous occupant. Being civil to the mad woman was particularly difficult. How could I even begin to have a conversation with her when just being in her company filled me with a chilling uneasiness. As we sat there silently eating our breakfast, I tried to think of at least one quality that she possessed that made her seem human, but I could think of none. And the only thing we remotely had in common was sharing the same father, and even he was a subject we wouldn't agree on.

As I glanced around the hall, I noticed there seemed to be some discontent amongst the resident's, many of them kept exchanging anxious looks as they muttered amongst themselves, ever so often glancing apprehensively at the mad woman as if they were afraid she would hear what they were discussing, or would notice something was wrong. Craddock and Wilding were leaning up against the far wall, their piercing eyes surveying the hall meticulously, but there also seemed to be extra guards standing in various spots around the hall. I had an undeniable feeling that there was trouble brewing.

The mad woman placed her arm over Noble's and clutched his hand. 'Will you be spending the day in the greenhouses my love?' She glanced at me. 'Effelia why don't you join him?'

117

The two of you must have lots to catch up on. You can tell Noble all about your happy family life with Gideon and that sweet little nephew of mine. How blissful it must be all living together in that grand old house.' She threw Noble a sideways glance. 'I expect Aunt Constance is over the moon that you've finally settled down with such an honourable man. I'm travelling through the mirror to Abercrombie in the next few days. Perhaps I should pay them all a visit.'

I could feel the familiar sensation of acute homesickness enveloping my heart with an unbearable ache. Feeling suddenly enraged I shot up from my seat and screamed at her. 'Stop it Verity. I can't bear it.' Faces were staring at me from their tables, but I didn't care. 'Why do you have to be so vile.'

Her whole body shook with laughter. 'Oh Effelia. I'm just having a little fun. That is all.' Without warning her amused expression changed to fury and she seized hold of my arm and put her face close to mine. 'You're so ungrateful dear sister. I went out my way to bring you here, so that you could have a break from motherhood.' Glaring at me her hand came up and pinched my cheek. 'You're looking so pasty and ill, perhaps a spell outside in the grounds will help.' Her high-pitched cackle was so loud that my heart leapt wildly in my chest. 'No, that certainly wouldn't do now would it? What would that loving husband of yours think if I allowed you to become torn apart by the trees?' Releasing my arm, she turned to Noble and gently ruffled his hair, kissing him lightly on the lips. 'Until later my love.'

I suddenly had the overwhelming urge to strike her, but I held back. Realising I must pull myself together and stay focused, I took a deep breath and tried to calm myself.

With a smirk she looked at me. 'Do have an enjoyable day Effelia.'

'Verity?' I said. 'What you told me yesterday about your discovery.' My voice sounded surprisingly controlled. 'I'm very intrigued and would very much like to see those ancient relics...and the mirror.'

She stared at me sombrely, her eyes narrowing. 'Yes of course Effelia, I will gladly show you them when the time is right.'

'When shall that be?'

'Soon dear sister, very soon.' From the look of amusement in her eyes it was blatantly clear she was enjoying herself. 'In the meantime, I have more important matters to attend to. I will be gone most of the day and quite possibly overnight.' Her lips twisted into a devious smile. 'Would you like me to give your love to Gideon and baby Gabriel, Effelia?' Without waiting for a reply, she roughly pushed passed me and headed away from the table. 'Do run along to the greenhouses with Noble, that's a good girl.'

I watched as she strode passed the residents without saying a word, her eyes fixed on the door. Hector had suddenly entered and was blocking the mad woman's way and appeared to be complaining to her about something. She yelled in his ear before shoving him backwards onto the floor. Without so much as a second glance she stepped over his crumpled form, and flinging the hall doors open she marched out the room. As Hector managed to stand up, I noticed Craddock and Wilding were beside him, cruelly laughing and prodding him in the stomach.

'I can't watch this a moment longer.' I uttered, glaring towards Noble in astonishment. 'How can you just sit there and allow this to happen.'

'Effie, please believe me it's not worth becoming involved.'

As I turned my attention back to the men, I saw one of the brothers push Hector onto the ground and to my horror they kicked the poor man as he crawled towards the door. As Hector gradually disappeared into the passageway he must have muttered something under his breath as one of the guards bellowed after him, telling him to cease complaining and get back to work.

I could feel a surge of anguish and fury rising in my stomach.

'You may not wish to become involved Noble, but that doesn't mean I can't.'

He firmly gripped my arm. 'Effie, no.'

With a scowl I wrenched my arm away and rose from my seat, and with my eyes firmly fixed on the brothers, I strode towards them. Hector had gone now and they were standing about laughing.

'Can you not see what monsters you are? No one deserves to be beaten up and pushed around, no one.' I could feel my face going red as they turned and gaped at me. 'I will see to it that you get punished for this.'

The two brothers exchanged glances, their bodies shaking with laughter.

'We do as we see fit Miss.' Said Craddock, running his thumb across his scar. 'That clown Hector is a trouble maker, and a nuisance to the mistress.'

My voice grew louder as the two brothers switched their attention to the residents, who were now slowly filing out of the hall. 'Well I think you'll find that your mistress doesn't actually have the final word in everything that happens at the monastery.'

Wilding threw me scowl, as if I was suddenly becoming irritating. 'You Miss don't know what you're talking about.'

I narrowed my eyes. 'Perhaps not, but I do know that Verity isn't your true leader.' My eyes glanced over to the top table where Noble was glaring at me. 'When Septimus passed away the title of leader would have passed to his descendant- his grandson Noble.'

Craddock came close, his large frame looming over me in a threatening manner.

'Yeah but mistress Verity's marriage changed all that.' He sneered. 'Has no one told you about her union with the old master?'

'What?' I exclaimed loudly, trying to be heard above the crowd.

They both stared at me in a somewhat strange manner. 'The marriage between Septimus and Verity.' Said Wilding with a confused laugh.

I went off into a world of my own for a moment, thinking what a fool I'd been for not figuring out the truth. My eyes drifted across the hall and focused on Noble, and as my eyes widened in bewilderment his expression became concerned. Still in a daze I turned away, and without really seeing them I stared into the crowd of faces.

Hearing raised voices I looked over to see Wilding shoving a man forward, telling him to get a move on and several of the residents began lurching towards the guard, shouting and screaming. Suddenly a young woman with platted hair grasped hold of my robes and began yelling in my ear, but in all the commotion I couldn't understand what she was saying, and just stood there staring blankly into her face. One of the guards came along and pulled us apart, shoving the woman in the direction of the door and pushing me backwards into the arms of Craddock.

'There, there Miss.' He said with a chuckle. 'I've got you now.' With ease he lifted me up and moved back against the wall, gently placing me back down. 'You stay with me until this rabble have left the hall. I'll take care of you.'

I shuddered as I felt his clammy hand on my arm and glared at him indignantly.

'I'm perfectly fine thank you.' Removing his hand, I very slowly inched away from him.

Wilding and several of the other guards were now forcing their way amongst the throng of people, clamping their hands on the one's causing trouble and dragging them roughly from the crowd. I observed how many of the resident's remained completely unflustered by the commotion, their pale faces staring vacantly into space, totally oblivious to what was happening around them. I wondered how they managed now without their daily dose of tonic, would they eventually wither away and die or would they struggle on until the bitter end, when the inevitable would happen and The Elders would put them out their misery. As a man was plucked from the crowd, I noticed how his bloodshot eyes were wild with desperation.

'You've got to help me Miss.' His hand reached out for me. 'I beg you Miss, save us. You're the sister of the mistress, you can stop this.' His face looked agonised as one of the guards began dragging him away. 'My name is Trafford Miss. Please try and persuade your sister to let us return home.'

'I shall try.' I uttered, automatically moving forward to help. 'I promise I shall try.'

It was a hollow promise, but nevertheless said with the very best of intentions. For it was a forgone conclusion that any attempt to chip away at the mad woman's conscience was futile. She didn't possess any concept of what was right or wrong and never would. Her heart was made of stone.

Without warning Craddock grasped my shoulders and hauled me back. 'I told you to keep away Miss.' He said fiercely. I found his hands creep around my waist and could smell his foul breath on my face. 'It'll do you no good to get involved.' As he gripped me with his sweaty hands, I desperately tried to release myself but with a mocking laugh he tightened his hold.

Noble was barging his way through the crowd towards us. His angry glare fixed upon Craddock. 'Take your filthy hands off of her.'

Craddock looked up in surprise as Noble headed straight for him and momentarily loosened his hold, giving me the opportunity to move away. Before he had a chance to react, Noble had punched him square in the face, sending him sprawling backwards against the wall.

'If you touch her again it's you who shall be fed to The Elder trees.' He snarled. 'I shall take care of it myself.' With a sudden movement he grabbed Craddock's throat with both hands. 'Now get out of my sight.' Releasing his grip, he shoved the guard towards the door. 'And take that brother of yours with you.'

Craddock glared at Noble sullenly, wiping the blood from the corner of his mouth with his hand. 'You've got no authority here mister. None at all.'

'That's beside the point. Your mistress won't be too happy when she finds out you weren't able to control a simple scuffle.' He glanced at me. 'And the fact that you manhandled her sister will surely not go in your favour.'

The entire hall had suddenly gone silent.

'What about the troublemakers? Asked Wilding. They need to be dealt with.'

Noble glanced around at the residents being held by the guards.

'Release them. They mean no harm.'

One of the resident's managed to free himself from the guards. He stumbled forward; his ashen face contorted in fury. 'Let us all go – back to our homes.' He yelled. 'We know what happens to anyone who defies the mistress.' He raised his hands in the air. 'Old Bernard went missing a few days ago and there's been no sign of Monaghan since supper yesterday. And that's just to name but a few. I travelled to Hartland on the promise of a new life but so far all I've seen is death. All these people who have disappeared haven't gone back home. They've been eaten by The Elder trees.'

Many of the resident's began to shout in agreement, and as the crowd surged forward, Wilding roughly grabbed the young man.

'Yeah, that's right. What a clever lad you are Stephens.' He got hold of a clump of his hair and yanked his head back. 'Your big mouth has now cost you your life.'

'Let him go Wilding.' I shouted in a rather quivering voice. 'Let us wait until Verity returns and then discuss the matter in a civilised manner.'

It was a senseless suggestion that I knew would result with the same outcome, but all the same it bought the resident's some time.

He turned his attention towards me. 'No offence Miss but you don't give the orders around here either.' A sickly smile appeared on his face. 'You're just the little weak sister of the mistress.'

Before I could respond Noble was taking my arm and leading me towards the door. And as we heard the guards sniggering, he turned back and glared at the two brothers, his face full of repressed anger. 'If you dare to harm any of the residents before the mistress returns, I shall see to it personally that you both pay for it with your lives.'

As he strode on ahead of me I could tell by his demeanour that he wasn't happy.

'I know you're angry.'

Without even looking at me he began yelling. 'I tried to warn you not to get involved. But you couldn't stop yourself, could you? Don't you see it's best to remain impartial to what goes on around here? Keeping a low profile means keeping alive.'

We entered a covered walkway with a series of tiny arches, which looked out onto a barren courtyard. Once upon a time I imagined there would have been a lily pond in the centre with a water fountain, and perhaps potted plants lining the edges. It would have been a beautiful tranquil spot where the monks could take some air and relax on the stone benches, their hands clasped in prayer.

Rather abruptly Noble came to a halt, and as we collided with one another my head smashed into his shoulder. He steadied me and looked down into my face, his eyes flooded with sudden concern.

'Effie I'm so sorry, did I hurt you?'

'No.' I stammered, looking up into his face.

As we held one another's gaze he moved his hands up either side of my head and began gently running his fingers over my hair. Still staring at me I noticed his eyes glazing over with emotion. One of his hands moved down and cupped my cheek and he very faintly murmured my name. As his face came nearer to mine, I thought he was going to kiss me but with a deep sigh he suddenly moved away.

'Let's just find the mirror and get you to safety.' He snapped. 'Sooner rather than later, especially after the commotion in the hall just now. Once Verity finds out what happened it will make the situation even worse.'

I sat down on the low wall underneath one of the arches.

'You have nothing to fear from Verity, she adores you Noble. I however am another matter.'

'Effie, I'm not worried about her, it's the guards I'm most concerned about.' He said sharply. 'Verity, as evil as she is, apparently doesn't wish to harm you. But I've seen how

Craddock and Wilding act, how they take matters into their own hands. And if they take a dislike to someone then that person either suddenly disappears or is bullied relentlessly, like Abel and Hector. Our actions a minute ago may have already cost us our lives. From now on the brothers will be watching us like hawks, just waiting for one of us to slip up or have another outburst, and then that will be it. They won't bother alerting Verity, they'll just dispose of us in any way they see fit, then toss our bodies to The Elder trees.'

I stared at him open mouthed, my body trembling. With a gulp I glumly bowed my head. 'I'm sorry Noble. It wasn't my intention to cause trouble, for either of us. I was just so outraged.'

He came and sat beside me. 'Effie, I know, I understand how you feel. I'm only angry because I'd never forgive myself if you came to any harm, and I thought it fair to warn you how dangerous those brothers can be.' He laughed. 'But somehow I think you already gathered that.'

Looking up at him I could see his anger had abated.

'I don't suppose you punching Craddock endeared him to you.' I said, giving him a weak smile. 'His probably after your blood now.'

'Of that I have little doubt.' He shifted a little and dreamily gazed out onto the courtyard. 'You know I never met my grandfather, and my mother Sabina would never really speak of him. But something tells me Septimus would be horrified at what's been happening at the monastery.'

We heard the faint sound of footsteps.

Noble swung his legs over the wall and landed in the courtyard. 'Shall we go outside and take some air?' he laughed.

'Yes, why not.'

Much to his amusement I leapt nimbly over the wall. Wasting no time, we quickly sprinted across the uneven cobblestones to the far side of the courtyard and hid in a shaded alcove in the wall.

'They must think we've gone to the greenhouses.' He muttered as several guards marched swiftly along the passageway.

'They won't find us here.' I replied with a shiver. A fine mist was passing slowly through the courtyard, concealing us from prying eyes. 'You were right what you said about Craddock and Wilding.' I said, glancing at Noble. 'I don't believe your grandfather would have tolerated them.' I gathered my sleeves and pulled them forward over my freezing hands. 'Septimus wasn't a good man. He gave the impression of being righteous and wise, but it was all just pretence. He was a weak old man desperately trying to preserve the unnatural way of life that exists here. After he gave up hope of finding the book that would grant him immortality, he set his sights on Gideon becoming his successor.' I watched as a single snowflake danced through the air then melted onto the cobblestones. 'But it wasn't to be. Then my sister appears when he is at his most vulnerable, and catches him like a spider ensnares a fly in its web.' Despite the cold I felt the heat on my face as I noticed Noble eyeing me intently. 'I felt so foolish in the hall when the two brothers told me about their marriage.'

'I did try and tell you last night in the library Effie, but then Craddock and Wilding made an appearance and it slipped my mind.'

'Don't worry.' The mist was rolling northwards now and I could see clearly across the other side of the courtyard. 'And at what point did you realise Verity was smitten with you?'

'I don't know.' Laughing he casually shrugged his shoulders. 'We spent a long while together in Briarwood after you left with Isaiah and Mace for Hartland, to seek out Gideon. For me it was merely a friendship, but looking back I can see how she may have taken my behaviour for something more.'

'Oh.' I exclaimed trying to make out I didn't care. 'Why, what did you do to make her think that?' I held my breath for his answer.'

His face broke into a sad smile. 'It was very innocent really. All we did was hold hands and occasionally hug. I enjoyed her company, and it was a blessed relief to spend my days in the company of a young woman who wanted me rather than wasting my time dwelling on a woman who didn't.' As he inclined his head towards me his expression was indignant. 'But then you returned to Briarwood and once again my life was thrown into turmoil.' He intentionally paused. 'Your visit however was fleeting, and then you were gone again.'

I sheepishly lowered my eyes. 'At what point did Verity travel to Hartland?'

He thought for a minute before answering. 'Well the strange thing is she left almost immediately after you returned to Briarwood. As I recall she wasn't happy with me. You were gravely ill and I was constantly at your bedside. She seemed so eager to leave that she barely said goodbye.'

'That must have been when she took the ledger and gave it to Septimus in exchange for Isaiah's freedom.'

He responded with a nod. 'For a while I didn't see her, and then completely out of the blue she turns up in the village. She immediately fell into my arms and burst into tears, bawling about being a widower so soon after her marriage. Father and I were naturally somewhat taken aback when we learnt whom her husband had been. But seeing how genuinely distraught she was about my grandfather I provided a much-needed shoulder for her to cry on.'

I raised my eyebrows. 'I see.'

His face turned to mine. 'Do you?'

With a frown I averted my eyes. 'What happened after that?'

'During her stay Verity persuaded me to visit the monastery, along with a few other of the villagers.'

'What about Mace, did she not try and talk him into leaving?

Noble laughed. 'Ah yes, my newly discovered little brother. At first he was adamant on coming with us but then for some reason he changed his mind. I never did find out why. Of course, if father had discovered what we'd been planning he would have insisted on us staying.' He lowered his head in shame. 'So, I wrote him a short note and left it on the kitchen table, then sneaked out in the dead of night and left with Verity and the others.' A lost look crossed over his face. 'And I've been trapped here ever since.'

There was an intense silence but it was broken instantly by the bellowing voices of men. Two guards who I'd recognised from the hall were pacing towards us at a rapid speed. I noticed the daggers secured to their belt buckles and as Noble shouted at the men to go away one of the guards removed the weapon and thrust it close to his face.

'The mistress won't be happy if you use that knife on me Hale.' Said Noble, staring sternly at the guard. 'I suggest you put it away before there's an accident.'

The guard, Hale seemed suddenly speechless and rather swiftly replaced the dagger in his belt. With a grunt he gestured for Noble and me to move. Exchanging looks we both rose and were chaperoned across the courtyard.

The greenhouses were more extensive than I'd realised and every available space was crammed full of plants, both on the tables and on the floor. As the two guards hurried us along, I noticed various residents hunched over the tables, wearily working. We were taken to the far end of the buildings where the only other person was a middle-aged woman with dark curly hair. She smiled nervously as we approached but swiftly turned away as the guards glared at her.

'We'll be letting you get to work then mister Noble.' mumbled the other guard. 'You can show Miss Farraday just how green fingered you are.' He grinned insolently, displaying two missing front teeth. 'We'll be standing close by just in case you decide to go wandering.' He looked steadily at me before mumbling something to Hale, and then they plodded along the other way.

'If we keep our heads down, we can hopefully steal out the side door in a moment without the guards noticing.' Noble muttered in a low voice. 'And then I can take you on a tour along the southern most part of the monastery. It's a good place to start our search for the mirror.'

I moved over to one of the long tables and gazed at the many rows of tomato plants towering up against the windows.

'You make it sound so pleasant Noble. As if we're on a fun day out.'

He drew close to me. 'Perhaps we should imagine we are.' With a smile he began watering some seedlings. 'Just like the ones we used to have in your home town by the sea.'

My face clouded over. 'I'm afraid I don't remember.'

'Sorry.' He said sombrely. 'How unmemorable it must have been for you.' he began to move around some of the wooden trays of seedlings, slamming them down noisily. 'However, I'm sure you recall your time spent with Gideon.' He bashed his knuckles down onto the table and was just about to speak again when long tendrils of root began winding their way around his left wrist, slowly creeping up his arm. With his free hand he frantically tore at them until they were all off before reaching for a pair of shears and violently hacking the roots into pieces.

That's when I noticed the tiny roots on the tables, around the plant pots, on the floor, and across the ceiling. From a distance they seemed harmless but as I looked closer, I noticed how they were slowly moving. I'm not sure how long they'd taken to spread, but little by little they were taking possession of the greenhouses.

Noble winced with pain as he held his wrist.

'Are you okay?' I asked

He let out a laugh. 'Yes, it's not the first time that's happened, and I fear it won't be the last. Day by day the roots seem to grow in strength.' His gaze travelled over my shoulder and when he spoke his voice was low. 'Now looks like a good time to sneak away. The guards seem preoccupied with something.'

We heard a woman suddenly begin to scream.

I turned around and saw the woman with the dark curly hair and the two guards gazing underneath one of the tables, their faces overcome with fear.

Noble took my arm. 'Don't look Effie. Whatever it is, it can't be good.'

Knowing my curiosity was going to get the better of me, I pulled away from him, and wandered across to where they were standing. With a cry I clamped my hand across my mouth. Lying beneath the table was a body, half entwined in roots. I couldn't see much of the face as it was obscured with the roots but it appeared to be an elderly man, his eyes gaping wide. As I observed the mass of roots around his neck and his half protruding tongue it was pretty clear death was caused by strangulation.

'That's old Bernard.' Exclaimed one of the guards with a strange laugh. 'I wondered where that crafty so and so had got to. Seems he didn't make it out after all.'

The woman began to whimper and with a stifled sob, fled from the greenhouses.

Noble stood beside me staring at the body. He glanced at Hale. 'You and Walters should remove the body.'

The guard looked blank. 'Where should I take him, down to the caverns?

'No.' said Noble with a deep sigh. 'Take him to the infirmary for now.'

Hale looked puzzled. 'But the mistress says that the trees should be fed whenever possible. She won't be rightly pleased when she finds out.'

Noble glared at him for a moment. 'Well, you can inform the mistress that's not going to happen. Bernard shall have a proper burial.'

The two guards gaped at one another in surprise and then proceeded with the difficult task of detangling the tendrils from the body. They began mumbling to one another as they cut away with the shears, and cursed as their hands kept coming entwined amongst the roots. They were so engrossed in what they were doing that they didn't notice Noble and I creep away down the far side of the greenhouses and out of the doors.

In the darkness we fumbled our way along a narrow passage until we reached a door that led us into what appeared to be a small chapel. There was the soft glow of candlelight coming from the altar, and for one moment it made the room seem warm and tranquil, a hidden sanctuary where one could hide away and forget their woes. However, as I stepped further into the room the peacefulness seemed somewhat unnerving and wrong. I sensed that the chapel had been abandoned long ago, and only the spirits of medieval monks would come and worship here now. I imagined they would pray for their once holy monastery to be brought back to life in an age when The Elder trees were merely saplings, and then they would take axes and hack them down until they were stumps, before they were strong enough to wreak havoc, before they destroyed entire worlds.

Taking two of the candleholders, Noble placed a small candle in each then held the wick up to the flickering flame of one of the large pillar candles until it was alight.

'Here.' He said handing me one. 'We won't get far without light.'

'I wonder who lit the candles.' I said realising that at least one person must be visiting this lonely place.

'I've no idea.' He said lighting the other wick. 'I never even knew this place existed until recently. None of the resident's or even the guard's, for that matter, seem remotely interested in holy worship. And I can't imagine Verity coming here to prayer.' Holding his candlestick up to my face he smiled poignantly. 'Perhaps it gets used for the occasional wedding ceremony.'

I stared at him without smiling. 'Septimus and Verity must have taken their nuptials here.' My eyes slowly drifted across to the altar. 'And my parents too.' I uttered grimly at him. 'I wonder if all the weddings that have taken place in this strange little chapel have resulted in such a disastrous outcome.'

He looked suddenly perturbed. 'Well I don't suppose I'll shall ever find out, as I'm never going to marry anyone.'

Not knowing what to say I ignored his comment and began strolling along each pew with my candle, pretending to look for a mirror that I already knew wasn't there, for it would be impossible to disguise it in such a small space. At the back of the chapel there was a side door leading to the vestry, but as we looked inside it soon became blatantly obvious, that apart from a few robes and discarded books, the room was empty.

Hearing an anguished sigh coming from Noble I turned and stared into his tortured face. 'You must really miss your home.' My eyes travelled to his hair and I suddenly had the urge to reach out and touch it. 'And then there is your father. You must be keen to see Caleb again. He's surely desperate for you to return.'

'Try as hard as you like Effie, but you won't persuade me to leave.'

I followed him as he strode out the vestry and watched as he slumped down dejectedly onto the front pew.

'But why stay when you clearly dislike the place. And don't tell me you're staying to keep an eye on Verity.' I took a large gulp. 'I...I don't believe you.'

'You're right Effie- I do hate it here, and Verity will do whatever she wishes, with or without me watching over her. But even if we found the mirror I would prefer to stay at the monastery and face my fate, rather than traipse back home and live in Briarwood without you. Father would come to terms with my absence, just as before.' He lowered his head, looking pensive. 'The true of the matter is Verity didn't talk me into coming to Hartland, I did it all by myself.' He gulped with emotion and looked up into my eyes. 'It seemed the only way I was ever going to get over you.'

Placing my candle on the altar I went and sat beside him. I bowed my head and gazed down at my hands and nervously began fiddling with my rings. When I spoke my voice was low, barely a whisper. 'And have you.... got over me?' As his arm brushed against mine a strange sense of longing flooded through my body and I felt myself flushing profusely.

'Look at me Effie.'

Very slowly I raised my head and met his eye.

'Our future together may be lost but it doesn't change the way I feel. Gideon may have won your love, and I've come to terms with that.' He looked deep within my eyes. 'But ever since I first saw you, I've thought about you every single day, I still do. I'm not over you Effie.' His voice became hoarse. 'I never will be.'

Suddenly I couldn't think straight. The intensity of his gaze was so overpowering that I believed he could see into the very depths of my soul. I averted my gaze and gradually edged away from him. 'We should continue looking for the mirror.' I mumbled, standing up. 'It...it must be somewhere.' I could still feel his eyes upon me, scrutinizing my face. As I reached the entrance to the chapel, I threw him a sideways glance. He was standing in the centre of the pews, rigid and unmoving, glaring at me. Like a frightened rabbit I scurried from the room and into the welcome darkness of the passageway.

Chapter 14

Completely immersed in my thoughts I wandered aimlessly along the dark corridors, not thinking or caring where I was going, or who or what I happened to bump into. I stumbled into a stone bench and rested upon it. There was no one about, and I was glad of it. With a drawn-out sigh I shut my eyes and tried to remove the vision of Noble's face, and to forget the words he had spoken. I was cold and hungry, but more than anything I was weary, in mind as well as in body. Without really thinking what I was doing I lowered my head onto the bench and lay there, and in no time at all I was asleep.

I dreamt there was a beach, a glorious beach, with sand as white as the purest perils. Barefoot I ambled along the seashore, gazing out onto the clear shimmering greens and blues of the ocean. Palm trees stretched on forever and the azure sky above me was cloudless. For a moment I closed my eyes and listened to the gentle lulling of the waves against the shore, and the sound of the gulls in the distance. I could feel the pure moist air spraying onto my face and body, enveloping me in the scent of the sea.

Suddenly from amongst the blond sand dunes a tiny figure came running towards me. To my delight I saw it was my son Gabriel, he was a little older now and ran with ease. We splashed our feet in the shallow water and collected shells and crabs in our buckets. As I looked southwards, I saw a man striding confidently towards us.

'Daddy, daddy.' Cried Gabriel in a joyous voice. He began skipping towards him, his dark curls bouncing in the sea air. 'I've missed you daddy.'

Gideon scooped Gabriel up in his arms and spun him round in the air. And then I ran to join them and all three of us stood there hugging. Gigantic sea horses appeared, galloping across the waves, and as they came nearer they turned into real animals and we clambered on and rode them along the seashore, then disappeared into the distant shoreline.

With a sudden jolt I woke up. Sadness filled my heart on leaving my dream. I suddenly wondered why there was no light, and then I remembered my candle was still in the chapel. I'd been so wrapped up in thoughts of Noble that all common sense had deserted me, and now because of my rash behaviour I was completely lost, and could barely see two feet in front of me.

'Noble, Noble can you hear me?' Panicking I stumbled blindly forward. 'Noble.' I said curtly as if it was his entire fault I was lost. 'Where are you?'

As I became increasingly disorientated the fear and anxiety inside me grew. Suddenly I lost my footing and stumbled down some steps, but luckily managed to grab hold of the rope running along the length of the wall. An odd stillness hung in the air that disturbed me, and I anxiously prayed that the silence wouldn't suddenly be broken by the groan of the trees. For although I wasn't directly in the tunnels that didn't necessary mean that the moving roots weren't close. They could easily latch onto my ankle or grab my throat, and just before dragging me to their lair they would slowly choke the life from my body, just like that poor man in the greenhouses. I wondered why the trees hadn't taken his corpse away, was he diseased or too old to risk eating, or perhaps they'd been overfed to such an extent that they were storing it there, to take when needed. However, I vaguely remember Gideon telling me how the trees in the wilds became sleepy in the sunlight. Could the trees at Hartland be affected in the same way if they were exposed to the sun? Even though this land was permanently smothered in an impenetrable covering of mist, the greenhouses were primarily made of glass, so even with a meagre amount of sunlight the environment was bound to be warmer, after all how would the fruit and vegetables grow without it. It was therefore possible that the roots in the greenhouses were weaker in the day than at

135

night, but that of course didn't explain how they still managed to strangle a man, and it was also unclear as to why they couldn't take the body come nightfall, when they'd sufficiently regained their strength. I realised at that instant that these theories were only floating around in my mind as a momentarily distraction, because even the grisly discovery in the greenhouses was preferable to my current situation.

As the steps came to an end, I carefully guided my arms along the damp walls, fearful of what I might stumble upon. My eyes had become more accustomed to the dark now and from what I could make out I was in some type of cave. 'Hello. Can anyone hear me?' Although my voice sounded pitiful and weak I was scared of calling out too loud just in case I alerted the wrong kind of attention- the unnatural sort that would kill me. There was a heavy dankness in the air, more so than up above. It was a medieval aroma of long ago that reminded me of a fortress I had once visited on a school trip. I cannot recall where and when this was but I remember becoming accidentally separated from the main party and standing alone in a cavern with only my overactive imagination for company. There had been soldiers there of another age who had valiantly fought and perished, and now their spirits were trapped in the midst of time. I remember being transfixed as the coldness of the air gradually crept across my bare arms like icy hands reaching out to touch me. As I recollect an exuberant Mace had suddenly bounded towards me exclaiming that I was in serious trouble with the teacher. Then he had pretended to fight me, and as his lanky body flayed about in different directions his mop of unruly hair flopped from side to side, causing his school cap to fly off his head. Despite my misery I couldn't help but chuckle.

Without warning I heard an object land by my foot, and as I bent low to retrieve it, I could just about see it was a small stone. I held it in my palm, twirling it around with my finger, and then tossed it back on the ground. It was colder still now, and I could clearly see my breath in front of me like a fog. I sensed something close, and as a bitterly cold hand ever so gently brushed my face I didn't jump in terror or scream, but instead I calmly took a step back, gazing around the cave. Standing in the corner I saw the solitary figure of a young girl.

'Lucinda?'

She remained very still, like a statue. 'Hello again Effie.'

I took a step forward. She looked so fragile and vulnerable that I wondered if the slightest movement or noise would cause her to vanish.

'I was wondering where you were.' My voice was gentle and low, like a mother soothing her child. 'How are you?'

As she soundlessly moved forward, I became a little apprehensive. It had been different before when I hadn't realised what she was.

'I am as well as can be expected thank you Effie.' She stared at me with her pale grey eyes that were surprisingly clear and bright. 'For someone who no longer walks amongst the living.'

I scrunched up my face and sighed. 'Lucinda I'm sorry. Asking you how you are was completely insensitive of me.'

'Please don't worry Effie. You needn't treat me any different just because I'm deceased.' Her hand touched my arm and I felt an icy chill through the cloth of my robes. 'I am still your friend.'

The realisation of the situation suddenly began to dawn on me and I felt my nerves begin to go. My eyes flitted over to the shadowy entranceway as the impulse to flee became overwhelming. But my body wouldn't move, so I simply stood there, trembling inside and out. My heart leapt wildly in my chest as she moved up close, her pale eyes staring into mine.

'I am so very sorry you've been sent back to the monastery but am exceedingly glad to see you all the same. We are still friends, aren't we Effie. I didn't mean to mislead you when you were here before; it's just that I thought if you knew the truth it might have frightened you away.'

I took a large gulp, trying not to show my fear. 'Just because you're....' I began to falter. 'You're still my friend Lucinda no matter what. And I'm very glad to see you too.' Despite my trembling lips I managed to give her a shaky smile. 'Do...do you still visit the library?'

'Yes, I do still visit the library. In fact, I was there last night, did you not realise?'

Trying to steady my nerves I took a deep breath. 'It was you wasn't it, who made the books fall off the shelves, in the library and in...in my room.' Unintentionally my voice grew more urgent. 'Why didn't you make yourself known to me?'

'I was too shy to show myself.' With a look of anguish, she held her transparent hands out before her. 'Please forgive me Effie. Please say you will.'

My initial instincts were to reach out and touch her hand, only how could I when she was no longer flesh and blood. But it was puzzling me how I'd been able to hug her and hold her hand previously. 'Calm yourself Lucinda.' I uttered in a low voice. 'You've done nothing wrong that I would need to forgive you for. I can't imagine that you ever will.'

Looking happier she smiled once more. 'I told Bertram how kind you are.' She came forward and pressed her hand into mine. 'I don't know how I'm able to make physical contact with you, but I am. Perhaps it's because you can see me when others cannot.'

I nodded in acknowledgment. 'You mentioned Bertram – is he the one that perished at the front gates?'

She looked melancholy, as her gaze drifted away from me. 'Yes. He and I both died that day, together. So, you see murderous Mundy really does deserve his nickname.'

I squeezed her icy hand. 'I'm so very sorry Lucinda. How much I wish I'd been there to help you.'

'Mundy was a young man in those days Effie. And you would not have been born. But thank you anyway.' She released her hand from mine and gave me a little smile. 'I however am in a position to help you get back to the hall in time for lunch. Your friend Noble has been frantic with worry, and has been searching the monastery looking for you.'

An ache crossed over my heart. 'Yes, I can imagine. We became accidentally parted when we were searching for the mirror.' My eyes looked eagerly into hers. 'Do you know about the portal mirror Lucinda, the one that Verity keeps hidden away?'

She giggled. 'Yes of course Effie. I've seen her disappear through the magic mirror many a time. Sometimes I wish I had the power to prevent her returning. What an exceedingly nasty lady she is.'

My faced relaxed into a genuine smile. 'Lady? I'd say monster is a far more accurate title, wouldn't you? But even if she became stranded in another land, someone else would have to endure her vile nature.' My eyes glazed over as I stared dejectedly down at the ground. 'If I didn't have to use the mirror to return home, I'd take a hammer and smash it to pieces, right this second. Too many lives have been ruined already, people from other worlds have been dragged to Hartland on the promise of a better life but have been tricked, and now they have no choice but to remain here with Verity to the bitter end, that's if they manage to stay alive.' Looking into her serene face it suddenly occurred to me what I should do. 'Perhaps we can somehow sneak people back through the mirror. We could all leave tonight, before Verity returns.'

She tugged at my sleeve. 'But Effie there isn't time for that, and it's too risky. It's vital that you leave the monastery immediately, and if you have others with you there's more chance of being caught.'

I inclined my head to the right, looking bewildered. 'Do I have something to do with Verity's plan- can my absence prevent it from happening?'

Her eyes looked downwards. 'Yes, something like that. It's a little difficult for me to explain. We should concentrate on the matter in hand.' She smiled weakly at me. 'The mirror is hidden below the monastery, deep underneath the tunnels, where even The Elder trees cannot reach.'

'Can you show me Lucinda?'

'Yes Effie, but we have to go through the wine cellar in order to get there. And the cellar is always locked.'

'And who has the key?'

'Verity keeps the key in her chambers.'

'But she would have taken the key with her Lucinda, when she travelled through the mirror. She'll need it to come back up from the wine cellar.'

'Your sister keeps a spare Effie. I can show you exactly where she hides it.'

I nodded slowly at her. It all seemed too easy; something would surely go wrong. All the same we agreed to meet directly after supper when most of the guards were generally preoccupied with clearing the hall of residents. Then, according to Lucinda, they would sit and eat their food and consume vast amounts of ale and mead, then doze off into drunken stupors.

Lucinda led me back to the chapel where I retrieved my candle, and then I followed alongside of her until we reached the door leading to the greenhouses, where she suddenly vanished without a word. Blowing out the candle I casually strolled through the greenhouses without making eye contact with anyone, hoping I wouldn't be noticed, but as I slowly opened the door and crept out, I felt a hand grasp my shoulder. It was Abel.

'There you are Miss. I be looking for you all over.' He wiped the sweat from his brow. 'I found her Miss. I found your friend.'

'You mean Clarice?'

He began jumping up and down in excitement. 'Yes Miss, she be in the kitchens.' He took my hand and pulled me hurriedly along the passageway. 'We must be quick. Most of the guards are in the great hall having lunch, but they'll be out and about soon. He poked his head around the corner to check on the hall door before dragging me past it and down a short flight of steps. 'The kitchens are down here Miss.' with a grin he patted my hand. 'I have to leave you here Miss and return to the hall, before I get into trouble.'

I drew in a deep breath and clenched my hands in his. 'I may have found a way out Abel. Where will you be later?'

'Oh Miss –what joy it will be to finally leave this place.' He began to shake my hand vigorously, his face bursting with enthusiasm. 'I shall be in the library Miss for the rest of the day and most of the night. The mistress has ordered me to clear it out.'

I looked puzzled. 'Why?'

He shrugged his shoulders. 'She didn't say Miss and I don't ask. No good comes of asking.'

My heart sank for a moment as I pictured all those precious books being carelessly tossed away as if they were worthless. I momentarily closed my eyes to try and rid myself of the image.

With a sigh I looked at him. 'Well I shall come and find you later Abel, after I know for certain we can escape.' I forced myself to smile at him reassuringly. 'And hopefully we can leave tonight.'

A loud voice bellowed along the passageway.

'Where ever you're hiding Abel get your behind in the hall otherwise you'll find my fist in your face.'

Abel shot me an ominous look. 'I've got to go Miss. It sounds like one of them brothers are after me.'

I watched as he lumbered up the steps then taking a deep breath, I entered the kitchens. The first thing I noticed was a wave of intense heat drifting over from the ovens that ran along an entire wall. It was a capacious room that was larger than the hall, and carried on right down the back where it narrowed slightly. Colossal cooking pots lay in the hearth being stirred by some young boys and in the centre of the room there were a mass of tables with people working amongst them. I also observed the five large carcases hanging from the ceiling on the far side, dripping blood upon the floor. From what I could make out they were deer, the once sacred creatures of Hartland.

Moving into the room I came face to face with Hector.

'Hello Miss Farraday.' He looked rather taken aback for a second before wiping his hands on a cloth then warmly shaking my hand. 'Come to visit us folk below stairs, have you?' He said with a chuckle. 'We don't get many visitors in the kitchens. As long as we provide food to the masses that's all the mistress cares about.'

I smiled politely at him. 'I've come to visit my friend Clarice. I...I believe she's here somewhere.' My eyes began scanning the sea of faces, which were now all staring at me in bafflement. There were many woman and young girls in aprons, with pallid faces and weary looking eyes. The sleeves of their robes were rolled up and they were hunched over tables laden with kitchen equipment and great bowls of vegetables and meats. A young man was half-heartedly kneading a mound of pastry with one hand, looking curiously towards me.

'Oh yes, young Clarice. Bless her.' Hector replied, wiping the cloth across his forehead. 'She's one of the tonic takers back when the old gentleman was in charge. There's still a fair few left at the monastery, but they stick out like a sore thumb with their blank expressions and dull ways. I'm afraid she won't be very forthcoming so don't be disheartened if she doesn't say much. And take care; they are prone to acts of violence. Living without the tonic has made them that way.' A high-pitched laugh erupted from his mouth as he nervously gestured me over to the far right. 'There's Clarice, as silent as the grave.'

The slender figure of a young woman was bent over a bowl, mechanically mixing its contents, her eyes glazed over. At first, I didn't think it was Clarice as her blond hair was cropped close to her head with a few unsightly tufts poking out here and there. However, as I tentatively approached, she slowly looked up and I recognised her large blue eyes peering back at me. They seemed lost within her face, almost sunken. With an exhausted sigh she turned away and continued her work. Feeling a tear run down my cheek I reached out and clutched the hand that was stirring the bowl and held it still. The wooden spoon she'd been holding fell into the batter.

'Clarice?' I squeezed her hand. 'It's me Effie. Your best friend.'

She stood there motionless, gazing into space.

'Look at me damn it, look at me.' I yelled in frustration. As soon as I released her, she plunged her hand into the batter mix and retrieved the spoon and carried on mixing.'

I moved away.

Hector was beside me, his face full of empathy. 'I feel your anguish Miss Farraday, really I do. They're sad cases indeed, what's left of them. After the tonic was banned many were so desperate, they went and collected the berries from the Rowan tree, and were never seen again.'

'What happened to her hair? Did Clarice cut it herself?'

'Nay Miss Farraday. The mistress orders the guards to cut it every week. She doesn't take kindly to someone finer looking than herself parading around the monastery. So, she either...' he paused for a moment and lowered his voice. 'She gets rid of them in whatever manner she sees fit or hides them away down here like hermits. Believe me, Clarice is one of the lucky ones.' He laughed again in the same high-pitched shriek. 'You be on your guard Miss, you maybe the mistress's sister but that don't mean your safe.'

'Ain't no one safe here Hector.' Said an elderly man close by. He picked up a mound of dough and slammed it back down onto the table in a fit of temper. 'I can't rightly remember where I came from and what it was like but no way could it be worse than this stinking place.'

Hector looked over at him and laughed. 'You're right about that Reg. I must have been barmy coming here.' He began hacking at a piece of meat on the table. 'The mistress promised us riches she did, and told us we could live forever, but instead I'm slaving away in this kitchen with a terrible dread that I won't make it through another day.' He took a glimpse at Clarice before peering into my eyes, his red sweaty face full of pity. 'Forget your friend Miss Farraday she's passed helping, or caring.'

I felt a lump come appear in my throat. 'I don't think I can do that Hector.' I uttered rather formidably. 'I'll never accept that all hope is lost.' I crossed over and smiled at her. 'My friend that I knew and loved is still in there somewhere.' Impulsively I reached out and stroked her hair. 'It's just a case of finding her.'

Clarice froze for a moment, the wooden spoon rigid in her hand. She began muttering something inaudible, and her head began moving to and throw. I jumped as she suddenly tossed the bowl across the kitchen and swiftly reached for a carving knife. To my horror she brought the point up against my chest and held it there.

143

'Go away and leave me alone I don't want you here Effie.'

I stared into her emotionless eyes. 'Clarice please-'

'This is my home, and this is where I shall find the tonic. If you dare think of dragging me away, I swear on my life this knife shall find a way into your heart.' She pressed the weapon further into my chest and moved it a little, making a cut in my robe. 'For I shall put it there.' She threw the knife on the floor and returned to the table, and began cursing loudly to herself.

'Hector took my arm. 'Like I said Miss Farraday. Your friend is beyond help.' His voice was grimly quiet. 'Go and seek out Mister Noble. He's your friend, he'll be nice to you.'

I gave a short, anxious laugh and glanced down at the ground. It was then I noticed the red stains smeared across the tiles, and wondered if it was from the bloodied carcases or if it was human blood. In this place either was possible.

Chapter 15

Noble was evidently furious with me and we spent supper in complete silence, barely making eye contact, and either one of us gracious enough to say sorry. I heard agitated whispers amongst the resident's and it was obvious from their concerned faces that the trouble from this morning was far from forgotten. I was however relieved to spot Trafford and Stephens in the crowd, and several others who had been involved in the fight. Perhaps the guards did take notice of Noble after all, but I feared their fate would still be sealed when the mad woman got to hear what had happened when she returned. I watched as Craddock and Wilding strolled around the hall, ever so often smacking someone about the head for talking. Then Craddock turned and stared at me in a horrible uncomfortable way that made my flesh crawl. I watched as he approached the head table carrying a flagon, his eyes directed at me.

'I see you have only ale on your table Miss.' He began pouring some of the liquid into my goblet. 'It's said the medicinal benefits of mead far outweigh its syrupy taste. You need to get some colour into that perfect pale complexion of yours Miss.' His eyes slyly travelled to Noble then back to me. 'Mistress Verity wants you to be in perfect health for the big day.' With a snigger he leant forward and slowly kissed my hand. Moving back, he gestured for me to drink then with a twisted grin, ambled back across the hall.

'What do you suppose that was all about?' I said to Noble, forgetting that we weren't talking.' I eyed him apprehensively, waiting for a reply. 'I'm sorry for running off this morning, but it actually turned out to be very productive.' I gazed at the mead before taking a gulp, hoping it wasn't poisoned. 'I bumped into a friend of mine and she knows where the mirror's kept, but first we have to get a key from Verity's room.' Becoming angry by his silence I got up to leave. 'If you'd like to help, we've arranged to meet at six outside my quarters.'

His eyes were suddenly wide and intent upon my face. 'And what if there's men guarding your door?'

My hand slid over the steak knife on the table and I discreetly placed the weapon under my sleeve. 'Then we shall deal with them.'

Verity's room was dark and foreboding, rather like the owner. It must have once belonged to Septimus and they must have used this room when they were married. I stared at the large four-poster bed on the far side of the room and noticed a bow and quiver full of arrows hanging above it. Every wall was enclosed with dark wooden panelling and covered with various paintings. On closer inspection it came to my attention that they were all portraits that used to be housed in the study. My face dropped as I cast my eyes over the canvases- each one had been slashed and scratched with a knife directly across the middle of the persons face, including the one of Sabina. But the most disturbing one of all was of Septimus, who had an arrow imbedded in the very centre of this forehead, and his eyes gouged out.

'Any luck yet?' asked Noble as he stood in the doorway looking impatient.

'No,' I said still gazing in disbelief at the portrait.

After tapping on my door after supper Noble had apologised for our little disagreement and volunteered to keep watch as Lucinda and I went into Verity's room. He didn't seem unsettled when I mentioned my friend Lucinda was a ghost, but sadly he couldn't see her.

'Do try and be quick, there's bound to be guard snooping about soon.'

I groaned. 'Please give us a minute Noble, we've only just arrived.' I glanced at Lucinda and rolled my eyes. 'Men eh.' I watched as she giggled like the young girl she was. I tried to forget she'd been alive before I was even born, and had been roaming the monastery for a good thirty years or so. It wasn't good to dwell on such things; it would drive one insane. 'They have no patience.' I turned and grinned at Noble but he'd already gone back outside.

On the dressing table was a large vase of crimson roses, and as I breathed in their sweet aroma a disturbing thought occurred to me. Flowers didn't grow around these parts, and I hadn't seen any in the greenhouses, therefore I wondered if she'd collected them from somewhere else, a place where there was an abundance of flowers- from my garden at home. For one brief moment I allowed myself to drift into a daydream, where a dear sweet old lady was pruning the roses, her face beaming at me in the afternoon sun.

I felt coldness on my hand.

'Effie. What's wrong?'

'Nothing. It's nothing.' I said softly, wiping my eyes with my cuff. 'I'm fine Lucinda.'

She took her hand away from mine and pointed to the portrait of Septimus. 'The key is behind there.'

I stood there quiet and still for a moment before moving my hand behind the portrait trying not to look at his ruined face. Unable to feel properly I took my hand from the back and lifted the canvas off the wall. 'I can't see the key.' I stammered urgently, searching the back of the painting thoroughly. My eyes travelled over the floor, just in case it had dropped down, but there was nothing. 'Where is it Lucinda?' I asked, beginning to become anxious.

Her eyes were filled with alarm. 'I...I don't understand Effie. She always keeps it behind the portrait of Septimus.'

With a frown I placed the portrait back on the wall and began searching behind all the other paintings, then I checked underneath the mattress and the bed. 'We're not going to find it.' Clambering onto the bed I looked behind the pillows before jumping down. Suddenly feeling disheartened I wearily walked across the room and checked in the drawers of the dressing table. Inside one of them was a tiny box, and when I opened it my eyes widened with astonishment.

'What is it Effie?'

'I've seen this brooch before.' Intrigued I took the piece of jewellery from the box and examined it closely in the palm of my hand. 'My...my Aunt has one just like this.' Feeling wretched I stared across at Lucinda. 'Verity must have stolen this from her room at...at the house where we live.' I banged my fist against my forehead. 'Rawlings, it's called Rawlings.'

Noble popped his head around the door. 'Hurry Effie, I can hear footsteps approaching. Get out of there.'

Rather disorientated I nodded frantically and quickly shoved the jewellery box back in the drawer and looked around the room. Several of the paintings hung crooked on the walls and the bed cover was all messy from where I'd been standing on it.

Biting down hard on my lip I turned and stared at Lucinda. 'Could we break down the door to the wine cellar?'

Lucinda shook her head. 'The door is extremely heavy it would take a giant to break through.' Her eyes drifted to the entranceway. 'We're too late Effie.' Her next words were faint and filled me with dread. 'Verity's coming.' With barely a movement she began to float through the far wall and then she was gone.

In a mad panic I rushed towards the door but Noble blocked the way.

'What are you doing here Effie? You should be in your room.' The tone of his voice was unusually loud, and when he roughly grabbed my arm I suddenly realised why. 'Let me escort Effie back to her quarters Verity.' He said widening his eyes at me.

The mad woman was standing behind him, eyeing me suspiciously. 'You've been searching for something haven't you?' Pushing her way past Noble she curled her lips into a smirk and brought her face up close to mine. 'Was it the ledger? You must know by now that I possess it. It was so thoughtful of you to mention its location in your tatty old notebook. Father told me all about it when he discovered it in your bag. My poor departed husband gladly released dear daddy when I informed him that the ledger was now in *my* possession.' She patted the top of my head. 'Now be a good girl and run along. As much as I'd enjoy a little chat it's been a long an exhausting day in Abercrombie.' She brushed her hand up against Noble's face. 'Yes, be a love and return my little sister to her quarters.'

Noble exchanged a fleeting glance with me before pulling me from the room. 'Of course, Verity.' Without looking at her he swiftly turned towards the passageway.

'Oh, and Noble. Do fetch me some mead from the kitchens. I'm parched after all that talking.' She cackled loudly. 'The good people of Abercrombie are particularly difficult to convince. But you'll be glad to know I've collected four people and they are now settling into their new accommodation at the monastery.' Her hand flew to her mouth. 'There would have been five but unfortunately one became lost during transportation when I purposely released her hand because she was screaming like a banshee.'

I glared scornfully at her. 'How thoroughly evil of you Verity.'

She clapped her hands together in glee. 'Well thank you dear sister, it was fairly easy to smuggle them into your study at home and through the mirror. Your Aunt was baking in the kitchen and Gideon was with baby Gabriel in the garden.' She pretended to yawn. 'Well goodnight Effelia, go and get your beauty sleep.' She glanced at Noble. 'We have a busy few days ahead of us.'

As she slammed the door, I felt a trickle of blood run through my fingers. It was from the brooch that I was clenching tightly in my hand.

The following morning after breakfast the mad woman linked my arm with hers as if we were the best of friends, and marched us out the hall. Perplexed, I turned to glance at Noble, who sat impassively at the table, watching me. After the disastrous attempt to find the key in the mad woman's room last night, he had escorted me back to my quarters without a word. And then he had muttered goodnight in a rather gruff voice, barely looking at me before turning to go. His ambiguous behaviour worried and also irritated me; sometimes when I looked into his face he seemed to have the weight of the world on his shoulders; there was real fear and anxiety behind his eyes, and a strange lost look that he displayed when he was trying to mask his emotions. Other times he was moody and uncommunicative, like a hurt and disgruntled animal that wanted to be left in peace.

We passed Abel in the passageway leading down to the library and he glanced at me sorrowfully before lowering his head to the floor. I noticed how he failed to make eye contact with the mad woman, and gave an anxious gasp as she shoved passed him as if expecting to be attacked.

'These are the old council chambers.' She announced, flinging open a set of double doors. 'Seeing as the council was disbanded years ago I took it upon myself to make it into an archery room.'

As she gave me an almighty shove forward, I stumbled and practically fell onto the floor of the large, spacious room.

'There's no need to push me, you know.' I said indignantly.

'Sorry dear sister.' Her eyes looked proudly around the room. 'Isn't it splendid?' She gushed. 'I designed it specifically for me.'

The room seemed rather empty with only a large target on the far wall and a selection of bows and arrows laid out on a table to the side.

The mad woman pursed her lips, her eyes darting to mine. 'Well, what do you think?'

'It's lovely.' I replied reticently.

'As you probably know I do enjoy a little archery.' A childlike giggle burst from her mouth. 'Especially when the target is live and moving.' Her mouth came close to my ear. 'And frightened.' She gestured to a chair by the table. 'Sit down Effelia and watch whilst I practice.' With an air of jubilation, she beamed at me. 'Do you recall that time at Rawlings when I almost pierced your heart with an arrow?' Without waiting for a reply, she trotted over to the table and selected a bow. 'I missed on purpose you know; I didn't really intend on killing you then; it was just a warning.'

I laughed drolly. 'Really. And what about the incident with Gideon, when he was injured with an arrow meant for me?'

Her fingers ran along the arrowheads. 'Oh yes.' Without looking up she laughed. 'That was meant to kill you.' Selecting several arrows, she put them in her quiver and strode towards me. 'Sisterly love eh? Squabbling over a man, a man torn between two siblings, a man...' she paused and glowered at me. 'A man who chose the wrong sister.' Her eyes narrowed as she continued to stare cruelly at me. She opened her mouth to speak but nothing came out.

'Don't worry Verity. You found love with Septimus did you not?'

'Huh.' With a huff she strode across the room with her bow and positioned an arrow ready for aiming.' Hearing a sudden knocking on the door she growled for the person to enter.

Hector hovered nervously in the doorway before gradually inching his way into the room. 'I'm sorry to both you mistress but ...'

'What is it now?' She snapped impatiently before releasing an arrow into the centre of the target.

I watched as he took one step backwards, placing his hands together out in front of him as if in prayer. 'Well mistress.' He laughed uneasily. 'There's been more trouble in the kitchens.'

Without looking at him the mad woman continued her archery. 'Well then deal with it you stupid man. Do I have to get the guards to do everything for you?'

He let out his high- pitched giggle. 'Oh no mistress. I beg your pardon mistress but I really think it should be you who comes and talks to them.' A simpering smile spread across his face. 'There's been a fight between one of the newcomers and one of the tonic takers.' He turned and glanced at me. 'Don't worry Miss Farraday it wasn't your friend Clarice.'

The mad woman immediately lowered her bow and gazed into my face. 'So, the Clarice girl is your friend.' She paused and began tapping her finger gently over her lips. 'Interesting.' With a chuckle she briefly looked at Hector.

'Well at least you're good for something.' With a sigh she took another arrow from her quiver. 'These tonic takers are becoming a nuisance. Perhaps we should dispose of them.'

My face became alarmed. 'No.' I shouted. 'You can't get rid of them just because they're causing difficulty. They can't help being the way they are, they didn't choose to take the tonic.'

The mad woman ran the arrow through her fingers. 'No but they are not improving dear sister, and they never will. Perhaps the kindest thing would be to end their suffering.'

Hector cleared his throat. 'Could I make a suggestion mistress. Would it not be wise just to let them have the rowanberries, it would ease their minds and bodies.'

She scowled at him. 'No Hector it would not. If we allow the affected residents to once again take the tonic, there's a real risk of the normal occupants becoming addicted too.'

'But mistress-'

'Do not contradict me Hector.' She shrieked. 'I don't want your opinion and don't care for it.' With expert hands she swiftly placed an arrow in the bow. 'Now get out of my sight.'

My eyes flickered over to him. 'You should go Hector.' I smiled apprehensively.

As his shoulders slumped forward he turned and proceeded to the door, but he hesitated for a second then swung round, his voice raised. 'Things can't continue the way they are mistress.' He shook his head despondently. 'And I certainly can't carry on like this.'

The mad woman looked at him with a cool reserved smile.

'Oh, you won't have to my friend.'

With one rapid movement she swung round and brought the bow up to her shoulders, and pulling back the string she aimed at Hector and released it. I watched in horror as the arrow plunged into his chest. Crying out in agony he clutched the arrow with both hands and collapsed to the floor, groaning loudly.

'Hector.' I screamed. Rushing over towards him I knelt down and took his hand, staring into his panic-stricken eyes. 'You're going to be all right Hector.'

He began to cough, with a weak choking sound. 'Am I Miss?'

A loud cackle of laughter came close to my ear and I looked up to see the mad woman standing over us. 'Isn't he dead yet?'

'No.' I uttered coldly.

'Never mind. He will be soon.' She marched towards the door, and then stood within the entranceway, bawling up the passageway. 'Wilding, Craddock, get here this instant.'

There was a strange gurgling sound coming from Hector as he attempted to speak. His face looked swollen and red, and as a trickle of blood seeped from his mouth, I noticed his bloodshot eyes gradually glazing over.

I put my hand on his shoulder. 'It's okay Hector you don't have to talk.' I smiled at him. 'Imagine you're back in Briarwood.' I uttered, stroking his forehead. 'You're happy there.' My voice began to break up. 'Amongst all the fields, meadows and woodlands.' I gulped with emotion as I saw the tears run silently down his cheeks. 'With the sun on your face and the wind in your hair, and...and the delightful sound of birdsong.' My hand moved slowly from his brow and gently closed his eyes.

He was dead.

The mad woman strolled up to us and roughly nudged Hector with her foot. 'Finally.' She cried. 'The big lump has been silenced.'

'Leave him alone.' I yelled, shielding his body with mine. 'He meant you no harm, why did you have to kill him?' I glared up at her, trying not sob.

She nonchalantly shrugged her shoulders. 'I needed the target practice.' Her lips began to tremble as she tried to stifle her laughter. 'And Hector wasn't exactly a valued member of the monastery.' An expression of deep concern suddenly appeared across her face and she bent down beside me. 'I will however miss the scrumptious cakes he baked, as will the others.' Rising she patted her stomach. 'It's for the best though, now's not the time for me to put on weight.' Her eyes darted across the room as Craddock and Wilding came plodding over. 'Remove the body' She snapped her fingers at them. 'Take him to the feeding spot underneath the monastery.'

I glared up at the two brothers. 'No.' I cried sharply, protectively cradling Hector in my arms. 'For pity sake, at least allow him a proper burial.'

'Oh sister. That's hardly a practical solution now is it?' Her lips curled into a smile. 'The trees need nourishment and feeding on this bulk should curb their hunger for a while.' She gestured to the brothers.

Wilding placed his hand upon my shoulder. 'Come now Miss, move away.' He grabbed the cloth of my robes and pulled me back.

I sat on the floor and watched as the two of them roughly hoisted Hector up from the floor as if he was a sack of potatoes, and casually chatting between themselves they carried him towards the door. Craddock glanced at me and winked.

The mad woman looked down at the floor in disgust then called after the brothers.

'Tell Abel to come and clear the blood off the floor, will you. And see how he's progressing with removing the books from the library.' Her eyes flitted to mine. 'It needs to be completed by tomorrow.' Looking sternly down at me she held out her hand. 'Get up from the floor Effelia and go and change, your robes are stained in blood.'

Feeling the mad woman's hand as she pulled me up made my skin crawl, it was like touching some repugnant creature that wasn't human. Standing there face to face with her I wanted to drag her down into the bottomless pit of the afterlife, where she would burn in hell for all eternity. I hated her, I hated her with every fibre of my being.

After washing and changing I found a comb in a small cupboard in the bathroom, and knowing it had probably belonged to Proctor, I washed it with the bar of soap on the sink before using it. Feeling numb I glimpsed at my reflection in the tiny mirror. My eyes were red from crying and my skin still looked pallid through lack of sleep and natural sunlight. I sighed as I tried to untangle the knots from my long auburn hair, all the while trying to make the lifeless body of Hector disappear from my thoughts. With an irritated sigh I took a pair of scissors from the cupboard with the intention of cutting my hair short, but just as I put the scissors to my head I heard a faint tapping on the door.

'Noble.' I said quietly as I opened the door.

He swiftly came in and shut the door behind him. With a startled face he stared down at the pair of scissors clasped in my hand.

'I hope you're not planning on stabbing me with those?'

I looked at him blankly unable to muster a smile. 'No, I...I was going to cut my hair into a shorter style.'

His eyes ran over my hair. 'Why?' He laughed softly as he reached out and smoothed it over. 'Please don't do that Effie.' Holding my gaze for a moment he suddenly moved away and went into the bathroom then emerged again with the comb. 'It just needs a little taming that's all.' Gesturing for me to sit down on the chair he took the scissors from my hand and threw then onto the bed, then slowly he began untangling my hair with the comb.

'You heard about Hector?'

'Yes.' He murmured softly. 'I'm sorry to say I'm not surprised. He particularly aggravated Verity with his constant bickering.'

'Well that's hardly an excuse to murder him.'

'No. You're right.' he knelt down and titled my chin so I was looking at him. 'Are you okay? I'm sorry you had to witness that.'

As I held his gaze I couldn't answer straight away. His eyes were so compelling that it was difficult to focus. 'Yes, yes of course.' Lowering my head, I placed my hands on my lap and began drumming my fingers nervously on my robe. 'I'm stronger than I used to be Noble. With all that's happened recently, I've had to be. And of course, being a mother tends to make one grow up.'

Without a word he swiftly rose and continued combing in silence. In the peacefulness of the room the soothing sensation of having my hair touched was causing my eyelids to flicker. Sleep had been difficult the past two nights, and I suddenly felt deliriously tired.

'There.' He uttered running his fingers through my hair. 'Your locks are smooth and tangle free.' Taking a step in front of me he examined me closely. 'You look even more stunning with your hair down Effie.'

Without replying I stared at him before rising and moving across the room, avoiding his eye 'Thank you for doing my hair Noble. I need to get some rest now.'

There was an uncomfortable silence.

I heard the bolt being put across the inside of the door and as he came and put his arms about me, we both clambered onto the bed and fell asleep.

Chapter 16

In the hall that evening I stared ahead with a fixed expression, not focusing on anything or anyone in particular. The strain and shock of this morning in the archery room still lingered hauntingly in my mind, and despite several hours sleep this afternoon I still felt listless. Noble sat beside me, but I found myself unwilling to meet his eye, slightly embarrassed and a little guilty at how I allowed him to rest with me on the bed. It had all been entirely innocent of course, however it didn't stop my face from burning up with discomfort.

A shrill cackle from the mad woman made me jolt slightly on my seat and I reluctantly came back to reality. Several members of the kitchen staff were serving supper and my eyes brightened as I spotted Clarice heading towards us, with a trolley full of food. Without a word or glance, she compliantly laid out the supper on the tables and turned to go. But before she had a chance the mad woman grabbed her hand and began scrutinising her face and hair.

'How scruffy you are Clarice. Be sure to go and smarten yourself up.' She pursed her lips, contemplating her next words. 'I shall instruct one of the guards to give you another haircut.' With a light laugh she raised her eyebrows and glanced at me. 'It looks like she's been attacked with a pair of shears.' Looking once more at Clarice her face became serious. 'Now off with you.' she said sternly, releasing her hand and pushing it away. 'Back to where you belong.'

For literally a second, I saw a glint of anger in Clarice's eyes but then it dimmed like the fading flame of a flickering candle. I was somewhat relieved when she left with the trolley. It seemed apparent that the mad woman was deliberately trying to provoke my friend, so she had an excuse to get rid of her, one less tonic taker to deal with. However, it was also clear that she relished the idea of taunting me, whenever she had the chance. It was all a game to her, a game where everyone played by her rules, a game of life and death, where she was the hunter and everyone else was the prey.

I caught Noble's eye and he smiled uneasily before tucking into his meal.

The mad woman had her back to me and was engaging in conversation with Stephens and Trafford, who oddly enough had been invited to join us at the top table, along with the other residents who had caused trouble that day. 'This is a particularly special wine.' She exclaimed excitedly. 'I brought it up from the wine cellar especially for you my friends.' Her head turned towards me. 'I have to keep the room locked at all times just in case someone takes it upon themselves to go a wandering.' Widening her eyes in amusement she switched her attention back to Stephens and the others.

It seemed the mad woman knew all along what we were up to, and that's why we couldn't locate the spare key. She had moved it.

Watching Trafford suddenly roar with laughter I wondered how he could be so oblivious to what was happening. With increasing apprehension, I peered at the mad woman as she poured the liquid into each of their goblets.

Suddenly she stood up. 'Let's all raise our glasses to these fine fellows at the top table and show them that we mean them no harm.' As she gestured for everyone to rise, I noticed her staring intently at Stephens and the others. 'Drink up gentleman this wine is not to be savoured.'

There was a slight hesitation from Stephens but watching the others knock the drink back he placed his lips to the goblet and drank the lot, wiping the scarlet juice from his mouth. With a broad smile the mad woman re-filled their goblets before serenely sitting back down, watching and waiting in silence, as if aware something was about to happen.

I moved the large chunk of venison over to the side of my plate and smiled as Noble pierced it with his fork and moved it across to his place and started to cut it up in large bite size

158

chunks. I found it amusing how eagerly he stuffed one slice at a time into his mouth, in quick succession as if it was the last meal he was ever going to have. Forgetting where I was for a second, I began to giggle. He turned and stared at me in surprise, his broad mouth breaking into a glorious smile, displaying his perfect set of teeth. But as he looked over my shoulder his happy face disappeared. Before I even looked at the mad woman, I felt her hard venomous eyes boring into me, and as she began to scrape her steak knife down the table, I felt a chill sweep over my heart.

'One of The Elder Trees is a yew.' She said, rising abruptly from her seat. 'Can anyone tell me about this very special tree?' her eyes scanned the crowd. 'Oh, do come on, surely someone is knowledgeable about such things.'

Wilding stepped forward with a smirk. 'The yew tree has berries mistress, red berries. Birds I believe like em, as do squirrels. But no such creature lives around these parts, they wouldn't last, not with them trees.'

The mad woman looked agitated. 'Yes, yes Wilding. I'm sure we're all well aware of that.' She began to run her tongue across her lips. 'But what if a human was to consume the berries?'

He scoffed, shaking his head. 'They'd be goner's mistress. The berries are poison, and death is swift if eaten in large amounts.'

She stood there contemplating for a moment then glanced up at the clock on the far wall. 'And how long do you think it would take for the poison to be effective if the berries were crushed into a pulp then added to liquid.' She pursed her lips then took an intake of breath then exhaled. 'Let's say for instance- a glass of wine.'

Wilding scratched his head. 'I don't rightly know. But I reckon ten minutes should to the trick.'

Several residents began to murmur between themselves and Stephens and the others suddenly looked nervous. I noticed one of them started to cough.

The mad woman swung round and stared at the men. 'Well, from my calculation the poison in your systems should start to do its job about now.' She began cackling as the men stared back at her open mouthed. 'Sorry gentlemen but your time is nearly up. Several residents lost their lives collecting those berries so at least show us that they didn't die in vain.'

Trafford suddenly lurched forward in his seat with a groan, clutching his stomach. Another of the men collapsed to the floor and began writhing about in agony, closely followed by another. Stephens however stumbled to his feet and made a beeline for the mad woman, holding out his hands as if to grab her neck. With a laugh she shoved him and he toppled onto the table in front of us, his eyes, red and bulging.

'Guards- remove these men this instant. Let them finish dying in the caverns. How pleased The Elder Trees will be tonight, to have such a feast.'

Several of the guards came forward with Craddock and Wilding, and muttering to one another they hauled the men from the hall. Raised voices came from the throng of people at the tables, and many looked shocked and frightened.

The mad woman clapped her hands loudly in the air. 'Simmer down everyone. I would advise you to stay seated, unless you too would like some special wine made from yew tree berries.' She stood there and carefully scrutinized the faces of the crowd. 'Those men who died here tonight did so for the greater good of Hartland. Disobedience of any kind will not be tolerated; it causes disruption and spreads fear amongst us. So, stay strong dear people and your loyalty will very soon be rewarded.

Lying on my bed that night I suddenly wondered what was wrong with me, why hadn't I warned those men that they were about to die? I suddenly hated myself for being so unresponsive and heartless. I'd just sat there whilst my best friend was cruelly teased, and said nothing to Stephens and the others as they drank their wine, knowing that it was poisoned. Once upon a time I would have used my shyness for an excuse, I would have been too scared to bring attention to myself, especially in a room full of people. However, things were different now, there was no longer an impenetrable wall holding me back. Nevertheless sometimes, when I least expected, that wall would creep back up, for although it was now a manageable obstacle, it would never truly go away. But as I lay there staring wistfully up at the ceiling, I realised that any sane person would have trouble acting normal in such an environment. I likened myself to a detached onlooker who was merely there to observe; I knew what was happening but didn't want to believe it. After all this was a land that should only exist in a storybook, it was too sinister to be real.

My thoughts turned to Noble, and suddenly all I could see was his face. My feelings for him had been carefully locked away, deep within my heart, where they remained safe and out of reach. But seeing him again had sent my emotions into turmoil. I told myself that my loyalty to Gideon should and would always be paramount; we were bound to one another through the sanctity marriage and I wouldn't allow anything to damage or destroy it. And yet laying there in the coldness of the room I came to a sudden realisation, a realisation that I believe I had known all along: I loved Gideon, and I always would, but I felt exactly the same way about Noble, and there was nothing I could do to convince myself otherwise.

When I eventually drifted off, I dreamt of Septimus. He emerged from the shadows of the afterlife, his face horribly contorted, and his pure white eyes glaring down at me, wide and frightening. With his skeletal finger he pointed down at me. Then I saw the blood, my blood seeping slowly from my body and onto the blanket, until the entire bed had become drenched in scarlet.

That morning after breakfast I found myself being taken through the greenhouses by Craddock and Wilding and towards the chapel.

'What's happening?'

'You'll see soon enough Miss.' Said Craddock giving me a little push through the doors.'

I heard muffled laughter from the two brothers behind me.

The mad woman was standing beside the altar in a flowing cloak. She turned as we entered; her eyes gleaming.

'Effelia, I'm so glad you're here to witness this auspicious occasion.'

'What occasion?

She unbuttoned the tiny clasp at the front of her neck and the heavy cloak slid to the ground. Underneath she wore an off the shoulder gown of pure white sheen that clung about the bodice. I suddenly noticed the style of her hair; it was piled on top of her head with a few wispy strands falling onto her bare shoulders. Apart from the usual coldness in her eyes she looked elegant and glowing, as any bride should be on her wedding day.

'You're getting married.'

A faint smile hovered around her lips. 'How observant of you dear sister.'

'And who is the groom?' I already knew the answer, but didn't want to believe it. Perhaps she had someone else stashed away, a lover who had already asked her to marry her.

'Well Noble of course, who else.'

'Are...are you sure?'

'Oh yes Effelia. It would have been Gideon but you already stole him from me. You should have seen the hurt in Noble's eyes when I informed him you'd definitely married his brother.' She gloomily shook her head. 'He was almost heartbroken.' She strode forward and stared into my face. 'But Noble's over that now and he's going to be mine.'

'Why does it have to be Noble?'

'Well why not. He's handsome and honourable, and rather more volatile than Gideon, do you not think? But that's part of his appeal.' She laughed mischievously. 'And I know you will be eaten up with envy.'

I could feel hot tears of indignation burning bright within my eyes.

She smiled self-righteously at me. 'Lost for words are we dear sister?'

Why oh why did it have to be Noble she married. I wouldn't have minded anyone else, just not him. I always imagined him settling down with a young woman from Briarwood, that's the way it should be, the way it was supposed to be, whether I liked it or not. But instead he would be stuck in purgatory for the rest of his days at Hartland, until his villainous wife became tired of him and ended his life.

Hearing raised voices at the entranceway I spotted Noble and Craddock discussing something, and then Craddock ushered him forward rather impatiently. Wilding came in too, his burly figure guarding the entranceway.

Noble stared from me to Verity, his face looking completely baffled. 'I...I don't understand.' He turned back to glance at the guards. 'Craddock tells me there is to be a wedding.'

'Yes, my love.' Uttered the mad woman. 'Our wedding.' She beamed with delight, as any bride would do. 'Do come forward and join me at the altar.'

He stared blankly at her before stumbling forward.

'Oh, do come on Noble.' she snapped. With a huff she strode forward and took his arm, forcing him up to the altar as if he didn't have a say in the matter. 'We haven't got all day.' With an impatient laugh she shoved passed me. 'Effelia has agreed to be my bridesmaid.'

I steadied myself against the pew. 'No, I most certainly have not.'

'I insist on it dear sister.' Reaching over to the front pew she produced a bouquet of dried flowers and shoved them in my hands. 'Here, at least have these.'

My eyes grew wide with astonishment. 'This is ridiculous.'

'Hold your tongue sister, before I have it removed.' Turning her attention back to Noble she roughly grabbed his chin and jerked it round so he was facing the altar.

He glared fiercely at the mad woman. 'Why didn't you tell me you were arranging this Verity?'

'I wanted it to be surprise my love.' She squealed with laughter. 'I know how you love surprises.' Taking his hand, he held it over the bible on the stone slab and began uttering the wedding vows.

I had an overwhelming urge to run up and drag him away from her, to implore him not to go ahead with this farce, but instead I stood rigidly against the pew, digging my nails into my clenched palms until they bled.

With a deep sigh he released her hand. 'I am truly sorry Verity but I cannot marry you. Had I'd been aware of your plans for today then certainly I would have warned you of how I felt.'

The colour drained from her face and her eyes became large and staring.

'You will marry me Noble. I command you to.'

I watched as a surly Craddock and Wilding suddenly came up behind us, their bulky arms folded across their chests.

Noble looked furiously at the mad woman. 'I am not your property and you cannot command me to do anything.' His eyes flickered to mine for a mere second before looking back at her. 'And then there is love.'

'Love?'

'I cannot commit myself to marrying someone I do not love. It would be sacrilege.'

For a moment she did not move, then without warning she flung herself forward into Noble arms. 'You'll grow to love me, I promise you. And the children we will have, you always wanted a large family didn't you my love.'

'No.' Gently but firmly he removed her arms and stepped back. 'That won't happen Verity. Not with me.'

She laughed a little, before turning her gaze upon me. 'You had a soft spot for my sister, did you not? Please don't tell me you still love her.'

My eyes darted to Noble, but he failed to return my stare.

'No of course not. You seem to forget she is married to my brother Gideon.'

She studied his face carefully, trying to decide if what he said was true. 'Then is there another you love?'

'No, there is no one.'

Taking a step towards him she placed a hand on his chest. 'Oh Noble, what a disappointment you've turned out to be.' She uttered in a quiet subdued voice. 'Such a terrible waste.' Her mouth moved over his face, caressing it softly before landing on his lips.

Noble pushed her away. 'Leave me be Verity.'

'You never objected to me kissing you before.'

He glanced at me before looking down at the ground.

'That's before I'd witnessed the true extent of your wickedness; how can I wed someone who deems human life to be so worthless.' He eyed her up and down in disgust. 'You utterly repulse me.'

Her eyes gazed icily into his. 'If that's how you feel then you are of no further use to me.' Her voice rose considerably louder as she clicked her fingers. 'Guards, take him away.'

Craddock and Wilding strode up to Noble. 'Where shall we take him mistress Verity?'

'Throw him in the cells for tonight. He shall be executed at dawn tomorrow.'

Noble's eyes met mine, widening in alarm.

Any dignity I might have been holding onto completely vanished.

'No. You can't.' I said in a screaming voice. Tossing my bouquet onto the floor, I barged my way between the guards and shielded Noble with my body. 'Please Verity I beg you, don't hurt him.'

Realisation flooded into her face. 'So, you do care for him.' Sniggering, she waved her finger in front of my face. 'What would your precious Gideon say?' She signalled to Craddock who firmly took my arm and led me away from Noble.

'Take me instead. Just leave Noble alone. Allow him to return to Briarwood.'

Suggesting such a thing was completely irrational but I couldn't help myself, I wasn't thinking straight.

'Don't say such things Effie.' Said Noble, his expression bleak. 'It's not your place to interfere in such matters.' Lowering his head, he strolled forward and brushed passed me. 'Now let's get out of this place.' With a fleeting grin he swiftly grabbed my hand and we charged towards the doors before the guards had a chance to grab us.

'Get them you imbeciles.' The mad woman bellowed.

A surge of excitement coursed through me but was rapidly replaced with dread as we spotted another man guarding the doors. Noble struck him in the face and he went sprawling to the floor, face downwards. But as we went to open the door, we realised it was locked.

Craddock and Wilding had reached the door, their smug faces grinning at us.

'Looking for this?' Asked Wilding waving a key in the air.

The mad woman began screeching with laughter. 'Take Noble away and bring my sister over to me.'

Noble struck Craddock with an almighty force, his fist catching him underneath the chin. The guard lost his footing and stumbled backwards against the wall, knocking the back of his head. As Wilding went to attack him, Noble grasped his neck and rammed his body against the door, wrenching the key from his hand. His eyes darted to mine as he handed me the key. 'Quickly Effie unlock the door.'

As I struggled to get the key in the lock something seized my waist in a vice like grip, and turning I saw it was Craddock, his face twisted into a smirk. As his body pressed up against mine, I dug and clawed at his hands then, with all my force, kicked backwards into his legs. He yelped like an animal and released his hold before coming for me again, his face contorted with rage. My eyes darted to Noble who was raining punches down on Wilding. With a sly smile Craddock lurched forward and grabbed my waist again, pulling me up against him. I tilted my body back and began tearing at his face with my nails, causing him to cry out in pain. As he wrenched my hands away, he lifted me up with ease and began swinging me around, and with an almighty growl he threw me across the chapel towards the mad woman, where I landed awkwardly on my back. As Noble briefly glanced over and shouted my name, Wilding brought his leg up and kicked him hard in the stomach, sending him sprawling backwards. He managed to scramble to his feet but the guards were already upon him; Craddock grabbed Noble's shoulders and neck whilst Wilding began punching him hard in the face and stomach.

I gasped in horror.

'Enough.' The mad woman roared, glowering at the guards with a steely gaze.

Looking decidedly disgruntled, Craddock released Noble and he collapsed to the floor.

'Well that was all very entertaining.' She said. 'And it got the both of you precisely nowhere, didn't it Effie?' Looking down at me she clutched a handful of my hair and roughly pulled me up. 'How dare you try and run away.' She brought her hand up and smacked me hard about the face.

'Leave her alone Verity.' Noble yelled in a hoarse voice, his face swollen and red. 'If you lay one more finger on Effie I swear I shall kill you.' He tried to rise but was kicked hard in the face by Craddock.

'Noble.' I screamed, as he lay motionless on the floor, his face covered in blood.

'Well I'm sure Effelia thinks that's valiant of you Noble.' The mad woman uttered with a cruel laugh. 'But I hardly think you'll be in the position to kill me now or when you're hanging by your neck with your body looking completely gruesome and lifeless.' She doubled over with laughter before shifting her gaze to the guards. 'Now get this man out of my sight. And make sure you chain him up.'

The guards grabbed his arms and heaved his unconscious frame from the floor.

'Please Verity.' I cried distraughtly. 'Don't allow this to happen...I... I shall do anything you wish of me.' With my eyes blinded by tears I stumbled towards Noble. 'He doesn't deserve to die.'

The mad woman grabbed my arm, pulling me back. 'Oh, don't be so melodramatic dear sister. You'll meet Noble soon enough...in heaven.'

As Craddock and Wilding began hauling Noble towards the entranceway, he regained consciousness for a moment and fixed his gaze upon mine, his eyes tender and loving. But then a dark cloud came over his face, a haunting despairing look of a man who knew he was about to die.

Chapter 17

My room had become my prison, even during supper they wouldn't let me out. I'm not sure how long I sat on the floor staring into the darkness. I wanted my mind to disconnect from reality as that would mean I wouldn't need to face the fact that Noble was about to die, it was too horrific. I hauled myself up and took the rosary beads from the vase, and crawling onto the bed I curled into a ball and closed my eyes; I began to pray like I'd never prayed before, the beads tightly clutched between my fingers. Wallowing in my torment I fell asleep.

Come morning I could hardly lift my head from the pillow. My sleep had been restless and several times I'd cried out in anguish. I crossed over to the bathroom and splashed my face with ice- cold water. Having a soak in the bath would have been preferable but I was too fretful to do anything; it wouldn't be right, not when someone I cared very deeply about had just been executed, or was about to be.

Breakfast had been a painful ordeal. Every time I glanced at Noble's empty seat beside me, I wanted to cry. The mad woman was unusually silent and every so often would eye me curiously to see my expression. She was waiting for me to break down in front of everyone; it would bring her joy to see me suffer. But I wouldn't give her the satisfaction. I would save my tears for later, in the quietness of my room.

As we were leaving the hall, she grabbed my arm. 'Come Effelia, allow me to show you the oldest part of the monastery.' She led me along endless passages then down a steep flight of steps until we reached a large door. 'This is where the wine cellar is Effelia.' Smiling she unlocked it and we entered a room full of dusty wine bottles, stacked neatly in their racks. 'Don't loiter sister. There's nothing interesting to see here.' Selecting another key from the chain around her belt we descended an extremely long spiral staircase, finally arriving in a large cave like hall.

'How much further?' I asked wearily.

'Not long Effelia, not long at all. What we are entering now is the most interesting part of the monastery. I stumbled across it whilst I was investigating. Can you believe that even Septimus knew nothing of its existence?'

I glanced around at the tapestries hanging from the walls; they had faded with age and looked rather moth-eaten. Draped across the floor was a large rug.

'Perhaps he couldn't get down here. He was after all not in the best of health.'

She let out an undignified grunt.

'Where do we go now? I asked curiously. 'There doesn't appear to be any other rooms.'

'Ah ha.' She exclaimed with glee. 'That's exactly what I thought but on closer inspection I discovered this.' Leaning forward she removed part of the rug, exposing a trap door. With a heave she pushed the wooden door back and jumped into the opening, disappearing from sight. 'Well come on Effelia. You're supposed to follow me you imbecile.'

I frowned. For a moment I was tempted to walk off and leave her. Perhaps I could find something heavy to put over the door, then she'd be trapped down there for all eternity, and I'd never have to look upon her repugnant face again. But *if* the mirror was down there, it would be my only means of escape, and the only chance I had to regain my sanity.

'Effelia.' She yelled sharply. 'I haven't got all day you know.'

I dangled my legs into the opening and jumped down. To my horror I came face to face with the mad woman. We were huddled together in such close proximity that I became panicked.

'Over here.'

I followed her through a small dark opening that we literally had to clamber into, before going down another set of steps. When we'd reached the bottom my first reaction when I glanced around was pure awe. We were standing in a magnificent church. It was much larger than your average place of worship, and in fact reminded me of a cathedral. The immense building had decorative symbols chiselled into the ceiling and endless rows of magnificent arches ran along the outer walls. There were great pillars that towered above us like giant statues flanking the pews. And at the very end of the building in the direct centre stood a gold altar.

'Breath-taking isn't it?'

'Yes.' I answered. 'It's truly splendid.'

I gave the mad woman a sideways glance and for one moment imagined we were just two sisters on a day out, enjoying the sights. We would spend an hour or two strolling casually around the cathedral before going for tea and cakes in the café by the cloisters. Then we would visit the little gift shop and purchase a small gift and a postcard with picture of the cathedral drawn in black ink. It was something that would never happen, not with her, but nevertheless I found it rather funny in a warped kind of way.

'Why are you staring at me Effelia, what is wrong with you?'

My eyes shot away from her. 'Nothing.' I bit down on my lip. 'Why do you suppose this place is hidden underground?

'Perhaps the monks needed a place of sanctuary. This church is a key symbol of their way of life, and a place that needed to be preserved.'

'Safe from the trees, you mean.' I said dryly. 'Surely they can't reach down here.'

'No.' she replied bluntly. 'They cannot.' Gesturing for me to follow her she strolled along the aisle and pointed over to the far left where several granite tombs were laid out. 'The original monks were buried here.' She turned and gave me an odd kind of look. 'They're still here, can you feel their presence Effelia? Even in death they walk amongst the living.'

I lowered my eyes to the ground. 'What's happened to Noble?' I took a deep breath and looked into her face. 'He...he hasn't really been executed, has he?'

She looked puzzled for a moment, studying my face closely. 'I was wondering when you'd pluck up the courage to ask me. Noble was strung up from one of the rafters in the games room at dawn this morning.' With a sweep of her hand she brushed her hair from her face. 'I would have allowed you to pay your respects but the guards took him down below for the trees.'

With a harrowing gasp I collapsed to my knees and buried my face in my hands. I felt as if my heart had been wrenched from my chest and replaced with a burning piece of coal.

'Oh, pull yourself together Effelia.' She yelled callously. 'I was rather enjoying our little venture before you mentioned his name, and now your happy mood has vanished and it will be all doom and gloom.' She hesitantly placed the tip of her finger on my shoulder. 'I know it's painful but believe me it's for the best. Noble was too much of a distraction for both of us, and now that he's gone, we can both focus on what's important.' She laughed rather flippantly. 'I've actually done you a favour.'

'What?' I uttered in disbelief.

'Well, your feelings for Noble will no longer cloud your judgement. In time you will forget him and be free to concentrate on your family.'

I struggled to my feet and forced myself to look at her.

'How like your father you are Verity, cold and heartless, ready to dispose of anyone who gets in your way.'

She blatantly she stared back at me, her dark eyes as dead as the night. 'So, what's wrong with that?'

'Have you ever stopped to wonder how many innocent lives you have taken Verity, and as a result how many families you've destroyed? Time may ease their pain but they'll never forget, their grief will be with them until the very end.'

She widened her eyes in fury. 'Have you quite finished your rant Effelia?'

'No.' I shouted, stepping towards her.

I watched as she leant back against a large statuette of a kneeling Madonna.

'You murdered Septimus didn't you?'

171

'Oh, Effelia really, that's cruel. It was a mercy killing -my poor husband's health was fading fast, and towards the end he was in constant pain. So, I plunged a knife into his chest and clasped my hand across his mouth and nose. He didn't put up much of a struggle, he was happy to finally depart this life. I sat and watched as the light gradually faded from within his eyes. It was a poignant moment that very nearly brought a tear to my eye.' She smiled.

'What did you do with the body?'

'I gave it to The Elder Trees. That's what he would have wanted. Then I told everyone he had died peacefully in his sleep. Of course, that busybody Proctor would have none of it. That vile woman would constantly go around the monastery spreading vicious rumours about me, saying how I'd murdered her beloved Septimus and how I'd only married him to gain control of Hartland.' She scoffed. 'I soon put a stop to that.'

'But Proctor was right, wasn't she?

'It wasn't a question if she was right or wrong Effelia.' She snapped indignantly. 'I'm sure the woman did it out of spite, you know. She was half in love with Septimus and couldn't handle the fact that he preferred me to her.' Her eyes flicked to mine. 'She was eaten up with bitterness and hate.'

I moved across to the long row of glass cases up against the far wall and pretended to look at the contents. My eyes swiftly scanned the various artefacts carefully displayed on a green velvet cloth, only half taking in what was there. There were several ornate daggers that caught my eye, and I noticed that one was missing. Out of the corner of my eye I saw her watching me, as if waiting for me to make a comment, or ask her another question.

'And how did you discover the ledger?' I asked, turning away from the cases.

'When I visited father in the crypts at Briarwood church, he told me you had it, so that night I came over to Caleb's, just before you left for Hartland, I searched your room, but couldn't find it. It wasn't until your return to the village that father communicated to me where the ledger was located.'

'But how, he was locked in the monastery cells?'

'By projecting himself through the power of the mind, silly.' She giggled. 'Alas our father isn't very good at focusing for very long, and it was barely a minute he was with me, but long enough to tell me the ledger was hidden away in the church behind that ghastly family portrait of yours. Without delay I rode with the book to Hartland on my eagle and confronted Septimus, and we came to the agreement that father could go free in return for the ledger. My only stipulation was that I be allowed to study the ledger whilst I remained at the monastery. In no time at all Septimus and I became extremely close.'

I laughed. 'I thought he was wise.'

'Even wise men seek love Effelia. And besides he was old and lonely.'

'Do you not think you took advantage of him in his old age?'

'Oh, most certainly. There's no fool like an old fool dear sister. Anyway, in a matter of weeks we were married and I could finally put the initial stages of my grand plan into place by becoming the ruler of Hartland.'

'Which you did so by disposing of your husband.'

'Septimus was a weak leader Effelia. He was rigidly set in his ways and truly believed that the tonic was the key to a controlled environment. But the residents either had a bad reaction to the medicine or became so incredibly dull that I just couldn't see the point of it all.' She laughed ironically. 'Of course, at the time I didn't realise that the tonic takers would become aggressive without their daily dose.'

'And what about the ledger, Septimus must have been keen to discover if it did indeed hold the key to eternal life.'

'Yes, but he was too eager. The mere idea of spending an eternity with a man such as Septimus made me shudder. So, I had to do something quick

I stared into her hard face. 'You didn't like him very, much did you?'

She gave me a knowing smile. 'Between you and I dear sister- I detested the revolting man. Noble on the other hand would have been a delight. Such as shame he had to die.' Her hand reached up to wipe an imaginary tear from her eye. 'Never mind eh?

An unbearable ache gripped my heart.

'Come.' She uttered, guiding me firmly by the hand. 'Let me show you the mirror.' As we went to the right of the grand altar, she unlocked the door to a small prayer room with stained glass windows and rows of benches around the walls. In the very centre stood the mirror. The frame was elaborately decorated with cherubs, beautifully carved into the wood, their little faces staring adoringly towards the glass.

She extended her arm towards the mirror. 'Your home awaits dear sister.'

As though compelled by an unknown force I took a few paces towards it. My family and home were so close now I could almost see them. It would be just like stepping from a room of nightmare into a room of joy. And after I had returned the mirror would be destroyed, for I would take a hammer and smash into tiny pieces. Only then would I feel safe, only then could I carry on living.

The mad woman's hand gripped my upper arm. 'No Effelia, not yet.' She said as if scolding a child.

'Why do you taunt me so?' I said through gritted teeth.

'Because that's what big sisters do.' She giggled. 'And it's so much fun.'

'I always wanted an older sister, but she wouldn't be remotely like you.' I swung round and glared at her. 'No one is like you.'

'Well thank you Effelia, I shall take that as a compliment.' Still holding my arm, she tugged me away from the mirror. 'Poor you eh. You must be desperate to see tiny Gabriel and that handsome husband of yours.' Her eyes narrowed with amusement. 'But then you have been distracted now haven't you, by the other handsome brother- God rest his soul.'

With an impulsive movement I tore away from her hand and blindly lunged for the mirror. Her hand grabbed the back of my hair and yanked my head back so I was looking up into her face.

'Older sisters are stronger Effelia, and also more astute. If you'd succeeded in jumping through that mirror in your present state of mind, you'll end up permanently lost between worlds.' She roughly pulled my head down further, tearing some hair from the roots. 'Is that really what you wish for you impetuous idiot?' You know I cannot allow you to leave, not yet anyway.'

'But why on earth not, what could you possibly need me for?'

With a great sigh she released my hair and shoved my head forward, causing me to stagger across the church. 'Let's go and view the paintings, shall we?'

I spotted the row of canvases along the wall each depicting distinguished looking monks. Unlike the paintings in the mad woman's room these one remained intact. There wasn't anything unusual about them, and as she watched me closely, I wondered what I was supposed to be looking for.

'Very nice.' I said in a low voice. 'You haven't ruined these paintings yet I see.'

A tiny stone landed at my feet, and I wondered if Lucinda was about.

She sniggered. 'Unlike the others these portraits actually hold some value. They show each and every monk that originally founded the monastery.' Her gown rustled along the stone floor as she came closer. 'You can see by the quality of the colours that these were painted by a proper artist, unlike those of your mothers.'

'Perhaps you're just envious that both my mother and I can paint.' I forced myself to look into her eyes. 'Have you even as much as lifted a paint brush Verity?'

She scoffed at me. 'Why would I when I possess far greater talents. Besides, a dagger and letter knife vastly improved the paintings in my room, especially the one of Septimus with the added addition of the arrow.'

'Why did you remove them all from the study?'

'Honestly Effelia, haven't you been told anything?'

I hesitated and shrugged my shoulders.

Her eyes flickered away from me. 'There was an incident involving the trees. I'd instructed several residents to clear out my late husband's desk. One of the idiots must have stupidly flung back the curtains and opened the windows. All this activity must have alerted the trees. As night fell, I decided to send Abel to go and check up on them, to see why they were taking so long. The room had practically been ripped apart, with the windows smashed and no one in sight.' She stifled a laugh. 'The only human remains were a severed hand on the rug. I took the paintings and had the room boarded up for safety.'

'How very awful.' I muttered underneath my breath.

'Yes, it was rather.' She chuckled. 'I really liked that study.'

I glared at her, deciding there was little point answering her back, only people with a heart had a conscience.

I turned away from her penetrating stare. 'You've showed me the church and the location of the mirror, and as you have no intention of allowing me to travel home, we might as well go back.'

'No, not quite yet.'

'Why ever not?'

'This is a church Effelia, and I must perform the sermon.' She casually went over to the pulpit and stepped up onto the platform. 'This is one of the discoveries I made whilst rifling through the building.' She bent down and produced a heavy looking book, thumping it down onto the wood. 'It makes for much more interesting reading than those dull books in the library.'

I began to cough as particles of dust went flying towards me.

'Do take a pew.'

'I'd much rather stand, thank you.'

'Suit yourself dear sister.' With a smug smile she opened the book and selected a page. 'Just in case you're curious, it's a diary. I've already read the relevant parts and can remember it word by word.'

'Then why are you referring to the book?'

She raised her arms and reached them out towards me. 'I thought you might find it amusing for me to stand up here and pretend to preach from a book, rather than just telling you.' Her nose wrinkled as she shook her head. 'To be brutally honest Effelia, you wouldn't understand the book, it's too complex for you. So, I shall tell you in story form, rather like a fairy tale I would tell to Gabriel.'

I stood rigid and still. 'However, you like Verity, I really don't care.'

'Once upon a time the kingdom of Hartland was discovered by a group of holy men known as monks. Together with their many followers they went about building their monastery, having faith that they would all live happily ever after. One bright sunny day five of the Brothers planted the great Elder Trees in a field behind the monastery, believing it to be a sacred and medieval spot. One such monk was Brother Carmichael, a peculiar looking young man who was naïve and very foolish, so foolish in fact that he took it upon himself to fall in love with one of the nuns from a nearby convent. Knowing there would be dire consequences if they were ever caught, they decided to flee under the cover of darkness with only the moon to guide them, and stole away into the night to start a new life together.'

She hesitated for a moment, drumming her fingers on the book.

'And?' I asked impatiently, trying to work out where this was leading.

'Oh, I don't know.' She shrugged her shoulders and slammed the book shut. 'They probably got married and had lots of children, in fact it is a certainty that they had at least one.'

With a strange fascination I watched as she produced my ledger from the pocket of her dress.

'Recognise this?' She asked with a knowing smile as she descended the pulpit and crossed over towards me. 'It holds more secrets than you can ever imagine.' Standing before me she opened it at a marker towards the end of the book. 'It states here that to begin the ritual one must procure the blood of a planter.' Rather abruptly she shoved the book in front of my nose, stabbing with her finger at the handwritten scrawl.

'A planter?' I exclaimed, unable to read the scribbled words.

She raised her eyes and scowled at me. 'If you silence your tongue for a few minutes I can explain.'

With a sigh I trudged over to one of the pews and wearily leant back. As the mad woman began to speak, I did my best to listen attentively, but her words sounded rather like an echo as my mind struggled to stay focused. She reiterated how the five monks planted the trees and how one of these monks went against his vows to God and left the monastery in disgrace. These monks became known as the planters, and they alone could control The Elder Trees. As the years slipped passed and the trees grew strong and began claiming lives, there was an increasing unease amongst the Brothers. Many feared the planters had created monsters and urged them to destroy the trees, before it was too late. But it was argued that The Elder Trees brought great strength to the land and were sacred to the monastery. Finally, it was decided that the trees should be saved, and any monks going against this decision would be forced to stand before the trees and face the consequences. One day a certain monk presented the Brothers with a book that he'd compiled, along with manuscripts that showed evidence of how The Elder Trees could become so powerful that their branches could completely wipe out the entire universe. Hartland would be the only land standing, and would become a kingdom of almighty wisdom and capability, bestowing upon its worshippers the gift of immortality. The five planters were so horrified at such an idea that they immediately ordered the book and all of the manuscripts to be destroyed. But somehow the book mysteriously disappeared before it could be burnt. And now it was in her possession, thanks to me.

My eyelids began to flicker and I felt my head lolling forward sleepily.

She walloped me across the head with the back of her hand.

'Pay attention Effelia, this is hardly the right time for a nap.'

I was suddenly reminded of one of my old school teachers, who would throw chalk at pupils who weren't concentrating on the lesson, or were dozing in their chairs. She had a grim and authoritative tone to her voice, and her steely glare was so intimidating and fearsome that the entire class loathed her. Mace used to joke she was a witch in disguise, and that if we didn't watch out, we'd be turned into frogs.

'I can't help feeling tired.' I murmured. I glared up at her as she stood over me threateningly. 'And besides, Septimus has already explained about the ending of all worlds Verity, before you brutally murdered him.'

'Not everything Effelia.' Her lips curled into a nasty smile. 'You haven't heard the best bit yet.'

'Does it have something to do with this Brother Carmichael, the monk who went against his sacred oath, is he at the centre of what you're trying to tell me?'

With a smiling compliment she reached out and patted my shoulder. For a moment her eyes almost softened, but then that familiar callous look crept across them, as if some evil presence was controlling her. 'Well done Effelia. Perhaps you're not such of a dunce after all.'

Choosing to ignore her comment I returned to our conversation. 'Are you saying that Brother Carmichael has a living descendant, and that you know who it is?' I caught sight of her face and my heart began to thump violently in my chest. 'You think it's me, don't you.' I laughed with an edge of nervousness. 'Please tell me I'm wrong Verity.'

For a while she stood there, quietly laughing, deliberately keeping me in suspense.

'You deserve a merit Effelia for such an effort.' She drew in a deep breath then slowly exhaled. Kneeling down beside me she took my hand in hers. 'So, when we have the ritual I will have to take a little of your blood. It shouldn't be too painful.' Her face came horribly close to mine. 'Although I'm not entirely sure how much blood is required, rather annoyingly it doesn't state the quantity in the ledger. So it may be a case of completely draining your blood, until there's hardly a drop

179

left.' Her expression looked suddenly contrite. 'Sorry about that dear sister.'

The church suddenly became dreamlike and distance as I drifted away from reality. Shifting away from the mad woman I rose and staggered rather unsteadily towards the portraits. As I came to the very last one, slightly set apart from the rest, I immediately realised that this must be Brother Carmichael. He was an ordinary looking young man with a pallid complexion and short auburn hair that framed his face with soft curls, rather like a halo. I observed how his green eyes glimmered, filled with animation and hope for the future; but there was also a deep shadow within them, an uncertainty of some sorts. Although it seemed we shared certain similarities it was hardly proof that we had the same bloodline, in fact the whole idea was ludicrous.

'Well?' Exclaimed the mad woman with vivid interest. 'Do you see it?'

'No.' I replied bluntly. 'Having the same hair and eye colour is hardly evidence that the two of us are related.' I said mockingly.

She was standing directly behind me now, like a forbidding shadow ready to whisper something frightful in my ear. 'Look at the hands Effelia.'

As my eyes drifted downwards, I noticed how the Brother clasped his hands neatly in his lap, just like me. There was a chain dangling through his fingers, with what appeared to be a locket attached. As I peered closer to the painting my breath caught in my mouth.

'It's a brooch Effelia. The brooch you stole from my room, the brooch I took from Aunt Constance's jewellery box. If you had bothered to look on the back you'd see it has an engraving – G A Carmichael.' She stood beside me, gazing at the portrait. 'I'll allow you to keep the brooch, it is after all a family heirloom of yours.'

I moved away, shaking my head. 'But you said that these planters had control over the trees. If…if what you say is true and I am a descendant of Brother Carmichael then what about that day at The Giver ceremony, the trees took me away and were going to kill me.'

'But they didn't kill you did they Effelia. Not when they realised who you were. Do you not think it strange how you succeeded in escaping their clutches more than once, how you've managed to be saved right at the last moment? The truth dear sister is that Gideon didn't save you from the trees; it was *you* who saved him. Without your presence on the day of the ceremony he would have been snatched away and devoured, along with that gawky friend of yours Mace.'

'You weren't there Verity. How can you be certain of what occurred?'

'My dearly departed husband told me the whole story before he passed away. My suspicions were alerted when he said how peculiar it was that the trees didn't harm you. I at once took it upon myself to solve this intriguing mystery, and was elated when I discovered you were a descendant of Brother Carmichael.' She hugged me tightly in excitement. 'How does it feel dear sister, to know your blood can make the ending of all worlds become a reality?' When she spoke again her voice was soft and lulling. 'Fear not Effelia, our wait is nearly over. Tomorrow evening it will happen, when the moon is at its highest. And afterwards we shall celebrate the creation of our new and improved world, and rejoice at our immortality.'

I was still gazing at the portrait, however now I was staring right through it into nothing. My mind had become disconnected from reality, like last night in the great hall, only now it hadn't just become separated but was floating far away to some distant land, where I couldn't seek it, and had no wish to.

Chapter 18

I sat numbly in the wicker chair in my room twirling the brooch around in my hands. The mad woman was right, it was engraved on the back with the name of my so- called ancestor. Whether I chose to believe this nonsensical belief or not didn't really matter, she was going to drain my blood either way, probably to the death. What a sorry state of affairs this all was, how much misery and heartache could one person take. The death of Noble played heavy on my heart and conscience, I would mourn his passing every single day for the rest of my life, however short it may be. And what about Gideon and Gabriel, would I ever see them again? Before I had been dragged back to Hartland, I had dared to believe the path of life was finally smooth, with a clear horizon beyond, and now...now the way was blocked with the mad woman, that evil being that foolishly believed some twisted fable could really become true. My choices were clear- I could either turn and flee back down the path, or go forward and face her head on, until the death.

I must have drifted off to sleep and only awoke when I heard the evening bell chime like a dull echo in the distance. As someone turned the key and unlocked the door I hurriedly scrambled up from the bed and stumbled to my feet.

'Evening Miss Farraday.'

I stared blearily into the eyes of Craddock.

'What do you want Craddock?'

He grinned at me. 'Supper is served Miss.' with a sickly smile he smoothed back his straggly hair and held out his arm. 'If you would care to accompany me.'

'I...I'm not feeling very well.' I said holding my arm across my brow. 'For tonight I think I shall skip dinner and rest.'

He gawped at me blankly. 'The mistress is expecting you.' For a moment he paused, looking down upon me. 'No disrespect Miss, but you need to keep your strength up. We don't won't you fainting on us through hunger now, do we?'

I lowered my eyes and pretended to laugh.

With the keys jangling on his belt buckle he turned to go, hesitating within the doorway. He turned to face me. 'I could bring you a plateful of food up later, if you like Miss Farraday, along with some mead.'

With a sigh I looked up and stared at the bunch of keys around his middle.

'Yes, yes that would be most acceptable.' I gulped, feeling my face begin to turn scarlet. 'I...I wonder Craddock. Would you like to join me? I'd very much like to hear more about your life prior to living at the monastery.'

With his eyes steadily fixed on mine he scratched his scar, looking rather taken aback. 'Very well then Miss.' His eyes ran over me appraisingly. 'Does...does that mean you like me Miss?'

I stared at him and began to laugh nervously. 'Well of course Craddock. I would very much like to be your friend.'

'Friend?' he looked dismayed. 'I was hoping to court you Miss, like a proper gentleman woos his sweetheart.' He took a stride towards me. 'We could take it slow like, if that's what you want.'

Taking another gulp, I made myself smile and look into his eyes. 'Yes, very well then.' I nodded at him. 'I shall see you later then Craddock.'

To my horror he picked up my hand and planted a slobbery wet kiss upon it.

'Until later then Miss.' without taking his eyes from me he reluctantly released my hand and moved back. 'I'll bring pudding too.' He winked and plodded towards the door, selecting the key to lock the door.

'Oh, and Craddock. I wonder if you'd keep the door open. I was hoping to go along to the cloisters for a spot of air to...to help with my headache.'

'Sorry Miss, no can do. The mistress gave strict instructions that you're not to go wandering.' He grinned, showing his discoloured teeth. 'And you must be here for our very first date.'

I turned away so he couldn't see my face. 'Yes, yes of course.'

'Until later then Miss.'

The door crashed behind him and I heard the key turn in the lock. Without delay I rushed to the bathroom and began scrubbing at my hand with the soap. The mere thought of his lips on my skin filled me with revulsion, and only when it was red raw did I pat it dry.

I began pacing up and down the room nervously wondering what on earth I had done. When I'd made the suggestion to Craddock to join me it was purely based on the assumption I could somehow pinch his keys, but now the whole thing seemed completely illogical. How would I manage to get the keys, what if it all went wrong? I sunk my face in my hands in utter despair and began to groan. I went and sat on the bed then rose and went over to the window, my heart thumping loudly in my chest. Mumbling to myself I began taking deep breaths in order to calm myself, as there was no way I could think rationally unless I relaxed.

As I tried to think up what I could do a strange noise came from the keyhole, and for one terrifying moment I imagined it to be Craddock returning early. I grabbed the china vase on the mantelpiece and raised it above my head, moving swiftly behind the door, ready to clout him as he entered. That way there'd be no need for another nauseous conversation, the deed would be done before I lost my nerve. And as the odious guard lay unconscious on the floor, I would take his keys and go. If Abel was in the library we could leave together by way of the wine cellar, and if one of the keys didn't fit, we would break it down, no matter how heavy it might be.

The sound of whispering voices could be heard as the lock clicked open. Was there more than one person, had they unpicked the lock? Trying not to become distracted I stared steadily at the door, and as it slowly opened, I held the vase above my head in readiness for my attack. As two cloaked figures entered something made me hesitate, and as they removed the hoods of their robes the vase slipped from my hands onto the floor with a thud. Standing there before me were Gideon and Mace.

'That vase would have worked you know E, especially on Gideon.'

With a cry I threw myself forward into their arms and we all stood there embracing one another.

'Good to see you E.' Exclaimed Mace, moving slightly away.

I smiled at him, my eyes filling with tears.

Gideon took my face in his hands and began to speak to me in between kisses. 'I'm so sorry to have taken so long Effie. I had to seek out your father to help me activate the mirror. Then once I'd arrived back in Briarwood, Mace and I immediately hurried to Hartland.' He caressed my face with his hands, wiping away my tears. 'Are you alright my love? Was it Verity who brought you here?'

Barely able to speak I gave him a nod. 'Yes, she…. she dragged me through the mirror.' My voice was hoarse and shaky. 'Are you okay. Is…is Gabriel well?'

He smiled reassuringly at me. 'We're both fine. Little Gabriel is safe with your Aunt Constance, but he misses you so.'

I stared into Gideon's dark eyes and flung my arms around him, burying my face into his neck. For a second, we clung to one another.

Mace cleared his throat. 'Excuse me you two, sorry to spoil the moment but I don't think we should hang about here longer than necessary. Not unless we want to meet a very grisly end. I've already had a brush with death on the way here, and don't intend to have another one.' He glanced at Gideon. 'I nearly sank into the mire reaching this place, didn't I big brother.'

Gideon smiled amusingly at him. 'Had it not been for me saving you.'

'Yeah, well it was me who managed to clamber out. You just gave me a helping hand.' He said, pulling a disgruntled face.

Looking at them both my face broke into a smile. It was strange hearing Mace calling Gideon brother, strange in a pleasing sort of way. As my mind automatically drifted to Noble, my face dropped.

'So, Effie my dear old friend.' Mace said cheerfully, draping his arm loosely around my shoulders. 'Quickly fill us in on what's been going on in this glorious place, and why you're here.'

As I sat back on the chair and told them both all about what had happened since I'd arrived, I purposely missed out the part about Noble. It was partly weakness on my part, I felt mentally incapable of informing them; I'd hardly had time to absorb his death myself, let alone tell his brothers. I didn't want to cause them pain, not now anyway. Perhaps it was a wrong and selfish thing to do. I should have learnt my lesson after the demise of Mace's foster parents, failing to let my friend know until sometime after had been a mistake. My only fear was Gideon and Mace finding out from someone else, and so I began praying that they wouldn't have the opportunity to bump into the mad woman, she would be the one who would take great pleasure in informing them of the sad news.

'So, where's Noble. Father seemed to think he was here.' Asked Gideon, looking somewhat perplexed.

My eyes flashed over to him, and not knowing what to do I simply shook my head, trying not to cry. I was actually relieved to hear a loud knock upon the door and as Craddock shouted out that he was just going to unlock the door my heart sank.

'Oh no.' I whispered to them both. 'It's the guard I was telling you about.'

A puzzled Craddock flung the door open muttering something about forgetting to lock the door, but before he'd stepped into the room Gideon struck him hard between the eyes with the china vase. The startled guard stared wide-eyed into my face before dropping into a heap at my feet.

'Quickly, we should tie him up.' Said Gideon, scanning the room. 'Have you something we can use?'

186

'There's some old rope in the spare room. Why don't we tie him to the chair in there?' I glanced down at his belt buckle and sighed. 'His keys, he must have removed them.'

'Don't worry about them now E. Let's just get this lump bound and gagged before he decides to wake up.'

As the two of them hauled his weight into the spare room I went outside to check no one was about. A tray of food lay on the table by the door, along with a flagon of drink and two goblets. Craddock must have been just about to bring it in. I shuddered at the thought of having to sit with such a man and having to endure him shrewdly watching me, like a hawk ready to pounce on its prey. And to think, without his keys, it would have all be in vain. I shakily picked up the tray and brought it into the room and laid it on the bed.

Gideon and Mace emerged from the side door.

'That was quick.' I commented.

'Yeah, well he's out for the count E.'

'The guard won't be going anywhere for a while Effie.' Exclaimed Gideon with a gentle smile. He came close and cupped my cheek. 'I think I know where the keys are kept. As I recall from when I was here before, the guards used to hang them up in a small storeroom on the west side of the monastery directly after supper, each and every night.' His face darkened as his eyes stared across the room. 'Grandfather was always a stickler for rules and regulations, I only hope this particular routine hasn't changed now he's gone.'

'What do you mean?'

He began stroking my hair. 'I shall have to go and fetch them Effie. I'm the only one that knows where they're located.'

'No Gideon, we...we shall all go. It's important we stick together.'

'Effie, there's less chance of being seen if just one of us goes. And besides, what other means of escape do we have, if the tunnels are no longer safe, we shall have to go through the wine cellar.'

I gulped nervously. 'But the keys might not even be there. Perhaps....' My thoughts drifted off to the mad woman. 'Perhaps Verity puts them away somewhere at night. Gideon we may never find them.' My mind began to race. 'Let's just go to the wine cellar and try and pick the lock. You managed it on this door.'

'Effie, I've been down to the wine cellar many a time, and the door...' A lost look crept over his face and he turned away from me. 'Grandfather used to have the tonic stored down there. I wonder...I wonder if there's any left.'

I clutched his chin and pulled his face round so he was looking directly into my eyes. 'Forget about that muck Gideon. You don't need it anymore, remember?' I kissed him firmly on the lips. 'You were saying about the door.'

He seemed bewildered for a short while and just stood there, gazing at me in a trance, but then his face brightened. 'Oh yes, the door, it has a reinforced lock that would be impossible to pick, and it's made of steel. Grandfather never mentioned the room beyond it and I suspect it was forgotten about.' With a heavy sigh he leant in close to me and breathed in my scent. 'I'll do my best not to get caught Effie, and I shall return before you know it. Hopefully with the keys.' He smiled weakly and kissed me.

'Promise me you'll come straight back.'

Moving towards the door Gideon chuckled. 'I promise to try.' He glanced over at Mace, who was lying on the bed, eating the food from the tray. 'Be on your guard both of you, and don't open the door to anyone.' He reached over to the outside of the door and retrieved the key that Craddock had left there. 'Make sure you lock the door after me Effie. I shall knock five times so you know it is me.'

I took the key from him and nodded.

'Take care brother.' Mace yelled, getting up from the bed. 'Don't go looking for trouble now.'

Gideon smiled at him then gave me another kiss. Then he was gone.

'He's a good man that husband of yours E.' Said Mace, still munching on the food. 'A little boring at times but decent.'

I swiftly locked the door and placed the key on the shelf.

'Don't call my husband boring.'

'Sorry E, only kidding.' He began scratching his back. 'I'd forgotten how damnably itchy these robes can be.'

'Where did you find them?'

'There were loads hanging up in the coat hooks by the entrance hall, so Gideon and I nabbed a couple, we thought it best we blend in.'

'Did you enter through the front gates?'

'Yep.' He replied picking up a chunk of meat and stuffing it into his mouth. 'Walked right in, just like last time.' Pouring some mead into the other goblet he passed it to me. 'Here, you look like you could do with a drink to steady your nerves.'

'Well, yes. The past few days have been rather harrowing - what with having to endure the madness of Verity, and her dark and murderous nature.' I laughed unsteadily before taking a sip of the mead. 'And now I've discovered I'm the key to her stupid plan. And...and well.' I took another swig from the goblet and stared up at the ceiling, trying not to cry. 'There's something else too Mace, something really tragic.'

'Whatever it is E you can tell me. I can keep a secret.'

We heard a loud groan from nearby.

'Craddock.' Exclaimed Mace, rushing over to the side door.

I followed behind him and a rush of fear hit me when I saw the guard peering directly at me, his eyes hard and callous. It was odd to see him bound and gagged, and with his blood smeared face and muffled groans he reminded me of a wounded animal.

'You rest there my dear man.' Exclaimed Mace, checking the rope. 'Because you're not going anywhere for a while.'

Craddock's moans became louder as he began to struggle violently in the chair.

'Well you're a feisty one, aren't you?' With a smile Mace turned to me. 'And according to my friend here you have a twin.' He stood there and folded his arms. 'Tell me - is your brother as ugly looking as you?'

The guards face was drained of colour as he glowered menacingly at him. If he were suddenly set free, he'd murder Mace where he stood, with his bare hands. For just like the stranger who had given him his scar, no one messed with Craddock.

Keeping my eyes upon the guard I pulled him away. 'Don't antagonise him Mace.

'Why ever not E?'

I dragged him from the room and locked the door. 'Because Craddock isn't the type of person to put up with it, believe me.'

Mace grunted. He poured the remainder of the mead from the flagon and knocked it back, then stuffed a large chunk of bread into his mouth.

'I was thinking of venturing down to the kitchens E, to get some food supplies.' He looked totally immersed in his own world for a minute, and when he spoke there was an air of uncertainty in his tone. 'Is Clarice really that bad E?'

'To be frank Mace, yes she is.' Catching sight of his gloomy face I went and sat beside him on the bed. 'But I'm certain that going back home will cure her, just like Gideon. We just have to find a way to make her leave.'

He slouched forward and rubbed his face. 'You know E, I was going to return to Hartland when Noble left the village to travel here, but Verity told me all the tonic takers had perished trying to collect the rowanberries. I should have trusted my instincts and come and got Clarice then, rather than listening to that crazy woman. If I'd got here sooner then perhaps her condition wouldn't have been so bad.' His eyes flicked to mine. 'Effie, I'm not courageous like Gideon or Noble; they're more of the strong silent type, whilst I can happily chatter away all day, but...but when it comes to doing anything courageous...well I'm weak and cowardly. That's the real reason I didn't come back before – I'm a chicken.'

I studied his face closely half expecting to see the glint of laugher in his eyes that so often appeared when he was toying with me. But his expression remained solemn and serious.

'That's completely untrue Mace. And besides you eventually came back to the monastery, surely that's brave. Clarice maybe lost in her mind, but you can save her, you can be her knight in shining armour.'

His face brightened a little. 'Thanks E. You are right.' With his fist he began banging on the tray. 'I can save her, and I will save her.' With a spring in his step he leapt up from the bed, emptying the contents of the tray all over the bed, and strode over to the door. 'Wish me luck old girl.'

'Mace wait.' I cried, holding out my arm. 'I didn't mean this minute.' I clambered off the bed and rushed over to him.

'Why not E? I know where her room's located. Come with me. We can smuggle her back here way before dawn, and then when Gideon returns with the keys, we can all scarper together, and be back home in time for one of Caleb's fry ups.' He looked puzzled. 'Or back in my old home that I can't remember the name of.'

'You make it sound so delightfully easy Mace.'

'Well you know me E, I'm an eternal optimist.' He furrowed his brow. 'I'm just a tad worried about travelling through that confounded mirror for the first time.'

I sighed. 'Let's worry about that later, shall we?'

With a grunt he kicked some of the broken vase across the room with his foot.

'Yeah you're right.' He grabbed my arm. 'So, are you coming with me?'

'Perhaps I should stay here and wait for Gideon. Just get back as soon as possible.'

'Will you be alright whilst I'm gone E?'

For a moment I hesitated. I was rather tempted to say no. The thought of being alone with Craddock filled me with dread, even if he was tied up.

'Yes, yes I shall be fine. If Craddock causes me trouble, I'll strike him over the head with something heavy, just like Gideon did with the vase.'

'Use the flagon E that should do it.'

I smiled as he tiptoed out the room into the darkness. As I closed the door it suddenly occurred to me that Clarice might have another room now, the mad woman might have had her re-located to a different part of the monastery. What if poor Mace couldn't find her, what if he got caught? Why oh why did I not think to warn him?

Gideon returned soon after, but hadn't been able to locate the keys. He was going to search for them in the mad woman's room but I persuaded him not to. She would have hidden them somewhere safe, a place only she knew about. We could of course have gone wandering aimlessly along the endless dark passageways of the monastery seeking a way out, or take our chances in the tree ridden tunnels, but ultimately, I knew we wouldn't get away. I think I'd known all along that my sister wouldn't take a chance on risking me escaping, I was too important to her, she needed my blood.

'When do you think Mace will return?' Asked Gideon with a soft smile.

I shrugged my shoulders. 'Who knows, he's probably made a detour to the kitchens for some food.' I smiled bashfully as his lips brushed my neck. 'Perhaps...perhaps he'll find Clarice still working there.' I felt myself being gently moved backwards towards the bed. 'And...and it's possible she sleeps in the kitchen and....' My words faltered as he silenced me with his lips.

A while later I emerged from the bathroom with a towel wrapped around me, my wet hair dripping on the floor, happily humming to myself. My eyes drifted across at the crockery and tray that lay discarded on the floor, I remember how Gideon had swept it off the bed last night. As I strolled across the rug, carefully dodging the broken pieces of vase, my feet almost stood on the rosary beads, I picked them up and began twirling them around my fingers. My face suddenly darkened as the voice of the tiny demon inside my head began to remind me of my failings, it was perched on my shoulder now, cruelly reminding me that I had no right to be happy. Noble was dead and Mace was missing, and he probably hadn't succeeded in saving Clarice. Gideon was here with me now, but for how long. When the mad woman drained my blood tonight that would be it. I would never see my husband again or my dear child.

I jumped as Gideon crept up behind me, his arms encircling my waist. He moved me round so I was facing him. Having already dressed in his robes, he immediately looked more in keeping with everyone else.

'You didn't waste any time.' I said, adjusting his hood. 'Are you that eager to return to your old life?'

He smiled endearingly at me. 'Only for today.'

'How is Craddock?'

'Snoring away most gentlemanly.' Gideon looked towards the side door. 'It's best we keep him tied up for now, one less guard to deal with.'

Chapter 19

It was rather strange strolling hand in hand with Gideon along the passageway, and as several resident's stopped in their tracks and stared at us, I nodded my head at them and smiled graciously. As we reached the great hall, I took a deep breath and together we marched in confidently, as if we owned the place. The dining area was already packed with people, and as we passed by, I observed them studying us curiously. The guards seemed naturally bewildered and began muttering between themselves, throwing us confused stares; I noticed how Wilding and one other guard trailed along behind us as we made our way to the top table. The mad woman stood up as we approached, looking completely stunned.

'Good morning Verity.' Said Gideon as we took a seat either side of her. 'I trust you slept well?'

Slowly sitting back down, she stared at him, her black eyes wide with shock. 'What are you doing here Gideon?'

He didn't answer her immediately but helped himself to a tankard of ale and some food. 'Let us eat first. I shall inform you directly afterwards.' Giving me a reassuring grin, he covered my hand with his and whispered in my ear. 'Relax darling. Everything is going to be alright.'

Wilding glowered at us suspiciously before turning to the mad woman. 'I need to talk with you mistress Verity.'

'It can wait.' She snapped, still glaring at Gideon.

'But mistress.'

'Oh, go away Wilding. Yes, I know your brother Craddock has gone missing. So, do be a good boy and go and find him then.'

'Thanks mistress.'

As he turned on his heel to go, I noticed how he threw me a rather strange furtive look. I gathered he knew his brother Craddock had visited me last night, and therefore would head straight to my room and discover him restrained in the chair. It didn't matter, sooner or later the guard would have been discovered; it was just a little sooner that I would have liked.

For a while everyone was silent as we ate, even the mad woman. I could practically hear her brain ticking over as she contemplated her next move. I was especially hungry due to Mace having eaten the entire tray full of food last night, and I eagerly tucked into the milky porridge and fruit. As I finished my drink, I felt Gideon squeeze my hand and nod his head at me as a signal. A complete feeling of dread came over me as I saw him rise from his seat and clear his throat.

'Good morning everyone, my name is Gideon and I am the grandson of Septimus, your once great leader. Some of you may remember me from when I resided here some time ago.' He paused for a moment as the mad woman huffed. 'My grandfather always intended for me to take his place following his death, and I therefore claim ownership of the chief ruler of Hartland.'

There were raised voices amongst the crowd and the mad woman rose abruptly from her seat and confronted Gideon, placing her face up close to his.

'This is a complete outrage. I am mistress of Hartland. My marriage to Septimus overrides your claim.' Her eyes switched to the crowd. 'This man maybe the grandson of my poor departed husband, but he is ill and doesn't know what he's talking about. He deserted this great land for a woman.' She practically shoved her finger in my face. 'This woman sitting here took him away and poisoned his mind against this great kingdom.'

I stood up, knocking my chair to the floor.

'Everything that comes out Verity's mouth is a lie. Septimus didn't pass away peacefully in his sleep- she murdered him by plunging a knife through his heart. And the other day she killed Hector.'

Several gasps of horror were heard around the hall.

Gideon took my hand. 'I ask you dear people, where does your loyalty truly lie: with your mistress who is a treacherous murderer and with whom you will most certainly die, or with me, a man of his word who will treat you fairly and with respect. I ask you all now to stand with myself and my wife, and together we will forge a new and improved way of life here, an environment where you don't have to be afraid, and where you can leave whenever you wish.'

The mad woman seemed unusually quiet, so quiet that it worried me. When over half the hall rose to their feet, she glared at them with a look of cool disdain.

'Don't listen to this foolish man. No one can leave this place. Everyone knows that it's easy to enter the monastery but impossible to leave it. The Elder Trees, as great as they are, are gradually taking ownership of Hartland, and before long they will completely possess it, and take our lives. Now I promised you all a solution, and a hold firm on my pledge. Tonight, dear people the ancient ritual will take place, a rebirth if you like of all the trees in every kingdom, far and wide. The trees will cleanse all other worlds and Hartland will stand alone, and all loyal residents of the monastery will be rewarded with the gift of immortality and The Elder Trees will protect and worship us just as we worship them. Isn't that what you all crave? Stand by my side dear people and live forever.'

I watched as many people rose to their feet, and rather worryingly some remained standing from when Gideon had asked them, which probably meant they had switched sides. I couldn't understand their logic. Did they truly believe what the mad woman was telling them?

I cleared my throat.

'If this ritual was to work, do you honestly think you will never die, and can you truly live with yourselves knowing that all other worlds have fallen. The mad....' I paused. 'Your mistress is the one who's not well, not Gideon. Can you not see how completely mad she is? I call her the mad woman because she *is* completely insane.'

Gideon leant forward and placed his hands on the table. 'Why don't we postpone this discussion until noon, this will give everyone time to go away and think about what myself, Effie and your mistress has said. All I ask is that you come back and show us who you will stand with.' He glanced at me; his face rather anxious then turned back to the crowd. 'Please see sense and stand with me, and make my grandfather proud.'

I watched as the mad woman gestured for the guards to come over.

Still feeling brave I faced the crowd once more. 'Your mistress will no doubt take us away now, probably to the cells, and you'll never see us again.' I shouted out desperately. 'Isn't that right Verity?'

She stared at me with complete indignation. 'No, no of course I won't sister. You have me all wrong.'

'Then give me your word, give everyone in this room your word that Gideon and I will return at noon, so we can settle this once and for all.'

The mad woman's face darkened as she glared at me. I could see she wished to strike me, to silence my tongue. But it would hardly look good in front of every one; in fact, it may be enough to make the resident's see sense.

'Very well dear sister I give you my word.' With an air of haughtiness, she glided across the hall and out the door.

The residents began filing out of the hall, closely watched by the guards.

Gideon's face came close to mine. 'You know this whole idea could all go disastrously wrong, don't you. We could end up worse off than before.'

'Unless we can reach the mirror, what other choice do we have?' I replied quietly so the guards couldn't hear. 'We should go to the library, Abel may still be there, and could help us with the key to the wine cellar. And then we should check my room and the kitchens for Mace and Clarice.'

He nodded, his dark expressive eyes looking tenderly into mine. 'Very well then darling, we shall do precisely that.'

I smiled lovingly at him.

On reaching the library we were dismayed to find it empty, empty of Abel and completely empty of any books. It was almost like someone had come along and ripped the very heart out of the room; it was deserted and forlorn now, uncared for and unloved. As we left the room I thought of poor Lucinda, and how devastated she would be. It was a little strange I'd not seen her for a while, there didn't seem to be any logic as to where and when she would materialise, but then why would there be, she was a ghost, a ghost that no one could apparently see but me.

As Gideon and I made our way pass the boarded-up study I heard a distinct voice coming from the room opposite, and as I pressed my ear up against the door it dawned on me who it was. Very slowly I opened the door.

'Effie. No, what are you doing?' exclaimed Gideon.

I smiled at him. 'It's okay I recognise the voice.'

The door creaked ominously as it came ajar. I took Gideon's hand and we both crept quietly inside. It was an odd little room, with several threadbare armchairs surrounding an unlit fire. Maybe it had been a parlour once upon a time, where monks would greet their guests by the warmth of the fire, and offer them refreshments.

A tormented cry came from the shadowy corner of the room.

'Be careful Effie.' Whispered Gideon cautiously.

Mace was leaning forward in one of the chairs, his large eyes looking at us with utter alarm. Clarice was on the floor by his feet, staring blankly into the empty grate, as if mesmerised by the invisible flames.

With small steps I approached them.

'Mace, what's wrong?'

Without saying a word, he peered down upon Clarice.

'That man deserved to die,' she said gravely, her eyes still focused on the grate.

'What man?' I stared at her, my voice becoming louder. 'Clarice what man deserved to die?'

Mace's eyes darted to mine. He slowly rose and shakily approached us. 'She gets agitated when someone raises their voice at her. It...it scares her.'

Gideon gently placed a hand on his shoulder and stared into his face. 'What happened Mace?'

'There...there was an incident in Effie's room.'

As he looked at us with an unblinking stare, he reminded me of a frightened little boy who'd just had a scary encounter with something awful, the sort of experience that would leave a lasting impression on you, and cause nightmares for years to come.

Hearing a sob come from Clarice I began moving towards her but Gideon held me back, firmly gripping my arm.

'It's not safe Effie.'

I stared at him indignantly before turning to Mace. 'So, you and Clarice returned to my room. What time was this?'

'He looked confused. I...I'm not sure. It was morning and the two of you had already left.' He gulped nervously. 'I heard a muffled moan coming from Craddock, so...so I went to go and check on him. Then...then.' He held his breath for a moment then rather shakily exhaled. 'Then Clarice slit his throat with a knife.'

With a gasp I covered my mouth and whimpered. My eyes flitted to Gideon, who was staring at Mace. We all stood there for a few moments and didn't speak. As my gaze slowly travelled across to Clarice, I noticed she had turned to face us, and it was only then I saw her bloodstained face and hands, and the front of her habit was splattered with patches of deep red.

'There was blood everywhere.' Mace screwed his face up in horror. 'It.... it just kept spurting out. I didn't know what to do, or where to go. So, we fled the room and hid in here.' His tone became choked up with emotion, and with a cry of anguish his head fell forward onto my shoulder.

I cradled his head in my arms.

Gideon began pacing around the room, deep in thought, ever so often looking at me and then turning away. 'We should move the body. With any luck it won't have been discovered yet.'

'Wilding knew his brother Craddock was bringing me some food last night, so that's the first place he would have gone to this morning.' I stared glumly down at the floor. 'It's too late to shift the body.'

Mace lifted his head and looked into my eyes. 'Clarice didn't mean it E. She's not herself. The tonic made her do it.'

I smiled sympathetically at him.

As Gideon strolled across the room, he took Mace's arm. 'You and Clarice stay here for now. We'll come back for you as soon as we can little brother.'

'What are you going to do?'

'Don't worry about that- you just concentrate on keeping safe.' He smiled reassuringly before turning to me. 'Effie and I have an appointment to keep in the great hall.'

As Gideon quietly closed the door I fell into his arms. 'Oh, poor Clarice.' I said in an agitated whisper. 'No one must ever know it was her that killed Craddock.'

I felt his hands stroking my hair, but no words came from his lips.

'Gideon?' I uttered looking up into his eyes.

'You can blame Clarice's behaviour on the tonic Effie, or lack of it, but whatever way you look at it she still took a life. And how do you suppose it looks for you Effie, if Wilding discovered his brother's body in your quarters, he'll automatically assume you murdered him.'

I moved away and stood there motionless for a moment. 'Well what do you suppose we do Gideon, go and tell Verity that it was Clarice? You seem to forget it wasn't that long ago you held a knife up to my neck, and if it hadn't been for Septimus intervening then...then.' My words faltered. 'What I'm trying to say is you were a different person then Gideon, just like Clarice, and you wouldn't have thought twice about killing me.'

He looked suddenly mortified. 'I...I didn't know that Effie. You never told me.' Clenching my hands, he pressed them against his chest. 'I'm truly sorry, I really am.'

I smiled softly at him. 'It's okay Gideon. I don't blame you for what happened, just as I don't blame Clarice. You are both innocent victims in all of this.'

We heard the sound of approaching footsteps.

Stealing a quick kiss, we stood staring at one another.

The mad woman came into view, flanked by several guards. They all shared a grim look of determination on their faces, as if they were on a mission of great importance.

I held Gideon's hand tightly within mine.

'Oh, here you are.' She said tersely. 'I was beginning to think you'd both tried to run away.' With a glassy stare she looked directly into my face. 'That would make you a coward as well as a murderer, wouldn't it Effelia?'

Gideon's face became enraged. 'Effie wasn't responsible for the death of the guard.' With a pause he stood there glowering at her, his face set in stone. 'I was the one that killed Craddock.'

'Oh Gideon, no...no.' I cried desperately. 'I won't allow you to do this.'

'Quite right Effelia.' The mad woman replied with a cool smile. She stepped forward and gazed closely at Gideon. 'Although your valiant attempt to cover for your wife's crime is commendable, I cannot hold you responsible.' Her finger flicked a strand of his hair. 'I see you have flecks of grey in your hair, I'm not surprised having married my grizzly little sister.' As he moved away, she grabbed the top of his robes tightly in her fist. 'You know Gideon, I believe there's a few bottles of the tonic left in the infirmary, would you like a glass?'

He wrenched himself away from her grip. 'Stop it Verity.' For a second, he began breathing frantically, and as his hand went to his throat he began to gasp.

In a panic I rushed over to him but the mad woman pushed me out the way.

'Leave him be Effelia, give the man some space.'

Gideon held out his arm. 'I'm alright honestly.' As his breathing steadied itself, he turned to me and nodded reassuringly, but there was a hint of apprehension in his eyes that he wasn't able to hide. 'Should...should we not go to the hall, it's nearly noon.'

The mad woman curled her lips into a devious smile.

'Well of course Gideon, if that is what you wish. But I do need to have a short conversation with your wife first, in private. Would you mind waiting for us in the hall, it shouldn't take long.'

Gideon's eyes flicked to mine, looking worried.

'Effie?'

'I shall be fine. See you in a minute then.' I murmured softly to him. 'You are okay, aren't you Gideon?' I placed my hand on his arm.

I felt my hand being wrenched away by the mad woman.

'Oh, don't fuss over him Effelia.' She began dragging me down the passageway. 'Gideon is a strong, healthy man.' Her eyes darted back to gaze at him. 'He just requires a few sips of the tonic as a pick me up.'

As we passed the archery room a sudden veracious roar could be heard from inside the room, it sounded like a man's cry.

The mad woman let out a wicked laugh. 'That's Wilding. We had to restrain him otherwise he'll attack you dear sister, and most likely murder you.'

My eyes became wide with shock. 'But I didn't kill his brother Craddock, nor did Gideon. I...I don't know who it was.'

'Well, it doesn't matter if you did or you didn't, you're still going to be blamed for it.' She sniggered. 'You cannot deny that you're the most likely suspect. At one time Effelia I didn't think you'd have it in you, but now I'm not so sure.' Her eyes narrowed as she studied my face closely. 'I wouldn't think any worse of you sister, you know, in fact I'd be rather impressed.' She gave me a quick hug. 'It would make us more alike.'

As the mad woman led me along the passageway, I realised we were heading for her room. As I peered into her laughing face it seemed she was hiding something from me, some delicious secret that she couldn't wait to tell me.

Coming to a halt by the door she lightly touched my arm and whispered into my ear.

'Sh...sh.' He might be asleep.'

'Who's he?'

Without a word she gradually edged open the door and gestured for me to enter. The room was in darkness and I had to strain my eyes to see. There was a woman sitting in the rocking chair by the bed, and she was cradling a child in her arms, my child.

'Gabriel?' I murmured in a disbelieving tone.

The mad woman caught my eye, her expression sparkling with a cruel joy.

'Keep your voice down silly. He's having a nap.'

As I approached the rocking chair my knees suddenly turned to jelly and I practically fell to my knees as I stared in wonder at my beautiful son. As an incredible feeling of love enveloped me, I had an overwhelming urge to scoop him up in my arms and run away with him. But although I was ecstatic to see my child, this was no place for Gabriel, and to run would be fruitless.

The sound of the mad woman sniggering brought me back to my senses, and I swung round to confront her.

'How dare you bring him here, didn't you realise how dangerous it could have been, travelling at such a young age, and surely even you can see Gabriel doesn't belong at the monastery, it's hardly safe.'

As she spoke her tone was icy. 'Because of that foolish talk you and Gideon gave this morning I had no choice but to bring Gabriel here. Now listen carefully. When we join the others in the hall in a short while, you're to do exactly what I say. You will inform everyone that you're mentally unstable and therefore didn't mean what you said about me earlier, you will admit to murdering Craddock in cold blood, you will say how Gideon is angry and bitter because he didn't become leader, and he doesn't care about any of the resident's and only wishes to leave Hartland at the earliest opportunity.'

'And if I don't do as you ask?'

'You and Gideon will never see your precious son again.' Her face came level with mine, her eyes vicious. 'And I mean *never.*'

'Surely you wouldn't hurt him?' I cried.

'Do you really want to take that chance dear sister?'

'No' I uttered in a weak, broken voice.

Gabriel began to cry.

The woman who was nursing him began to gently rock him to and fro in her arms, but he suddenly began to sob.

I automatically reached for him. 'Let me take Gabriel.'

'No, said the mad woman sharply. 'He wants his Auntie Verity.' Shoving herself in front of me she hurriedly took him from the woman and held him up against her chest. 'There, there my sweet. There's no need to cry Gabriel.' She sighed as the sobbing became louder.

'Please.' I asked hoarsely, my eyes beginning to sting with tears. 'Hand him to me.'

'Oh, very well then.'

As she passed Gabriel to me, I tenderly held him in my arms and kissed the top of his head, moving my cheek against his hair. 'It's okay, mummy's here.' Rather bewildered he looked up into my face, and rubbing the sleep from his eyes, he beamed at me.

'There, he just wanted his ma.' Exclaimed the woman as she hunched forward in the rocking chair, smiling sweetly. But as the mad woman glowered at her the smile slipped from her face.

I reluctantly glanced at the mad woman.

'If I agree to your demands, do I have your assurance you'll give Gabriel back to me?'

'You have my word. That is as long as you survive the ritual, and I don't have to take too much blood.'

I touched noses with Gabriel, gazing steadily into his exquisite eyes, and then impulsively began smothering his perfect little face with kisses. He grinned at me, and began chuckling with mirth.

As the mad woman began rambling on excitedly about tonight, I tried to drown out the noise of her grating voice and concentrate solely on my son, my dear son who meant more to me than anything in the entire world. I had no choice but to go along with what she wanted, I couldn't take any risks, for if anything was to happen to my child, I'd never forgive myself.

'Very well then Verity, I will do everything you ask of me.'

She snorted scornfully. 'I thought you would.' Her eyes softened as she gazed at Gabriel. 'Pass the child to me now Effelia.' She ordered, still looking at him. 'I want to give him one last cuddle before we go to the hall.'

I sighed, reluctantly passing my son to her.

'He's such a cutie pie, isn't he?' She lifted him up into the air and swung him around. 'Yes, yes, you like that don't you.' her face nuzzled up against his. 'Auntie Verity loves you, yes she does.' He squealed with laughter as she threw him up once more.

There was a light tapping on the door. A guard entered, immediately lowering his eyes submissively. 'Pardon me mistress but it's almost noon. They'll be waiting on you in the hall.'

'Yes, yes.' She snapped. 'I hardly need reminding by one of the guards, now do I.' Looking agitated she handed Gabriel back to the woman. 'Be sure to take great care of him until I return. And don't unlock the door to anyone but myself.'

The woman nodded frantically at my evil sister before gazing at me, and for a mere second, I detected a shadow of compassion in her eyes.

'Oh, and Effelia?' The mad woman said tapping me on the shoulder to gain my attention. 'You are not to breath a word about all this to Gideon, he must not know his son is in Hartland, do you understand?'

I nodded sorrowfully.

I'd barely had a chance to say goodbye to Gabriel before the mad woman was pulling me towards the door; my eyes stayed upon my son until it slammed shut and I heard the key turning from the inside. As I was marched along the stone floor, I heard him crying in the distance, and my heart began to ache.

It hadn't meant to go this way; Gideon and I had planned on winning over the residents and overthrowing the mad woman and her guards, we would then be free to go on our way, never to set foot in this vile place again. However as is often the way with plans, they very often go wrong; and as I stood there that day, all eyes upon me, I felt like I was a prisoner forced to admit her wrongdoings before a jury, crimes of madness and of murder; with no choice but to go along with the pretence of being guilty. But what hurt me the most was deceiving Gideon. I could see him watching me out the corner of my eye, his face blazing with anger and bafflement. Not once did I look at him, knowing if I did he would see the pain behind my eyes, and would guess the truth; at one point he cried out my name and asked me what I was playing out, but I just stood there stoically like a living statue, staring ahead at the sea of bewildered faces before me.

For a few moments a silence fell upon the hall.

'And what does the grandson of Septimus make of all this?' called out one of the residents.

Reluctantly Gideon tore his eyes away from my face and stared forlornly at the crowd. When he spoke his voice sounded strained and uncertain, and even though he implored them to accept him as leader of Hartland I'm sure everyone sensed his resolve gradually waning. The situation worsened when the mad woman took his arm and whispered into his ear, something I imagine about the tonic. Like a broken man he suddenly slunk down into his chair.

The mad woman faced the crowd, her expression full of triumph.

'Are you with me good people?'

When the incessant cheering began, I closed my eyes. Their mistress had become victorious, they wanted her to remain leader, and they wished madness to rule.

'Wilding will want revenge.' Yelled one of the guards, glaring at me viciously before looking at the mad woman. 'Miss Farraday took his brother's life and therefore her life should be for forfeited.'

The mad woman's face lit up with pure elation.

'No truer words have been spoken, young sir. The blood of the accused *will* be spilt tonight at the ritual, the ritual we've all been waiting for, when our beloved trees will be unleashed through the doors to all worlds.' Her voice became raised. 'Our greatness is almost upon us, dear people. Can you feel it?'

A huge cheer echoed throughout the hall, followed by rapturous applauds from the residents, whose faces were full of nervous excitement. The tonic takers however remained silent and unmoving, like shadows of their former selves.

I felt myself being forced forward.

'Until then my sister shall be kept in the cells.' Taking my arm in a grip of iron she looked directly into my eyes. 'I'm sorry Effelia but as you are supposed to have murdered one of our esteemed guards, I must be seen to be doing the right thing. I'm sure you understand.'

'Yes.' I uttered in a subdued tone.

The mad woman's voice dropped considerably. 'And do not get any silly ideas of trying to snatch the little one, my room is under lock and key and two men stand guard outside.' Suddenly looking concerned she tilted her head so her ear was by my mouth. 'What's that you say dear sister I can hardly hear you. Ah yes, I see.' A nasty cackle came from her lips. 'You cannot go anywhere because you'll be locked in the cells, Noble is dead and Gideon, well Gideon is as good as lost, now the tonic is within his grasp.'

'You seem to have it all worked out don't you Verity, in that strange evil head of yours. Father will be so proud when he discovers your latest achievements.'

She raised her left eyebrow. 'Is sarcasm the only weapon you have left to fight with, Effelia? How very sad.' Clicking her fingers at the nearby guards, she barked orders at them. 'Take the prisoner away.'

Gideon caught my eye, peering at me with a dazed expression. It reminded me of when I'd found him in his grandfather's study that day, just after he'd destroyed my painting, saying how it wasn't a true reflection of who he was anymore; he truly believed I'd purposely deceived him.

The guards took me away, and rather apprehensively led me through the greenhouses, their frightened eyes darting around the place nervously. The tree roots had taken hold now and smothered the ceiling, walls and floors in a mass of tightly knit tendrils; they reminded me of snakes, coiling together for warmth, ready to attack and throttle its victim, before dragging it away and devouring it whole. One of the guard's feet became tangled in some tendrils, he produced a knife from his belt buckle and began frantically cutting it away, before stamping violently on the roots. We ran after that, only stopping when we'd come through the far doors that Noble and I had crept out of only recently. As we proceeded along the cold passageway, I realised we were heading for the little chapel.

'Why are we going this way?'

The shorter guard half glanced at me; his expression completely apathetic. 'Tis the safest way to the cells Miss.'

As we entered the chapel a hunched figure of a man was cowering on one of the back pews, and as we came closer, I saw that it was Abel. In a fit of panic, he shot up from his seat and stared at us.

The taller, square-jawed guard began to laugh at him mockingly.

'So, this is where you've been hiding away like a craven. The mistress has been looking all over the monastery for you.'

The other guard sniggered. 'I didn't take you for the praying type Abel.'

'Nay, I'm not.' Abel replied gloomily. 'What are you doing with Miss Effie?'

The guards proceeded to tell him about my confession in the hall.

Abel stared at me looking flabbergasted. 'No, Miss, no. I don't believe it.' He impulsively grabbed my arm. 'You're not the kind to commit murder.'

I drew a breath and sighed. 'Well actually...'

The tall guard barged in before I had a chance to finish my sentence. 'Enough of this foolish talk.' He groaned at Abel, removing his hand from my arm. 'Let's get you down to the cells Miss.' Placing his large hands firmly on either side of my shoulders he swiftly moved me forward.

Abel briefly glanced at me before facing the two guards, his face twitching slightly with nerves. 'Let me take Miss Effie down to the dungeons. You fellows have important work to do for this evening. I'll make sure she's locked in proper.'

The two guards exchanged glances then handed him a bunch of keys.

'Yeah.' One of them replied, looking rather relieved. 'You might as well make yourself useful.' He nodded sullenly at me. 'Until later Miss.'

I stared blankly at them as they turned and left the chapel.

'Those two are a couple of cowards Miss. They'll do anything to get out of going underneath the monastery.' His eyes widened with concern. 'You don't really want me to take you to the dungeons, do you Miss, not when I can show you a way out of here.'

'I didn't realise there was another way out...a safe way.'

His eyes looked cautiously towards the door before guiding me down to the very back of the chapel. 'Oh yes Miss. I discovered it all by myself, I did.' With a sudden burst of energy, he went around the back of the altar and lifted up a large section of cloth, draping down behind it. 'It's down this way Miss.' Taking a lantern he began descending a rather narrow set of steps directly underneath where the altar was situated. 'It's a bit of a tight squeeze, especially for big old Abel.' He chuckled.

'The mistress and guards only thinks these steps leads them to the dungeons, but I went exploring the other day and stumbled on an old tunnel.' He looked back at me. 'Come on Miss, watch your step.'

As we arrived at the bottom of the steps we turned a sharp right and travelled down a uneven pathway until we arrived in a large cave-like opening with various tunnels leading in different directions; it reminded me of when I'd become lost the other day, and had stumbled across Lucinda, in fact I was almost certain they must be in the same vicinity. It seemed all the caverns at the monastery were very similar- they were cold, damp and chillingly unwelcoming, with a horrid environment where you felt nearer the dead than the living.

Abel shone the lantern up ahead.

'Now, you don't want to be wandering left Miss. That way is a favourite place for them trees. We take the middle tunnel, which brings us out by the dungeons.' He paused. 'Or cells as most folk call them now.' He suddenly raised his voice considerably. 'And it was whilst I be coming along this way that I happened to trip over something.' Coming to a direct halt, he pointed down to the ground. 'Fell flat on my face, I did.' He kicked away some rubble with his boot, revealing a square wooden cover, protruding very slightly from the floor. 'I had to hide the door with bits of stone Miss.' with a heave he lifted the cover up with his hands and dropped it backwards with a crash. 'Didn't want anyone else finding my secret way of escape.' A grin spread across his face. 'There's a flight of steps that leads to a mighty long passageway that's too far underground for them trees, and once at the end you'll be beyond the gates of the monastery.'

I stared vacantly down into the darkness of the hole.

'Miss Effie?'

'Huh? I replied looking up into his face.

'What's wrong Miss, you've hardly strung two words together since bumping into me in the chapel. You need to cheer up Miss. Don't you see, we can leave now.' He gulped with excited apprehension. 'You can go and grab that friend of yours and we'll all be free.'

'Abel, I can't leave the monastery yet.' I said in a clear calm voice. 'Please don't ask me to explain. I wonder though if you would help my friends escape, they should be in the little parlour room opposite the study. Then all three of you can leave together.'

His face dropped. 'What about you Miss?'

'I can meet up with you all later.' I said, avoiding his eye so he didn't see my pained expression. For now, however I must go to the cells.'

'I don't like it Miss, I don't like it one bit.' He moved the piece of wood back over the hole and shuffled some gravel back over it.

As Abel guided me further down the tunnel, I told him how clever he was finding another way out; his freckled face went slightly red and he began to chuckle like a boy being paid his first compliment. I imagined he hadn't been praised very much in his life, not since living at Hartland. I made him give me his word that he would leave this evening, whatever happened; after all he deserved a better life, a fresh start, a chance to be reunited with the family that Isaiah had torn apart all those years ago.

'Here we are Miss.' He said solemnly as he unlocked the cells. 'I'll try and come back and see you later before.... before.' With a stifled sob he sunk his face into his hands.

I placed my hand upon his shoulder.

'Abel please, it's all right. I withstood The Giver ceremony and I will make sure I survive this silly ritual.' I purposely smiled merrily at him as he gazed down at me. 'Keep strong and stay positive.' I nodded at him and smiled once more. 'Promise me you'll go and seek out my friends, they need someone brave like you to rescue them.' I pictured Mace's response if he was standing here now, how aghast and indignant he'd be.

The cell door creaked open and I strolled in.

'I give you my word Miss. Now you take care.'

As he locked me in, he peered through the bars. 'At least you have company Miss.' His eyes looked across my shoulder. 'A friend of yours I believe Miss.'

Feeling puzzled I nodded and watched him disappear into the shadows.

With trepidation I slowly crept along the straw covered floor towards the figure huddled in the corner. It took me back to when I'd joined Isaiah in the cells, and for one nonsensical moment I believed it really to be him. But as I drew closer the figure rose its head and I stared into a pair of imposing eyes.

I sank to my knees with a cry. 'Noble, Noble is that really you? My heart skipped frantically in my chest as I pondered whether he was a ghost. 'I...I thought you...' Suddenly afraid of his answer, my voice trailed off. 'I thought you were dead.'

'No Effie.'

A strange laugh escaped my lips as he reached out and took my hands in his. They were warm. I studied his face carefully, noticing the unhealthy pallor of his complexion.

'What happened Noble?' I asked quietly, sinking down into the straw beside him.

'Verity wanted you to believe I'd been executed. But the truth is I've been in this cell since the day she tried to marry me. I don't think she intends to set me free, but wishes me to rot down here, alone and forgotten.' He picked up a piece of mouldy bread from the plate on the floor and tossed it across the cell. 'I've accepted my fate but you....' his large eyes looked bemused. 'Why are you here Effie?'

Noble stared into my eyes and listened attentively whilst I told him the events that had occurred since we'd last met. I noticed his face cloud over when I mentioned Gideon, but his expression swiftly turned to distress when he learnt about little Gabriel.

'I'm so sorry Effie. None of this was supposed to happen.'

Laughing softly, I rested my head against his shoulder and sighed. 'No, no it wasn't.' I rather shyly looked up into his face. 'But I'm so happy to know you're still alive Noble. When Abel returns he can set you free and you can flee the monastery.'

With a sudden movement he pulled me closer, clutching me tightly in his arms. 'No Effie, I'm not going anywhere, not without you.' His fingers began caressing my hair. 'I shall remain at Hartland until the bitter end.'

As the tears fell silently down my cheeks, I closed my eyes, trying desperately not to think of his lips upon mine, for despite knowing it was wrong my resolve was fading fast, and I knew that attempting to pull away would be futile.

Chapter 20

If only I had the power to suspend time, for then it would allow me a few more precious moments before I faced the ritual. But as I mulled the thought over in my mind, I felt my eyelids becoming heavy, and before I knew it, I had drifted off to sleep in Noble's arms.

I dreamt I was standing upon a narrow bridge, where the veil between worlds is gossamer- thin. On the other side lay delightful other worlds beyond all dreams, where one could live another lifetime then step back into their own world where merely a day had passed by. As lightening flashed across the sky I saw before me an eerie white mist, glowing green, and as I felt a deep vibration in the damp earth beneath my feet, I knew the gates to the underworlds were opening. I could hear the birds, the heralds of the other world, they had already awoken the dead with their enchanting song and were now coming for the living, suspending earthly time by lulling them into a deep sleep. I saw wondrous spirits from shimmering heavens emerging from the mist and then fearful armies came forth, set loose from their brooding hell they rode on magnificent horses, ready to unleash their wrath upon all living worlds. As Hartland lay sleeping amongst the fallen Elder Trees, I prayed that I would be forgiven for what I had done; for I alone had caused this, and all it had taken was a few drops of my pitiful blood.

'Effie, Effie wake up.'

My body jolted as I came back to consciousness. Noble was staring poignantly into my eyes. I wanted to stay there in his arms, where it was safe and warm. There were two burly looking guards who I'd not seen before standing in the entrance to the cells.

'Is it time?' I asked hoarsely.

Noble lifted me up from the ground. 'Yes.'

'You won't cause trouble, will you?' I whispered close to his ear. 'Remember, Gabriel's life could be put at risk.'

He nodded solemnly.

As the guards ushered me forward one of them grabbed Noble and bound his hands behind his back. Apparently, the mad woman wanted him to be present at the ritual. They pushed us forward into the tunnel and we all made our way back up into the monastery. It occurred to me then that Abel had not returned; whether that was a good sign and he had managed to reach Mace and Clarice, remained to be seen. As Noble was led away I was taken to a small room where two women were waiting. They dressed me in a gown, clad in brocaded silk, and over it a green hooded tunic with elaborate gold embroidery on the collar and cuffs; my hair was plaited and piled neatly on top of my head, pinned in place with diamond encrusted pins. They told me I looked stunning, but as I stared back at the image in the mirror all I saw was a stranger staring back at me, this wasn't me, this wasn't how I dressed, and then I realised this was my sacrificial clothing, the attire I would more than likely perish in after giving up my blood.

As the two women escorted me across the icy fields I was reminded of the time before at The Giver ceremony when I'd taken this path, a dangerous and foreboding path that would only lead to one outcome...death. Only unlike before there was a strange ball of yellow light, flickering through the trees up ahead, like a beacon of brightness; at first, I thought it was the sun going down, but then I remembered it didn't come out in Hartland. We were nearly at the barrows now, where the trees had taken me before.

One of the women, who had a genial face, placed her hand gently on my arm.

'Stop here a moment Miss, whilst we remove the cover.' Placing her lantern on the grass they both knelt down and lifted a piece of iron grating from the grass. 'There's a ladder leading down to an underground tunnel that will bring us out to where we need to be.' She gestured for me to enter. 'After you Miss.'

I nodded impassively and grabbed onto the iron bars of the ladder, staring down into the darkness.

'The tunnel's well-lit Miss. You'll see when you're down there.'

As we travelled along the passageway the women told me that this was the route used by the pickers who collected the rowanberries for the tonic, and how half of them never made it back. They spoke as though the incidents happened years ago and there was no longer any danger from the trees. Even if their mistress had filled their heads with nonsense and lies in order to proceed with her plan, I couldn't understand how they seemed so calm about the whole thing; did they truly believe we would be safe? As we emerged from the other end of the tunnel, I saw we had arrived near a large bonfire and standing around it were the residents of Hartland carrying blazing torches. Several people were throwing what I thought to be firewood into the flames, however as I looked closer my heart sank, for it wasn't firewood they were using but books. Now I knew why Abel had been asked to empty the library. The five great trees were in clear view and surrounded us like gargantuan monsters, the light from the moon illuminating them in a mysterious glow; I gazed at them with a mixture of awe and dread as their moving branches reached out like clawing hands ready to lay claim to its prey.

I froze.

One of the women coxed me forward. 'We're quite safe Miss. The trees don't like the fire.'

With a nod I walked forward towards the crowd of people and immediately spotted the mad woman and Wilding, impatiently waiting for me to join them. Just behind them stood an unsmiling Gideon and Noble, restrained by several guards. A little further to the right, away from everyone stood a stone table with a cauldron in the centre, embossed in silver gilt, and lying beside it was a small dagger which I surmised she'd taken from the display cabinet in the underground church.

Feeling everyone's eyes upon me I gulped nervously, and the colour flamed into my face.

The mad woman began to laugh. 'Welcome dear sister.' Her eyes ran over me. 'Your costume is splendid for such an occasion. It's a shame the colour makes you look washed out.' She beckoned me closer. 'I won't bite Effelia.' A short burst of laughter suddenly exploded from her lips as she grasped my chin tightly with her hands, forcing me to look into her eyes. 'Remember to do precisely what I ask of you and your son will not be harmed.' Releasing her hold, she turned to face the crowd. 'The moment is upon us dear people; our time of greatness has finally arrived.'

There was an unenthusiastic cheer from the crowd

Without warning I felt arms encircling my waist and I was suddenly lifted towards the stone table; as the grip became tighter, I became aware of hot breath by my ear.

'You murdered my brother Miss, and I'll make sure you pay with your life.'

I turned my head to meet Wildings gaze, chilled by the pure look of hatred within his eyes.

When I spoke, my voice was soft and low. 'I didn't kill Craddock.'

He spat in my face. 'Liar.'

'Let go of my sister you imbecile.' Snapped the mad woman. 'I shall take it from here.' Methodically she rolled up my left sleeve and held my bare arm across the cauldron. 'Effelia's descendant helped bring life to our trees and now she will give her blood for them.'

I could hear Gideon shouting behind us, pleading with the mad woman to stop. But she was steadfast in her task. She suddenly reminded me of a witch with her lank dark hair and pallid complexion, and eyes that bore into you with such intense wickedness that one would be frightened of meeting her gaze for fear of being struck down dead, or being turned into a toad, or some such creature.

She picked up the dagger and placed the blade flat against my arm.

'Effelia Farraday – do you willingly surrender your blood?'

An eerie silence fell upon the field.

'Yes.'

'Do not agree to it Effie.' Yelled Gideon. 'Why are you doing this?'

'She is no longer beholden to you Gideon and now her only wish is to make her contribution to Hartland. Isn't that so dear sister?'

Once again, I had no choice but to agree. I glumly nodded my head.

'Please Effelia, whatever's Verity's said or done you mustn't do this.'

The mad woman glanced back at him. 'Oh, do be quiet.' As she signalled to the guards one of them struck the side of Gideon's jaw and he went sprawling to the ground.

Without warning she sliced my arm with the blade, cutting deep into my flesh.

I gasped with pain.

Rather roughly she grasped my upper arm and held it steady, watching in morbid fascination as the blood began to pour into the cauldron, and as it became a mere trickle I winced as she squeezed her hands tightly around the cut in order obtain more, but barely a drop came out.

'Now the question is should I make another cut for good measure?' She stood there contemplating for a moment then turned to the crowd. 'What do you think everyone, have we enough blood?'

No one spoke, no one except Wilding.

'Allow me to make the cut mistress. It is better to have more blood than not enough. We should slit her throat, just like she did to my poor dead brother.'

In the background I could hear Noble yelling, but as my head began to spin the sound of his voice seemed to fade. To my amazement the mad woman must have decided against draining any more blood and I found myself being roughly dragged back by Wilding, his fingers purposely digging into my wound. The mad woman began to stir the pot, reading something from the ledger about a magical broth, her words made little sense as she rambled on in an unknown tongue.

Perhaps it was my imagination but the trees became still.

The mad woman slammed the ledger shut.

'Bring her forth Wilding.'

The guard suddenly shoved me forward and I nearly collided with the mad woman. She looked at him sternly and then nodded to someone in the crowd and a woman moved forward and handed her a wooden bowl.

'You Effelia must fill this vessel with the brew. Then you must imprint each tree with the potion, allowing it to soak into the bark.'

'How?' I asked perplexed.

'With your hand dear sister.' She handed me the bowl and gestured for me to fill it. 'Be quick now. And be careful not to spill the contents.'

Once the bowl was full I hesitated for a while, staring dauntingly at the trees, pondering over my chances of successfully applying the potion without being harmed; if I was part of Brother Carmichael's bloodline, was that enough, would I be granted immunity from their clutches or would they snatch me away as soon as I touched their precious bark.

'Move Effelia.' The mad woman ordered harshly.

As I was jolted back to reality I began to shiver uncontrollably. My legs felt like jelly, but somehow I managed to stumble forward, trying desperately not to drop the bowl from my shaking hands. Everybody was watching in silence, waiting to see what would happen. It struck me odd that the trees were unmoving, almost as though the mad woman's words had lulled them into a trance. But their behaviour unnerved me; it was like the calm before the storm.

A stifled groan came from the yew, and as I stepped closer my first reaction was to cry out in terror. There was a pair of blinking eyes peering out at me from the base of the tree; the rest of the face appeared to have been absorbed into the bark, along with the body. It must have been one of the residents. Unable to look I turned away knowing it was too late to help the poor soul. Taking a deep breath, I dipped my entire hand into the potion and placed my palm flat against the trunk and held it there, so that the liquid soaked into the bark. Then I made my way around to the next tree and did the same, and so on, until I'd arrived at the very last tree, the Rowan, I think. For one surreal moment I leant my head against the trunk and breathed in its ancient aroma, trying to understand what it was feeling, and what it wanted. I suddenly felt its pain and torment, and suffering, so much suffering. The Elder Trees didn't wish to exist in this manner, they didn't want to take human life...they wanted an end to their misery, they wanted to die. As the tears ran down my face, I found myself sympathising with their intense anguish, I sensed it, almost as if I was one of them.

Gradually I turned away, hiding my face underneath my hood.

The mad woman began to cackle. 'Come back and stand with us Effelia.'

With a heavy heart I trudged back towards the blazing bonfire. Suddenly I recognised the burly figure of Abel frenziedly fighting his way to the front of the crowd; he grabbed onto Gideon and yelled something in his ear. Wilding suddenly appeared and began smacking Abel across the head and face, screaming obscenities at him. My first reaction was to run forward and help him but then I noticed Gideon and Noble attacking the guards, along with several other resident's. As the crowd surged forward more people became involved in the fight, and as some of the guards were overpowered many of the tonic takers joined in too.

'In the name of Hartland- stop.' Bellowed the mad woman, her eyes darting alarmingly amongst the crowd. 'This is not the time for fighting.' With an exasperated sigh she turned towards me. 'If this is your doing dear sister then I pity your poor son, having to be torn away from his mother, and all because she wouldn't follow simple orders. All you had to do was to behave until after the ritual, and then you would have been reunited with Gabriel. But now...'

Feeling infuriated I watched as the entire crowd continued to fight. I noticed Gideon held one guard in a headlock, whilst Noble and Wilding were kicking and punching one another relentlessly. People were screaming with panic as someone furthest away from the bonfire was lifted up into the air by a branch and flung across the field.

I gulped. 'This is not my doing Verity. I knew nothing about it.'

'Do you really expect me to believe that?' She smirked looking in disgust towards the crowd as they continued to battle with one another. 'It doesn't matter now anyway.' A sly smile crept over her face as she looked at me. 'You have done what I asked of you Effelia, and now you are of no further use.'

'So, I can go and get my son?'

As we stared at one another I noticed she still held the dagger in her hand.

'Well of course Effelia. But before you go, please stay and witness this once in a lifetime event. Then I will personally escort you to your son.' With a laugh she wrinkled her nose. 'I shall give you a send-off you'll never forget, as long as you live.' She let out a cackle and began swinging the dagger from side to side.

Without warning there was a peal of thunder, followed by a distant rumbling beneath the earth. Everyone stopped fighting and stood motionless, looking frightened and bewildered.

The mad woman curled her thin lips into a smile. 'It has begun.'

Gideon came forward, stepping over an unconscious guard. 'It's okay Effie, Gabriel is safe with Mace and Clarice.' He extended his hand. 'Let's leave this instant.'

'Are you sure?' I asked looking surprised. 'I...I didn't think you knew about our son being here.'

'I didn't Effie, not until a minute ago when Abel told me.'

'You've got Lucinda to thank for that Miss.' Said Abel in a laughing voice. 'She was the one who told me about your son.

So, after I got your friends from that room by the old study, we all went and rescued him.'

'Oh, Abel what are you gibbering on about.' Exclaimed the mad woman.

Ignoring my sister, he stared into my face.

'It's true Miss Effie. They overpowered the guards and went and took the little one. They're all hiding out in the chapel, waiting for us.' He looked alarmed as he met the gaze of the mad woman.

There was a roaring and a thunderous pounding, as if some great beast was trying to break through the earth, and as the ground began to tremble, people began to cry out in anguish, and I saw Abel lose his balance and tumble backwards. Perhaps my dream of earlier, where the dead had been restored to life was becoming a reality, or maybe the ritual had actually worked and the deep roots of the trees were preparing for their onslaught on all worlds. Either way it couldn't be good.

The mad woman looked victorious. 'That's it my precious trees. Go forth and take back control of your lands.'

Staring into the leaping flames of the bonfire a strange clarity enveloped me, and I suddenly realised what must be done. Taking a deep breath, I gave the mad woman an almighty push and she tumbled to the ground, and seeing the dagger drop from her hand I swiftly picked it up and placed it in my tunic. Hurrying forward I took two blazing torches from a couple of perplexed residents then ran swiftly towards The Elder Trees, and stood in the shadow of the yew, a torch in each hand.

When I spoke, my voice was loud and clear.

'My forefather started their life and I shall end it.'

The mad woman had picked herself up from the ground and was looking decidedly uneasy.

'What do you mean?'

'All this time Verity, you've always thought of yourself, but have you ever stopped to think what The Elder Trees want. For centuries they have stood on this land, unable to live like normal trees, and having to take subsistence from human life in order to survive. But just because they exist in this manner doesn't mean they like it. They do not want this life, or any other life for that matter.' I gently ran my hand over the bark. 'It's time for them to be cremated.'

'No...no.' she screamed. 'You can't Effelia.' She began searching for her dagger, then realising it was missing she let out a ferocious growl and began making her way towards me, only to be restrained by Gideon. 'You're too late dear sister. The ending of all worlds has already begun. The Elder Trees will soon bury deep underground and reach the other worlds where they will join together with every single tree that exists, and then they will claim back their lands.' With a sudden smile she snuggled back against Gideon. 'You cannot stop it dear sister, no one can. Now move away from the trees and join your husband like a dutiful wife.'

'Oh, do be quiet Verity.' I shrieked.

With a stifled cry I swung the torches high up into the yew, managing to ignite a large bough, and as the flames began spreading a strange groaning sound came from the tree and its branches began shifting wildly in every direction.

A blood- curdling scream erupted from the mad woman's mouth.

One of the boughs headed straight for me and I ducked my head just in time; it travelled over to the crowd, and people began screaming as several residents were thrown across the field by the massive branch. Gideon ran forward, dragging me back towards the centre. I saw Noble and some of the residents casting blazing torches towards the trees, and watched in horror as one man was picked up by a branch and tossed into the bonfire. The trees were completely ablaze now and clearly in distress; a deep groan reverberated across the field as several branches came crashing down to the ground, writhing in agony and reaching out to the fleeing crowd. As the ground began to shake, I saw immense roots emerging from the icy ground and heading straight towards us.

'Run.' I screamed.

As we made our way around the side of the crowd, I felt Gideon pulling back.

'Where's Noble?'

My eyes darted around the field looking for him, but all I could see was a multitude of roots intermingling with the residents, winding and securing themselves about their bodies, and pulling them towards The Elder Trees, that were now engulfed in flames.

A rising dread came over me.

'I saw him a second ago, but...but he's gone.'

'Go and find the others in the chapel Effie, I shall join you shortly.'

'No.' I screamed at him. Both of us will search for Noble.'

He gripped my arms and stared into my tearstained face. 'Please Effie. Trust me, I shall find him.'

I nodded blindly. 'Hurry Gideon, please hurry.'

For an instant his mouth met mine and we clung to one another.

I rushed down the field and back to the monastery. I wasn't scared of the trees coming for me anymore, if they were going to take my life they would have done it before when I stood amongst them, or when I set them alight, but they were angry now, I could tell. As I reached the greenhouses, I noticed every pane had been broken and a large root had smashed its way through one of the walls. With trepidation I stepped over the rubble and into the building, and as the root slowly moved along the floor like a snake, I saw how the tendrils that had previously made their home in this room had attached themselves to it. Cautiously I edged my way along the side of the building until I reached the far door and went out into the dark passageway. Despite not having a lantern I somehow reached the chapel, trying not to become distracted by the crumbling ceiling. One solitary candle was lit at the altar, and sitting on the floor, bound with rope were Mace and Clarice.

My heart started to pound in my chest.

'What happened, where's Gabriel?'

Clarice turned to me. 'The mistress took him.'

'What?' I screamed. I could feel my stomach begin to churn as an overwhelming sense of realisation washed over me. When I'd left the field, the mad woman was nowhere to be seen, I realised now she must have heard what Abel said then rushed to the chapel.

As Clarice glared at me with a crazed look in her eyes she looked almost feral.

'I stabbed one of the guards in the chest.' Her gaze travelled over to the front of the pews where a body lay face down on the stone floor.

I stood there for a moment feeling dazed. Then coming back to my senses I rushed forward and examined Mace. He had a gash on his forehead and his nose and lip were bloodied.

'Are you all right Mace?

He smiled feebly at me. 'That cursed woman E, she took Gabriel.' His head fell forward for a second then came back up. 'I'm sorry E, we did all we could, but there was four of them and they gave me a right old bashing.'

I ruffled his hair. 'I can see.' With trembling hands, I began to undo the rope. 'You're covered in blood.'

As the rope fell to the ground, I looked at them both. 'Wait for me here, I'm going to get my son.'

'But E you don't know where Verity's taken him.'

I looked steadily into his eyes. 'I have a pretty good idea.'

I ran up the passageway and came face to face with Wilding brandishing an axe. He smirked when he saw me, his piercing eyes glowering at me with repulsion.

'Well, that's a stroke of luck Miss. I was looking for you.'

'Get out of my way Wilding.'

I moved the other side of him to pass but he blocked my way.

'You and me have got unfinished business.' He scraped the axe along the floor then swung it up over his right shoulder, grinning at me with his discoloured teeth. 'I've got this axe for protection from the trees and it will do a good job decapitating you Miss. Think of me as your executioner.'

As I took a few steps back he pushed me onto the ground and stood over me with the axe.

'Any last words before I strike your head from your shoulders?'

'Yes. There is.' I mumbled, reaching into my tunic pocket. 'You're going to rot in hell, just like your brother.' I shot up and plunged the dagger into his leg and began to run up the passageway.

I felt something fly past close to my face and realised it was the axe, and as I turned back, I saw Wilding limping after me.

'You're a coward Miss. Come back and face me.'

I stood there contemplating whether or not to run, but I knew he'd only come after me. With a sigh I retrieved the axe and swung round to face him.

He grinned. 'That axe is no good with the likes of you.'

'Really?' I replied.

Taking aim, I lifted up the weapon and threw it with all my might, never believing for one moment it would strike him, but to my astonishment it caught him in the shoulder. He staggered back clutching the axe with his hands and fell to the ground, groaning in agony. I went and stood over him, watching him squirm with pain and humiliation.

'You'll not get out of here alive Miss.' He mumbled. 'Them trees will rip you apart, limb from limb.' He gasped with pain. 'See you in hell.'

Without a word I left.

Chapter 21

My journey to the church was relatively easy. Luckily for me the mad woman must have fled in a rush, as the door to the wine cellar was unlocked. When I finally reached the church, I felt completely panicky and overwrought, fearing that my sister had already travelled through the mirror with my son. I pictured her taking Gabriel to some distant land and starting a new life, she would fill his head with dark thoughts, and he would turn out to be as evil as her, incapable of love or compassion, with a heart made of stone.

At first it appeared the church was in darkness but then I spotted a flickering golden glow emanating from the altar. Should I allow this tiny light to give me a glimmer of hope, hope that they were still here in the magnificent church; this was of course an irrational notion, as seeing a blazing lantern meant nothing, an yet in my heart I suddenly knew that I wasn't too late.

The mad woman stepped forward from the shadows, her face a deathly white.

'Well, look who it is. The descendant of Brother Carmichael who believes she has put a standstill to the ending of all worlds.'

Never before had I been so glad to see my sister. With a spring in my step I rushed over to where she was standing.

'Where's Gabriel?'

'He's safe Effelia. You know I wouldn't harm my little nephew.'

'You risked my son's life by bringing him through the mirror, and now he's in mortal danger.'

'Well that's your fault Effelia- If you hadn't harmed The Elder Trees, he'd be perfectly safe, your actions may have completely jeopardised all my hard work and put all our lives at risk.'

'So, you admit your ludicrous plan might not have worked.'

She shrugged her shoulders. 'I really cannot say dear sister. You see there's nothing in the ledger about the trees being destroyed by fire. For all we know the ritual will work.' Her gaze drifted up to the ceiling as dust began to fall from up above. 'We should know by morning.'

'Then why are you leaving Verity? As mistress of Hartland should you not stay and stand with your people.'

'Oh, but I am Effelia. But Gabriel and I shall be spending the night at Rawlings.' She wrinkled her nose. 'My son's safety comes first.'

'Your son? What are you talking about Verity' I swallowed nervously. 'I'm his mother.'

She crossed over and glared into my face. 'You *were* his mother.' Her head titled to the right and her eyes became wide with amusement. 'You'll be dead soon and who better to look after Gabriel than his Auntie Verity.'

'You'll never be a mother to my son. You wouldn't know how.'

'I can learn - how difficult can it be. Surely, I can't do a worse job than you, or even my own mother for that matter.' Her eyes suddenly became distant. 'How she constantly moaned and criticised me, but it was when I accidentally killed my friend William Hind that mother really went berserk. She was going to tell the entire village.'

I suddenly remembered the villager who had shouted out at Isaiah's trial that day in church.

'You killed that boy, the brother of Merrick Hind. All the time he'd thought Isaiah was responsible when really it was you?'

'I told you it was an accident.' She shrieked. 'One day William and I climbed a tree in the woods. He was being rather annoying so I gave him a little push. He fell to the ground and died. I never meant for it to happen, not really. Father buried his body there in the woods, and we had to pretend that William had gone wandering off and we didn't know where he was.'

'That's...that's awful. If it was an accident then why didn't you tell his parents the truth?'

'Oh Effelia, they would never have believed us, nor would the villagers. My own mother didn't even believe me when I told her it was an accident. So, I took a hammer and bludgeoned her to death.'

My eyes glazed over.

'You....you were the one responsible for her death, not Isaiah.'

'Yes, it was me. Father never forgave me for what I did.' She said, suddenly looking venomous. 'You've always been his favourite, but now I have a chance to redeem myself. 'If the ritual fails then Gabriel and I shall take up residence at Rawlings, and when father sees how wonderful I am with his grandson he *will* finally forgive me.' With a light laugh she whispered in my ear. 'I shall enjoy taking your place, with your son and your husband. You see Gideon always belonged to me Effelia, he's the one I've always desired, and he's the man I'm going to have. I pray that he has not been harmed tonight, for he and I will be man and wife. Together we shall produce more siblings for Gabriel, and live a long and happy existence as one big family.' For a moment she closed her eyes and shook her head. 'It's a shame your old Aunt has to go, but if we decide to permanently live at your home she'll just get in the way. You understand, don't you dear sister?'

In a fit of fury, I slapped her across the face. 'Your madness holds no bounds Verity.'

She looked incensed. 'Any madness I possess is overshadowed with brilliance; a brilliance that will one day make me great. Whilst you, with your ignorant stubborn nature, will never amount to anything.'

'Go to hell Verity.'

Without warning she grabbed my hair and shoved my head back so it crashed against the corner of the stone altar. I fell to the ground, lying there in a crumpled heap. A searing pain shot through my skull and my head began to spin, causing an acute wave of nausea to come over me. I could see her moving back a little, laughing mockingly. Somehow, I found the strength to get up and for a second I stood there unsteadily on my feet before losing my balance and falling back painfully against the centre of the altar. I cried out in agony before managing to steady myself with my hands.

Suddenly a shuddering groan reverberated through the church, sending with it a series of tremors.

Verity began to cackle. 'We're safe down here Effelia. Nothing can harm us.' She laughed again. 'Or let me rephrase that – nothing can harm *me*.'

Through the darkness I could see her coming closer, in steady purposeful strides. I opened my mouth to speak but instead began to retch. I swallowed, desperately trying to keep myself from vomiting.

When she spoke again her voice sounded strange, like a distant echo. 'What a terrible shame it has come to this, dear sister.'

I groaned, still unable to respond.

Her face was up against mine. 'Can't speak? You never did have much to say.' Reaching up with her hand she began stroking my cheek. 'Gideon may be a touch distraught when he learns of your death, but I shall be there to comfort him.' She sniggered scornfully. 'And to take care of his son.' Her fingers travelled to my hair, and grabbing a handful she twisted it and yanked my head back. 'How greedy you were loving both Gideon and Noble.' A screaming laugh escaped her lips, emphasizing her madness. 'Only now you'll never see either of them ever again.' Releasing my hair her hands drifted down and encircled my throat, and as her dark eyes stared unwaveringly into mine with a chilling look of steely determination and pure hatred, she began to squeeze.

My eyes widened in sheer panic and I let out a pitiful whimper. In desperation I begin tearing at her hands, struggling to release them from my neck, but her hold on me was like iron.

She smiled, her lips curling into a snarl. 'I've always wanted you dead Effelia, and had it not been for having to keep you alive for the ritual you'd be long gone.' She spat into my face. 'Daddy's beloved little daughter who could do no wrong.'

I winced and then tried to answer but was unable to move my lips. Frantically I ran my hands along the altar, trying to find something to clout her with, but it was futile.

'But daddy's not here to save you now, is he?'

The pressure of her hands was becoming unbearable and little by little I felt myself weakening. It would have been so easy just to give up, to fade away. But that would mean she had won, and I couldn't allow that to happen. I began to feel around again further along the altar, and this time my fingers grasped a heavy object, a candlestick, I think. Mustering the only strength, I had left I swung it up in the air before bringing it down onto the side of her skull. She eyed me strangely for a second, and I watched a trickle of blood run down her face, then releasing my neck, she collapsed into a heap on the floor. I gasped, trying to get my breath back, my hands protectively covering my neck. Without removing my eyes from her body, I gradually edged around her and made my way across the church.

A sudden whimper coming from the far right of the building made me cry out.

'Gabriel. Gabriel is that you?'

Rushing frantically in the direction of the noise I went into the prayer room and lying in a basket was Gabriel, wrapped snugly in a blanket, fast asleep. He must have cried out then settled back down. I kissed him tenderly on the forehead and arranged his cover. Then I saw the mirror, standing there invitingly, waiting for me. I was suddenly filled with indecision- would it be best to deliver Gabriel through the mirror to the safety of home then join him later, or should I keep him with me and go and meet the others in the chapel. Both had their risks: with my head injury I still felt weak, and without sufficient concentration we could both end up travelling from the mirror into a shadow world where we'd be roaming like lost souls forever; and if I took him through the monastery we risked being injured or killed by the trees or falling masonry.

With a frustrated groan I momentarily closed my eyes, but just as I did so a crack appeared in one of the stained-glass windows and a gnarled branch came coiling down towards the mirror. Instinctively I moved the basket away and out of the room. A tremendous crash suddenly filled my ears followed by the smashing of glass. Peering back into the prayer room I saw part of the ceiling had caved in and fallen on the mirror, it lay amongst the rabble, smashed and ruined.

I let out a harrowing sigh. 'Looks like we'll be taking the longer route home.'

Taking a moment, I knelt down and checked on Gabriel and was just about to lift up the basket when I noticed something rather disturbing. The body of the mad woman had disappeared. Foolishly I'd believed her to be dead, foolishly I was wrong; when I heard a movement behind me my heart began hammering loudly in my chest. With a gasp I rose from the ground and turned to see her bloodstained face, made all the more chilling by the paleness of her skin and the blackness of her eyes.

'Please tell me you're a ghost.' I said in shaky voice.

'You can't get rid of me that easily dear sister.' With a twisted smile she brought her right hand forward, holding a knife rather near to my face. 'Lucky for me there's a complete variety of weapons housed in this church, just waiting for me plunge into your heart. Now move up the aisle, away from Gabriel.'

Rather carefully I stepped away from the basket.

Baring her teeth, she snarled at me. 'Prepare to die.'

As she lunged for me with the knife, I managed to dodge her for a moment but as she came for me again, I wasn't quick enough and the knife sliced into my arm, right next to the cut from the ritual. I grimaced with pain and staggered back.

'Just accept defeat dear sister. You know I'm stronger than you.'

As I glared into her cruel, unforgiving eyes, I knew that one of us was going to die tonight, and it was probably going to be me.

'Yes, you are stronger than me, but you're also pure evil.' I took a step towards her. 'And there's no place in this world for the likes of you.' Without thinking of the consequences, I lunged for her and swiftly grabbed her wrist before she had time to thrust the knife into me, and held it fast. As she tried to regain the use of the weapon I felt her nails clawing at my skin, and her fingers dug into the wound on my arm. I cried out in pain and released my grip on her wrist. I pushed her then, and as she grabbed hold of me we both tumbled to the floor. I wasn't aware of the blood immediately, but then I felt it seeping through my tunic. Looking down into the face of my sister I saw her eyes staring unnaturally wide into mine; there was nothing behind them anymore, nothing but emptiness; they were dead eyes.

A loud rumble could be heard directly overhead.

With an air of panic, I rolled myself off the body and clambered to my feet, momentarily staring down at the knife deeply imbedded in the mad woman's chest. It must have pierced her heart when we fell, instantly killing her. Trying not to look at her face, I took one of the long cloths draped over the altar and covered her body. There wasn't time to say a prayer, and what prayer would I say for such a person.

'Goodbye Verity.' I croaked; my voice barely audible. 'May you rest in peace.'

I heard a sudden cry.

'Gabriel' I yelled. 'Oh, Gabriel I'm sorry.' With haste I went and picked him up. He was awake now and staring blearily at me with his wide eyes. 'You're safe now, everything is going to be alright.' I planted a kiss on his cheek. 'And mummy's never leaving you again.' I held him against me fiercely. I smiled reassuringly into his soft little face, his rich dark eyes, staring at me innocently from underneath his curls.

As the far side of the roof caved in, I stumbled backwards, glaring up at the snake-like roots forcing themselves into the church. I cradled Gabriel close to my chest, covering his head with my arms.

'Time to leave little fellow.' I uttered, withdrawing further away from the roots.

Swiftly I rushed up the back of the church carrying Gabriel and we went up the narrow set of steps and made our way up through the trap door and into the wine cellar. Several bottles had crashed to the ground, turning the floor crimson; I stepped carefully over the broken glass, trying to ignore the creeping tendrils that seemed to have suddenly spread through the room. Emerging through the door I breathed in sharply. A mound of tangled roots had invaded the passageway and several of the stone columns had fallen to the ground; residents were running about screaming, and I saw several bodies lying on the floor.

I held Gabriel close.

An elderly looking man approached me and jabbed his finger into my shoulder.

'You caused this.' He shouted viciously. 'The mistress was going to give me eternal life then you come along and set fire to the trees.' With a cry he kicked away a root that was trying to grab his ankle. 'And now I'm going to die.'

I stared into his bloodshot eyes, not really sure what to say. 'I'm sorry.'

'Sorry, is that all you've got to say for yourself?'

As the man continued to shout at me someone let out a scream behind us as a colossal root came smashing up through the floor, heading directly towards where we were standing.

'Look out.' I yelled at the man, but he either didn't hear or wasn't prepared to listen. Tugging his hand I swiftly ran over to the far left but he refused to move. What happened next would be permanently imprinted on my memory, for the root impaled the man through the stomach and out through his back, lifting him up in the air, before ripping him in half. With a whimper I closed my eyes and pressed my face against Gabriel's head, wrapping my arms around him protectively. Luckily, he'd been looking the other way and hadn't seen a thing. Half stumbling I ran for my life, not knowing what direction I was heading. It was becoming apparent that the trees had completely taken over the monastery, whether this was my doing or the mad woman's, I couldn't be sure, but it now seemed certain that they were out to destroy us. As I stepped over bodies and fallen stonework a hoard of residents came rushing past me, closely followed by a mass of twisted roots. Pressing my back up against the wall I stood there and watched in horror as several people tripped and fell over an upturned stone slab lying across the floor and were instantly caught up amongst the roots and dragged along the passageway with them.

Gabriel began to cry and I rocked him softly from side to side.

'It's okay, we'll be home soon.'

Rigid with fear I suddenly couldn't move, but what frightened me the most was what the elderly man had said to me before he perished. Had I really caused this because I'd set the trees alight, or was it the outcome of the ritual, triggered by my blood. Was this the beginning of the end? My eyes glazed over for a moment, for I was painfully aware that, either way, I was responsible for this tragedy that was unfolding right before my very eyes.

'Effie, Effie over here.'

The voice seemed distance and familiar. I half turned my head and saw the faint outline of a young girl. It was Lucinda.

I gave her a poignant smile.

She drifted closer. 'We haven't much time.' As she approached me a deep look of concern crossed over her face. 'This isn't your doing Effie. Verity didn't realise what the true outcome would be. You see the ritual written in the ledger was never meant to destroy other worlds, it was meant to destroy Hartland.'

'When did you discover this?'

'I've known all along Effie. That is why I was so eager for you to leave, as without your blood the trees would not be capable of destroying the monastery.' Her face became grim. 'Although I do believe they were gradually taking it over.' She placed a cold hand on my shoulder. 'By igniting the trees you have hopefully put an end to their reign.'

I looked bewildered. 'But they are still alive.'

'No Effie, they are slowly dying. You have to remember that they are no ordinary trees.'

A thunderous crash sounded to the right.

'Come. With any luck I can lead you both to the chapel.'

I followed on behind her. There were bodies everywhere now, and with care I stepped over them.

Thank you for speaking to Abel, I had no idea he could see you too.'

She giggled. 'Oh yes. I befriended Abel in the library when he was collecting all the books for the bonfire. He helped me come to terms with their loss.'

We took a sharp left and travelled down an exceedingly narrow corridor, and as we emerged out the other side I recognised where we were.

Lucinda stood in front of the chapel door.

'Abel and your other friends are waiting for you in here.' Her expression had a tinge of sadness about it. 'This is where I leave you Effie. You are in safe hands now.'

Instinctively I touched her cold cheek. 'Thank you, Lucinda, thank you for everything.' My heart wanted to say more but my head urged me not to. One couldn't tell the dead to take care, or invite them to join you. 'I shall miss you.'

She smiled warmly at me. 'I will miss you too Effie. And your little boy.'

I nodded graciously at her and entered the chapel.

'Hello?' I said staring into the empty room. 'Gideon?' With a quick sigh I crept towards the altar, and jumped in surprise as a figure sprung up from behind it.

'Thank the Lord Miss, you're safe.'

'Abel.'

He peered down behind the altar. 'It's alright you two it's Miss Effie.' He chuckled. 'And her little son.'

I laughed apprehensively.

Mace poked his head around the side of the stone table. 'Come on E. Let's get the hell out of here before we get done in by those demonic trees.'

'What about Gideon and Noble, are they not with you?'

Mace and Abel exchanged glances before lowering their eyes.

'Where are they Mace? I said with a rising sense of panic.

'I don't know E.'

Gabriel began to cry.

Clarice's head poked up from the top of the altar. 'They're probably dead.' She uttered in a monotone voice. 'No one stands a chance against the trees.'

'Now, now Clarice, don't be so negative.' Retorted Mace.

The door began to bang as if a giant fist was thumping against it.

'Come on E.' he said eyeing the door cautiously. 'We've got to go.'

'Perhaps I should wait for Gideon and Noble.' I stared down at Gabriel. 'Would you like to go with Uncle Mace? Mummy will join you very soon.'

'No Miss Effie, no.' Roared Abel in protest. 'It don't make sense Miss for you to stay.' He pointed at the door. 'Any time now that door will be blasted apart by one of them trees and the roots will come and drag you away.'

Mace put his arm around me. 'Abel's right E, listen to the big man.' His eyes widened underneath his unruly hair. 'You may be related to Brother what's his name but that doesn't make you invincible.' He began to drag me towards the altar. 'Gideon and Noble wouldn't expect you to wait for them, and besides they've probably fled another way.'

As the door crashed apart a root came slivering along the floor towards us.

I stared at Mace. 'Let's go.'

We all made our way down the steps into the cave, and in silence ran down the tunnel that led to the deep underground passage that Abel had discovered. Being so far down was scary and claustrophobic, and I had difficulty breathing. Despite it being free from roots I heard a distant rumbling above our heads and sensed they were coming. As we emerged in a field, I was relieved to feel the cool night air upon my face. Away in the distance I could see the shimmering glow of the fire as it continued to consume the trees; it had spread now and was lapping up against the perimeter, and creeping up the root laden gates. But the trees weren't going quietly, and I watched aghast as colossal roots smothered the monastery, smashing through the stonework as if it were made of paper, and there was screaming, lots of screaming.

Gabriel stirred in my arms.

'Let me take him Effie.' Said Mace softly. 'I'll rock him back to sleep.'

I responded with a pitiful nod. 'Thanks.' I handed him Gabriel. The poor thing must be hungry by now and I was certain he needed changing. The most practical thing would be to return home to Briarwood immediately but instead I sat on the grass, dazed and exhausted. 'Make sure he keeps warm, won't you Mace.'

'Right you are E.'

I watched as he carefully sat close beside me with Gabriel in his arms, nestling him close to his chest.

Clarice was pacing about restlessly.

'Why are we waiting here for, survivors? No one else would have made it out alive.' She began wringing her hands. 'We should get out of here while we still can.'

Mace peered at her. 'Now, now Clarice, calm down.' He said soothingly. 'Sit beside me and rest for a while. We've a long journey ahead of us and need some sleep.'

With a frown she lowered herself to the ground and sat somewhat away from him.

Looking downcast, Abel joined us. I smiled gently at him then glanced into Mace's sombre eyes, and noticed he was struggling to smile through the tears. With a heavy heart I placed my head on his shoulder and stared at Gabriel. Feeling numb I closed my eyes.

The first thing I noticed was the brightness of the morning. For one blissful moment my mind was clear, and then the realisation sunk in and an overwhelming ache crossed over my heart like a cruel dark shadow.

Several deer were roaming nearby, peering curiously our way, wondering what we were doing on their land.

I heard a giggle.

A sleeping Mace was lying next to me, cradling Gabriel, who was wide-awake, his large eyes staring into mine. With a smile I carefully picked him up in my arms and kissed his nose, holding him close. I started to cry.

'Daddy.' He squealed.

I gasped, gazing at him lovingly through my tear stained face. How ironic that his first word should be that of his father.

'If only daddy was here darling.'

I rose from the ground and turned round, staring in astonishment at the view before me. The fire had burnt out now, and the monastery lay in a complete ruin amongst the remains of the tree roots in the dying embers. The Elder Trees still remained standing but their unnatural life had finally come to an end; and they were now merely burnt out shells, charred and withered like dead creatures perpetually entombed in their grave. As the years passed by visitors would come from far and wide to look upon the shrine of Hartland, and the history of the land would be revered and romanticized. Only people such as myself would know the truth.

'Look.' Exclaimed Abel pointing up to the sky. 'The sky is blue and the sun....' he remarked excitedly. 'The sun has come out.'

As we all stood there marvelling at the change in the weather my eyes were drawn to the entrance of the monastery – the roots still clung to the iron railings, despite being entirely blackened from the fire, and the colossal gates seemed to be moving. Suddenly transfixed I carried on looking as various roots broke away from the gate as it swung open, and to my surprise several figures emerged from within.

'Here Miss Effie, let me take the little one.'

Thanking Abel, I handed him Gabriel.

I felt Mace clasp my arm. My eyes flashed to him then back to the gates. Hardly able to watch but knowing I must, I waited with baited breath, my heart pounding unsteadily within my chest.

At first, we saw no one we recognised, and there didn't appear to be many survivors, just a few men and woman with young children, but trailing behind were two more men, one had his arm draped over the other, his head drooping forward.

A strange noise erupted from my lips as I saw who it was and I instinctively placed my hand over my mouth. Feeling elated I bounded towards the figures with tears flowing down my cheeks. As soon as I reached Gideon my arms came about his neck, then I gazed into face.

'I thought you were dead.' My eyes travelled to Noble who seemed barely conscious. 'Is...is he badly injured?'

Gideon's face was pale and his breathing sounded laboured. 'I'm...I'm not sure. He was trapped by a branch, but I managed to free him.'

Mace came leaping forward, grinning all over his face. 'What took you so long brother, we thought you'd got lost.' He grabbed Noble's other arm and hauled it across his shoulder.

'We had to wait underground, until the worse of it was over.' He paused to catch his breath. 'Good to see you Mace.'

I watched as they hugged one another. Very gently I lifted Noble's head and peered at his blood -splattered face. For a brief second, he half opened his eyes and we gazed at one another before he lost consciousness. I stepped back so Gideon and Mace could carefully lay him down on the grass, and as the two brothers crouched down beside him, I found myself moving further away. If Noble was too badly injured there was a chance of me falling to pieces in front of Gideon, and he may realise my true feelings for his brother. Looking

239

at the three siblings I suddenly wondered how different their lives might have been if they'd all grown up together, if Noble hadn't gone wandering off after his mother at such a young age and Mace had been brought up by Caleb. They would have forged a long-lasting bond that could never be broken, and perhaps, just perhaps Gideon wouldn't have dreamt of me, and in their eyes I would never had existed. They'd never had to be here at Hartland if it weren't for me, I had caused all this, and if Noble died, I would be responsible.

Mace came plodding over, looking miserable.

'Noble's still out for the count.'

I gazed down at the grass. 'He doesn't look too well.'

He shook his head gravely. 'He's not.'

My heart sank.

I glanced back at Abel; he was pulling faces at Gabriel and making him giggle. Clarice seemed agitated, and was pacing up and down the field, ever so often stopping to stare at the monastery. A couple of the survivors had wandered off as if they knew where they were going, whilst a man and the women and children were milling about looking lost; I suspected these were the ones who'd been tricked into travelling through the mirror, and could possibly originate from my home town, the name of course had slipped my mind, if this were the case then I would help them return.

My thoughts drifted to the journey ahead of us. The idea of us all trekking back to Briarwood through the wilds was a real concern. Noble needed urgent attention and poor Gabriel would soon grow weak. If only we had the calling whistle, if only Croft was still alive.

I frowned, staring at Mace. 'We have a hell of a journey ahead of us. Noble will have to be carried on a makeshift stretcher for one thing and-'

Mace barged in before I could finish my sentence. 'Help is on its way E; didn't Gideon tell you? He managed to reach Caleb last night by using that neat mind thing that he does, Caleb's on his way with a couple of his furry friends for transport.'

Chapter 22

It is said that the dead don't truly die but linger by the living, watching them coming and going on the earth. I sense the inhabitants of the monastery haven't travelled to the silent land of death, not yet. They languish amongst the ruins, where the wind howls like a pack of tormented hounds. And if you should hear a whisper in the gloom, a haunting laugh, or a sense of chilling unease, you know you are being held in their chilling embrace.

I consider myself one of the lucky ones, along with my friends. We fought and conquered Hartland, and escaped with our lives. But although the monastery has gone, along with its draconian and murderous ways, its memory is still fresh. Eventually I hope to reflect on those dark days without fear, but that day hasn't yet come to pass, for although my physical scars have faded my mind is not so easily healed. Almost every night I awake drenched in sweat, believing I can't breathe. My nightmares take me back to the monastery, where the trees are slowly consuming me. Brother Carmichael is there with Septimus, watching from afar whilst I gradually suffocate amongst the bark, and when I am near death and only my blinking eyes are visible, they kneel before me and pray for my soul, then with blazing torches they ignite the trees. On other occasions I find myself in the underground church with the mad woman, a mournful laugh is etched across her decomposing face and her eyes are bulging and transparent. Her skeletal hands are about neck and this time she succeeds in strangling me.

Once upon time being in Briarwood was like being in a sunny dream that you never wanted to leave, a place that filled your heart with gladness. But now...now my mind is no longer at peace. Perhaps too much has happened to carry on without any worries, or perhaps I have finally grown up and in doing so have taken on the burdens of an adult. Either way my demons could no longer be banished. And so, I began to question whether there really *was* an enchanted spell covering the land, or if Briarwood was simply a sweet little village of yesteryear.

In the caring hands of his father, Noble soon made a full recovery, and only had a faint scar running across his temple as a reminder. Gideon had saved him that night, removing a branch that lay across him and dragging him to safety; somehow this act cemented their relationship as brothers, and they were now much closer. Since returning to the village they had spent time talking about their younger days, and resolving issues regarding their mother, Sabina. The tension between Noble and I was still there, and now and then we would catch one another's eye and give each other a knowing look. I found myself having to avoid him, but it wasn't easy in such a small cottage. I knew in my heart that we couldn't survive in this manner for very much longer, one of us would have to move out. It would be cruel and unjust to expect him to leave his home, so I began seriously contemplating the idea of moving somewhere else in the village with Gideon and Gabriel. After all, we were a family and needed our own home.

As I stood there gazing out the kitchen window, I smiled to myself. Caleb was in the garden giving Gabriel a piggyback, they were chatting and laughing to one another as they went around the vegetable patch. Caleb doted on his grandson and Gabriel thought the world of his grandfather.

Gideon came in and wrapped his arms around my waist.

'And what are you daydreaming about today Effie?'

I was thinking about taking a stroll. Why don't you join me?'

He didn't answer straight away and just nuzzled his face into the nape of my neck. 'Not today darling. Why don't you ask Mace or Clarice to accompany you.' he paused for a moment. 'Or even Noble, I think he's back from the market. If you like I can go and find him.'

I swallowed. 'No, no I don't think so.'

We were both silent for a moment.

I cleared my throat. 'Clarice always feels calmer after a walk, but she's having a nap at the moment, and I don't wish to disturb her.'

'How is she today?'

'The same.' I replied rather gloomily. 'She'll have to return home Gideon, it's the only way to improve her condition. Perhaps I should have a quiet word with Mace to see when they're leaving. He really can't keep putting it off.'

'And you, what will you do about seeing your Aunt?'

My voice became faint and uncertain. 'I'm not sure.'

With a drawn-out sigh he removed his arms from my waist and trudged slowly to the table and sat down. As I turned to gaze at him, I noticed a distant look in his eyes.

Gideon, is there anything wrong?' I asked feeling concerned.

'No darling, you run along and find Mace.'

I continued to stare at him; unable to shake off the feeling he was keeping something from me.

Mace came barging into the room, with his face lit up in amusement. 'Where's Caleb? That old Miss Bowers is here again requesting to see him. Apparently, her latest ailment is a sprained ankle.' He grinned cheekily. 'Any excuse to visit her beloved.'

'I heard that.' Said Caleb, coming in through the back door with Gabriel. He wiped his feet on the mat. 'I hope you invited her in Mace?'

'Well of course. I told her to go and wait in the parlour.'

A rather wobbly Gabriel came running towards me and his father, and Gideon scooped him up into his arms.

Mace smiled broadly at his father. 'Don't you find it odd that she's here every week with something or other bothering her? I tell you Caleb she has a soft spot for you.'

'Come on now son. Don't you think your imagination is running away with you?' Suddenly looking bemused he placed his hand on Mace's shoulder. 'And I've told you enough times. Call me father, not Caleb.'

Mace looked shamefaced. 'Okay...father.' He grinned sheepishly at him. 'I just hope I don't have to call Miss Bowers 'mother' soon.'

Caleb burst out laughing as he headed for the door. 'No son there is nothing romantic in my thoughts towards that sweet old lady. Your mother was the only woman for me.' He paused for a moment with his hand on the doorknob. 'She may be gone but she will always be my wife. Now if you'll excuse me, I need to go and attend to Miss Bower's ankle.' Rather abruptly he left the room.

'Play, I want to play.' Announced Gabriel with a giggle.

'Okay little nephew.' Mace said, sticking his tongue out at Gabriel, much to his amusement. 'Want to spend some time with Uncle Mace?' He asked, ruffling his hair. 'We can play hide and seek again.'

Gabriel exploded into a fit of giggles and began clapping his hands together with glee. 'Hide, me hide.'

'Alright little one.'

I cleared my throat. 'Actually, Mace I thought we could take a stroll together.'

He pulled a face at me. 'Really?'

'Come on Mace it'll do you good to get some colour into those pallid cheeks of yours.' Said Gideon turning to me. 'And I shall play with Gabriel, darling. You go off and enjoy yourself.'

I half smiled at him. 'You'll have to play hide and seek with him, you know.'

He threw me a reassuring grin. 'Perhaps another day; we'll do some drawing at the table instead.' With a sigh he widened his eyes at Gabriel and placed him down onto the floor. 'That will be fun, won't it son.'

'No, hide, hide.' Exclaimed Gabriel rather wilfully, stamping his feet.'

Gideon smiled gently at him. 'Very well then son, but just for a while as daddy's a little tired.' For a moment he locked eyes with me before gulping and staring solemnly down at the table.

'Come on then E, stop standing there like a dummy.'

My eyes lingered on Gideon before switching to Mace.

'Actually, perhaps we should go another time. I....I think it's raining.'

Mace scratched his head in puzzlement. 'Make up your mind woman. And anyway, when has a little rain ever stopped you. Are you afraid of your hair going frizzy?'

'No, not at all.' I laughed. 'It already is frizzy.'

'Exactly.' Replied Mace, his eyes full of amusement. He took my hand and dragged me towards the door.

We passed over the cornfields and headed to the clump of yew trees up ahead, then through the woods, following the tiny brook that ran alongside it. Once we'd reached the edge we came out upon open countryside. The shower had passed over now and the landscape was basked in the mid- morning sunshine which streamed down between the clouds in the cool airy sky. After striding across a field I pointed westwards.

'Look, a tiny path.'

'It probably leads to nowhere E.'

I grabbed his hand. 'Oh, come on Mace, where's your sense of adventure.'

He pulled a face. 'I left it behind today.' He began dragging me back. 'Why, all of a sudden do you want to walk miles E? I would have been quite happy just going for a normal walk, rather than trekking through the unknown wilds of Briarwood.'

'Well....a long walk always clears my head.' I replied pulling him towards the path. 'And we've hardly gone that far.'

'E, is something bothering you?'

'Oh just a few niggling worries.' I said, slowly going along the uneven stone path. 'One of them concerns you and Clarice.' I stopped and faced him. 'Mace I don't understand why you are delaying taking her home. If I'm right all traces of the tonic will be obliterated once you've both left.'

His face clouded over. 'Truth is E, the idea of travelling through that mirror makes me shudder. What if something goes wrong? I've been thinking it might be better to stay in Briarwood and hope Clarice improves with time.'

I carried on walking. 'Mace I'm hardly an expert on these matters but from what I've learnt the tonic doesn't just wear off. Don't you think Clarice deserves a chance of recovering and of being reunited with her mother? And don't worry about the mirror, I'm sure it will be fine.'

As I heard him mutter on his voice seemed to fade into the background. I let out a small gasp as we reached the end of the path. Down a bank stood a sweet little cottage, nestled amongst the trees. For some particular reason it looked familiar, and yet I was certain I'd not been here before. I noticed the dark wooded area to the right of the cottage with meadows to the front and wide sweeps of pastureland to the rear of the property. And as we drew nearer, I saw the creepers, smothering the brickwork and wallflowers growing up against them. A low green hedge ran around the front of the garden, which was filled with an abundance of wild flowers and weeds.

'I wonder who lives here.' Commented Mace, staring curiously at the cottage. 'Perhaps the owners will invite us in for tea and cake.'

'I think its abandoned Mace.'

He groaned. 'Let's go back E'

'No, we're here now, and might as well take a peek inside.'

With another groan he walked alongside me.

Going through the tiny gate my dress brushed passed the flowers that had drooped considerably in the rain. I pushed the door open and ventured inside. There was a peaceful atmosphere within the cottage, a lingering stillness. The rooms downstairs seemed surprisingly large and roomy, although the low beams made them seem a little dark.

'So, you've definitely not been here before then?' Said Mace, following after me.

'No, I don't believe so.'

'It's a bit spooky, isn't it E?'

I looked at him and raised my eyes. 'No, the cottage is just lonely and needs some tender loving care.'

'You make it sound like it's alive Effie, like something out of a nightmare.'

It was at that precise moment I became aware of why it was so familiar. I *had* seen the cottage before, only it wasn't in person, it was in a dream, a dream that I'd had ages ago of being here with my ancestor Florentine.

'No Mace, more like a dream.'

With a smile I headed for the kitchen. Suddenly I had the idea of moving here with Gideon and Gabriel. With a little work it would make the perfect family home. Perhaps that's what Florentine was trying to tell me in the dream, either that or it was a warning. But the cottage gave me a sense of happiness and belonging, and I took that as a good omen.

I let out a contented sigh. 'The place has such a good feel about it, don't you think Mace?'

'No, it gives me the creeps.'

'Well I think it would make the perfect place to live.'

'But what about going home, don't forget about that Effie.'

'Home? Mace I am home.'

Mace took my hand. 'I mean our proper home, away from Briarwood. The truth is Effie you're allowing this land to completely cloud your judgement.' He titled my chin so I was looking into his eyes. 'You owe it to yourself as well as your Aunt to go back home to see her. If you don't go back now, you'll totally forget about her, and probably never see her again. So as your friend I'm asking... no I'm telling you to come back with Clarice and I...just for a while.'

Feeling suddenly weak I went and sat down on one of the old chairs.

'But that would mean leaving Gideon and Gabriel. I've already been parted from them once, when I was taken to Hartland, I'm not sure I can bear it again. And I can't take them with me, it would be far too dangerous. Only the other day Caleb told me how Verity should not have taken Gabriel through the mirror, as it could have serious repercussions for one so young.'

He knelt down beside me, peering into my face. 'Gideon will understand, and will be perfectly capable of taking care of his son in your absence. I on the other hand will have my hands full with Clarice and need you with me for moral support. And your Aunt will be overjoyed to see us. I can't even remember what her first name is E, isn't that terrible.'

I stared into space. 'Yes.'

Abruptly he rose to his feet and shuffled slowly over to the dusty dresser.

'One of the reasons I've been delaying the trip is because of my foster parents. Going back home will be a painful reminder that they're gone. And if I see Isaiah there's a chance I might murder him.'

I stared at him in shock. 'You...you think he was responsible for their deaths?'

'Don't you?' Pursing his lips, he moved his head from side to side.

I nodded slowly. 'Yes, yes I suppose so.'

'It was too unusual to be an accident E, and who else would do such a thing on purpose but that heinous father of yours.' He shrugged his shoulders. 'So, it might be a good idea for me to keep out his way.'

'Perhaps yes.' I replied, without smiling.

'So, what's the verdict E, are you going home?'

I stared thoughtfully into his face.

Home was like a foggy dream where all my memories were out of reach, and if I did attempt to reach them, they would run away from me, as if taunting me, as if they didn't truly belong in my mind; they belonged in the other world, and I wasn't allowed to reclaim them, not unless I went back. Caleb was right when he said travelling across worlds was bad for you, the repercussions could be catastrophic. But ultimately, I knew in my heart what my answer would be.

'Okay Mace, I will come home with you, but only for a short while. I must see Aunt one last time, before I return to Briarwood for good. You never know I may be able to persuade her to come back with me.'

'Stranger things have happened E.' Smiling softly he kissed the top of my head. 'Just promise me we'll go soon, before I chicken out.'

I gave him a faint smile. 'I shall have to speak to Abel and the others, to give them the option to come back with us.'

He nodded unsurely. 'That's rather a lot of passengers E, are you sure we can all go through together?'

'I think so. Verity travelled with four or five at the same time, so I'm sure we can do the same. I shall ensure everyone knows what to do, including you. It just takes a little concentration that is all.'

'Able may not be able to get through, you know. No offence E, but he doesn't strike me as someone who can focus for very long. He could end up taking a dangerous detour to a ghostly world of no return.'

'It's a risk, yes.'

I walked away from him and began pacing up and down the room in deep contemplation. Abel had been staying with my brother Gilbert, and the two had got on surprisingly well, and were great company for one another. I would visit them frequently and enjoyed their cheery, if rather simple chatter. As far as I could tell Abel seemed happy and content in his present home and part of me was reluctant to drag him away, but the chance to reunite him with his family must surely take precedence, and he deserved to have that opportunity. Gilbert didn't miss his sister, Verity and seldom mentioned her, much to my relief; perhaps if he knew the true story of the mad woman's demise, he wouldn't be so civil towards me- I basically told him she had perished at the monastery with all the other unfortunate victims, and left it like that. Out of the other survivors, one had moved on and the rest were staying with Miss Ingram in the village, a kindly old lady who didn't frown on newcomers and was happy to put them up.

'What about the mirror, you don't know how to activate it, do you E?'

'Gideon knows, Isaiah showed him when he came back for me.' I paused. 'He won't mind showing us.'

Mace gave me a nudge. 'So, what else is bothering you?'

'What?' I replied in a daze.

'Clarice and I were one of your niggling worries, what else?'

I stared at him blankly before lowering my eyes and laughing nervously. 'Nothing, it's nothing.'

'E, can we walk back home now?' He said as we went into the hallway. 'This place might feel homely to you but I feel on edge, and keep expecting someone to jump out and scare us both half to death.' He suddenly whacked my arm. 'Don't lie, I know you've been here before. Who else would have written that in the dust? And don't try and say you wrote it when we just came in, because I would have noticed.'

I followed his eyes as he gazed at the mirror on the wall. My name had been written in the dust, right across the glass.

As we approached the front door, I spotted Caleb tidying the garden.

I took Mace's arm and whispered to him.

'Promise not to say anything yet about us leaving. I'd like to tell Gideon first, in private.'

'Okay E, whatever you say. Caleb's not going to take it well, you know.'

'He won't mind *me* going, it means he can spend more time with his grandson. But you....'I sighed. 'No Mace, he won't be happy about that, and I can hardly say I blame him.'

After I'd fed Gabriel and put him to bed, I joined the others for dinner. Caleb sat there beaming with pride as his three sons sat there helping themselves to food, with Mace taking the bigger helping. What joy it must have brought him to have them altogether like this, and with Gideon free from the tonic, the tension in Caleb's face had dispersed. I knew how terribly fond he was of Mace, I could see it in his eyes, his cherished youngest child, who by some phenomenal piece of luck had found his way back to his father, after all these years; only now Mace had to leave and once again the family would be torn apart.

Gideon smiled at me as I sat beside him and gently squeezed my hand.

'Did he settle down alright?'

'Surprisingly well, yes.' I replied helping myself to some casserole. 'You must have tired him out with hide and seek.'

Caleb chuckled. 'I think you'll find it's the other way round.'

'Pass the potatoes Noble.' spluttered Mace with a mouth full.

'You have enough on your plate greedy guts.' Retorted Noble with a smile.

Caleb laughed again as he picked up the dish and passed it to Mace. 'Oh, let him have more, he's a growing lad.'

'Thank you, Caleb...I mean father.' Pulling a face at Noble he piled three more potatoes onto his plate then glanced at Clarice. 'You should tuck in my girl, build your strength up.'

She threw him an odd look. 'Shall I need my strength for the journey ahead?

My knife and fork cluttered to the plate.

Caleb looked startled. 'What journey?'

'We were going to tell you.' I said rapidly, my eyes darting to Mace.'

'Mace is taking me home.' Announced Clarice sharply. For one brief moment I thought she was intentionally being spiteful, but glaring at her I realised she didn't mean to be, it was only the tonic, or lack of it.

Caleb glared at Clarice and then from me to Mace. 'What do you mean?'

Mace's eyes looked slowly towards Caleb. 'Effie and I have to take Clarice home in order to cure her condition.' His voice became fainter. 'We shall return father, I promise.' Looking sheepishly at me he tried to smile. 'Sorry E, I only mentioned it to Clarice to cheer her up a bit. I didn't realise she'd blab about it at dinner.

'When are you leaving?' asked Caleb, in a low voice.

'Soon, very soon.' I replied grabbing Gideon's hand and looking into his face.

We all turned to stare as Caleb banged his fists on the table and abruptly rose from his seat, his eyes boring into mine. 'I will not permit this again Effie. Too many times you've taken my sons away from me. First of all I almost lost Gideon, then Noble left Briarwood for the second time, which I know you had something to do with, and he barely made it back alive from Hartland, and now you want to take my youngest son away with you again, just because this friend of yours has been sent mad by the tonic.' His eyes flickered to Clarice. 'She doesn't need Mace; you take her Effie.' As he leant forward over the table his face was crimson with fury. 'Only this time don't bother returning.' Once more he crashed his fist down, and then with a groan he left the room.

Mace rushed after him, shouting his name.

'Father will calm down Effie.' Said Gideon, leaning in close. 'He didn't mean what he said.'

I could see that Noble was staring at me but when I looked his way he glanced down at the table, his lips sternly compressed. With a sudden movement he rose up from his seat and strode out the room.

Clarice stared vacantly at Gideon and I. Bending her hands she began cracking her fingers rather aggravatingly.

Trying to ignore the sound I turned and faced Gideon.

I purposely spoke in a whisper. 'I was going to tell you Gideon, later this evening.'

'It's okay Effie. I understand. You can go with my blessing.'

'Won't you miss me?'

'Of course I will. I don't want you to go, but I fully understand that you need to spend time with your Aunt. And I also know you will come back at the first opportunity.' He smoothed my hair away from my face. 'You should try and get her to return with you this time.'

'Yes, yes I will.'

Clarice continued cracking her fingers as if it was a newly discovered pastime.

I grimaced.

'Why don't you retire to your room Clarice, and get some rest.'

She stopped moving her fingers and glared sullenly at me. As her hand hovered over the knife by her plate, I suddenly became anxious. No matter how hard I tried the mere idea that she'd really murdered Craddock and one of the other guards in cold blood seemed positively ridiculous, and yet it was true, the tonic had turned her into a murderer, and murderers often killed again.

I placed my hand lightly on Gideon's sleeve and gradually rose to my feet.

'Shall we turn in darling?'

He nodded silently.

As we both left the room I glanced at the knife in her hand. Holding it like a weapon she began repeatedly stabbing the leftover food, and all the while she stared at me, her eyes dark and menacing.

That night I locked the door. Gideon said he'd be happy to show me how to activate the mirror, and that it was easier than I thought. When he'd dropped off, I lay there in the crook of his arm, staring up at the beams. Gabriel was fast asleep in his crib and every so often let out a contented sigh.

It was becoming blatantly clear that our trip home should be very soon. Clarice was beginning to scare me; my poor friend was in there somewhere, but in the meantime we'd all have to be cautious of her volatile behaviour and would have to watch her like a hawk. All of a sudden, I pictured her blackened body being pecked to pieces by crows, just like the murderer Noble had told me about, who had been placed in a gibbet in the village square as a warning to others. Evidently this would have been Isaiah's fate had he not craftily managed to wrangle his way out of it. If Clarice was to suddenly snap and murder someone, she wouldn't stand a chance amongst the bigoted minds of the villagers, she was an outsider, and they knew nothing about tonic takers, and what the muck could do to your brain. I would plead with them to let her go, but had a feeling they wouldn't listen. I had to take action before it was too late; tomorrow I would inform the others she must be locked up until we leave, for her own safety and everyone else's.

Chapter 23

The following day, after an extremely bad night's sleep I decided to venture into the village to inform Abel and the other survivors of our plans to leave. Caleb was barely speaking to me and seemed to have taken possession of Gabriel for the day, and Gideon was working on the allotment, with a little help from Mace who was rather grumpy at having to keep Clarice locked up like a prisoner.

Abel came over with a tray.

'There we go Miss. Here's a nice cuppa and a slice of ginger cake.'

'Thanks.' I murmured taking a sip of the tea. 'You know Abel, you can just call me Effie, if you like.'

As he eased his frame down into the armchair opposite me, he chuckled. 'Right you are Miss...oops.' He covered his mouth with his hand. 'Sorry Miss...I... I mean Effie.'

I began to laugh.

Gilbert came shuffling into the room and took a seat beside us.

'Save some cake for me Abe.'

'Course I will Gil. What you take me for, some type of piggy woofer?'

Gilbert didn't reply for a second and just sat there munching on his cake, spilling crumbs down his shirt.

'Well, yeah.'

They both eyed one another sternly before bursting into laughter. I joined in, my eyes widening in amusement. We sat and talked for some time, mostly about Abel's culinary skills and the village folk. I gazed at Gilbert in alarm when he asked me if I'd paint Verity's portrait, saying how he should have a picture of our sister up over the fireplace. Despite how she would bully him, he thought it the right thing to do. I looked

255

at Abel and raised my eyebrows. 'Perhaps one day.' I felt my cheeks turning red. It was a lie of course, as even though the memory of her face was very much clear in my mind, I could never bring myself to paint the mad woman.

'Be a pal Gil, go and get me soup off the stove.'

With a drawn-out sigh I reached forward and took Abel's hands in mine.

'I'm taking a trip home in the next few days, are you coming with me?'

He was suddenly speechless and sat there staring at me, his mouth wide open.

'Abel?'

'No, Miss, No, I be staying here if it's all right with you.'

'I wrinkled my forehead in confusion. 'But...but I thought you wanted to go home?' My face became grave. 'What about your parents?'

'Now there Miss. Don't you go fretting about that.' He began to swing my hands to and thro in his. 'Big old Abel don't want to be moving homes again.' He glanced towards the door. 'And what would Gil do without the likes of me to keep him out of trouble. He's like the little brother I never had, and it would break his heart if I upped and left him in the lurch.' Releasing my hands, he reached into his trouser pocket and produced a crumpled up letter. 'I thought you be going soon so I wrote this here note to my parents. Would you pass it to them Miss? It be short and badly written but it says what I need to say to them.' His eyes drifted over to the fire. 'Least they'll know that their son Abel is alive and well, that be all that counts.'

I felt my eyes filling with tears.

'Don't cry Miss. I don't like to see me friends sad.'

'Sorry.' I sniffed. 'It's...it's just.'

My niggling doubts of yesterday were still festering in the darkest corner of my mind, and were so well hidden that even I couldn't reach them, and had no wish to. They were too painful and torturous, and I was too weak to face them.

He grabbed my hands. 'What be wrong Miss, you can tell Abel.'

I dabbed my eyes and cheek with the sleeve of my dress.

'Ignore me Abel, I'm just rather emotional at present. The harrowing experience at Hartland has left me a little out of sorts.' I made myself smile. 'You on the other hand have adjusted marvellously.'

Gilbert came bursting back into the room.

'What's up sis? Has Abe been upsetting you already?

'Enough of that you blighter- Miss...Effie and me have been having an important talk.' Said Abel, grinning at me. 'And you're fine, aren't you Miss?'

I looked at Abel then gave Gilbert a reassuring smile.

'Yes...perfectly fine.'

Miss Ingram greeted me with a welcome smile and was eager to invite me in. I stayed for a while and tried to listen attentively as she sung Caleb's praises; apparently his medicine had done wonders for her arthritis and she insisted I take a basket of rhubarb from her garden as way of thanks. I managed to have a quiet word with the survivors from the monastery. Evidently, they were not remotely keen to leave Briarwood. I suppose, just like me, they had immediately been captivated by the charm of the village, and were content to stay. However, I knew from personal experience that strangers were not welcome here, and seldom remained. Village folk saw them as a threat to their unique way of life and were wise to what would happen, as sooner or later something would spark the visitor's memory of home and reality would strike them in the face, and with haste they would return to whence they came. Ultimately, they didn't belong here, this wasn't their world, and it wasn't mine, even though I was determined to make it so.

I returned home another way and found myself in a deep lane overhung with trees, making it shady and dark. As the branches swayed in the soft breeze, they made strange patterns on the mottled ground and the shadows formed imaginary figures, lurking ominously further on up the lane. It reminded me of the ghostly passageways in the monastery, and for one foolish moment I allowed terror to overwhelm me and I began to run. In a panic I darted amongst the trees and fell headfirst into a gorse bush, badly scratching my face and arms. Groaning in pain I began to crawl on my hands and knees to the field beyond, pulling at the strands of my hair that had become tangled up in the shrub. As I picked myself up and brushed the pieces of greenery from my dress, I noticed some villagers meandering through the field with several dead rabbits slung over their shoulders. At first, I didn't move, hoping they wouldn't spot me, but as they passed by one of them glanced over and smiled, nodding at me from underneath his cap, and as he began mumbling to the others, they all turned to stare with laughing eyes.

One of them called over. 'Are you alright there Mrs Thoroughgood?

'Yes, yes thank you.' I uttered in a surprised voice. 'I've…I've lost my way.'

'Just go across this field here and you'll see the church steeple that be near Caleb's cottage.'

I nodded in acknowledgement

'Enjoy the rest of your day Mrs Thoroughgood.'

Smiling, I watched as the men merrily went on their way then went to retrieve the basket of rhubarb.

I didn't mind that they'd been amused by my wild appearance and would most likely go home and tell their wives, for it seemed the village folk were finally accepting me as one of their own, rather than throwing me strange stares, thinking I was the ghost of Florentine Heatherington. What was also rather perplexing was how they suddenly seemed to turn a blind eye to me twice leaving Briarwood, and then returning. Gideon seemed to get away with it, but he wasn't a newcomer. I could only ascertain it was because I was now married to a villager.

Approaching the church, I decided to rest on the bench for a while before returning to the cottage. Everyone had been so jovial before Clarice's announcement at dinner last night, but now that happiness had been shattered, and I didn't want to rush back. I dreamily strolled slowly around the side of the building and came to a standstill. Noble and a woman were sitting on the bench, laughing and chatting to one another. They stopped and stared at me.

'Oh.' I exclaimed rather taken aback.

Noble rose up from the bench. 'Effie. What happened to you?'

My voice seemed to have dried up and all I could do was gape at them. The woman was about my age with dark blond hair arranged neatly around her head. She smiled graciously at me, and I noticed what kind eyes she had.

I ran my hand over my hair in an attempt to smooth it down. 'I ah...I fell into a gorse bush.' My eyes widened and I shook my head, laughing rather nervously.

'You're badly scratched.' He said, running his eyes over my face and arms. 'Let me take you home, father has some special lotion that will ease the pain.'

'No' I exclaimed rather bluntly. 'Thank you Noble but no, I shall be perfectly fine on my own.' I forced a smile at the woman. 'Good day.' Then I turned on my heel and marched away from the church and into the cornfield.

In an uncomfortable silence I sat with Caleb at the kitchen table whilst he tended to my wounds.

'Try and be more careful next time Effie.' Said Caleb dabbing my check with some cloth.

'Ouch.' I exclaimed.

'Sorry. The lotion may sting a little at first but will soon sooth the scratches.' He sighed wearily as he began to apply more of the liquid. 'You've scratched yourself next to the wounds.' He commented, examining my arm. 'Luckily they have almost healed.' With a frown he stared at the cuts. 'Are you sure this was Verity's doing?'

'Yes.' I murmured.

His eyes fixed on mine as he studied my face as if he were given me an interrogation. 'Are you *sure* you didn't provoke her?'

Since our return Caleb had been unwilling to accept the mad woman had done anything wrong; in his eyes living in such a hideous place had brought on her deplorable

259

behaviour, and none of it was her fault. 'We mustn't speak ill of the dead.' He would exclaim sombrely.

'No.' I uttered. 'I've told you what happened Caleb. The mad....Verity hated me, and wanted me dead.'

He began soaking my arm in the lotion, holding the cloth firmly over the cuts.

'Verity's been through a lot Effie. To lose her mother so tragically, and then to discover that vile father of hers was responsible for her death.'

I swiftly looked up and met his gaze. 'Is that what she told you happened?'

'No, but the whole village knows Isaiah murdered Violet.'

My eyes widened in response but I didn't see the point in telling him the truth, and I'm not sure he would believe me anyway.

'Verity's always been envious of you and Gideon, perhaps that hasn't helped. But once the two of you were wed, I thought she'd moved on. At one stage I thought her and Noble were becoming close but I have a sneaking suspicion his heart lies with another.'

My arm instinctively jerked in his hand.

'Perhaps there's someone from the village?'

He hesitated. 'Oh, I'm sure of it. Many a young woman in Briarwood would be only too happy to become his wife.' As he examined another scratch on the side of my chin, I noticed how he stared directly into my eyes as he spoke. 'It's only a matter of time before he's married.'

My eyes lowered so he couldn't see my reaction.

He cleared his throat. 'I'd like to apologise Effie, for what I said at supper last night. It was very wrong of me. Mace made it clear that he wanted to leave with you and Clarice.'

'Thank you, Caleb, but I do understand your concern. Mace will return, as will I. My home is here now with Gideon and Gabriel.'

'His face became animated. 'That little grandson of mine is the joy of my life, as well as my sons of course.' He chuckled. 'Promise me you'll not take Gabriel away from Briarwood.'

I placed my hand over his. 'I promise.'

As I reached the top of the stairs that evening Noble and I collided on the landing and my face made contact with his. Instinctively he put his arms out to steady me and for one brief moment we stood close together, staring into one another's eyes. Then we both lowered our gaze and drew apart. Trying to laugh casually I headed for the bedroom and on reaching the handle I turned to see him looking at me with such intensity that my heart gave a sudden lurch.

'Effie...today at the church'

'It's okay Noble you don't have to explain.'

'But...'

'Goodnight Noble.' I mumbled softly before he had a chance to finish his sentence. I hurriedly went into the bedroom and shut the door.

'The three of us must spend the day together tomorrow.' Said Gideon as we lay in bed that evening. I want to spend as much time with my beautiful wife as possible before she leaves.' His lips gently touched mine. 'Perhaps I should come back with you Effie. I may be alright this time.'

I raised my head from his chest and stared tenderly into his eyes. 'Gideon, please. Last time you very nearly died; I will not risk your life again. And I certainly don't wish to beg Isaiah to part with more of his blood.'

'You remember that then?'

'Funnily enough, yes. Certain events cannot be wiped from my memory, no matter how many worlds I travel to.'

He laughed.

'Gideon?'

'Yes.'

'Your heart...is it okay?'

He didn't answer me immediately and I started to become concerned.

'Effie, of course it is. I just become a little short of breath at times, that is all, nothing to concern yourself about.' He rose himself up a little and rested his head on his hand. 'Now you mustn't worry about me, I am made of sterner stuff than you give me credit for.' With a loving smile he lowered his lips to mine.

The following day Gideon and I prepared a picnic together and as mid-morning approached, we packed it up in a basket and took Gabriel for a stroll in the cornfield by the church. He was taking his first few steps by now, and took great delight in stumbling a few paces before falling down in the corn, then with a squeal of laughter he would pick himself up again and repeat it. We laid out a cloth and ate the food before resting in the afternoon sun, whilst Gabriel took a nap. The sun shimmered across the corn like waves in a golden sea, glimmering across our faces and warming our souls. I suddenly felt rejuvenated and completely at peace with the world. And whilst our child slept, we laughed and chatted together about when we were children and the fun we'd have in the forest, that mystical forest that only existing in our dreams. It was one of those afternoons when everything was completely perfect and special, an afternoon that should carry on forever.

'There's Noble.' murmured Gideon as we were making our way slowly back to the cottage.

My heart did a lurch as I saw he was with the same woman from yesterday.

'Noble.' shouted Gideon, putting the picnic basket down for a moment. 'Come and join us.'

They both glanced over and Noble mumbled something to the woman and gave her a hug, and then she waved at us before strolling across the field in the other direction.

'Who is she?' I asked staring after her.

'It looks like Maisie Fellows from the village.'

Noble was pacing directly towards us looking serious. He gave Gideon a little smile before looking at me.

'Effie, I've just seen Abel and Gilbert. They're upset because they think you're going to leave without saying goodbye.'

'I will pop in and see them.' I turned to Gideon. 'Will you walk with me?'

'You'll take her, won't you Noble.' he paused. 'You can collect that crate of preserves from Miss Bowers whilst you're there. I'll take Gabriel back home and feed him.' With an endearing smile he looked at me. 'Just promise to be quick.'

Noble and I glanced at one another.

As my face reddened, I glanced at Gideon. 'Really, there's no need. I...I can collect the crate.'

'You'll break your back trying to carry it Effie. No, Noble will walk with you. You don't mind brother, do you?'

Noble stood there despondently. 'No...not at all.'

As Gideon gave me a peck on the cheek, he took Gabriel's hand and they very slowly began walking towards the cottage.

We hardly spoke to one another as we strode to the village. Noble looked moody and preoccupied, as if having to walk with me was a severe inconvenience. Abel and Gilbert were overjoyed to see us and insisted we stay for a cup of tea. As I tried to ensure them both I wouldn't be away for very long, my eyes flickered to Noble who was staring intently at me in his usual manner. On the way out of the village we stopped off at Miss Bowers and she gave us the crate, it was full of homemade jam with fruit she'd picked from her garden. We thanked her and swiftly went across the cornfield in silence. Suddenly I spotted something a little way off in the corn. It was the picnic basket; Gideon must have forgotten about it.

'Just a minute Noble.' I said, bounding over towards it. 'You go ahead.'

With a groan he rather violently put the crate down on the ground. 'No. I'll wait, just hurry up Effie.'

Something inside of me snapped and I swung round to confront him.

'What on earth is wrong with you Noble? Can we at least try and be civil to one another.'

'Why.' He retorted. 'You're leaving tomorrow...again. And don't pretend you're only going to be gone a few days, we both know that's not true.'

'Why can't you be more like Gideon and accept that I have to go? And for your information I most certainly intend to come back to Briarwood immediately.'

He took a step nearer and began to shout. 'Well I'm sorry I can't be more like my brother, Gideon. He's always been the placid, understanding type, and I've always been the disagreeable one with a temper, especially when it comes to you.

I glared at him. 'Well keep away from me then, and go and spend more time with your lady friend, Maisie.' Shaking with anger I marched up to the basket and grabbed the handle.

Hearing the sound of laughter, I half turned to look at him.

'What's so funny?'

'Your jealous, aren't you Effie.'

'Huh. Don't be ridiculous.' I began walking away.

I felt his hands grab hold of me and swing me round so I was looking directly into his face. The basket dropped from my hands.

'Admit it. You hate the idea of me being friendly with another woman. I saw it in your eyes when you thought I was marrying Verity, and I see the exact same look now. You can't bear the idea of me loving anyone but you. You'd like me to hang around pining for you whilst you carry on your life with Gideon.' The grip on my shoulders got tighter. 'You're selfish Effie, you might not realise it but you are.'

In a daze I stared into his face.

'Well perhaps I am selfish but I don't mean to be. I've never asked you to wait around for me Noble. It doesn't matter what I do or say to try and dissuade you from loving me, you never take a blind bit of notice. You're stubborn Noble, as stubborn as a mule.'

To my annoyance he began laughing again.

'Perhaps I am...and a hopeless fool for loving you.'

'Seeing as my attempts to make you move on are futile, I might as well tell you the truth.' I found myself pausing for thought, suddenly fearful of saying the words out loud, and knowing I probably shouldn't. 'I do love you Noble...I've loved you for a long time, and God help me I've tried not to.'

He smiled gently. 'I know you love me Effie, I've always known. You're not very good at hiding your emotions, your face always gives you away.'

264

I glared at him in disbelief.

'You told me at the monastery that you would never get over me, but you *must* find a way. Gideon is my dearest love and he is your brother, and we both know we could never betray him.' I could feel my voice choking up with emotion. 'So, we *must* put an end to this entire situation before it destroys us.'

'And how do you suppose we do that Effie?'

'We need to distant ourselves from one another. There's this lovely little cottage on the edge of the woods, surrounded by pastureland. On my return I fully intend to move into it with Gideon and Gabriel. I've not said anything to your brother yet as I wanted it to be a surprise. But it...it should make everything easier.'

'Should it?'

I tried to give him a genuine smile. 'Yes, yes it will Noble. Now I want you to promise me you'll seriously consider marrying your lady friend.'

'But Effie.'

'Please don't interrupt Noble I haven't finished. You don't want to spend the rest of your life alone, lamenting on what could have been. I want you to have a family and live a long and fulfilling life.' I swallowed hard. 'Now promise me.'

He remained silent for a moment, staring into my eyes.

'I promise Effie.'

'Good.'

Slowly he released my shoulders. 'We should be getting back.'

I nodded in agreement and picked up the basket.

He went and retrieved the crate and together we strolled back to the cottage, once again, in silence.

When we arrived in the back door Caleb was standing over the table with his sleeves rolled up, making pastry.

He looked closely at us. 'Is everything alright?'

When I spoke my voice was faint and a little shaky. 'Everything is fine.' I plonked the basket down on the floor.

Noble put the crate on the side before glumly gazing down at the table. 'What are you making father?'

Caleb narrowed his eyes, looking rather puzzled. 'I'm making rhubarb pie.'

As Noble hovered beside his father I slipped out the room and up the stairs.

'Hello darling.' I exclaimed in a hushed voice. Even though he was half asleep I couldn't resist scooping him up in my arms. 'I missed you, did you miss me?' he began rubbing his eyes, and smiled when he saw me. I nuzzled my face up against his then began smothering him in little kisses. 'Daddy in garden.'

'Is he, you clever boy.'

As I glanced out the window, I spotted Gideon leaning up against the front wall, staring out across the fields. Even though I couldn't see his expression I felt in my bones that his face was deeply troubled. My first reaction was to run down and join him, but something held me back, and as I continued to stare out at him the tears came, streaming down my face and onto Gabriel.

Dinner was over and we were all clearing the plates away, apart from Mace who was slouched at the table spooning Miss Bowers jam into his mouth.

'You're not supposed to eat it out of the pot like that son.' Said a laughing Caleb.

'Why not?' he mumbled. 'I'm desperate for sugar, all the cakes gone, so unless you have a bar of chocolate hanging about this is the next best thing.'

'Chocolate?'

'Yes father.' Said Mace rolling his eyes and looking at me 'It's made from cocoa beans?'

Caleb shook his head looking mystified. 'There's plenty of rhubarb pie left.'

'I hate that stuff.' He began to shudder.

Noble and I reached for the same dish by accident and as his fingers brushed mine our eyes met. In retrospect I wasn't sure that declaring my true feelings for him was wise, but at that particular moment in the cornfield it had seemed the decent thing to do, he knew I loved him anyway, and even if I'd denied it, he wouldn't have believed me.

As Mace went and dropped his plate into the washing up bowl, he splattered water all over Noble. He cried out at him in annoyance then flicked some soapsuds all over his brother and laughed as it rested in his hair. Mace retaliated by doing the same to him, smearing soapy water all over his face. Caleb stood in the corner laughing.

Gideon came and put his arm around me and suggested the two of us go and sit in the garden and watch the sun go down. I nodded at him eagerly, and we sneaked outside and left them to it. For a while we snuggled up to one another, drinking in the last remnants of the day before it inevitably faded in readiness for the next. As I lay there that night in Gideon's arms my heart ached at the thought of having to leave him and Gabriel, and for one strange second, I almost padded down to the cellar to destroy the mirror, putting an end to it once and for all

That morning we all ventured down to the cellar where the mirror was housed. As Caleb stood there holding Gabriel he reminded me that travelling to and from the mirror could be detrimental to my health. I found myself thinking of the mad woman, and how frequently she would flit between worlds with ease, physically she had seemed normal but mentally of course she was abnormal, and always had been. But with her death any lasting damage caused by the travelling would never be known.

Gideon and I clung to one another and as he took my face between his hands, he kissed me tenderly. 'Bring yourself back safely Effie, and soon.'

Between tears I nodded and buried my face into his shoulder.

As Gideon turned to say goodbye to Mace and Clarice, I tentatively approached Noble and took his hand and held it tight within mine. With a sudden movement he tugged me forward into his arms and held me there before I pulled away.

Caleb noisily cleared his throat. 'Take good care of yourself Effie and make sure you return my youngest child to me.' He uttered with an agonised stare at Mace. 'He's very special to me.'

Mace came and stood close to Caleb. 'Oh, father please. I'm not a child, and I've already assured you that I'll be back. You can't get rid of me that easily.'

With a sad smile Caleb embraced him.

Lastly, I took Gabriel from his grandfather and smothered his little face in kisses. 'Mummy shall be back before you know it. And I shall bring a new toy back for you, a teddy bear perhaps.'

'His large dark eyes gazed into mine. 'Bear...bear.'

I held him close to me. 'Yes of course sweetheart, if that's what you'd like.'

As Gideon reached forward to take him I felt my heart was being wrenched from my chest. A stifled sob escaped my lips.

'It's best we return upstairs now.' Said Caleb. 'Our being here whilst you have to travel through will be far too distracting.' He gestured to Gideon and Noble. 'Come on sons.'

'The two of you go up I need to show Effie how the mirror works.' Said Gideon with a small sigh. In a serious voice he told me to twist each cherub to the left, rather like one would turn a handle, until it clicked. Once this was done to all four of them the gateway would be opened. 'It works precisely the same way on the other mirror at your home Effie.' He watched whilst I followed his instructions then winked at me. 'See, easy.' Giving me another kiss, he turned and trudged up the wooden staircase with Gabriel in his arms.

My eyes followed them up the stairs, and when they'd reached the top Gideon looked back at me, his eyes glistening, then mouthing goodbye he disappeared behind the door with Gabriel.

'I'm...I'm not sure if I'm ready for this E.'

Trying not to sob I took a large gulp then gazed wide eyed from Mace to Clarice. Her bloodshot eyes bore into mine as she busily clicked her fingers, as if sensing it aggravated me. She seemed undaunted by what we were about to do; either that or she was totally oblivious.

'It's not too late Mace. If you'd rather stay...I can take Clarice home.'

'No, no E.' he replied adamantly. 'Just give me a minute.' He slunk to the floor and began taking deep breaths.

Clarice began picking up herbs from the table and suddenly started to rip them apart.

'Stop that Clarice.' I uttered sternly. 'It's time to go.' I was beginning to become impatient and eager to get this over and done with. 'We must all hold hands, and whatever you do don't let go. You must both focus on home. I know we can't remember it very well, but try and picture something from your past, the face of your mother for instance Clarice...' I hesitated and glanced at Mace. 'You could think of your foster parents and where they used to live, or another place that's familiar.'

Mace leapt to his feet. 'I can see the promenade E. The promenade from our home town.'

'Good Mace, that's good.'

I held out my hands to them both.

'All I see is red.' Said Clarice. 'The red of the tonic, and blood, blood that I have spilt.'

Mace and I gave one another a look.

'Stand in between us Clarice. We're taking you home to see you mother, the mother who loves you dearly.'

We all linked hands and edged our way towards the mirror. There was a faint glow emanating from within the glass, like the sun trapped behind mist on a winter's day. Once again, I searched my memory for one snippet of information about Aunt, and suddenly recalled how she would meticulously clean the kitchen each and every week until it sparkled, but it wasn't enough, it wasn't clear. I found myself travelling up a spiral staircase and entering an attic room- it was hauntingly eerie, a good place to lurk if you were a spirit who wanted to scare the living. I could see a stack of boxes and a mannequin dummy, then my eyes rested on a strange wooden toy with a ghastly unnatural face poking up amongst a pile of books.

'Hold on tightly to Clarice's hand Mace.' I shouted. 'This is it; we're going.' Taking a deep breath, I stepped through the glass.

Chapter 24

How effortlessly I should have slipped back into my old life, my familiar and unchanged life with everything in its rightful place, the same routine, the same scenery and the same old Aunt. But on returning I discovered a dark shadow had settled over my home, and now everything would be different, and my happy little existence at Rawlings had vanished forever. For my dear Aunt was gravely ill, with only a few weeks left to live. She sadly had an inoperable brain tumour. I cannot describe my heartbreak at finding her so poorly, she was painfully thin and her face looked drawn and pale from the terrible headaches she was suffering from. The doctors of course gave her medication to ease her discomfort but ultimately, they could do no more for her. Many times, I asked her if she would travel back with me to the other land, where I thought it might be possible to cure her. However, she was quite adamant that she wanted to spend the remainder of her days at home, the only home she'd ever known or ever wished for. So, with her typical stoicism she struggled on, despite me complaining that she should rest. She would rise and dress as usual and insisted on doing light chores around the house. But often she would retire to her bed early and I would sit reading to her by the bedside. As the days drifted past, she spent more time confined to her bed, mostly sleeping. When I had a spare moment, I would find solace in the garden, lamenting over those far off memories when I was a child with my Aunt.

It was a strange, lonely period of my life when my world was centred on caring for my Aunt, and all other aspects of my life seemed to fade into the background. Mace was there with me when he wasn't helping Clarice. Mrs Lapworth had been overjoyed when we turned up with her daughter and it gladdened my heart to see the both of them reunited. Oddly enough on our return Clarice had been frightened and confused, and progress with her recovery had been slow. Some days she would insist on crouching on the floor in utter silence, other days she would become overly anxious and Mace would have to pacify her by reminding her that she was now in the safety of her home. Thankfully she no longer had violent outbursts and I prayed my friend was no longer a danger to society. For even without making notes I remembered she had killed at least one person, a rather unpleasant individual who probably deserved what he got, but all the same she had committed murder.

Isaiah had made a few visits, frequently turning up on the doorstep with flowers that I suspected he'd collected from the garden. 'My Aunt still won't allow you in.' I'd say in a solemn voice. 'I cannot go against her wishes Isaiah; it would not be right.' He would throw me a disgruntled look before trudging back down the driveway, his head bowed. I was almost tempted to invite him in for a cup of tea. But something told me once he'd stepped over the fresh hold, I would never be rid of him. And my Aunt certainly wouldn't be pleased; she still venomously detested him.

'Come close Effie.' Said Aunt one morning, her breathing ragged and shallow.

I closed my book then leaned forward over her. 'What is it Aunt?'

'Underneath the geraniums.' She stopped for a moment to catch her breath.

With sad eyes I nodded at her. 'Yes Aunt?'

'To...to the far side of the back garden buried in a rusty old tin, that's where the rest of the money is kept...and there's lots of it Effie.' She clung weakly to my sweater, pulling me closer. 'Be sure to put it somewhere safe, somewhere he cannot reach it.' With half closed eyelids she peered at me, barely able to keep awake. 'Your father's an evil man Effie. Be sure to be on your guard.'

'I will Aunt.' I said in a sad whisper.

She released her hold and flopped back against the pillows; her eyes closed. 'You're a good girl Effie.'

With a smile I pulled the blanket up around her and smoothed down her hair. I kissed her forehead and got up to go and make myself some lunch.

With a gasp she opened her eyes wide and glared at me. 'Don't leave me Effie, not yet.'

'I shall be back in just a moment Aunt. I promise.' Reaching forward I clutched her hand. 'Can I get you anything?'

She stared at me then slowly shook her head. 'My time is near Effie. I feel it in my bones.' With a cough she winced with pain then began shifting in the bed. 'I...I had a visitation from your mother Effie. She was looking down upon me, just as you are now, only she wasn't really there.'

Trying not to show my alarm I squeezed her hand. 'It's probably the medication Aunt, the doctor warned you of the side effects. Don't think about it. Just rest now.'

She suddenly looked distressed. 'Don't.... don't you see why your mother was here? She was coming for me, coming to take me away with her to the spirit world.'

'Please Aunt, stop this talk, you're not going anywhere.... not for a while anyway.'

For a moment her eyes became animated. 'But it's alright, I will be happy to see my dear sweet Freya. No longer will we be parted.'

All I could do was smile at her, not really knowing how to react. If my Aunt truly thought my mother had come to take her away from the mortal world, then so be it. I wouldn't take away a dying woman's beliefs.

'Very well then Aunt.' I carefully removed my hand from hers. 'Now you lie there and take it easy. I shall go and fetch your medication.'

It was cloudy with the threat of spring showers when my Aunt passed away. I remember thinking that from this moment onwards a tinge of sadness would forever linger within my heart, for with her passing nothing would be the same anymore, and no longer would Rawlings feel like my home. How thankful I was to be with her in the last few days, I only wished we could have spent more time together.... before the end.

In the days to follow an unnatural quietness descended upon the house, and Mace and I would sit in silence, our thoughts full of sorrow. All kinds of people came to pay their respects, amongst them Aunt's friends from the committee. With their sad faces and words of sympathy they came laden with elaborate wreaths, flowers, home cooked meals and cakes, keen to assist with the funeral arrangements. I would nod at them blankly, pretending to listen, but really I was lost in a strange melancholy-like stupor that wouldn't leave me. When night fell, I would seek solace in my room, collapsing onto the bed and crying into my pillow. Agitated and restless I would toss from side to side unable to rest.

At the funeral I managed to keep composed by tightly clasping Mace's hand. My fortitude nearly gave way as I heard an old friend of my Aunt's give a reading, describing Constance as a loyal, kind-hearted friend who would be sadly missed. She went on to say what a dedicated member of the committee she was and how she excelled in her charity work and the goods deeds she undertook within the community. In addition to this she mentioned what a keen gardener my Aunt had always been, and was exceedingly proud of Rawlings and of her niece Effie. I gulped when she mouthed my name, suddenly wondering if I should say a few words, but as the congregation rose and we went onto the next hymn I realised that to do such a thing would cause me to break down and sob. As we trundled out the chapel, I spotted Isaiah sitting at the very back, his eyes apparently welling up with tears. He stared at me in anguish like a pitiful stray dog trying to gain attention.

'Just ignore him Effie.' Said Mace, pulling me towards the doors.

Disregarding him was easy for today, but ignoring him afterwards would be an impossibility, for it was a forgone conclusion that sooner or later he'd come knocking on my door, expecting to move back into Rawlings, and laying his claim to my home.

My Aunt's coffin was lowered into the ground next to the plot of her mother, and her mother before her. It was somehow fitting that they should all be together, reunited in death.

As we walked away the rain began to fall, and I caught sight of a lone figure standing back from the mourners, a woman I think, her face obscured by a hooded cloak. She was watching me.

'Coffee Mace?' I asked, as he lay stretched out in a chair on the terrace, shielding his eyes from the morning sun.

He grunted 'Yeah, make it a strong one E.'

Giving him a little smile, I wondered back into the house.

Last night, after the wake, and everyone had gone home, Mace and I had toasted my Aunt with some whisky. We sat there together at the dining table, talking about her, laughing poignantly at the mischievous pranks he would play on her, and how she would scold him. 'But Connie could never stay angry for long, not with me.' He bragged cheekily. 'She'd always send me home with an extra-large slice of cake.' As I cleared away the empty plates and glasses, he helped himself to some wine left on the table, as well as various uneaten sandwiches and cakes. 'Considering the amount of people that came this afternoon I'm surprised there's any food left.' Taking a gulp of wine, he'd watched as I gathered the dishes together. 'At least that abominable father of yours didn't make an appearance.' Looking anxiously at him I smiled. After taking the remainder of the food in the kitchen I'd given Mace a peck on the cheek and bidden him goodnight.

'So how much did you drink last night?' I asked, handing him a mug of coffee.

He yawned. 'Not much E. Just a few glasses, but my head is a little sore.'

I sat down beside him with my coffee and looked out upon the lawn. 'Mace, I meant to ask you yesterday, did you notice that cloaked woman at my Aunt's funeral yesterday. She was standing away from the rest of the mourners.'

He took a slurp of his drink then plonked it down onto the garden table.

'No E, I didn't.' he raised his left eyebrow and peered at me from underneath his mop of hair. 'You don't think it was that insane sister of yours, do you? Perhaps she's returned from the dead to seek her revenge.'

A frightening vision of the mad woman suddenly popped into my head, glaring at me with her terrifying eyes. Since returning home my dead sister would haunt my dreams, evading them insidiously, and in them my Aunt's death came upon me strongly and with considerable force.

With a shiver I shook my head violently. 'No, no it wasn't her, or her apparition. It was someone else.'

He looked pensive. 'Perhaps it was someone who wanted to pay their respects, but didn't wish to disturb us. Either that or it was just some random spirit roaming around the graveyard. That is their final resting place E.'

I war wrapped my cardigan around myself. 'I suppose so.' I laughed. 'Putting that to one side, how is it that you remember my dearly departed sister so easily? Do you sit in bed each night and read your notes on what happened in the other world.'

'Yes. I read them at least once a day Effie.' His face became concerned. 'You may have casually discarded your notes but I'm obviously a little more sensible than you are.' He said in a slightly mocking tone. 'I'm also wiser…and taller, and more handsome.'

I smiled slowly. 'Well yes, you are taller. And in regards to making notes, I've no need, not when I remember Gideon and Gabriel without them.'

He pondered for a moment, holding his finger to his lips. 'But what about everyone else E? There's Caleb and Gilbert your simple brother…. and someone known as Noble.'

Suddenly I began to cough and splutter on my coffee. I placed the mug on the table and put my hand over my mouth.

'Cough it up chick.' He smiled at me with a glint in his eye. 'Do you not remember that night in the village green when a couple of the locals were celebrating their wedding? You and Noble sneaked off when no one was looking and got a little.... friendly. And those long lingering stares you and he always give to one another. Gideon may be blind to it but I'm not.' Reaching for my hand he began moving around the emerald ring on my finger. 'Noble loves you Effie, do you not remember?'

'Oh, do stop it Mace.'

'Why?'

With a sudden impulse I snatched my hand away and rose from the chair. 'I really don't see why you're dredging all of that up Mace, it's hardly constructive now is it?'

He sighed. 'Oh, E I'm sorry. It's just that having two older brothers is a big responsibility, and I feel very.... very protective over the two of them. I just don't want the situation to be exactly the same when you go back, that's all. Because sooner or later someone's going to get hurt.'

'Yes, very well Mace, point taken.' I retorted coolly. With a huff I reached for my coffee. 'I should go back inside.' Proceeding to the patio doors I turned to glance at him. 'I have a lot to do before I go back home to Gideon and Gabriel.'

It was whilst I tried to busy myself in the bedroom that I heard a commotion outside. Pacing over to the window I saw Isaiah holding Mace in a headlock, shouting at him. Muttering underneath my breath I raced downstairs, through the kitchen and out the back door.

'What's going on Isaiah?' I asked, emerging swiftly onto the terrace.

'This ignoramus has just accused me of murdering his foster parents.' Said Isaiah, releasing Mace and pushing him away. 'The audacity of it. It's true to say they were infernal busybodies, who I didn't much care for, but murdering them - huh. No, it was a gas explosion, pure and simple.'

'You *were* responsible Isaiah I know you were.'

'Prove it boy.'

Mace lurched at him, punching him in the stomach, causing him to cry out and collapse to the ground.

With a scowl Isaiah glared up at him. 'Get off my property this minute boy or I shall call the police.'

'What? Exclaimed Mace, falling about in hysterics. He looked across at me. 'This father of yours has finally lost his marbles E. Best give that lunatic asylum a call and have him committed.'

As Isaiah rose to his feet a sly smile spread slowly over his face, and he locked eyes with me. 'Effelia, dear daughter don't you think it's about time you told the boy what's going on, or would you rather I gave him the happy news?'

I gulped. 'Please Isaiah, if we could keep this conversation for another time, I'd....'

Isaiah's voice came booming over the top of mine. 'No, no Effelia that really won't do, now will it.' With a jubilant grin he went up to Mace and prodded him in the chest with his finger. 'You see boy, my daughter here very kindly agreed to sign Rawlings over to me in exchange for saving the life of her beloved Gideon. And now that her precious Aunt Constance has departed this world, I shall be taking possession of my new home.' He shoved him across the terrace. 'Which means *you* boy are no longer welcome in this house, or the grounds. So, I suggest you leave before I have you charged with trespassing.' His hand rested on his stomach. 'And assault on the owner.'

Mace's stood there, his mouth open wide. 'This...this is insane.' He glared at me looking completely perplexed. 'Please tell me it's not true E?'

'I'm very much afraid it is Mace.' My head was pounding and I was beginning to feel sick. 'Now if you don't mind, I'm going back inside the house. I'm really not in the mood to squabble over such matters when my Aunt has only been gone a few days.' Feeling the tears come I turned from them both and stormed inside.

The remainder of the day I was on my own in the house. Mace had returned to Clarice's and Isaiah was probably preparing to move back into Rawlings.

For some time, I rested on the bed, seriously contemplating going back through the mirror right that minute. I felt my time in this world was over, there was nothing left for me here anymore. Most days since coming home I'd had a yearning deep inside of me, a powerful force of nature so mighty and compelling that I felt incapable of resisting. It was pulling me back to the land where I now belonged. For although the deep, impenetrable fog of forgetfulness still lingered in my head, I was aware that Gideon and my son existed, and were waiting for me. All I had to do was step through the mirror in the study and I would be reunited with them. The only snag was I'd already promised Mace that I would stay for his birthday celebrations the week after next, and it would be cruel of me not to. In the meantime, I would try my best to keep myself occupied.

After Ambrose had finished in the garden for the day I sneaked outside and went and found a shovel from the new shed to the side of the property, and marched down to the back of the garden, to where the geraniums grew. Aunt had loved her geraniums, she always said they were easy to maintain, and now they were still here and she was not. In a fit of frustration, I began yanking them up roughly with my hands, not caring if I tore them from their roots, then I took the shovel and began to dig. For some time I couldn't find anything at all and then suddenly I hit something hard. With a tingle of excitement, I reached into the earth and pulled out an old rusty tin. Brushing the soil from the lid I opened it and gazed down at the considerable number of notes inside, enough I imagine to keep Rawlings maintained for several generations to come. I'm not sure if all the money was what Isaiah had obtained from vulnerable old ladies, I would never know unless I asked him, and I was hardly about to do that. But nevertheless, I would have to decide what to do with it all before I went home. Swiftly I covered up the hole and replanted the flowers as best I could, although I had reservations about them lasting. Going back inside with the tin I stuffed it underneath my mattress.

Chapter 25

Mr Goring of Webster's visited a couple of days after the funeral and read the will, bequeathing Rawlings to me. It came as no surprise when Isaiah burst into the room directly after the reading and shoved my written testimony right under Mr Goring's nose.

'So, you see young man. The house now belongs to me.'

Looking somewhat perturbed Mr Goring studied it quizzically before looking from Isaiah to me. 'Is this right, Miss Farraday. Do you not wish to contest this?'

I glumly shrugged my shoulders. 'No sir, not in the least, Isaiah and I had an understanding.' I bowed my head. 'And I stand true to my word.'

He studied my testimony further. 'Well I shall have to verify the signatures of the witnesses, and if it is all in order then I suppose...'

Isaiah interrupted him. 'You suppose nothing young man.' he angrily tapped the testimony. 'It *is* all in order.'

'Well...yes.' Replied Mr Goring rather hesitantly. 'But...but I need to....'

'Oh, do stop dithering. Perhaps I should contact your superior, as you're obviously incapable of dealing with such matters.'

Mr Goring looked bewildered. 'I can assure you that Ms Webster; my superior will agree we should check the authenticity of the document.'

Before Isaiah had a chance to bite back, I darted in between the two of them.

'Isaiah and I completely agree Mr Goring,' I said in a reassuring voice. 'You must do what you have to do.'

'Quite Miss Farraday, quite.' He eyed me closely for a moment, a slight smile on his lips. 'If you change your mind and wish to contest your testimony then please do not hesitate to visit our offices. I'm sure you will have a case, and a real chance of claiming back your home.'

I smiled placidly at him and nodded. 'Another cup of tea Mr Goring?'

'I'd love to Miss Farraday but I really must be going.' He was staring at me again, making me feel nervous. 'Perhaps I may call another time?'

Isaiah eyed his slyly. 'Yes, perhaps when my daughter's husband is present.'

He looked startled. 'I do apologise Miss Farraday if I'd known you were married I...I wouldn't have addressed you by your maiden name.'

Lowering my eyes, I found myself blushing. 'There's no need to apologise Mr Goring. I should have informed you when we first met today.' I laughed sadly. 'Sometimes I forget that I am no longer Farraday.'

'Yes, it's Mrs Thoroughgood to you young sir.' Said Isaiah, rising from his seat. 'Please, allow me to escort you out the house.' He hovered over him impatiently as he stuffed the paperwork back into his briefcase. 'Be sure to return my testimony when you've finished with it and don't get any idea about mislaying it, as I have several copies with my solicitor.'

As Mr Goring reached the living room door he turned back and gave me a meek smile then waved goodbye. Without warning Isaiah nudged him forward, urging him to hurry home before the storm began.

I heard the door slam loudly.

'What an annoying young man.' Isaiah said in a bellowing voice as he returned to the living room. He quickly limped to the window and watched as Mr Goring drove off in his car. 'The sort of person one would like to strangle with their bare hands then bury their body in the garden.' He snorted. 'If one could get away with it.'

I crossed over towards the door.

'That's an awful thing to say Isaiah. You're only upset with him because he wants to check the authenticity of my testimony. And he's obviously rather bemused why I would agree to hand over my house to you.'

Isaiah grunted, still gazing out the window.

'Yes, I suppose it would seem a tad strange to an outsider.' With a loud laugh he followed me as I went into the hallway. 'Strange but true, eh Effelia?' He declared jubilantly. 'Rawlings finally belongs to me.'

'Yes Isaiah – congratulations it's yours.' My voice began choking with emotion. 'You've finally achieved what you've wanted all these years.' I turned away and made my way to the staircase, running up them two at a time, trying desperately to hold back the tears, tears for the loss of my beloved home, and tears of sorrow for my Aunt; how very sad it would make her to find her cherished Rawlings now in the hands of the man she totally despised.

The days that followed were full of mixed emotions. For some reason I felt anxious and jittery, with a distinct feeling that something terrible was about to happen. With Mace frequently at Clarice's and Isaiah not yet properly moved in, I had gotten into the habit of wandering aimlessly around Rawlings, unable to rest. The memory of my Aunt was everywhere, imprinted within its very foundations, deep within its soul. I sensed a strange melancholy stillness within the rooms that I hadn't noticed before, almost as though it was weeping. Occasionally I would sit in the garden, underneath the shade of the great oak, dwelling on old memories of my childhood and lamenting over the happy times with Aunt. Other times I would stay in my room, sprawled out on the bed, staring up at the ceiling, and drift off into my own little world, or hide in the quietness of the library, breathing in the ancient scent of the books and wishing I could lose myself within their pages.

I heard a hammering on my door and Mace barged in with a piece of toast in his hand.

'Wake up sleepyhead, the ignoramus that is your father has just rung to rudely inform us that he won't be visiting his newly acquired property today as he's busy.'

'Right.' I mumbled sleepily. 'Why, what's he doing?'

'He's toddled off down to the village hall to have a chin wag with all his old biddies. Apparently, they're all dying to know the latest news and it's going to take him the best part of day to explain how he managed to worm his way into procuring Rawlings.' He took a bite of his toast. 'I expect he'll tell them a sob story that's a complete fabrication of the truth.'

I swung my legs out of bed and laughed. 'Well, he can hardly tell them what really happened, can he.'

'Oh, I don't know, he could twist it so it makes him look good. I imagine he would say something like -Effelia my darling daughter was so grateful to me for saving the life of her beloved Gideon that she gave me Rawlings as a thank you gift. I of course flatly refused the offer but she insisted that I have her home and told me how happy it would have made Constance.'

Wrapping my dressing gown around me I chuckled. 'Yes, he probably will say something similar.' I gave him a half-hearted smile. 'I'll see you downstairs in a moment. Put some toast on, will you?'

'Sure Effie, I can do you a full English if you like. I'm now a master cook in the kitchen, you know.'

'Is that true Mace? I asked with a grin. 'Have you been taking lessons from someone, such as Clarice or her mother?'

He didn't answer.

'Mace?'

His large eyes grew wider. 'No, it wasn't them. It...it was my father Caleb.' With a huge sigh he rubbed his eyes, beginning to laugh and cry both at the same time. 'I've just realised I miss him.'

I smiled serenely. 'Well maybe you *should* come back with me. You and Clarice.'

'Oh E, you know I want to, but it's Mrs Lapworth, Clarice won't leave her.' He paused. 'And I won't leave Clarice, not now she's finally getting better.' With a sigh he leapt towards the door. 'All this talk of food has made me ravenous.' He disappeared out the door. 'I'll go and put some nosh on.'

After a quick bath I dressed and ran down stairs to join Mace in the kitchen, and had barely finished my breakfast when I heard someone rapping on the front door.

'I'll get it Mace.'

'If it's Isaiah then tell him to go back and join his lady friends.'

With a laugh I opened the door to see a slight young woman standing there. She must have been a little older than myself and her round face was framed with brassy looking hair, styled into a long bob. When she spoke I noticed her lips were smothered in a rather garish red lipstick.

'Hello, you must be Effelia.'

I stared at her blankly. 'Do I know you?'

The woman let out a high-pitched laugh. 'That's typical of him isn't it? Not to mention me.' She rolled her eyes. 'I'm Isaiah's wife- Lillian.'

In a daze I continued to stare at her. 'Pardon?'

She began to look uncomfortable. 'Well aren't you going to invite us in?'

'Us?' It was only then I noticed several children darting around the garden. 'I'm sorry, it's just that Isaiah didn't mention he had another wife.'

The woman burst out laughing before realising I was being serious, and then she became stony-faced. 'I'm hardly another wife. Isaiah and I have been married for years, and I'm his one and only.' She inclined her head towards the children, who were now pushing passed her and into the house. 'As you can see, we have four children together.' Not waiting to be invited in she slid passed me into the hallway. 'I've come to inspect my new home.'

In astonishment I watched on as she wandered up the hallway, taking in her surroundings.

'I can already see that this old house will need a major overhaul.' She giggled nervously, grasping my arm then releasing it. 'If you don't mind me saying - it's so old fashioned.' She whispered in my ear, as if the house could hear her. 'And the name Rawlings, I really don't care for it. I've already told Isaiah I want to change it.' She gazed up at the ceiling and twisted her lips, deep in thought. 'I was thinking of renaming it The Homestead.' Her eyes flicked swiftly to mine. 'What do you think, classy eh?'

I was speechless.

'He told me you didn't stay here much and that it was the old lady who used to live here – Connie, wasn't it?'

'Constance.' I answered sternly. 'My Aunt.'

She glanced at me properly for the first time, her eyes swiftly running over me. 'Oh yes. I'm sorry for your loss.'

I nodded my head slowly but said nothing.

With a groan she brushed passed me and hurried over to the foot of the staircase where one of her children was busily crayoning on a painting. 'Patrick! Stop doing that this instant.' He dropped the crayon and darted down the stairs, before his mother could grab him. 'Come back here now.' She shouted after him, but he was already out the door. 'Patrick likes to draw moustaches and things on anything that has a face. Never mind though eh. All these ancient looking paintings can be sold off.' She giggled again and momentarily squeezed my arm. 'Isaiah says you're an artist, are any of these yours?'

'A couple, yes.'

'Well, you can take them when you move out, can't you.'

I stared at her in alarm. 'Is that what Isaiah told you'

'Yeah, he said you had another home, somewhere overseas and that you'd be returning there shortly and not coming back.' Yet again she touched my arm. 'I think it's for the best, don't you?

I spoke through gritted teeth. 'Well probably yes, but I may still return to Rawlings and…and besides I'm sure Isaiah will want to keep the paintings.'

'We'll see.' She replied in a clipped tone.

I watched in disbelief as she began poking her head around all the rooms downstairs one by one, and making disapproving comments as she glanced inside. Lastly, she tottered into the library. I trailed behind her, briefly glancing at the children as they raced towards the kitchen. They must have gone out the back door as I heard it slam loudly.

'Oh, what a stuffy room, so dark and depressing.' Another high-pitched laugh, rather like a squeal, escaped her lips. 'And all those dusty old books will have to go.'

I felt myself kneading my hands together, trying to hold back from slapping her face, or worse still punching it.

'I would appreciate it if you'd leave them alone, I said between gritted teeth. They're very precious to me.'

Her loud grating voice came close to my ear. 'You'd better take them as well then.'

Taking a deep breath, I crossed over and glanced out the window. The children were outside, being chased by Mace. I watched as they turned on him and got hold of his jumper, pulling him down to the grass. They then threw themselves on top of him and began to playfully punch his stomach.

'The gardens are a bit impractical with all those flowerbeds and trees. Best we clear it all. I was thinking of a large swimming pool to the rear, with a patio area, and the rest could be grass with a large play area for the children.'

I could feel the rage building up inside of me, ready to explode.

'Is that a summerhouse I see in the distance? She gasped. 'We could make it into an art room.'

Surprised, I turned to look at her. 'Really?'

'Yeah. The children can draw and paint to their hearts content. And as it's so far away from the house it won't matter if they wreck the place.' She laughed. 'Perhaps we could re- use the canvases from some of the old paintings hanging in the house, the kids would love to paint over them, especially the portraits.'

Perhaps if she hadn't clasped my arm again, I may have gone easier on her, but as she reached out to grab it I dug my nails into her flesh.

'Get out, get out you awful woman.' I shrieked, grasping her upper arm and roughly dragging her towards the door. Have you no respect for the dead? My poor Aunt has only recently passed away and already you want to move in and ruin our home.' Ignoring her whimpers, I continued to haul her into the hallway and over to the front door. 'Well you're not living here, not now, not ever. I'd not even met you until a few moments ago, and it was certainly an experience, one I have no wish to repeat.' I gave her a little shove out the door. 'And just to let you know, you're not Isaiah's legal wife.'

'I saw her mouth gape open wide. 'What do you mean?'

With a look of defiance, I stood there, my arms folded. 'By law he's still married to my mother.' Following her outside I noticed Mace and the children standing there in astonishment. 'And don't forget to take your brood of children with you.' Without another word I turned on my heel and went back into the house, slamming the door behind me. I charged to the kitchen and slumped down in a chair.

Mace poked his head around the back door. 'Is it safe to enter?'

'Yes. Why wouldn't it be?'

'Well you were a bit enraged at minute ago E.' He tentatively stepped into the kitchen. 'You were so petrifying that I almost left with Isaiah's missus.'

I rubbed my eyes with the back of my hand then looked up into his eyes, unable to laugh even though he had grass in his hair. 'She's gone then?'

He drew out a seat and sat opposite me, arms outstretched on the table. 'She hasn't just gone; she's fled in tears.'

'Ah.' I tried to compose myself. 'Well what did you expect me to do, welcome the woman with open arms?' I could feel my anger returning. 'She comes to my house out of the blue and reels off a list of abhorrent changes she's going to make to Rawlings when she moves in with her children.' I banged my fist on the table. 'The audacity of the woman.'

Narrowing his eyes, he slowly shook his head. 'But E, you're forgetting one major point – Rawlings isn't yours anymore is it. You signed it over to Isaiah, remember?'

'Yes, and it torments me every single day. But I had no choice.' I gazed wistfully down at the table. 'Gideon would have died otherwise.' Playing with my wedding ring I looked up into Mace's face, his large gentle eyes studying me compassionately. 'I just wish Isaiah had thought to mention his family. I obviously would have still agreed to the testimony, but it wouldn't have been such a shock today.'

'Yeah, the crafty old goat, having two wives on the go is bigamy, you know.'

'Yes, I'm well aware of that Mace.' Concern spread over my face. 'I hope I didn't upset the children. I'm sure they heard me speaking about the marriage not being legal.'

Mace waved his hand with an air of dismissal. 'Don't worry about that E. Kids are resilient little devils. And what- the oldest one must be ten, eleven. They'll probably too young to understand.'

We heard someone putting a key in the front door.

'That must be Isaiah.' Mace exclaimed, dashing over to the back door. I'm going over to see Clarice's. See you later?'

I nodded, half smiling.

He turned and grinned cheekily at me before dashing out the door. 'Have fun with daddy.'

To my amazement I began to laugh. The sudden thought of Isaiah having four young children to contend with was funny. I pictured him playing with them and reading bedtime stories when they were good and scolding them when they were naughty. I wondered if he sought sanctuary at Rawlings to get away from them, for some peace and quiet. And were all those business trips merely a fabrication, when what he was actually doing was spending time with his family.

I rose slowly from the seat and trundled out the kitchen.

Isaiah glanced over at me as he removed his raincoat.

'It's beginning to drizzle out there.' Taking off his hat he placed it on the coat stand and grimaced, rubbing his leg. 'This wet weather plays havoc with my bad leg. If only I had my diaries to hand.' He gazed at me with pleading eyes. 'I implore you Effelia to see sense and have them returned to me. I am a shadow of a man without them.'

I scoffed. 'That's a little difficult when my Aunt never informed me who's in possession of them.'

He approached me slowly. 'But then we must surely find out.' He reached out and gently placed his hand on my cheek.

'Your poor Aunt is no longer with us Effelia. Let us retrieve my diaries and put an end to this whole sorry business.'

Pushing his hand away I looked at him sullenly then marched along the hallway and into the library, where I began to search through the books. He followed me into the room.

'Effelia, what are you doing?'

'I'm saving my books.'

He laughed anxiously. 'Whatever do you mean?'

Unable to contain myself any longer I swung round and faced him, staring steadily into his eyes. 'I'm saving them from being destroyed by your wife.'

Without uttering a sound, he stood there, studying my face in bewilderment, and when he finally spoke his voice was unsteady. 'Do you mean your mother, has...has she made contact?'

I laughed. 'No, not that *wife* silly, the *wife* you have here in Abercrombie. The *wife* that visited me today with your four children.'

Yet again he became silent, allowing the realisation of what I had just told him to sink in. He smiled, a nervous, anxious smile that was ingratiatingly sickening.

'Effelia, allow me to explain.'

I extended my arm, gesturing for him to sit down. 'Please do.' I uttered without emotion. I positioned myself in the armchair adjacent to his.

As he began to explain his face looked mostly crestfallen, but there was a hint of shame in his eyes too, the guilty shame of a man whose closely guarded secret had just been revealed. 'How wretched and lonely I felt when Freya, your dear mother had gone from my life.' He said. Quite by accident he had met Lillian and they had married in secret some years later and started a family. He'd always wanted to say something to my Aunt and I, but was frightened of upsetting us and didn't think we'd understand. I hardly raised an eyebrow when he relayed to me how miserable she made his life and how many a time he contemplated "bumping her off" but he didn't wish to leave the children motherless and couldn't possibly take on the sole burden of responsibility of caring for them. Bending forward he took my hands in his and swore to me Lillian had only been made aware of Rawlings existence a short while ago, after she had supposedly read his mail by accident. And he was mortified that she had visited the house without his permission.

I withdrew my hands from his and placed them neatly in my lap.

'So, what happens now?'

'Nothing will happen Effelia. Under no circumstances will I allow my family to take up residence at Rawlings.' He said, smiling and shaking his head. 'As much as I love them...' He paused. 'As much as I love the children, they cannot come here to live.' He raised his hands in despair. 'Can you imagine what they would do to our lovely home? And that's just the children.' A cool, faraway look appeared in his eyes. 'That woman would destroy its entire character and turn it into something vile and modern. She would rip out the heart of Rawlings just like I'd like to rip out her heart.'

With a sigh I rose up from the armchair and made my way to the door, leaving him sitting there in the musty old library, deep in thought.

Mace slung his jacket over his shoulder and ambled across the hallway, a slice of half-eaten toast hanging from his mouth. 'Are you sure you won't come E? He asked, temporary removing the toast from his mouth. 'I know you're leaving soon but it will still do you good to get away from Rawlings.'

I emerged from the kitchen with a vase of flowers.

'Thanks Mace, but no, I really must sort through those books in the library.' I placed the flowers on the oak cabinet in the hall. Since my Aunt's passing we had been inundated with cards, flowers and wreaths from people wishing to pay their respects. It was all very well but there were so many flowers in the house that I was running out of places to put them all. 'And Isaiah is due to move in today, I should be here to greet him.'

'What a good and dutiful daughter you are Effie.' He said in a low voice. 'It's just a shame your father is such a murdering lowlife whose stolen your home and committed bigamy.'

I burst out laughing. 'Oh Mace. What would I do without you.'

He saluted me, stamping his feet and knocking them together. 'I'm here to serve you, my lady.'

I smiled after him as he stumbled out the door, tripping up on the mat as he went.

'Have a lovely day Mace.' I shouted after him. 'And don't forget about tonight.'

It was Mace's birthday today and we'd decided to dine out this evening, just the three of us. Clarice, apparently, was looking forward to it. She was coming on so well that I began to have hope, real hope of her returning back to normal. Sometimes I would see an animated spark within her eyes, and it reminded me of the bright- eyed young woman that I remembered.

Suddenly I felt my spirits lift, and feeling positive I made my way to the library to gather more books together. After the unexpected visit from Isaiah's new wife I'd already moved some items of sentimental value over to Clarice's house, including the portrait of my mother. Although Isaiah had reassured me that nothing would be sold or destroyed, I still had a niggling doubt, and being one of those types who was extremely sentimental the thought of anything disappearing from my home was heart-breaking.

As I carefully positioned myself on the ladder, I selected some of the dusty old books from the higher shelves and piled them with the others in a cardboard box on the floor, coughing from the dust particles that floated in the air. Amongst the books I'd chosen to take away from Rawlings was the tin full of money that I'd retrieved from my mattress earlier on. I was also very concerned about leaving the mirror in the study, as with Isaiah moving back in, I suddenly felt it was no longer safe at Rawlings; he would probably take a hammer and smash the glass, just so he could prevent me from leaving. I rarely went in the study, for it was a reminder of my other home, but I would go there today and put the mirror in the car, ready to take to Clarice's house later.

I heard someone yell out my name. It was Isaiah.

'It's me. I'm home.'

'I'm in the library.' I called out calmly, descending the ladder and brushing the dust from my skirt. Rather hurriedly I picked up the box of books.

He bounded into the library, beaming all over. 'I have my luggage and I'm already to move in Effelia.'

Completely reticent I nodded at him and headed for the door with the box of books. 'I shall give you a hand with your luggage.'

'I see you've been stealing books from my library.'

Standing in the frame of the door I swung round. 'There's only a few here. I didn't think you'd mine.' I said softly. 'Besides, you may own Rawlings now but the contents of the house still belong to me.'

He waved his finger in front of my face. 'It doesn't state in the testimony that I'd be excluded from owning the contents. Which therefore gives me the right to take full ownership of all the possessions kept at the property.' With a huff his eyes travelled down to the box of books. 'I order you to put them back on the shelves, this instant.'

My eyes became wide with shock. 'No.'

Without warning he began to rock with laughter, his whole body shaking. 'Oh, you should see the look on your face, it's a picture.' He wiped his face as a tear ran down his cheek. 'I wasn't being serious Effelia. Of course, you can take the books.'

Not amused I marched into the hallway.

'I see you've already taken your mother's portrait; I'm perfectly fine with that of course.' He called after me, still unable to contain his laughter. 'Take whatever you can find, including that frightful dummy.'

Placing the box beside the oak cabinet I pressed my hand across my temple and briefly glanced at him. 'I've got a headache.' I mounted the stairs. 'I'm going upstairs to my room.'

'I thought you were going to help with my luggage?'

'You can manage.'

Reaching the landing I cautiously peered over the banisters to check Isaiah couldn't see me, then raced along the passageway to my Aunt's room. I don't know why but there was something in his tone that bothered me. 'Take whatever you can find.' He said, which made me wonder whether he had already *found* what he wanted. With bated breath I crossed over to her dressing table and opened the top drawer, knowing that this was where my Aunt kept her jewellery box. It clicked as I opened it and I stared down at the velvet base- it was completely empty. 'No, no, no.' I muttered frantically. In a fit of panic I fell to my hands and knees and began searching through each drawer at a time, hoping to find at least one piece of jewellery, or her watches, or anything that had been handed down from generation to generation, but nothing was left but a few scarves and handkerchiefs

'I needed the money.'

I jerked my head around to see Isaiah standing there, leaning up against the door.

'So, you thought you'd just sell all my Aunt's jewellery, without even asking me. You only had to ask I would have given you some money.' I said coldly, rising from the floor. 'Why didn't you consider doing that Isaiah, why?' I demanded my voice becoming angrier by the minute.'

He stared at me coyly. 'I do have my pride you know. What kind of father would ask his own daughter for money?'

'Well surely that's better than stealing from your daughter, because that's what you've done. That jewellery belonged to me.'

'So, you would have taken it with you when you leave, eh?' He sniggered. 'I think not. It would all sit in that jewellery box gathering dust, never seeing the light of day.'

'That's hardly the point.'

I heard a sudden noise downstairs. Someone was hammering on the front door. Grimacing at him I left the room and charged down the stairs, flinging the door open wide. I'd expected to see Mace standing there and was a little taken aback when I saw a strange man in a hat and coat, carrying a rather shabby briefcase. He was a slightly built man with horn-rimmed glasses and a thin face.

'Can I help you?'

'Miss…. I mean Mrs Thoroughgood?

'Yes, that is I.'

'I'm with a law firm known as Bishop and Smith and my name is Mr Cartwright.' He removed his hat and smoothed down his hair. 'I wonder if I might have a word with you and…' He looked over my shoulder into the house. 'And your father Mr Penhaligon.'

Hesitantly I stepped back. 'Yes of course. Do come in Mr Cartwright.'

'I apologise for not visiting before, it's just I only become aware of your Aunt's passing a few days ago.' He smiled compassionately at me. 'My sincere condolences to you and your family.'

I lowered my eyes. 'Thank you.'

I took his hat and coat, and placed them on the coat stand then showed him into the living room where he sat rigidly in one of the armchairs with his briefcase in his lap.

'Can I get you a cup of tea?'

He waved his hand dismissively. 'No thank you, but I wonder if I may have a glass of water?'

Before I had a chance to reply, Isaiah came storming into the room, his face like thunder. 'Who are you, and what do you want?'

Mr Cartwright looked aghast.

'This is Mr Cartwright Isaiah and his with a law firm. He needs to speak to the both of us about something.'

Without removing his eyes from Mr Cartwright's face, Isaiah flopped down in the armchair opposite him. 'Well, what is it man?'

I threw Isaiah a look of disdain. 'Wait, I said in a clipped tone. 'I'll just go and get your water Mr Cartwright.'

When I returned with the water there was an uncomfortable silence, and Isaiah was still glaring at the poor man as if he was going to attack him.

'So, what's this all about?' I asked, passing Mr Cartwright the water and sitting down beside them.

He took a sip of water then rather shakily put the glass on the side. Pushing his glasses further up his nose he began looking through his paperwork from his briefcase.

'It's regarding the passing of your Aunt.' He momentarily stared at me before turning his attention to Isaiah. The late Constance Farraday. We act on her behalf and....'

Isaiah interrupted in a loud voice. 'Whoever you are, you're too late. Constance's solicitors have already read the will and everything has been finalised. So, I think you'll find you've had a wasted journey.'

I'm very sorry Mr Cartwright; please excuse Isaiah's rudeness. Just ignore him and carry on.'

The man cleared his throat nervously and gave me a weak smile. 'Thank you, Mrs Thoroughgood.'

'Please, call me Effie.'

A deep groan came from Isaiah. 'Enough with the niceties just get to the point man.'

Mr Cartwright shifted in his seat, looking on edge. 'Constance had appointed two separate solicitors to deal with matters concerning her estate. I believe you had a visit from Mr Goring of Webster's recently.' He coughed. 'He was the gentleman who brought her death to my attention, and you have him to thank for me being here now.' Rather nervously he glanced at me.'

'What are you blabbering on about?' Growled Isaiah.

'Well you see Constance also hired Bishop and Smith, the firm I work for.' He pulled out an envelope and held it out to Isaiah. 'Constance instructed we pass you this letter, Mr Penhaligon, following her death.'

Isaiah snatched the envelope from his hand and ripped it open. Having read the letter, he passed it to me, looking sullenly at Mr Cartwright.

Dear Isaiah

If you are reading my letter then death has taken me.

Knowing you the way I do it seemed right and just to put in place a legal procedure that will categorically make sure you never again reside at Rawlings. Therefore, should you attempt to worm your way back into my home following my death, then the evidence that I have against you will STILL be passed on to the police and you WILL be arrested forthwith. This order applies until the end of your natural, miserable life.

Constance Farraday

Having read the contents, I passed it back to Isaiah who immediately screwed it up and tossed it into the fire before Mr Cartwright could object.

Mr Cartwright exchanged a glance with me before warily looking at Isaiah. 'I'm afraid destroying the letter was futile. We hold the original at our offices along with a signed statement from Constance that lays out her wishes.'

Isaiah leant forward in his seat, glaring aggressively at him. 'Is that so?' He sniggered. 'Well I shall contest it. I shall prove that dear Constance had lost her marbles when she agreed to such an idiotic suggestion. And surely as I am now the legal owner of Rawlings such an agreement would be irrelevant.'

Mr Cartwright laughed nervously at Isaiah. 'It makes no difference whether you own the property or just live in it; the result will be the same. It's a non-negotiable order that therefore cannot be contested. And I can assure you Constance was of sound mind when she made it.'

Isaiah looked morosely at him. 'Do not ridicule me sir.'

He shifted in his chair, looking uneasily at Isaiah. 'May I point out Mr Penhaligon that the evidence in our firm's possession is damning enough to ensure that you spend the remainder of your life in prison. But lucky for you Constance insisted that the order against you would only be acted upon if you ever lived at Rawlings, otherwise you would remain safe from the law. Most people would be grateful to have their freedom.'

'I'm not most people Mr Cartwright. I may be a free man but without Rawlings....' His voice trailed off for a moment and his eyes flickered over to mine. 'It seems your dear Aunt Constance is determined to make me suffer Effelia, even from beyond the grave.' Isaiah's expression turned grim as he slunk forward in his chair, staring glumly down at the floor.

A thought suddenly occurred to me, it was a farcical idea, one that went against all my better principles, but somehow it made sense.

'Could Isaiah's wife and family move into Rawlings?'

Isaiah suddenly looked up and stared at me in alarm. 'Effelia?'

Mr Cartwright widened his eyes in surprise. 'I wasn't aware that he had any other family. But yes, if he has a marriage certificate then yes it could be a possibility.'

I was tempted to tell him the wedding wasn't legal because Isaiah was still married to another woman- my mother. But she was either dead or lost forever in another world.

'I'm sure that Isaiah has the certificate safely hidden away somewhere.'

Mr Cartwright's face brightened a little. 'Then I shall look into it for you.'

Isaiah threw himself forward and hid his face in his hands. 'No, please don't worry yourself. My family cannot live there without me.' His voice sounded strange, tearful, and as he looked up at me, I saw the torment in his eyes. 'What should I do Effelia?' he uttered distraughtly, grasping my hand.

I placed my other hand over his. 'You could always sell Rawlings.' I said in a low uncertain voice. 'And buy another grand house elsewhere.'

The old Effie wouldn't dare utter such words; she would believe it to be a betrayal of Aunt and Rawlings itself. But selling Rawlings or having it ruined by Isaiah's new wife, either didn't matter. I had changed, life had changed me, and I could no longer allow my heart to rule my head.

He shook his head violently. 'No. I will never sell my home. Of all the worlds I have visited, of all the places I have seen, nothing, I mean nothing can hold a torch to Rawlings.'

Mr Cartwright's face looked uncomfortable and confused. 'Well, I should be leaving.' He collected his papers and put them back into his suitcase. 'If you change your mind Isaiah about your family living at Rawlings, then please let me know.' He glanced at me hesitantly. 'I hope you don't mind me saying Effie, but why don't you stay on at Rawlings. It's such a shame not to keep it in the family.'

'I have another home Mr Cartwright, where my husband and son are waiting for me.' My voice was quiet as I spoke, as a wave of heartache washed over me. 'But I will be greatly saddened to leave Rawlings.'

He pursed his lips and nodded then looked directly at Isaiah. 'Please see to it that you vacate the premises by noon tomorrow. A colleague will be making random checks on the house, and will alert the police if they find you here and hand over the diaries.' He hesitated. 'I'm very sorry.' Looking apologetic he extended his hand for Isaiah to shake but he was unresponsive. 'Good day.'

I saw Mr Cartwright off whilst Isaiah languished in the living room, to dejected to even move. Returning to the living room I went and stood beside him for a moment, and watched as he poured himself a large whisky.

'Are you alright Isaiah?'

'No.' he murmured, staring ahead as if in a trance. 'It's always been a dream of mine to own Rawlings, my dearest dream. And for one brief period of time it came true.' His voice sounded weak and odd. 'But then that dream was snatched away from me. And now I have nothing.'

'Look Isaiah, I'm sorry about Rawlings, really I am. However, my Aunt could have taken those diaries of yours to the police when she found them, and you'd be locked up now in a prison cell. But she allowed you clemency, she allowed you to carry on with your life, knowing that you were a murderer, amongst other things. So as Mr Cartwright said, you should consider yourself a fortunate man. You have your health and a loving family, and if you could bring yourself to sell Rawlings you could buy another house. So please don't mope about feeling sorry for yourself when there's really no need to.'

He took a gulp of his whisky. 'Thank you for that dear daughter, but your words of wisdom cannot help me.

I stared into his face. He looked lost and defeated, as if all his fighting spirit had deserted him.

'I'm popping out for a while.' I bit my lip and gulped. 'Perhaps we can talk some more on my return.' I moved my hand with the intention of resting it on his shoulder but then thought better of it. 'You will stay at Rawlings tonight, won't you?'

He turned slightly in his armchair and his eyes widened as he stared at me endearingly. 'Yes. This is where I belong Effelia.'

With a contented sigh he poured himself another whisky and gazed into the fire, watching the flames dance in the grate.

Chapter 26

The pleasant music drifted softly through the restaurant.

'Do you remember when we used to play hide and seek at Rawlings and you Effie, you...you would always find the best places to hide.' Said Clarice, stuttering a little as she carried on. 'And...and Mace would always get annoyed and give in.' A hint of a smile crossed over her face. 'He would go and sulk in the kitchen and help himself to cakes.'

Mace clapped his hands at Clarice.

'Yes, yes that's right.' His arm slipped around her shoulder. 'However, I think you'll find it was Effie that sulked after failing to seek me.' He chortled. 'And I didn't need any excuse to eat cakes, especially home-baked ones from Connie.' A tinge of sadness showed in his face as his eyes glazed over. 'She was a brilliant cook.'

With tears in my eyes I reached out and squeezed his hand.

'Do you have to leave tomorrow E?'

'Yes, it's time Mace. I've already stayed away far too long.'

He gave me an answering smile. 'What I would have given to see the look on Isaiah's face when he realised he had to leave Rawlings. Good on old Connie eh.' Said Mace chuckling. 'She was an astute woman E.'

I smiled wistfully at him. 'The thing is I almost feel sorry for him, and he would have taken care of Rawlings you know, protected its history.'

'Yes but E, you know he would've moved that wife and children in sooner or later. He wouldn't have lived in a big old house all on his lonesome.' Finishing his meal, he cheekily took a potato from Clarice's plate and stuffed it into his mouth. 'With only the spirit of Connie to keep him company.' Mace peeked sheepishly at me. 'You didn't mind me saying that did you Effie?'

I laughed and shook my head. 'I can just imagine her floating about from room to room, keeping an eye on her property. And if Isaiah had moved in, she would surely have haunted him.' Looking pensive I lowered my eyes and began fiddling with my napkin. 'Dear, sweet Aunt.'

We were silent for a while.

Suddenly the lights went dim.

'Oh, you didn't.' exclaimed Mace, covering his face within his hands. 'E, you know how embarrassed I get being the centre of attention.'

I roared with laughter, exchanging glances with a smiling Clarice.

Several members of staff were approaching our table with a birthday cake full of candles and as we all began to sing happy birthday, Mace stood up with a big grin all over his face.

'Thank you, kind citizens of Abercrombie.'

Leaning forward he blew out the candles and the whole restaurant began to applaud. He then proceeded to bow to everyone before planting a kiss on Clarice's lips. She looked aghast for a moment before relaxing a little, her face turning scarlet. As the other guests began returning to their meals, Mace began tapping his spoon against his crystal wine glass.

'I will, if I may, make a small speech.' He caught my eye and smiled. 'This woman sitting before me is called Effie Farraday. Since young children until the present day she has been my best friend. We have had our ups and downs over the years, but with my patience and understanding our friendship has endured. With my guidance and assistance, she has grown into the woman you see before you.' He paused, staring into my eyes. 'A beautiful, kind and courageous young woman who I am proud to call my friend.' His voice began to break up with emotion. 'Sadly, all good things must come to an end, and Effie is leaving tomorrow and I may never see her again. But I want her to know she will be forever in my thoughts. However faraway she may be.... she will never be forgotten.'

A hushed silence spread across the restaurant.

With tears in my eyes I rushed over to him and flung my arms around his neck.

'Oh Mace. Of course, we won't forget one another.'

'I know.' He whispered into my hair.

'I shall always remember you too Effie.' Said Clarice. Nervously she rose and we gently hugged one another.

Everyone had settled down now, and began talking amongst themselves.

To my embarrassment Mace once again tapped his wine glass.

'I would also like to commend my girlfriend Clarice. Against all odds she overcome her illness and returned to reality, and in doing so our love for one another has flourished.' He cleared his throat. 'This flaxen haired beauty is the woman I wish to spend the rest of my life with.' Dropping to one knee he gazed anxiously into Clarice's eyes. 'Will you therefore do me the very great honour of becoming my wife?'

All eyes were on her now, and as I stared into her face, I noticed how radiant she appeared.

'Perhaps.' She uttered in a muted tone.

That was enough for Mace. Rising from the floor he grabbed her hands and kissed them fervently. 'That's a start, a very good start.'

As we all sat down again the manager approached us, looking rather embarrassed. He asked Mace to kindly refrain from making any more speeches as it was disturbing the other guests. Looking indignant he glowered at the manager and apologised through gritted teeth.

'Are you sure you don't mind staying at Rawlings tonight Mace?' I asked as we were heading home in the car. I don't know why but I had a niggling worry that wouldn't leave me.

'Huh huh.' He murmured. 'Clarice looked elated tonight; don't you think E?'

The brakes screeched as I changed the gear, jolting us forward. 'Yes Mace, she surely must have been pleased with your proposal.'

To my relief we had reached the turning for Rawlings and I could soon park the car. Driving was somewhat of an ordeal for me, and I was rather happy to be saying goodbye to it. The dark tunnel of overhanging branches from the great oaks loomed above us like a contorted mass of outreaching arms intertwining with one another, and when we emerged back out into the open, I spotted a peculiar orange glow in the distance. A momentarily lack of concentration caused me to lose control of the steering wheel, and the vehicle swerved a sharp right, landing us in a small ditch at the side of the gravel driveway.

Mace began to scream at me. 'What on earth are you doing Effie? The house is up ahead, not in this ditch.'

Without really hearing him I clambered out the car and began staggering towards the house, then as I came nearer, I broke into a run. Mace was shouting after me but I was suddenly oblivious to everything around me, everything except the glimmering brightness up ahead. For one moment I was frozen to the spot, mesmerised by the leaping flames as they danced and lapped through my home. My heart was thumping frantically in my chest as I struggled to catch my breath.

I heard raised voices from behind me.

'Hurry Ambrose, for God's sake hurry.' Shouted Mace. Coughing and spluttering he came to join me. 'Ambrose is cycling to the Armstrong's to telephone the fire brigade.'

Returning to reality I tore my eyes away and glared at Mace. 'But...but that's two miles away.' I cried in anguish. 'They'll never reach us in time.'

'What else can we do? I can hardly produce a phone from thin air, now can I E.'

A flicker of annoyance swept across my face. It never ceased to amaze me how Mace would turn to sarcasm whatever the circumstances.

'Yes, I'm well aware of that.' My mind drifted off for a second and in one abrupt movement my hand covered my mouth. 'Isaiah...what about Isaiah? What if he's still in Rawlings?'

'Ambrose saw him leave the house earlier.'

'Is he sure?'

'Wait here Effie, whilst I run and ask Ambrose.' He replied mockingly. 'Or perhaps I could drive after him.' He lightly slapped his forehead. 'Oh no I can't do that as you drove the car into a ditch.'

'I'm...I'm sure we could shift it. Then you could drive to the Armstrong's and ring.' Feeling panicked I began pacing up and down the grass. 'That would be quicker.'

'E...you're not thinking straight.' He grabbed my shoulders and held me still, pulling my face round so he could look me straight in the eye. 'Effie, even if we did manage to remove the car from the ditch by the time I'd driven over there, Ambrose would have already reached the Armstrong's.' His voice suddenly sounded hoarse and emotional. 'It's best we stay here.'

I stared into his face then began to nod slowly. 'Yes, yes you are right.'

With a harrowing sigh I turned my attention back to Rawlings. Wafts of smoke were billowing towards us as the blaze raged uncontrollably through the house like a ferocious beast leaping out at every angle, destroying everything within its path. I shuddered as the window of the study shattered, sending shards of glass soaring through the air, close to where we were standing. As we instinctively took a few steps back a sensation of utter dread swept rapidly through my body, totally enveloping my heart in an unbearable ache. The mirror... I had to save the mirror. With all that had occurred today I had forgotten to remove it from the study.

'Oh no.'

'Effie, Effie what is it?'

Without answering I automatically began charging towards the flames, oblivious of the searing heat upon my face. But something was grabbing my waist, holding me back. I recall screaming at Mace, digging my nails into his flesh until he cried out in pain, but still he wouldn't release me. I became hysterical, screaming my lungs out in frantic despair. And then I began to sob, great heart wrenching sobs that I couldn't seem to control. Mace released his grip on my waist and grasped my shoulders, and then swinging me round to face him he began to shake me roughly.

'Stop it Effie, stop it.' He slapped me hard across the face and I became silent, staring like a wild woman into his tear-stained face. 'We're safe, that's all that matters.'

In a fit of fury, I gave him an almighty shove and he toppled to the ground.

'Nothing matters if I can't get back to my child.' My voice was hoarse and dry from the smoke and it hurt to speak, but I didn't care. 'The mirrors gone; don't you see?' I yelled, pointing at the house. 'I can't go back; I can't return home.'

Mace was mumbling something to me but I didn't hear. Suddenly I was lost in my very own nightmare. My home…. it was waiting for me, my family were waiting for me, and I had patiently waited to return to them…and now it transpires I had waited *too* long. A sensation of complete and utter hopelessness washed over me as I had a sudden realisation of the misery and suffering that I would have to endure, knowing I could never see my family ever again. For one strange moment I wished to lose myself amongst the flames, and without realising it I began stumbling forward as if unnatural forces were beckoning me to join them.

'What are you doing E?' Mace screamed at me, pulling me back. 'You need to keep away.' He grabbed my face in his hands, forcing me to look at him. 'The mirror's safe, I moved it into the summerhouse a few days ago.'

'The…the summerhouse.'

'Yes, yes you silly woman. Go and check if you like, but I promise you it's there.' He still held my face, staring into my frantic eyes. 'I had a hunch that it wouldn't be safe in the house. But it is safe in the summerhouse, the fires not going to reach right down the back of the garden, now is it?'

I began to laugh. 'Mace, oh Mace.' Taking his hands and removing them, I instinctively reached forward and started planting kisses all over his face. 'Thank you.'

'All right Effie, there's no need to overreact.' He began rubbing his hand across his face. 'I'm not the right person to practice your kissing on.'

Forgetting the fire, I began howling with laughter, both hysterical and joyous at the same time.

Mace began to mutter underneath his breath. Gently tapping me on the arm he pointed up to the very top of the house. I couldn't see anything at first as the flames were lapping up against the windows, but then I saw him, leaning over the windowsill in the attic...it was Isaiah.

I drew in my breath, clasping my hands over my mouth.

'Well I'll be damned.' Exclaimed Mace. 'Ambrose must have made a mistake.'

'Why is he in the attic?' I asked in disbelief. 'Isaiah, get out, get out.' I yelled, waving my arms up in the air to get his attention.

He was shouting, trying to tell me something, but I could hardly hear him above the roar of the fire. However, for a sudden moment his voice became audible, and I heard him cry out. 'I'm locked in Effelia, he's locked me in.' He pointed down towards us, muttering something else, which I couldn't quite catch. I think I heard him crying but then I realised he was laughing hysterically.

My eyes darted to Mace a puzzled look on my face.

'Don't look at me. I didn't lock him in.'

'Well I can't imagine it was Ambrose.' I retorted.

'Perhaps he's finally gone mad.'

I strained my eyes, trying to see him through the smoke. 'Hold on Isaiah.' I shouted, even though I was sure he wouldn't hear me. 'The firemen are on their way.' An acute feeling of sickness was gradually building in the pit of my stomach as I realised they weren't going to reach him in time.

Mace took my hand and held it tight.

We both watched in horror as the top part of the house suddenly collapsed, making a tremendous crash. Smoke and dust rose up into the air filling my lungs, and we both started to cough violently.

'We should stand back further E,' Mace said softly.

My eyes frantically scanned the front of the flame filled house, looking for Isaiah, but I could no longer see or hear him. A lump came to my throat as I felt my eyes fill with tears.

Unable to look one moment longer I turned away; it was too torturous. My gaze momentarily focused on the garden seats behind us, Ambrose must have moved them away from the terrace earlier to prevent them catching alight. My breath caught in my mouth as I saw who was sitting right in the centre seat with his usual grotesque grin. His large protruding eyes were staring fixedly ahead, as if he was watching a show – it was Gilbert.

I can only recall snippets from the remainder of that fateful night. My tears were all spent and now I just felt numb and emotionless, I was like a sleepwalker aimlessly wandering through a living nightmare that just went on and on. The firemen came too late, there was nothing left to save. Rawlings had gone, it was a burnt-out shell, a skeleton. My dear home, my Aunt's home had finally crumbled to the ground, taken away from us by a raging fire. After it was over, Mace had tried to get me to leave, but I couldn't sleep or settle. I have a vague recollection of asking him to go away, to leave me be, but he insisted on staying, and there we both sat in silence, staring into the dying embers of the fire. He left me on my own for a while, draping an old shawl from the car around my shoulders, as he went and spoke to Ambrose and the fire crew. Dawn broke and the warmth of the early morning sun gradually penetrated through the trees onto my back, I could feel it on my shoulders and my neck, like a comforting blanket of support. The remains of the smoke were swirling through the wreckage like tendrils of hate, hurtfully reminding me of what had happened to my beautiful house, and to my father.... It was somehow fitting now to call him by his proper name. Finally, I had drawn a line under his misdemeanours, and in doing so I was able to forgive him, I would think fondly of him now, and I would mourn his death, as a grieving daughter would do.

I heard a movement behind me.

'The police are here Effie. They've already spoken to me and Ambrose, and now it's your turn.' Said Mace.

My heart sank. 'Is it really necessary for me to speak to them now?'

'It won't take long E.' His tone was unusually soft and quiet. Gently he placed his hand on my shoulder. 'Please E, remaining here isn't healthy.'

I sniffed and shakily rose from the ground. Glancing at him I noticed the ghost of a smile on his face. I nodded at him and cleared my throat. 'Where are they?'

'Over by the summerhouse.' He said, wiping a smear of dirt from my face. 'You look like hell Effie.'

I rubbed my hand across my cheek and tried to laugh but nothing came out. Without a word I turned and staggered down the back of the garden with Mace trailing behind me. As I approached the policemen, they were deep in conversation and it was only when I cleared my throat that they noticed me. We sat in the summerhouse whilst Mace lurked about outside. My heart began thudding loudly in my chest as I saw how close we were to the mirror, and I was suddenly worried that one of the policemen may accidentally knock it over and smash it. I began to fidget nervously in my seat. 'I hope this won't take too long, I'm...I'm not feeling very well.' I stammered in an oddly strained voice. They seemed concerned and apologised for bothering me at this difficult time and conveyed how sorry they were about my loss. They questioned me about my movements yesterday then asked about Isaiah. 'We were led to believe by Ambrose...my late Aunt's gardener that my father wasn't in the house' I told them quietly. 'But then we discovered he was stuck in the attic room.' They exchanged glances then turned their attention back to me. My gaze lowered to the floor as I told them how the door has a habit of jamming. It was a lie of course, but what would be the point of mentioning that someone had locked Isaiah in. I must have misheard what he'd said over the noise of the fire. They asked me if I had any idea how it started and I told them it may have been down to the faulty wiring. I could see by their faces that they weren't convinced, and yet again they looked at one another as if they didn't believe me. Looking extremely serious they informed me that there'd have to be a thorough investigation into what had happened and I must let them know an address where I could be contacted. One of the policemen had his elbow right next to the mirror and in a fit of panic I shot out of my seat and announced I was feeling faint and could they please leave now. Impatiently, I stood by the open door and ushered them outside. And once again expressing their condolences, they bid me goodbye.

'Well they were a bit gloomy, weren't they?' Mace declared looking closely at my face. 'Effie?' he said, taking my arm. 'You're looking a tad weary. Come back with me to Clarice's house and get some sleep.'

I looked wistfully at him and smiled weakly. 'For a while yes I will, thank you.' I linked my arm with his. 'But then I must come back here.' My eyes drifted to the summerhouse.

I had only meant to sleep for a little while, but through sheer exhaustion I fell asleep that afternoon and didn't wake to the following morning. It had been a dreamless slumber and on awaking I felt refreshed and surprisingly hungry. After breakfast Clarice and her mother went off into town and Mace and I made our way back to the house in my car, which the firemen had kindly helped Mace to remove from the ditch. My instincts were telling me to return to Rawlings, not that anything could be done, but we were going to collect the mirror and move it to Clarice's house, and then I would leave....

As we approached the house, I found myself averting my gaze so as not to look upon the ruin, it was too painful. We exited the car and slowly strolled towards the summerhouse.

Unexpectedly Mace chuckled and began running over towards the garden furniture. 'Gilbert! How did you get here?' He picked the dummy up in his arms as if he was a baby. 'Effie?' he swung round and stared at me, looking rather perplexed.

'I don't know Mace. He was sitting there during...during the fire.' I gulped. 'But I have no idea how he got there. I'd not moved him from my wardrobe.'

Mace stood there contemplating what I'd said. 'Perhaps he crept out your room, slid down the banisters and scurried out into the garden.'

'Who knows, and quite frankly who cares' I said marching towards Mace. 'We should take him with us, I suppose.' Reluctantly I reached out and took the dummy from him and adjusted his threadbare jumper. Something came loose and fell onto the grass. 'What? I exclaimed in puzzlement, bending down I picked it up. 'It's...it's a key.'

'A key?'

'Yes.' I replied in disbelief. I recognised it immediately. It was the key to the attic.

An absurd notion suddenly entered my mind – what if Gilbert had locked my father in the attic and then started the fire?

'A key to what E?'

I let out a short laugh and placed the key in my pocket. 'Oh, I don't know Mace. It hardly matters does it?'

'Okay E, there's no need to take that tone. You're far too good natured for sarcasm.'

'Sorry Mace, I didn't mean to speak to you like that, the pressure must be getting to me.'

He smiled rather sweetly at me. 'Effie?' he asked with a hint of apprehension. 'There's something I've been meaning to ask you.'

'Yes Mace, what is it?'

'It's been bothering me...since the fire.' He scratched his head. 'Has it occurred to you that Isaiah may have started the blaze?'

I pondered thoughtfully for a moment. Gazing towards the house an intense pain crossed over my heart. It hadn't entered my head before but hearing Mace say it, suddenly it made sense. Isaiah's disposition seemed far from stable when I'd left him that night. *'This is where I belong Effelia.'* He'd uttered dejectedly, as if he had no intention of ever leaving Rawlings. Perhaps it was my fault. If I'd stayed with him then none of this would have happened.

Mace came closer and peered into my face. 'Well, what do you think?'

'It's possible, yes. Rawlings was everything to him. And if he couldn't have it then no one could, not even his wife and children.' I looked puzzled. 'Let's just say, for arguments sake, that he did cause the fire, surely he intended to leave afterwards?'

He looked pensive. 'But why go to the attic, and who locked him in?'

My eyes fell onto Gilbert. 'Perhaps that's where Isaiah started the fire, and he had meant to leave but couldn't escape the room.'

'I never liked that attic.' Mace exclaimed, shaking his head vigorously. 'It always made me feel like some malevolent presence was lurking amongst all that heap of junk you stored in there, watching and waiting for the right moment to attack.'

I think he expected me to laugh, but I didn't.

'Well, whatever happened that fateful night, we shall never know the truth Mace.'

'Not unless Isaiah visits you as a spirit and tells you the whole story E.'

I eyed him coldly.

'I'm sorry E. That was insensitive of me.' He screwed his face up, looking frustrated. 'I just can't help myself sometimes, it just comes spewing out.' With a smile he glanced at Gilbert. 'I blame this little freakish fellow of yours.' He exploded in laughter. 'I mean how the hell did he turn up in the garden? Perhaps he locked Isaiah in the attic, and hid the key up his jumper.' Puckering his lips, he slowly turned to face me, looking decidedly amused. 'You knew it was the attic key, didn't you Effie?'

'With a bashful smile I nodded.

After carrying the mirror carefully to the car we returned to collect some paintings that I'd done in the summerhouse whilst Aunt was ill. They weren't anything special, just a couple of landscapes, one of golden cornfields and an old church shrouded in great yews, and the other of a quaint little

310

stone cottage surrounded with pretty wallflowers and wild daisies. Mrs Lapworth, Clarice's mother, had been very obliging in allowing me to keep so many possessions at her home. Only recently I'd wondered what else I should take, without cluttering up her house too much, but that didn't matter anymore- everything had gone, and was little more than a pile of ash. Thank heavens my favourite books were safe, and my mother's portrait, amongst other things.

'Are you sure that's everything E?' Mace asked, carrying the canvases underneath his arm.

'Yes, thanks Mace.'

We'd already propped Gilbert up on the back seat. I would take him with me when I left. This mysteriously terrifying creature had been passed down through generations, and whether I liked it or not he belonged to me. One day perhaps I would discover the reason for the dreams we shared, and what they meant. Sometimes I truly believe he was trying to help me, in his own twisted way, but other times I also think he genuinely wanted to scare me.

'Do you mind if we spend a few moments here, before we leave Mace?' I smiled sadly. 'It may sound strange but I'd like to say goodbye to the house.'

Loading the canvases in the boot he slammed the lid and laughed. 'E, everything you do is strange. Why change a habit of a lifetime.'

'Perhaps spending too long in your company over the years has made me that way.' Laughing I glanced at him, expecting him to respond immediately, but he was silent. 'Mace?'

His gaze had drifted away from mine, focusing on something behind me. I became startled as an odd look of intense alarm crossed over his face, causing his large eyes to grow even wider.

'Mace?' Mace whatever is wrong?'

As still as a statue he continued to stare over my shoulder without saying a word, his face pale and mouth gaping wide.

I began to laugh nervously. 'Is this one of your silly little tricks?'

With a gulp he frantically shook his head, his eyes still locked on something behind me.

I was suddenly frightened to look; terrified of facing whatever it was that had Mace in such a state of shock. For it had to be profoundly astonishing to render him speechless. But with every second I could feel my curiosity mounting until I could no longer stand it. With an anxious sigh I shakily swung around and looked directly into the gleaming eyes of a woman, the same woman who had been lingering in the background at Aunt's funeral. Only now I could see her clearly.

'It's alright Effie.' She said in an unsteady voice. Don't be afraid.'

When I spoke my voice was weak and quiet. 'Mother?'

The woman began to nod, laughing and crying at the same time. Tentatively she began to approach me. All of a sudden, I felt myself plunging into a daydream type of state. My mind was telling me it was a hallucination that the apparition would simply vanish any second now.

'Oh Effie.' She whimpered. 'I've waited so very long to be reunited with you.' Without warning she reached forward and placed her arms about me, holding me in a tight embrace. 'I'm sorry, I'm so sorry we've been parted all these long years.' With a cry she released me and gently cupped my face with her hands, her luminous eyes carefully scanning my features. 'It is true. Constance told me how lovely you were.' Her eyes grew serious. 'Please believe me- it was your father who was responsible for my long absence. He...he came one night and took me away, to a land I couldn't reach you.'

My face broke into a slow steady smile. 'I know, I know...mother.' I gazed in wonder into her tearstained eyes. 'You are here now, and that's what matters.'

She clasped my hands. 'And here I shall remain Effie. By your side.'

Beginning to sob I clung to her, weeping like a little child in her mother's arms.

Those final few days in Abercrombie seem so strange and indistinct, and yet I do recall the overwhelming joy at finding my mother, an event I had not anticipated. It shone like an unexpected light of happiness, overshadowing the grim darkness of grief and gloom that had clung to me for so long.

Mother came and stayed with us at Clarice's after it transpired she'd been sleeping rough in a nearby forest. We spent hours together, discussing every subject imaginable, and every so often she'd gaze into my face, her green eyes bright with exultation, and tell me how much she'd missed me.

The world where she'd been trapped for so long with Noble had been unbearable and grim. Once there had been forests and woodlands, but they had long since ceased to exist, trampled over and destroyed by the hand of man. She couldn't bear the noise, the crowded streets and busy roads, with a constant stream of traffic, the endless rows of concrete buildings; some so high that they overpowered what little trees were left. But against all odds they had found a gateway that would get them out. For reasons she couldn't remember, my mother had been delayed in the other world and had urged Noble to travel first on the understanding she would join up with him in a few days. It was risky, very risky, but apparently she had no choice. Just before she departed through the gateway my mother had briefly visited Aunt in the library at Rawlings, leading the poor woman to believe her sister was an apparition from the spirit world. My mother truly believed and hoped she would arrive back home, but as she journeyed through the gateway a great force pushed her into another direction, causing her to land in another time and place, a horrid world that she couldn't bring herself to speak about. I remember how my father had destroyed the portal in Browning's Wood, just after he'd disposed of Mace – it made sense that my mother must have been travelling through when the explosion occurred, veering her off course. Somehow it seemed pointless telling her this. However badly behaved my father was in life, he had gone now, and I had no desire to speak ill of the dead. Since his passing I'd constantly dwell on his family, deeply concerned for their welfare, wondering what I could do to help. And when the answer came to me, I made enquiries as to where they lived and went for a visit.

Lillian Penhaligon resided along a rather drab street in the neighbouring town, in a little terraced house.

With some trepidation I knocked on the door, and waited a while before someone answered. As the door swung open, I saw immediately it was Isaiah's wife.

She stood there glaring at me coldly. 'Yes, what is it?'

I could see she'd been crying, as her eyes were red and blotchy. Unlike previously she wasn't wearing a scrap of makeup, and her hair looked lank, as if it hadn't been washed in a while.

'Good morning Lillian...I...I'd just like to say how dreadfully sorry I am for what happened to Isaiah.' I glanced over her shoulder into the passageway. 'How are you and the children coping?'

After a moments pause, she edged away from the door, gesturing for me to enter.

'Not good at all, if you must know.' She muttered padding along the narrow passageway in a pair of fluffy pink slippers. 'You'd best come into the living area.'

I followed her into the room and narrowly missed tripping over a train set laid out in the centre of the floor.

'Where are the children?'

'With their grandma.' She ambled across the room and threw a pile of clothes off the sofa. 'Take a seat. Sorry for the mess, but with four kids in the house it's not easy to keep tidy.' Her eyes drifted over me with contempt. 'Still, I'm sure you'll not be wishing to stay long, not after your unnecessary rant at me the other day.'

I reddened slightly with awkwardness and agitation. It's true I suppose, I was rather cruel to her that day at Rawlings. On the rare occasions I lost my temper I would always feel guilty afterwards, wondering if I'd overreacted, and in the end I would invariably back down and apologise, but observing her cool displeased manner towards me now I found myself becoming enraged: Lillian had lost her husband, and yes I felt sorry for her, but I had lost my Aunt, my father and my home, and yet she showed not one shred of compassion.

'No, I won't take up much of your time.' Sitting on the edge of the sofa I looked directly into her eyes. 'Here.' I said sharply, handing her an envelope. 'This is for you and your children.'

Without saying a word, she took the envelope and casually opened it. She paused for a moment her expression unchanging, then pulled out the thick wad of notes inside.

'Why are you giving this to me, where did it come from?'

I found myself struggling for words. How could I say it was Isaiah's money, money he'd supposedly acquired through murder. And even if I didn't mention the murder part, surely she would find it odd that her husband should possess such a large amount of cash. Thank heavens I had the foresight to remove the tin of money before the house went up in flames. For wherever the money originated from I was pleased to put it to good use. Lillian had a good chunk and the remainder I would leave at Clarice's house on the kitchen table in an envelope addressed to Mrs Lapworth. I'm sure she'd be thankful for a little extra money, and would no doubt spend some on her daughter Clarice and Mace.

Lillian cleared her throat. 'Well?'

I began to fidget on my seat. 'I...I found it buried in the garden at Rawlings.'

With a scowl she shoved it back into my hand. 'I don't want it. It belongs to you.' Retrieving a handkerchief from her pocket she began dabbing her eyes. 'And if you're giving it to me out of pity then don't. I'm not a charity case.'

Tentatively I reached forward and covered her hand with mine. 'No, please believe me, that's *not* the reason.' I'm going away soon and... and the money, well it...it. Well let's just say I won't be needing it.'

She threw me an odd stare. 'Why?' A small laugh escaped her lips. 'Everyone needs money.'

There was a long silence.

Why waste time trying to explain to her when I wasn't even sure myself; not having my notebook had put paid to that. All I knew was I wouldn't require money.

'I ....I have plenty enough money of my own. So please take it.' I handed her the envelope once more. 'There's more than enough there to build a new house on the land where...where Rawlings used to be. I've already had dealings with my solicitor and he should be visiting you shortly to get your signature to the deeds.' I paused for a second. 'And then it's yours, all yours.'

Her eyes were full of disbelief and bafflement. 'But why are you doing this? You don't even like me.' She cried, standing up and walking over to the window.

'No, that's not true.' I shot up and went over to her. 'I was in mourning for my Aunt.' My voice became emotional. 'I still am. And you turning up like that, out of the blue, well it was rather a shock. You see, Isaiah never told me about you.' I took in a deep intake of breath then exhaled. 'So, when you started telling me the changes you were going to make to Rawlings, the house that's been in my family for generations, I became a little upset.' I gently placed my hand on her shoulder, trying to be strong. 'But now, the house I knew and loved has gone.' I began choking on my words. 'And it's time I let go of my sentimentality and make a fresh start. A lovely new home can be built, a family home for my little brothers and sisters...and you.'

There was another awkward silence.

Quite unexpectedly she let out a heart-wrenching sob and fell forward onto the carpet. 'Oh, Effie I miss him. I miss Isaiah so much.'

Throwing the envelope on the coffee table I knelt down beside her and placed my arm about her. 'I know. Me too. But I'm sure he'd be happy to know you are being well looked after. Of course, if you'd rather stay here then...'

'No.' She shouted between her tears. 'I can't stand being here when it reminds me so much of him. It's too painful.' With a shrug she removed my arm and rose from the floor.

'And besides, it's so cramped in this house, and the garden is tiny.'

Getting up I smiled sympathetically at her 'Well then what are you waiting for.'

'I can't believe it.' She let out a shrill laugh. 'Are you sure about this....Effie?'

'Yes.' just promise me you'll get that swimming pool.' I grinned. 'And a play room for the children.'

Without warning she embraced me. 'Isaiah was right about you. He always said how kind you were.' Drawing back, she smiled warmly at me. 'He was very proud of you, you know.'

I lowered my eyes forlornly. 'I should be going.' With a deep sigh I turned towards the door. 'Please send my best wishes to the children. I'm sorry I missed them.' As I headed down the hallway I noticed Isaiah's raincoat hanging up on a peg. I stared at it for a moment, remembering how he used to love wearing it.

Lillian was standing close by and when she spoke a shiver went down my spine.

'They didn't actually find a body, you know...in the remains. Don't you think that's strange?'

I stood there on the spot without turning. 'The fire...it probably wouldn't have left anything....' My voice trailed off.

'I suppose you're right.' She uttered sadly, as I opened the door.

'Well goodbye Lillian.' I turned and gave her a small hug. 'Do take care.'

'You too Effie, and thank you for what you've done.' Her voice was choked with emotion as she spoke. 'I shall never forget it.' She reached out and touched my arm. 'Will you be attending Isaiah's memorial service next Friday?'

'No, I'm sorry Lillian, but it's imperative I leave for my trip as soon as possible. I do hope the service is not too harrowing for you.' With a plaintive smile I turned and headed down the pathway.

'Where are you going to live Effie?'

'Oh, in a village someway off from here.'

317

'Well do come back and visit won't you. I'm sure you'd like to see my four cheeky little brats. After all you are their big sister.'

I stared back at her. 'Thank you, Lillian that would be wonderful.' Holding back the tears I gave her another smile and went out the gate.

After returning to Abercrombie I visited the cemetery with my mother and we placed a fresh lot of flowers on Aunt's grave. She was buried under a great oak, similar to that in the garden at Rawlings, it was somehow right that her final resting place should be underneath such an ancient tree, and it eased my mind to know that this would make her happy. Kneeling there I told her all that had happened, all about Rawlings and Isaiah and of finding my mother. I'd like to think she would have approved of me giving the money to Lillian, for her children were my siblings and were therefore family. I imagine a very different house would soon be standing in the grounds of Rawlings, but rather that than a skeleton of an old house, a haunting shadow of what used to be.

It took me a while to find Abel's parents. They were buried right at the far corner. It was only when I'd been packing my rucksack for the trip back that I pulled out the crumpled letter, and I suddenly remembered what I was supposed to have done. A few days ago, I'd made enquiries and it didn't take long to discover they had both sadly passed away. How glad I was that he hadn't returned with me, for it surely would have been greatly distressing for him to discover they had died. With tears in my eyes I put their son's letter beside the grave and placed a stone upon it. I told them I was sorry they never got to see their son again, but he was happy and safe, and they weren't to worry anymore. I comforted myself that if they could somehow hear me, they could rest in peace.

'All packed?' asked Mace looming over me, holding his hands behind his back as if he was hiding something.

'Yep, I think so. I just need to choose a few more books to take.'

He made a noise. 'Of course, you do E,' suddenly he produced Gilbert and thrust him in front of me. 'I'm glad you've decided to take this little fellow with you.'

'Ah.' I exclaimed, staring at the hideous looking dummy. 'Thanks Mace. I left him under the bed for safekeeping and totally forgot about him.' I laughed softly. 'How did you know where to find him?'

His face grew puzzled. 'Gilbert was perched up against your rucksack, waiting to go. You *are* going to take him with you, aren't you E?'

'Yes, yes I am.'

With a gulp I stared into the dummy's eyes, and for a brief second, I imagined he swiftly winked at me. I would never know the truth about Gilbert, had he been trying to warn me all this time, or did he really mean me harm, had he locked Isaiah in the attic and burnt down Rawlings, who knows. But one thing was very clear, and had been for a long while now. He was no ordinary little dummy and didn't wish to be parted from me.

'Gilbert belongs with me.'

'Good woman.'

I smiled.

It was naturally sad to leave Abercrombie for the last time, and we were all very tearful, especially Clarice who clung to me like a child. I think she had gotten used to me being here, and didn't like change. Mace carefully took her from me and held her tenderly in his arms, then reached out for me and all three of us stood there hugging one another.

'This isn't goodbye forever Effie.' He said in a choked-up voice. 'I'll be seeing you soon.' He turned to my mother and they hugged. 'Have a safe journey both of you.'

With tears in my eyes I thanked Clarice's mother for everything she'd done.

As we approached the mirror, we all said one last goodbye, and Mace and I began to cry. Feeling both anxious and excited I turned to my mother and took her hand and together we left my old home forever.

Chapter 27

At first everything went well in Briarwood. I was reunited with Gideon and Gabriel, and we made preparations to move into the cottage on the other side of the woods. Caleb had chuckled when I'd told him where it was and how to get there. Apparently, I hadn't realised there was a shorter way to reach my new home, by going through the village then passing over the meadow.

My mother was surprisingly shy when she met them all and I realised how alike we were in that respect. She was so lovely and gracious that everyone immediately liked her, especially little Gabriel who was delighted to have gained a grandmother. When we moved into our new cottage, she came to live with us, and for some time Gideon, Gabriel, mother and myself had a wonderful time doing the place up, and making it a proper home. We cleaned up all the furniture and tidied the gardens. Gideon created a large vegetable plot out the back and we discovered a small apple orchard in the field beyond, as well as an abundance of blueberry and gooseberry bushes. When it was all finally finished, we invited Caleb, my brother Gilbert and Abel over for tea in the back garden, and everyone was full of joviality.

The only ones absent from our lives were Noble, Mace and Clarice. On our arrival back in Briarwood I discovered Noble had left the village some time ago, after informing his father he had the urge to travel, and no one had seen him since. Then there was Mace and Clarice, who I hadn't seen in a long while, but hoped one day they would return to our little village. Caleb was naturally upset at not having his youngest son back in Briarwood, but was banking on him coming back soon. 'Otherwise, I'll go through that damnable mirror and drag him back myself.' He had exclaimed angrily.

The wagging tongues of the villager's seemed to have finally ceased, and they no longer gaped at me as if I were a ghost. Luckily the title of witch had not befallen me and all in all I had finally been accepted. I had even made friends within the village, among them was Maisie the young woman who'd I'd seen chatting to Noble outside the church and in the field a while back. It soon became evident that there had never been anything between the two of them, as her heart had always belonged to someone else in the village. Their meetings were entirely innocent and not at all of a romantic nature, for although she thought him very attractive he really wasn't the type of man she wished to marry. 'And anyway, he's entirely smitten with someone, and has been for a long while.' She said. 'Other women have lost interest because of it, as they know they'll wasting their time.' I averted my gaze when she told me this, so she wouldn't see my face turning crimson.

Then came the day I was hoping would never arrive. For so long now I had buried my niggling worry at the back of my mind, hoping it would just go away and never return. Only things such as that seldom do, they come back to haunt you, and sometimes destroy you.

'How are the beans coming along? I asked Gideon as he watered the plants.

'Really well thanks darling. They should be ready to pick soon.'

Beaming, I wrapped my arms around him and gazed into his face. 'You should take a break; you've been out here for ages.' I paused. 'You look a little tired, why don't you come in for some tea?'

He kissed me. 'In a moment, I just need to check on the lettuces in the cold box.' With a weak smile he wiped the sweat from his brow. 'Then I'm all yours.'

I smiled back at him. 'Well hurry up, before Gabriel scoffs all the lemon cake that my mother's made.' Laughing I turned to go.

'Effie?'

'Yes.'

'You know I love you very much, don't you?'

322

'Of course.' I furrowed my brow. 'Why do you ask?'

'No reason, I...I just wanted to say it, that's all.'

'I love you too Gideon.' For a moment I gazed into his dark eyes, then with a short laugh I swung round and made my way into the cottage.

My mother and Gabriel were sitting at the table, reading together. She greeted me with a welcome smile.

'Come and sit with us Effie, I'll pour the tea out.'

'Cake grandmother, what about the yummy cake?'

'All in good time little one. Why don't you read another page of your book and then you can have a slice.'

'Oh, do I have to?' Gabriel complained.

My mother and I exchanged a smile.

I went to pour out the tea. 'Let's read the next page altogether Gabriel and then you can have some of the yummy cake.'

He beamed from ear to ear. 'Yes mummy.'

We sat there for a while and helped Gabriel with some difficult words.

'Well done darling, your reading is coming along brilliantly for someone so young.'

He clapped his hands. 'Cake, cake.'

My mother laughed. 'Isn't Gideon coming in for a break Effie?'

'Yes he...he was going to.' My words trailed off. 'I'll go and get him.'

Rather slowly I approached the back of the garden and went around the corner to the vegetable patch.

'Gideon? Gideon come in for....' My heart suddenly went cold and I cried out. 'No, no.'

He was sprawled out on the grass face downwards.

With a whimper I knelt down beside him and gently moved his face so I could see it. 'Gideon, wake up.' My voice became hysterical. 'Please, wake up.' I leant over him and as my cheek touched his I realised it was stone cold. As I cradled him in my arms my body began to rock with hard wrenching sobs. It suddenly began raining, torrential rain that would go on for some time. I remember thinking they were tears from heaven, tears for my beloved Gideon.

It seemed to me I had had my fair share of heartache and loss to last me a lifetime, or at least it seemed that way. I cannot say how long I grieved, or if indeed I will ever stop grieving, for the pain never truly goes away, it only lessens in time, and somehow you learn to live with your sorrow.

Gideon's final resting place was at his favourite part of Briarwood, a location with the most incredible views stretching far and wide down into the valley. He would often go there and contemplate life when he was living, and now he was gone it was a good spot for him to rest in peace. Many a time I would take flowers and lay them on his grave, then sit there and talk to him about life, about our life. Somehow it made me feel close to him, and if I closed my eyes, I could almost imagine him sitting beside me. Occasionally I am blessed with seeing him in my dreams, we are in the forest again, just like when we were younger, and as we hold hands, I tell him what Gabriel's been up to and how things are progressing in the cottage, and all about the goings on in the village. He assures me that heaven is real and is full of joyful spirits who have also passed over, including my Aunt, who he visits regularly. Whether it is real or not I cannot say but it greatly eases my mind to believe that their happy and not alone in the darkness, where there is nothing, where everything is dead.

Caleb passed me a letter after the funeral, a letter Gideon had written to me some time ago and given to his father to keep safe until the time had come to hand it over. As of yet I cannot bring myself to read it, so it lays unopened in my dressing room table.

It transpired that Caleb had known all along about his son's condition, and that's why he didn't like Gideon travelling. 'Sadly, he was the unlucky one out of my sons that inherited his mother Sabina's heart complaint.' He told me forlornly. 'That's why she was so eager to take him to

324

Hartland when he was a child. She foolishly thought she could make him better, you see.' He held back a sob. 'Noble always thought it was because she loved Gideon more, but that's not the case. Sabina loved all her children equally, I'm certain of that.'

Mother helped me tremendously after his death, she would be there for me all the time, caring and comforting me. She would sit with me and we would talk for hours about anything and everything, and sometimes we would laugh and other times we would cry.

Gabriel was my shining star, he cheered me up when I was feeling low and kept me occupied as young children do, stopping my mind from dwelling on sad thoughts. In the evening when he was tucked up in bed I would sit there and paint. I took it upon myself to do a portrait of my Aunt, and then of Rawlings, my old home. How funny it was that I was able recreate them in oils when I could barely recollect anything at all from that time. Now I would never forget them, they were always there on my living room wall whenever I needed reminding. 'That's a beautiful house mummy.' Gabriel once said. 'Can we go and visit it?' I smiled sadly at him and said it was no longer there. He also asked me about the woman in the painting and I told him that she was his great Aunt, a lovely lady who was watching him from her garden in heaven.

Probably the strangest thing of all was how Gabriel formed an instant attachment with my childhood dummy, Gilbert, he would carry him around everywhere and snuggle up with him at bedtime. Never again did I dream about the dummy, although he still alarmed me rather when I looked into his face.

It was on a particular day in mid-summer that we had an unexpected visitor. My mother had taken Gabriel gooseberry picking for making preserves whilst I did some chores around the house. I'd already tidied the living room and was just about to put the washing outside on the line, when I heard a light tapping on the front door.

'There's no need to knock Caleb, just come in as usual.' I shouted, thinking he was here to see Gabriel. He tended to call most days so I naturally assumed it was him at the door.

They knocked again.

Cursing underneath my breath I stepped over the basket of washing and made my way to the door and flung it open. I stared at the man standing there as he gazed back at me. He had grown a beard since last I saw him and his hair was considerably shorter.

'Hello Effie.'

'Noble. What...what are you doing here?'

'I've come to pay my respects. I would have come sooner but I...I only learnt of Gideon's death when I returned to the village a while ago.' He let out a harrowing sigh. 'Effie I'm so very sorry for your loss.'

I lowered my eyes. 'Come in Noble.'

As we both sat at the kitchen table, he explained that if he'd been aware Gideon was so gravely ill he wouldn't have left in the first place. It was never his intention to come back to Briarwood, but in the end, he had an overwhelming urge to return to his home. As he stopped talking, he took a deep breath and delved into his pocket.

'Father gave me this letter that Gideon had written to me before...before he died. I read it on my return to the village.' He produced a folded piece of paper and placed it on the table in front of me. 'I thought you might like to read it.'

I sat staring at the letter, trying to keep composed. Suddenly I wondered if it was a similar letter to the one Gideon had left me, the one that remained unopened in my dressing room table upstairs. With shaking hands, I took the letter and began to read.

My dear Noble

Firstly, I would like to say that despite our differences I have always looked upon you with the deepest affection.

I have known for some time that you and Effie love one another and I am perfectly fine about it. I write this letter to ease my mind and to make you aware that my greatest wish is that the two of you marry when I am no longer here. I should hate for Effie and Gabriel to be alone, for they both deserve to have someone good and decent in their lives, and who better than you dear brother. I will of course understand if this is not what you wish for, but promise me you'll watch over them.

Love always
Gideon

Without showing any emotion I handed the letter back to him and rose from the seat. 'Would…. would you leave now please Noble.'

He looked perplexed as he took the letter and got up from his seat. 'Naturally it's a lot to take in. Shall I come back and see you another time?'

'No.' I shouted at him. 'Do you honestly think it will change everything because we have Gideon's approval to be together? He may have been gone a while now but that doesn't mean you can just take over where he's left off.'

'Effie please I…. that wasn't my intention. You must know I could never replace Gideon.'

'That's right Noble, you cannot. I charged over to the door. 'Now please leave.'

He brushed passed me and went towards the front door, his head bowed. For a moment he half turned to gaze at me, but I immediately looked away from him. As I ran up the stairs I barely heard the slam of the door. Going directly to my dressing table I retrieved the letter from Gideon and tore it open.

My dearest Effie
If you are reading this letter then sadly I am no longer here. I think I've known for some time that my heart is failing, and I have come to terms with what will happen.

Sorry I didn't warn you Effie but I knew that nothing could be done for me, and I didn't see the point in worrying you.

Words cannot express my heartache at having to leave you, but alas I do not have a choice. Thank you, my darling, for being in my life, I was truly blessed when I met you all those long years ago and have always treasured our love.

This is a new chapter for you now Effie, and you must promise me that you will not be sad. Life is for the living, and I want you to embrace it and be happy. Our wonderful son is so precious and I know you will continue to shower him with love and affection.

I'm aware that Noble loves you and I believe you love him too. If this is indeed the case then please know it would make me truly happy for the both of you to be together. More importantly follow your heart Effie.

Know that I will always love you my darling.
    Forever yours
    Gideon
      xxx

I cannot tell you how long I remained sitting on the bed. Reading his letter was like speaking to Gideon beyond the grave, only despite what he'd written I just felt numb inside. Many a time I'd almost read his letter but something had stopped me and I'd shoved it back into the drawer. Maybe I had sensed all along that he knew the truth about Noble, and would write about us in the letter. Nevertheless, despite Gideon's blessing, to me it would *still* seem like the worse kind of betrayal. To move him out the way and replace him with another was completely wrong. My feelings on this matter wouldn't seem to budge, and ultimately, I no longer had the ability to follow my heart because it had now turned to stone.

Epilogue

I was standing on a chair, trying to reach up to the very top of the dresser so I could get a jar of pickle. We were having a picnic today and the others had already gone up ahead with the baskets of food.

'Oh, mother do be careful. Let me get it for you, I'm sure I can reach.'

'It's alright Gabriel, I've got it.' I handed him the jar and carefully clambered down from the chair. 'It'll be a while before you're as tall as me darling.' I said with a grin.

'I am almost. Grandfather says I'll be towering over you soon.'

'Well I'm sure his right.' With a warm smile I took his arm. 'Come on, the others will be wondering where we've got to.

Holding hands, we slowly made our way up the bank and along the overgrown pathway. I stopped at the top to catch my breath.

'Uncle Mace.' Cried Gabriel running towards him. 'I hope you've not eaten all the food.'

I watched as the two of them began to play fight, and as Gabriel fell on the grass Mace started to tickle him relentlessly.

Smiling broadly, Clarice came pacing over towards me and gave me a hug. 'We thought you'd got lost Effie.' She looked closely into my eyes. 'Are you feeling better than yesterday?'

I nodded. 'Yes, thanks Clarice, my mother took care of everything whilst I got a good night's rest.'

She raised her eyebrows and glanced over towards the picnic. 'I hope she's not the only one helping out.'

'I laughed. 'No, no he helps too.'

'Good.' With a chuckle she linked her arm with mine and we made our way over to the others.

Mace and Clarice had come back to Briarwood after Mrs Lapworth had passed away. They were married now and living with Caleb in his cottage.

It was the strangest thing, but a few days before returning to Briarwood, Mace had visited one of his old school friends, who lived a few hours drive from Abercrombie. As he was travelling home on the bus, he swore he saw Isaiah sitting in a little tearoom, chatting to some elderly ladies. It was impossible of course, for not even my father could have escaped that fire.

Abel stood up to greet me. 'Hello there Miss.' He went to shake my hand but I gave him an embrace instead.

Many a time I'd told him to address me as Effie, but he could never quite get the hang of it, so in the end I simply gave up asking him.

'Glad you could make it Abel. Don't forget you and Gilbert are coming over for tea tomorrow.'

'I won't Miss, I surely won't.' He began to giggle as he glanced at Gilbert, who was sitting on the grass talking to my mother. 'He be the forgetful one, not me.'

Gabriel went to give Caleb a hug. Since Gideon's death the two of them had become inseparable. My mother had become dear friends with Caleb, and recently I began to wonder if it was more than mere friendship between them both, as now and then I would catch them looking at one another in a certain manner, a deep lingering stare that I knew all about.

I stood there for a moment gazing at my husband, and we gave one another a knowing smile. As it transpires my heart hadn't turned to stone after all. After reading Gideon's letter once more I had sought out Noble and it wasn't long before we decided to marry.

'What took you so long?' He asked with a grin. Lifting our daughters, Bessie and Matilda up in his arms he strolled over and kissed me on the lips. 'I was just about to come and find you Effie.'

'Daddy, daddy let me down. I want to go and play with Gabriel.'

'Me too daddy'

Laughing he lowered them onto the ground. 'Go on then girls.'

They both gave me a little hug then darted off to pounce on their big brother.

I let out a contented sigh. 'Hopefully they'll get tired out.'

He wrapped his arms about me. 'I wouldn't count on it darling.' Grinning he glanced down at my swollen stomach. 'Father has concocted a new remedy for your morning sickness, so hopefully you'll feel a little better soon.'

Smiling, I rested my head against his chest and he kissed the top of my head. We had already decided that if we had another girl, we would name her Hetta, but if a boy, he would be named after Gideon. I still thought of him often, as we all did. A while ago I painted his portrait and it was now displayed with the other paintings in the living room.

'Come on you two.' Yelled Caleb. 'Food's ready.'

As he gestured for us to join them, I observed Mace shovelling an entire scone in his mouth then reaching for another one. Clarice lightly slapped his hand and scolded him, and he gave her a bashful smile. As Noble and I went to sit beside my mother and the others I pondered if there was ever a time I had felt such happiness.

Many villagers believe there is no longer an ancient magic covering the land of Briarwood; some say it disappeared with the demise of Hartland, but deep in my heart I *do* still feel the enchantment of the village, I always would, for this land truly is the most wondrous place imaginable, and where I truly belong, it is my home.

THE END

Printed in Great Britain
by Amazon